Praise for

WORDS ON WATER

"Each character . . . is riotously believable, and together contributes to a circus flavor of monumental size."

≈ Dr. Jerry Henderson, author of *Here & Now, Then & There: A Collection of Short Stories*

"The feel, the smell, the power of the ocean . . . "

≈ Joseph L.S. Terrell, author of *the Harrison Weaver Mysteries*

"A delicious array of stories and poetry from a collection of extraordinary talented writers . . . entertaining and (a) keenly observed look at life and the human heart."

≈ Alana White, award-winning fiction author

"The Harpeth River Writers bring a feast in a blend of poetry and prose that will captivate you and keep you reading, story after story."

≈ Louise Colln, author of *Woman Of The Land*

"Something special happens when you put together a collection of stories by these well-respected southern writers. As each unique story is told, a picture is painted in your mind, leaving you feeling a variety of emotions, always satisfied."

≈ Carole Webb Slater, author of *Letters from the Heart, 1943-1946*

"This Outstanding collection is bursting at the bindings with creative talent . . . Thoroughly entertaining and engaging."

"An immensely talented new collection. Each story involves water, whether it's the bright blue ocean that surrounds the Island of Anguilla, the waterways of Charleston or the gentle rain around a rural homestead. Beautifully written (with) well-conceived characters and suspenseful endings."

"A canny and wholly riveting anthology . . . a tour de force of how imagination is shaped by the lore and mystery of water. It's a wonderful blend of poems and short fiction. Whether dehydrated, plain thirsty, in desperate need of a cooling plunge, or even hydrophobic, this collection is absolutely essential."

Words On Water

Words On Water

A HARPETH RIVER WRITERS ANTHOLOGY

HARPETH RIVER WRITERS

Dedication

Water: the human body is composed of sixty-five percent, and the planet's surface is seventy-one percent. Mahatma Ghandi proved we could survive without food for twenty-one days, but only four without water. Despite our symbiotic relationship, dedicating our collection to it seems too impersonal. Better to thank real people whom we rely on to survive—our friends and family for their support and others who gave feedback to our words and ideas. And to the reader—we appreciate you plunging into this book.

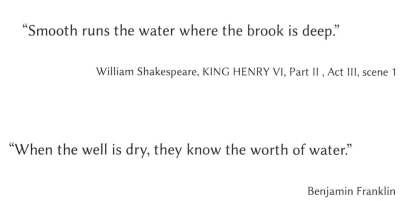

"Smooth runs the water where the brook is deep."

William Shakespeare, KING HENRY VI, Part II , Act III, scene 1

"When the well is dry, they know the worth of water."

Benjamin Franklin

Contents

Lake

Rain

Ocean

River

Delta

Introduction

Water is our first home. It is through water that we first feel our mother's heartbeat, and through water we connect with her, heart to heart and soul to soul. In the womb, we breathed it, and for the rest of our lives, we depend on it for our very survival.

Water is life.

But beyond that, water is mystery.

Who hasn't felt the wonder and power of the ocean? Or stood beside a mountain stream and marveled as the tension of the modern world drained away? Who hasn't known the joy of splashing in puddles, the rage of a summer storm, the salty taste of sorrow? We are drawn to water, in part because it holds the whole of human history inside it.

Think about it. There is the same amount of water today as there was four billion years ago. That bottle of artesian refreshment you drank this morning may once have rained on Napoleon. As Da Vinci said, when you put your hand into a flowing stream, you touch the last of the past and the first of the future.

Water is magic.

And so are words. If, as Kahlil Gibran suggests, a single drop holds all the secrets of the oceans, a single story can convey the secrets of a human heart.

When the Harpeth River Writers decided to collaborate on an anthology, they wanted a theme that would reflect their group identity, give the book a unified feel, and allow for a wide range of creative expression. What could be more unifying, yet boundless, than "water"?

The resulting anthology contains thirty-plus stories and poems by nine different authors, each written with the unifying theme of water, yet as different as a ripple is from a tsunami. Here, you'll find humor, tragedy, motorcycle gangs, vengeful spirits, fractured relationships, and more. The final story, "The Many Names of Jillyn," weaves all nine voices into a single narrative that, like droplets in a stream, merge to form a seamless whole.

So dip into this collection and let these words wash over you and through you. Let them touch your heart. You'll be glad you did.

—Jaden Terrell is a Shamus Award finalist and the internationally published author of the Nashville-based Jared McKean mysteries. She is a contributor to the "Killer Nashville Noir" anthology, to International Thriller Writers' "The Big Thrill" magazine, and to "Now Write! Mysteries." A recipient of the 2017 Killer Nashville Builder Award and the 2009 Magnolia Award. This former special-education teacher is now a writing coach who offers live workshops and online courses.

Droplets

LAUNDRY DAY

Micki Fuhrman

Presoak

The Clothes Encounter was quiet for a weekend. Stephanie fed a handful of quarters into a slot, leaned over the aging washing machine, and stuffed the tub with two days' worth of laundry: a few t-shirts and pairs of jeans, an armload of sour-smelling onesies, baby blankets, burp cloths, and bibs. *Only two days? How can one small human create such an enormous pile of putrid laundry?* She held out a V-neck top she'd just bought at T.J. Maxx. A dried patch of baby spit-up adorned the left shoulder. Another infernal white spot. Every garment she owned bore traces of them. Stephanie shoved the blouse into the washer, poured in blue-flecked powder, and the tub began to fill with a loud hiss.

Kyle was doing his best 747 imitation, lips curled into an engine cowl, dipping and tip-toeing in circles while holding little Aiden over his head.

"Kyle! Ceiling fan!"

Kyle quickly lowered the baby's altitude. "Oh. Sorry."

Stephanie flopped into one of the mismatched chairs and picked up a grubby *Better Homes & Gardens* magazine. She turned it over and began flipping through the back pages of Christmas cookie recipes and instructions for making wreaths out of pipe cleaners and wine corks. *Geez, it's August already.* She nudged through the magazine pile with one finger, searching for a warm-weather issue.

"How come you always look at magazines backwards?" Kyle held Aiden in the crook of one arm and raked his hair smooth with his other hand.

Stephanie sat up straight and side-eyed Kyle. "What's wrong with the way I look at magazines? All the important stuff is in the back."

Kyle shrugged. "Just a little weird is all. Magazine publishers put all this thought into laying out every issue—what goes in and where it's placed. Then you read it backward. I dunno—it defies logic, don't you think?"

Stephanie laid the magazine in the chair beside her. She opened her mouth, but no answer forthcame. A slight flutter in the pit of her tummy turned around on itself a few times, then formed a small, heated ball. Kyle glanced over and caught her side-eye, head on. His left eyebrow arched. *He always does that when he's about to make a smart-ass—*

"Hey, don't take it personally, Steph. It's no stranger than the way you do a lot of things. Like . . . like, when you take a bite of something you think tastes horrible, then you say, 'Ewww, this is horrible. Taste this!' Then you stick a forkful of it in my mouth. Now that's just weird. Why would I wanna taste it?"

It shouldn't have bothered her. Kyle was a comical guy, always trying to make her laugh. But not usually at her expense. Stephanie felt her heart beating in her ears.

By now, the OxiClean had done its damnedest, and a few million particles of deli mustard, chili sauce, bicycle grease, perspiration, vomit, and feces loosened their holds on the strands of cotton, polyester, and microfiber and floated out into the surrounding warm water. The old Maytag, bought during the Clinton administration, heaved once, jolting its pulleys and belts into motion for the next cycle.

Power Wash

"And the way you turn the radio down when you're driving and looking for street signs. Like you can't see because of the music. That's kinda funny, actually." Kyle's eyebrow still arched smart-assedly.

"Is it now?" she said.

Maybe it was the five months of sleep deprivation and all those peanut butter sandwiches half-eaten on the fly. Or maybe the gaping absence of daily adult human contact, or the fact that she hadn't worn mascara or shaved her armpits since Valentine's Day. The tiny heated ball in Stephanie's tummy gained in volume and intensity until it shot a stream of igneous lava up her throat and onto her tongue, where it transmogrified into words—the kind of words that sear the heart, brand themselves onto the brain, and can't be recanted by a lifetime of apologies.

"I had no idea I'm such an embarrassment to you," she said. "So . . . I suppose it's perfectly normal to do things like—oh, I dunno—blow your nose into a Kleenex, then open it up and *look at it*?"

"Well, just keeping tabs on my health, babe. You're supposed to check the color of your—"

"Never mind! As if it could get more disgusting. So, what about the way you witch-cackle every time you see my mom's number on caller ID? I don't consider that typical husbandly behavior."

"Oh, you just don't know." Kyle tickled Aiden's chin with his pinky. "Does she, little man? We guys commiserate over these things."

"Our son will have a mother-in-law someday. Don't teach him to disrespect her."

"Don't have to. That skill is buried somewhere on the Y chromosome. And, besides, you nicknamed all my friends—and me—after the seven dwarfs. What's so different?" He began rocking Aiden slowly back and forth to the rhythmic churning of the washing machine. The baby worked hard at a pacifier, and his eyelids drooped with sleepiness.

Stephanie chewed her lip. The magazine was rolled up tight in her hand and, also in rhythm, she began slapping it on the arm of the chair. "When you go in the bathroom to take a shower, you put clean underwear on your head like a turban. I'd call that a little weird."

Kyle's eyes scanned the laundromat. "You don't have to say that so loud. I just do it to be funny."

"Your mom said you always did that. Even when you thought no one was looking." She knew it was mean, but it just slipped out.

Kyle's expression darkened. "You sing Barry Manilow songs in the shower. His career was over before you were born."

"And you think Kim Possible's mom is hot."

"Well, she kinda . . . is."

"She's a *cartoon*."

Kyle seemed to be pondering the moral issue therein, and didn't appear to reach a conclusion. "So . . . you can't read a gas gauge. The tank is empty every time I get in the car."

"Every time? I don't think so. You know, I really don't get out much these days, in case you haven't noticed. I stay home and wipe a baby butt all day while you're chatting up cute little teenage girls who need new iPhones."

"Yeah, like that's really what I wanted to be doing with my life," Kyle mumbled.

"Excuse me?" Stephanie's eyebrow assumed an arch of its own. A plump woman in a floral sundress stopped her clothes-folding and gawked at the feuding couple. Aiden's eyes popped open for a moment. The pacifier bobbed a few times, and he slowly blinked back to sleep.

"I don't mean it that way. It just—it gets old, Steph. Really pretty boring, you know, hanging out in a Verizon store all day, listening to the same music, looking at the same carpet, giving the same spiel. *Upgrade today and get a hundred dollars off a new phone. Unlimited data, unlimited lines, unlimited every kind of crap you can think of.*" Kyle sighed deeply and turned around to look out the laundromat window. "Unlimited boring crap."

Stephanie stared at Kyle's back. "I would welcome that kind of boring crap. At least you get to talk to people."

"Am I not a people?"

"You know what I mean. You're, you're my . . ."

"Yeah, I'm just your husband."

Drain

The old pump kicked in and dirty water began draining noisily from the washer drum. The impurities of the last two days were sucked downward through a hose and into a rusty pipe encased in the concrete slab, then swept into an underground labyrinth of sewer lines.

"So that's how it is," said Stephanie. "You married me and then found out I have all sorts of annoying habits."

"And likewise, I guess."

He sounded tired. She *knew* she was tired, and had been for months, maybe longer. Baby-birthing did unspeakable things to a body, things no one bothered to mention in any of the dozen books she'd bought in preparation for becoming a mother. Stephanie felt like a birthday balloon, four days after the party—slack and sagging, skimming just above the floor line, occasionally bumping into furniture and walls.

Rinse and Spin

With a sharp click, the washer drum spun into motion, accelerating until it reached a blurry state of high-speed rotation. Punctuated jets of clean water pelted the clothing. The sundress lady stacked her folded A-line skirts, ruffled blouses, nylon slips, hiphugger underwear, and mint green cardigan inside a rectangular laundry basket. She stretched her Revlon "Pink in the Afternoon" lips into a brief smile in Stephanie's direction, then hefted the basket onto her hip and trundled out the door.

Kyle stood at the window, feet planted apart, gently pivoting at the waist, rocking the baby. At the bend of his elbow, Stephanie could see a curly tuft of Aiden's hair.

For a moment, she could see Kyle on the day of their wedding. His jet black hair was perfectly styled, and he tugged at the ascot of his rented tux. His best man, Tyler (aka "Bashful"), broke into a lopsided grin when she walked down the aisle, but Kyle—Kyle looked dead serious when he caught sight of her. She couldn't be sure, but she thought she saw his bottom lip quiver, just for an instant. His green eyes were riveted to hers, even after the minister began his opening remarks, which she now failed to recall.

A poly-fill baby quilt embroidered with pastel-colored jungle animals, a gift from Kyle's sister, had migrated to one side of the washer. The angry *whump-whump-whump* shattered Stephanie's reverie. Aiden awoke in full gut-scream mode. Cradling him like a football, Kyle sprinted to the washing machine, nearly colliding with Stephanie.

She flung open the lid so hard it slammed back down on her fingers. More lava words spewed from her mouth. Together, they tugged at the wadded ring of wet clothing until they pulled the sodden quilt free. Giving it a shake, Stephanie tucked the quilt evenly around the agitator and restarted the machine. She and Kyle exchanged a long, bone-weary look. Aiden's screams had not let up.

"I'll go feed him," she said, taking the baby and shuffling off to the relative quiet of the Subaru.

"I . . . appreciate . . . you," Kyle said, "really, I do," but the glass door had already closed behind Stephanie. He stood there until the Maytag's frenzied spin came to a stop.

Dry

Stephanie sat in the passenger seat long after Aiden had finished nursing. She did the thing she never tired of doing—gazing at her son's face. The dark lashes, the adorably puckered lips, the strong little fingers wrapped around her thumb. These details were also missing from the dozen becoming-a-mother books on her bedside table.

She peered through the bug-splotched windshield. A few minutes before, Kyle had moved the laundry to one of the big dryers along the back wall. Now he sat tipped back in a chair, eyes closed. *Good idea. Got about thirty-five minutes.* Stephanie let herself relax against the headrest.

A passing dump truck woke her up. Kyle stood at a waist-high table inside, folding a crib sheet. Aiden stirred and stretched his legs, tiny toes spread apart.

"Come on, little monkey. Let's go help Daddy." She knew Kyle saw her come in and strap Aiden in his carrier next to the chair, but he didn't acknowledge her. Without a word, Stephanie joined him and picked up a yellow bath towel, hooded to look like a rubber ducky. It was still warm from the dryer and smelled fresh. April fresh.

"You remembered the dryer sheet," she said.

"Yep."

A pair of her pink and black panties clung to the rubber ducky's bill. As Stephanie peeled them away, she heard a couple of static crackles. Looking around to confirm there was no one else in the Clothes Encounter, she ducked her head and slipped the panties over her hair, tucking her ponytail under the elastic.

It took Kyle only a few seconds to notice. His face melted into dimples and crinkled green eyes. "You look like an alien. But a cute alien." He grabbed the yellow ducky towel from her hand and wrapped it around her, pulling her close. "*My* cute alien."

Stephanie closed her eyes to better absorb the sensory wonder of the moment. Clean laundry, Kyle's aftershave, strong arms, cooing baby, and the mechanical applause of surrounding dryers and washing machines.

"Guess it all comes out in the wash, huh, babe?" said Kyle.

Stephanie snuggled closer.

"Dopey."

THE BOOLABURG

INCIDENT

John Neely Davis

Mid-afternoon. Satellite trucks from the three major networks, Fox News, and CNN squatted near the perimeter of Boola County Mercenary Stadium, antennas hoisted skyward like giant insects searching for prey. Vanderbilt's medivac choppers swarmed like Technicolor mosquitos, landed briefly, elevated, and swung westward toward Nashville. Tennessee's governor cut short his speech at Fall Creek Falls State Park, and his helicopter arrived minutes before two Tennessee Highway Patrol Jet Rangers and a Kiowa. Fort Campbell sent a Huey loaded with medical supplies and two trauma unit teams. The air, stirred with rotor wash from the choppers, shimmered with grass clippings, dust, sandwich wrappers, and gold and red confetti left over from last night's pep rally.

≈≈≈

Jim Farron had been dead for fifteen years. He had grown up in a family of coal miners. He knew the dangers: cave-ins, explosions, roof failures, electrocutions, bad air. However, the pay was good, and his seniority guaranteed that he could always work the day shift. His wife, Hazel, stayed at home, and he was proud of that—proud that she didn't have to work at the shoe store or at the shirt factory like so many other wives. Then the mine roof collapsed and along with it, Hazel's way of life.

The day after Jim's funeral, Hazel sat at the kitchen table and pondered her options. Naturally, the happiness of their sons, Silas and Paul, came first, but she could no longer sit at home. Everyone would have to make sacrifices. The boys worked after school and on Saturdays at the ice plant and the lumberyard. It took three years for her to get her associate's degree, working after classes and on the weekends at Boolaburg Women's Wear. Jim's mother, God bless her, helped with the boys. The day Hazel got her diploma, they felt as if all four of them had graduated.

Now, her sons were successful, traveling globally and working in pharmaceutical development for an international company.

It was a typical school day for Hazel. Her clock radio came on at 6:15; local news announcer with WCAV, Charlie Colson, gave the weather report: *Partly cloudy and mild, possible PM showers.* She bathed, brushed her teeth, pulled on her blue terrycloth robe, and went out into the carport where the morning paper waited. Back in the kitchen, she scanned the headlines and glanced at the obituary page—did not recognize anyone—and declared the day off to a good start. She watched the blue flame caress the bottom of the teakettle and popped two slices of whole wheat into the toaster. It was her workday breakfast: toast, no butter or jelly, one cup of decaf—black with no sugar. As she ate, she packed her lunch—always a brown bag with half a broiled chicken breast in a baggie, a cup of plain yogurt, an apple, and two vanilla wafers dabbed with a smidgen of peanut butter.

Hazel tidied the kitchen and then made her bed. Her clothes were color-coordinated in the small closet; it was soothing to see the hues as they gradually changed. She chose a blue dress and black sensibly heeled shoes, flossed and brushed her teeth again, then applied makeup. She studied her image in the mirror. *Gotta make an appointment at Autry's and get something done to this awful-colored hair. Stop by Chic's Salon; get Evelyn to give me a manicure. Wrinkles, good Lord, look at the wrinkles.* She placed her hands on the sides of her face and tightened the skin. *Can't anyone help with these wrinkles?* She gathered the cell phone from its charger on the bedside table. The keys to her five-year-old Chevy hung by the door—they had never hung anywhere else. She took them, dropped the phone into her purse, walked out, and locked the door. In the car, she checked the adjustment of the rearview mirror, fastened her seat belt, and started the engine. She waited for the red lights on the instrument panel to fade before backing out of the driveway.

Two blocks from her house at the intersection of Anthracite Avenue and Second Street, Chief Deputy Juno Lang sat in his patrol car, eyes flitting across the onboard radar system. He smiled at Hazel and waved—seven twenty-one and thirty-four miles per hour—she was right on time. As usual.

It took twenty minutes to drive to the school. She would be at the principal's office fifteen minutes before he arrived; Principal Bashette would bet his next week's paycheck on that. He had hired her almost ten years ago—best secretary in the entire state system, he bragged. "I could go fishing for a month, and the school would continue to run without missing a beat," he told the school board. Frequently.

She was a uniformed, no-nonsense woman.

Hazel unlocked the principal's office suite, turned the lights on, and walked into the abbreviated kitchen where she filled two plastic pitchers with tap water. From the mini-fridge, she took a plastic ice tray and divided the contents into the pitchers, placed one pitcher on a large coaster on Mr. Bashette's desk, then crossed the room and adjusted the air conditioner to seventy-two degrees. Principal Bashette liked it that way.

She sat at her desk, poured water into a glass etched with a cursive world's best secretary, and flipped open her Day-Timer. Oscar Simpson, the new chemistry teacher, had an 8:00 a.m. appointment with Principal Bashette. Oscar was a ratty, exceedingly hairy, prematurely balding little man with buck teeth and a five o'clock shadow that appeared within an hour after he shaved. In addition, his personal hygiene was less than acceptable. She heard his students referred to him as "Stinky." He was not married and as far as anyone knew, had never dated.

Outside, Mr. Bashette parked in his reserved space, and she heard the door to his Ford slam as Oscar Simpson entered her office and stood awkwardly at her desk. His shirt was already damp at the armpits, a tuft of body hair peeked from his unbuttoned collar, and the third shirt button from the top was missing.

She stood, sipped the water, and holding the coolness of the World's best secretary glass against her cheek, said, "Mr. Bashette will be with you momentarily. Won't you please have a—" She did not finish the sentence, but instead, stumbled forward onto the startled chemistry teacher.

Oscar recoiled from the spilling water and breaking glass, then reached out for the falling woman with the grace of a man trying to grasp a wet dog without touching it.

Hazel gasped twice. "The water . . . it's . . . can't get a . . . ." She convulsed twice and stopped breathing.

≈ ≈ ≈

The barber's sign with its helix of red, white, and blue stripes commenced spinning. The neon open sign in the front window of Clipper's Cuts came to life. Five minutes earlier, Clipper Duncan had finished his shave, soaked his face with a steaming towel, and applied Pinaud Lilac Vegetal to his meaty jowls. It was the morning ritual before opening the shop. Clipper made it a habit to get to the barbershop at least thirty minutes before opening. He liked to shave where he had plenty of hot water.

The scanner on his work shelf flashed through a dozen channels and stopped on the Boolaburg police frequency.

Boolaburg Dispatch: All units 10-33 at the high school.

Clipper rinsed his straight razor under the faucet and looked at the scanner. He tapped the button on the face of the radio that would hold the frequency for forty-five seconds before starting another scan. The minute hand on the clock with the Gillette razor blade advertisement jumped: Eight eleven.

Tommy Heitz limped in the front door. He was the second-chair barber, a former welder who lost his left foot in a mining accident. He had confided to Clipper: "Screaming, twisting kids ain't nothing compared to having a continuous miner roaring in your face all day." Clipper took him at his word and always arranged a trip to the restroom when Mrs. Dodd brought her five-year-old triplets in for their semi-annual haircuts. That would be three restroom trips for Clipper in fifteen minutes.

"Something going on down at the high school. Just before you came in, Dispatch sent out a 10-33. Believe that is a 'Need immediate assistance.'"

Tommy turned his barber chair to face the front window of the barbershop and leaned back into the aged leather. "Bet it's that Juky Patton kid acting up again. Just 'cause he scored three touchdowns the other night, he thinks he is the cock of the walk. He'll be damn lucky if he finishes his senior year. I don't care if the Vols are recruiting him; he is a royal pain in the ass. But I reckon he come by it honest; his daddy was, too."

Boolaburg Dispatch: All units 10-39 to the high school.

Clipper moved to the sidewalk in front of his shop just in time to see Deputy Juno Lang skid around the corner, siren wailing, blue lights flashing. The deputy was leaning forward, mic at his lips, and didn't acknowledge Clipper.

"Whoa," Tommy said. "Didn't think Jeff had a foot near that heavy. He's not careful he'll spill his coffee."

Back in the shop, the two barbers stood staring at the scanner, mesmerized.

Car Three to Dispatch: 10-52 Everything available.

"Damn," Clipper said. "That's a call for an ambulance. No, not an ambulance, he wants all ambulances. Sure ain't the Patton boy causing all that trouble, I can tell you that."

≈ ≈ ≈

The short, yellow school bus stopped at an unpainted concrete block building. Identical signage on both: boola county senior development. The accordion door opened and seven adult men came out in single file, like kindergartners; the first man rested his hand on the bus driver's shoulder, and each succeeding man placed his right hand on the shoulder of the man in front of him.

Once the file of men entered the building, two men holding hands scurried from the bus and turned left toward downtown Boolaburg. Although both dressed in bib overalls, white T-shirts, and black tennis shoes, because of their dissimilar physical appearance, no one would have guessed them brothers.

The leading man wore a baseball cap with *bob* in capital letters stitched across the front. He had a flat, wide face and short, thick neck. His eyes, behind plastic heart-shaped sunglasses, scanned the sidewalk, and their movements were unsynchronized. He extended his tongue with each crab-like step, as if the effort took full concentration.

The second man, Eli, was taller and leaner, wore aviator sunglasses, and walked with his head tilted back like a timid animal testing the morning breeze. He clutched the overall galluses of the shorter man and followed a step behind, matching his gait with Bob's lurches.

With their talents combined, the Stanford brothers were mentally and physically equal to most residents of Boolaburg.

Bob walked with short, choppy steps and leaned against the pull of his brother. "Come on, Eli," he said, his speech slurred. "I need a 'nanner. I got this 'un yesterday, and it's about wore out."

Bob always carried a banana in his right front pants pocket. It protruded like an old western gunfighter's pistol—*Lash LaRue's*, Bob thought. When stressed, he would pull the banana from his pocket and point it toward the provoker. Mrs. Below at the high-school cafeteria gave him a fresh fruit each day. Bob called it "reloading." Eli worked—kinda. Each day after the cafeteria stop, Bob led Eli to the barbershop and seated him next to the shoeshine chair. Eli took a worn whetstone from the bib of his overalls and waited. "I'm a world champion knife sharpener," he said each time the front door opened. "A dime a blade. Or a quarter for three. Guarantee you can shave with any blade you give to me." There would be a three-second beat, and Eli would finish his chant, "Or the sharpening is free."

His lack of eyesight did not affect his touch, and he ran his thumb deftly down the freshly sharpened knife-edge.

But this morning, they didn't make it to the cafeteria. A stream of howling police cars and shrieking ambulances blocked their path, and the two men stood at the town's single traffic light, Eli repeating, "What's happening—what's happening?"

Bob did not answer, but instead danced with excitement and didn't notice as the banana fell from his pocket to the concrete.

≈≈≈

Charlie Colson struggled. His degree in communications from Tech was useless as teats on a boar hog—while he didn't quite understand the phrase, he used it often because he thought it made him sound worldly.

Working at wcav was one step up from standing on a street corner shouting through a megaphone, because wcav—1480 am on your radio dial—voice of the plateau—had a range of ten miles during daylight hours and three miles at night.

The station featured country music—none of the current country-western boys with soul patches, earrings, and cutoff sleeveless shirts—with traditional performers like Kitty Wells, Lonnie Glosson, Wayne Raney, Lefty Frizzell, and radio performances of the renfro valley barn dance.

Charlie was almost a celebrity because he hosted the noon time radio swap shop where farmers traded bales of hay for goats and women swapped crocheted doilies for hen eggs. He also made on-air, happy-birthday announcements and sold radio advertising in thirty-second chunks for everything from hog feed to Washington Dee-Cee bib overalls. The station furnished him with a battered and un-air conditioned Ford Pinto with the radio's logo in peeling letters on the driver's side door. He was a news stringer for WSM and dreamed of the day when his voice would be broadcast over the mighty 650.

≈≈≈

Oscar Simpson loosened his grip on Hazel and turned awkwardly away as she slid to the floor, her dress slipping up to the top of her thighs, revealing shocking-red panties. For a second he stood looking at the lifeless woman, then wiped his palms against the sides of his trousers as if he'd been touching something unclean and raced down the corridor to intercept Mr. Bashette.

The principal studied his reflection in the storm door and adjusted his foulard tie. After school today, he planned to drive down to Nashville and attend a Special Ed meeting at the state office building. He looked forward to the trip, having a nice meal and a cocktail, and if the timing worked out, perhaps spend a few hours with his widowed mother. The tie had been a Christmas gift, and Mom would appreciate seeing him wearing it.

Oscar Simpson flung the door open and staggered toward the startled principal. "It's the water. It's . . . it's . . . it's killed Hazel . . . and I'm dying, too." Oscar dropped to his knees before the principal, retched twice, and then fell face forward onto the sidewalk.

Principal Bashette took two quick steps back from the convulsing man and stared at the foam collecting in the corner of Oscar's mouth. He fumbled at the latch of his briefcase before opening it and spilling a jumble of ballpoint pens, textbooks, and a plastic bag containing an egg-salad sandwich on the parking lot pavement. He found his flip phone and stabbed 911 onto the keypad.

≈ ≈ ≈

"But we were here first, you sumbitch." Clothed in a tattered fire-engine red suit, Brother Aaron Solomon stood at the edge of the Boola County Fairgrounds watching a Blazer Brothers Circus roustabout unloading a cage containing a scrawny lion from a flatbed eighteen-wheeler.

Willie Johnson was Supervisor of Streets in Boolaburg and in addition, held the honorary position of Chairman of the Fair Board. Although his annual compensation from his fair work was only three free tickets to any event held at the fairgrounds, he did not believe he should take a cussing—especially from the overweight, balding, self-proclaimed, miracle-making man screaming in his face.

"Now, Brother Solomon, don't talk to me like that. Watch your tongue. You just get a grip on yourself and remember that you're a man of God. Christians share; love their fellow man."

Willie had never attended a single gathering of the brother aaron solomon's restoration revival. Driving by the fairgrounds this morning on the way to work, he had seen the bagging, open-sided tent hovering over a sawdust floor and five-dozen metal chairs. Naked sixty-watt bulbs dangled from electrical cords suspended from tent poles, and a single floodlight was poised to focus on the raised platform at the front of the tent. A gaudily painted wooden lectern embossed with the letters basrr in a gothic font commanded the center of the platform. Two fiberglass porta potties lurked at the edge of the parking lot, a respectable distance from the tent, assuring freedom from embarrassing sounds and even worse, smells.

Solomon came closer to Willie and amped up his volume. "These circus people—have you seen them? Men running around without shirts, hairy bellies hanging over their pants. Women with their faces painted, hair done up on the top of their heads, bosoms shoved up till they almost touch their chins."

Willie's knowledge of basrr was contained in a pamphlet he'd taken from a convenience store counter last night. According to the pamphlet, fifty years ago as a five-year-old child, Brother Solomon had a vision while recovering from a serious bout of scarlet fever. A voice told him he would bring salvation to the Appalachians and would raise a great temple to the glory of God. Brother Solomon had never married and had devoted his entire life to fulfilling the prophecy.

The Chairman of the Fair Board eyed the basrr bedraggled canvas tabernacle and the two porta potties. He wondered if The Voice would settle for a tent and not hold Brother Solomon accountable for not building a temple.

Willie had arrived at the fairgrounds in response to a frantic phone call from Brother Solomon. The Chairman of the Fair Board had seen a dozen sweating, shirtless men unfurling a canvas circus tent. However, he had not seen the high-bosomed women, but nevertheless, felt it was his obligation to do so—'specially since he was Chairman of the Fair Board and a community pillar.

Boston Blazer stepped down from the cab of the Diamond Rio tractor and wondered why the fat fellow was screaming at the skinny man dressed in a baggy white-and-lime seersucker suit. Boston wiped the sweat from his forehead, then adjusted his aviator sunglasses. His khakis were stained with ferris wheel grease, and his work boots—in deference to the hot weather and steaming humidity—were loosely laced. Although it was still early in the carny season, he was tired—tired of jerk-water towns, small crowds, and the constant headache of dealing with rubes.

"There," Brother Solomon shouted toward Willie and pointed to Boston Blazer. "Go on over there and tell him we were here first, and he can load up his tent and that mangy lion and just move right on out."

Boston slammed the truck door and crossed the parched clay of the fairgrounds. He extended his hand. "Hey, Mister Johnson. Remember me? Boston Blazer. We talked last month. Got the permit from you, and here we are just like the permit says. Finished a very successful run up at Scooterton. Looking forward to entertaining the fine folks here in Boolaburg."

"Now see here . . ." Brother Solomon's words trailed away when he saw the spider web tattoo on Boston's elbow and the tattoo of a handless watch on his left wrist—the preacher knew prison tats when he saw them. Boston pulled a folded copy of a document from his shirt pocket, flattened the wrinkles, and handed the permit to the Chairman of the Fair Board.

Solomon's stomach experienced a butterfly flutter when he saw Boston's tattooed knuckles: stay on the right hand and down on the left.

While Willie pretended to scrutinize the permit, Boston turned to watch the roustabouts raising the tent. He ran numbers through his head—lately, he had started doing this a lot. *Twelve men at sixteen dollars a day. Fifty dollars for the permit. Hundred thirty-eight dollars for fuel. Twenty-five dollars for groceries.* He had left Scooterton with four hundred and twenty-nine dollars in his trucker's wallet. *Three night's work for a measly four hundred and twenty-nine damn dollars. Then there was the lion. He needed meat scraps. Or a big chunk of meat. For God's sake, the lion's hair was falling out.* Last night, Boston had shared a baloney sandwich with the big cat.

Brother Aaron, sweat darkening the back of his red coat, was yammering at the Chairman of the Fair Board again. "You've dropped the ball. You've over-permitted the site. This is all your fault."

Boston looked at Brother Aaron, mentally measuring the shouting man's height and girth. *Probably be enough meat right there to feed the lion for three days.*

≈≈≈

Principal Bashette stepped across Oscar Simpson's twitching body and ran down the long hallway. Hazel was sprawled awkwardly on the floor in her office. He knelt beside his secretary and checked her pulse. In all the years they had worked together, this was the first time he had noticed how fair her skin was. Now it was dry and cold.

At his desk, he cleared his throat and moistened his lips before speaking into the PA system's microphone. "Good morning, this is Principal Bashette. Please exit the building in an orderly fashion and assemble on the football field where I will give you additional instructions. On your way out, avoid the water fountains—I repeat—avoid the water fountains."

The principal dashed down the hall and stood at the school's main entrance, monitoring the orderly flow of students. He was a strict disciplinarian, and the stream of students moved calmly past him.

The evacuation would have been successful had the red-haired Warren twins not arrived for classes ten minutes late. Habitually tardy, they were accustomed to evading detection by sneaking unseen into the school by the end door. But this morning, they almost stumbled over Oscar Simpson as the chemistry teacher struggled to regain his feet.

"Don't go in there," Simpson said, his usually weak voice now weaker. "Mrs. Hazel has been poisoned. She's dead. It was the water."

The twins jerked the door open and sprinted down the hall to the principal's office. Through the doorway, they could see the unmoving body of the secretary, the wet floor, and the broken glass.

In his finest hour, patriot Paul Revere could not have spread the word as joyously and effectively. The Warren brothers charged into the mass of calmly evacuating students shouting, "The water is poison. It's done killed Mrs. Hazel, and Oscar Simpson is lying out on the sidewalk, dying. We saw both of 'em. It's awful."

For the first time in his career as principal of Boolaburg High, Mr. Bashette lost control of the three-hundred-member student body and most of the teachers. Later, while he was in the Boola County Hospital's chaotic emergency room being treated for a broken arm and two fractured ribs, he confided to his wife that he had feared being trampled to death.

≈≈≈

At the football field, the closely shorn grass between the twenty-yard lines was almost hidden as milling students gave wide berths to those who seemed to be in the most serious condition.

The Boola County Mercenaries were one week into their two-a-day practice sessions, and the entire football team had been consuming copious amounts of water, trying to ward off heat exhaustion and debilitating cramps. Four offensive linemen, three safeties, and a linebacker lay on their sides, retching.

Two sobbing cheerleaders sat crossed-legged on the grass encircled by the rest of the squad, who were consoling them.

The entire first-period home ec group, who had just completed washing their hands for the salad prep class, sat near the bleachers, crying uncontrollably.

Ms. Felder, the humanities teacher, had collapsed out near the forty-yard line. Two of her students and the second-period math teacher were laying their hands on the unconscious teacher and beseeching God at the top of their lungs to spare Ms. Felder's life.

Contagion came into effect and students in varying stages of unconsciousness crumpled onto the field. Mercenary Stadium resembled a third-world country under an Ebola attack.

Within thirty minutes of the Warren twins' terrifying announcement, every emergency vehicle from Boolaburg and the surrounding counties was on the scene at the football field or en route. Three of Vanderbilt's medivac helicopters had risen from the hospital's helipad and were hammering eastward toward the stadium.

The Tennessee Highway Patrol, anticipating overwhelming emergency traffic, rerouted all westbound I-40 traffic between Boolaburg and Nashville. Tennessee's Lieutenant Governor, the Director of Tennessee Emergency Management Agency, the Area Commander of Nashville's Salvation Army, the Regional CEO of the American Red Cross, and the Major General of the Tennessee National Guard loaded into Air Guard choppers and left Nashville.

Boolaburg Chief of Police, Herky Payne, reported that six thousand feet of yellow crime scene – do not cross tape was needed to enclose the campus. In addition, local law enforcement officers secured the perimeter and were restricting ingress and egress to authorized personnel only.

≈ ≈ ≈

Unaware of the chaos, at the Boola County Fairgrounds, Chairman of the Fair Board Willie Johnson was proud of the peace he'd partially negotiated and secretly wondered if he should run for a city office—alderman, or maybe mayor.

Boston Blazer suggested that he might open the circus only on Thursday

and Saturday, leaving Friday night and Sunday afternoon for basrr. Brother
Solomon disagreed. Thursday's crowd had never been robust, and Saturday night's services were better attended. Prudent women knew Saturday
night was the time their husbands were most likely to get all likkered up.
A man in church on Saturday night was not likely to be a man in jail on
Sunday morning. Still, Sunday's gatherings, while painfully small, were
always the most generous. Brother Solomon even had a special sermon
based on the widow's mite and another about streets paved with gold.

"If we can come to an agreement on this allocation," Chairman of the
Fair Board Johnson said, "I think I can arrange for one of the city's street-
washing trucks to come out and sprinkle the fairgrounds. Hold the dust
down. But I must have assurance that there will be no further conflict
between the two of you."

"Give me a few minutes to go to my Lord in prayer about this matter,"
Brother Solomon said, as he removed a sweat-stained and worn Old Testament from his coat pocket.

Chairman of the Fair Board Johnson and Boston Blazer moved to the
shade of the basrr tent while Brother Solomon dropped to his knees and
consulted with the Higher Power.

A battered Dodge eight-passenger van with basrr emblazoned on the
driver-side door slowly crossed the fairground parking lot and came to a
jerking stop at the side of the tent. A young woman carrying a Styrofoam
cooler emerged from the van's sliding-door opening and was joined by
the driver, who was carrying a bag of ice. Blazer and Johnson exchanged
bewildered looks. The women were identical twins, even to their crooked
teeth and crossed eyes.

"Been to the ice plant. Gonna fill the cooler with ice and put some bath
cloths in there. Brother Solomon and one of the women on the mourn-
ers' bench like to got too hot last night. Oh, guess I oughta introduce
myself. I'm Annie, Annie Penguin," the woman with the ice said, "and this
is Nannie. We're sisters. Twins. Plumb alike, 'cept she don't talk. Lessen
it's absolutely necessary."

Although the twins were wearing white smock-like dresses, Boston's discerning eyes noted that all the protuberances and dips were in the right places. "Y'all kin to Solomon?" he asked.

Nannie poured ice into the cooler and waited for her sister to respond to Boston's question. Annie sat in a folding metal chair and folded white bath cloths into precise squares. "Oh, no, we joined BASRR up in Hungry Gap last week."

"Hungry Gap?" Boston said.

Annie stacked a dozen bath cloths on her lap and gave them a final smoothing. "Guessing you've never been there. It's in West Virginia. On the Tug Fork River. 'Bout five miles from Welch."

"I've heard of Welch."

Nannie opened a folding chair and sat beside her twin.

Annie patted her sister's shoulder. "We was both saved. Brother Solomon preached to us. Showed us the error of our ways. We'd been turrible sinful."

The young woman stretched the last word out so long that Boston wondered what in the heck they'd done.

"We spent most of two nights on the moaner's bench. Everybody was crying and singing and praying. Then the Holy Ghost come over us. It was such a wondrous feeling that I just rose up and started shouting—they said I was speaking in ancient tongues. Nobody 'cept Brother Solomon could understand me, and I didn't know myself what I was saying."

Chairman of the Fair Board Johnson turned from the twins and muttered to Boston, "Folks start that shouting and speaking in tongues shit—I'm outta there. Next thing you know, they open up a wooden box and drag out a copperhead or a rattler. Hold that snake in front of their face and sway back and forth. I'm telling you, it'll make the hair rise up on the back of your neck."

"Where y'all staying?" Boston asked.

"We stay in the van. It's right comfortable in there."

"The three of you?" Boston questioned.

Annie smiled. "Oh, no, that wouldn't be proper. Me and Nannie sleep in the van. Brother Solomon always stays in a motel. Right now, he's staying at the Elgin. He needs to have a good cool place so he can study the Bible without being bothered. Then, of course, he's got to shower and shave so he'll look good while he's preaching. When he goes to eat breakfast, we can go in the room and wash up. Sometimes . . ." Annie's cheeks flushed, and she halted in midsentence.

Boston brought a cigar stub from his shirt pocket and sniffed the stale tobacco. "And what, Annie? What were you about to say?"

Annie looked to her sister for support, but Nannie would not meet her gaze. "We . . . well, I . . . sometimes . . . Brother Solomon needs . . . he's a man of God and . . . but sometimes he needs . . . he says it's all according to the—"

Boston raised his hand. "You don't have to go on. I understand." He dropped the unlit cigar, and with his heel, ground it into the dirt, then waited for the red-swirling in his brain to go away. "How old are you, Annie?"

"Sixteen. We're both sixteen," she said.

A squadron of Tennessee State Troopers cars swooshed along the highway at the front of the fairgrounds, sirens whooping, emergency lights pulsating, long antennas slicing the morning air.

The radio hanging from Willie Johnson's belt sputtered with static intermingled with the dispatcher's voice. "Mr. Johnson . . . you to come . . . worst thing . . . dead people . . . ."

≈≈≈

Mid-afternoon. Satellite trucks from the three major networks, Fox News, and CNN squatted near the perimeter of Boola County Mercenary Stadium, antennas hoisted skyward like giant insects searching for prey. Vanderbilt's medivac choppers swarmed like Technicolor mosquitoes, landed briefly, elevated, and swung westward toward Nashville. Tennessee's governor cut short his speech at Fall Creek Falls State Park, and his helicopter arrived minutes before two Tennessee Highway Patrol Jet Rangers and a Kiowa. Ft. Campbell sent a Huey loaded with medical supplies and two trauma unit teams. The air, stirred with rotor wash from the choppers, shimmered with grass clippings, dust, sandwich wrappers, and gold and red confetti left over from last night's pep rally.

Bewildered, Chairman of the Fair Board Johnson stood slack-jawed at the edge of the high school campus.

Weeping mothers, enraged and red-faced fathers, and anxious siblings waited in the stadium's parking lot, restrained by law enforcement officers from entering the stadium. The National Guard set up a mess tent. Red Cross handed out bottles of water. The red-haired Warren brothers snatched four cases of water from the Red Cross supply and were peddling bottles for a dollar each. Two pre-teen boys sold boiled peanuts from a wooden wheelbarrow. The local funeral home distributed five hundred wooden-handle fans. Four independent candidates for county constable worked the crowd, handing out flyers and bumper stickers.

Boolaburg Chief of Police, Herky Payne, raided the poolroom and swore in ten new, completely unqualified deputies.

≈≈≈

"Ain't no need of hanging around here." Clipper Duncan levered his barber chair to the upright position, then stood and faced the front window. "Why don't you turn out the lights while I go take a leak. Might as well go down to the stadium and join the crowd."

Tommy Heitz locked the barbershop and favoring his bad leg, hobbled along the sidewalk behind Clipper toward the stadium.

A block from the school, they encountered the mass of people. "Looks like a bucket of creek minnows flopping around," Clipper said.

Tommy leaned against a telephone pole and looked at the milling crowd. "Damn," he said. "I've been to the Gator Bowl and a stock car race at Bristol, but I ain't never seen a crowd like that."

≈≈≈

Eli Stanford looked upward, blind eyes searching for the source of the noise. The whining of the helicopter engines and the *slap-slap-slap* of the rotor system in such proximity was frightening and disorienting. "Bob. Bob, tell me what you see," he shouted as his hands fluttered through the air frantically searching for his brother.

Bob removed his plastic heart-shaped sunglasses, extended his tongue, and followed the path of three helicopters as they roared over the street at an elevation of less than two-hundred feet. "War," he said. "War. They coming."

A four-by-four concrete box culvert had been constructed under the street—one end opening on the south side of Monroe Street and the north end opening near the receiving ramp at the side of the high school cafeteria. Bob dragged his brother into the culvert, and they squatted in the semi-darkness with their hands covering their ears as the 101st Airborne's Huey hovered over the street, waiting for ground operations to radio a landing zone.

≈≈≈

WCAV's Charlie Colson had arrived—this was the big event needed to launch his career! He was in heaven but still alive. Awed and struggling to stop his mouth from hanging open, he stood looking up at the forest of antennas. Already he's seen WSM's cute little female anchor, two prominent CNN correspondents, one of those Fox guys who covered every disaster from starving dogs in Kenya to lost Eskimo children, and a *Tennessean* sports reporter, Tom something-or-other, who was on his way to Hicksboro to cover The National Rolley Hole Marbles Championship and Festival.

Charlie wore a tattered yellow polo shirt with—WCAV 1480 on your am radio dial Voice of the Plateau—silkscreened on the back and wandered through the crowd, sucking on a bottle of Red Cross water.

Trailed by a cameraman, CNN's Janice McCormick extended her hand toward Charlie. "You live here?" she asked.

Charlie intended to use his professional radio voice, but his words came out with the tenor of a mid-puberty, pimple-faced boy. "Yes, I'm Charlie Colson with WCAV," he squeaked and turned so the reporter could see the back of his shirt.

"Do you have a moment?" she asked, and without waiting for an answer, made a circular motion with her index finger to the cameraman, and spoke into the microphone. "This is CNN with breaking news, and I'm Janice McCormick. We are live in Boolaburg, Tennessee, where earlier today, hundreds of high school students were poisoned. I am speaking with Charlie Colson, Program Director, with WCAV. Mr. Colson, can you tell us what happened and verify the number of casualties?"

Charlie was regaining his composure, but his recovery was compromised by Janice's cleavage that seemed to simultaneously press against both sides of his nose. That and the new title of Program Director are things dreams were made of and would keep him awake tonight.

He cleared his throat and tried to fill his diaphragm with air just as he'd been taught in radio announcing school. "Far as I know, only the school secretary died, but Oscar Simpson is feeling poorly."

This was not what Janice McCormick was seeking. "I understand," she said, trying to ignore a drop of sweat moving down her cheek and angling toward her chin, "the entire football field is littered with dead or maybe dying students. Can you confirm this?"

Charlie was conflicted. Immensely. But his mama had hammered into his heart: "To thine own self be true." He answered, "No, ma'am, I hear there's a bunch puking and rolling around, but I ain't seen no dead folks come out of there yet."

Janice looked at the camera and jerked an index finger across her throat. She nodded to Charlie and followed by the cameraman, elbowed her way into the crowd.

Charlie knew he had blown his chance to be on national TV. He did not know what he had done, but it must have been bad. However, it had not been a total waste of time. He had seen Janice McCormick's cleavage up close. Real close.

≈≈≈

Alice Linden was the first woman mayor of Boolaburg. Her training as a pharmacy tech did not qualify her to handle a major disaster or hold a press conference. But here she stood on a flatbed trailer, blinking into the raging illumination of a dozen floodlights.

She had chosen a tan business suit and a white blouse for the occasion; her dry mouth was an unintended accessory. Behind her stood Tennessee's Lieutenant Governor, the Director of Tennessee Emergency Management Agency, the Area Commander of Nashville's Salvation Army, the Regional CEO of the American Red Cross, the Major General of the Tennessee

National Guard, Boolaburg Chief of Police, Boola County Sheriff, and two midget door-to-door Bible salesmen who had gotten caught up in the dignitaries rushing to the stage.

Alice looked out onto the sea of upturned faces—*My God, I wish I were back at Walgreens raking opioids into childproof amber plastic bottles.* She cupped her hand over the microphone, and the feedback caused the sound system to shriek at the decibel level of a low altitude flyover of the Blue Angels.

The scream of the PA system ceased when she moved her hand. "Sorry, sorry," she said. "This has truly been an extraordinary day in Boolaburg. I will try to give an accurate update of today's events. We have one known fatality, Mrs. Hazel Farron, a secretary at the school. Perhaps as many as a hundred students and eight teachers have come down with an illness of undetermined origin. Our local emergency room and hospital have been overwhelmed. Many of the ill are being treated in place by the 101st medical team at Mercenary Stadium. The more serious cases have been transported by ambulances and helicopters to either Nashville or Knoxville. We are unsure of the nature of the illnesses. Early speculation is water contamination from unidentified bacteria."

As if choreographed, the crowd gasped and every cup and bottle of water slipped from instantly paralyzed fingers and splashed onto the parking lot surface. A shuffling of bodies swept through the crowd as everyone tried to move away from the spreading liquid.

Alice continued. "Perhaps the only comforting information I have is we believe the bacteria is confined to the school's water source. As many of you know, ten years ago the city drilled a well here on the campus. So there is almost no possibility that the city water supply is infected."

Somewhere in the back of the crowd, a man shouted, "Hallelujah."

On stage, the midgets high-fived.

"And finally," the mayor said, "our medical team has reached the conclusion that those individuals on campus when the unfortunate incident occurred this morning will be quarantined here until further notice."

There was an agonized roar from the crowd, and seven mothers sank to the ground as if they'd been shot.

Alice visibly flinched before continuing. "The school building, including the cafeteria and gymnasium, will be off limits to anyone unauthorized and not wearing a Hazmat suit. Tents and shelters are being brought in, and of course, meals will be furnished. Are there any questions?"

Like panicked birds, frantic hands fluttered above the crowd. As if in response, the diesel engine running the generators powering the floodlights sputtered once, coughed twice, and shut down. Darkness was overwhelming and immediate.

≈≈≈

With all the excitement, the economy in Boolaburg reached a level not seen since the mines closed fifteen years ago. Food trucks swarmed the little town like flies to a dead possum. Fruit stands and vegetable vendors crowded against the sidewalks. Both motels were one hundred percent occupied. In less than an hour, seven T-shirt vendors sold out of silkscreened shirts with an enormous red bug—the artist's conception of a bacterium—stenciled on the back. Hillbilly entrepreneurship surfaced as local residents rented bedrooms to the influx of media and the out-of-state curious. Overnight, Grady Watson's cow pasture adjacent to the city limits sprouted pop-up tents and camping trailers like dandelions. Henry's Hamburger Heaven ran out of ground beef before noon, and Sam's Soft Serve ice cream machine caught fire. Even the cells in the county jail were standing room only.

At the Boola County Fairgrounds, Brother Aaron Solomon and Boston Blazer decided there were enough people to fill both venues.

The Blazer Brothers' rickety ferris wheel turned until midnight with only an occasionally empty seat. Boola County schoolchildren gathered around the lion's cage and stared with awe in their eyes; the lion returned their stares with hunger in his.

Brother Aaron Solomon's Restoration Revival had some of the audience rolling in the aisles—literally. The fiery sermons about the Holy Spirit and the Power of the Blood were drawing spectators who had never witnessed a tent revival. While Brother Solomon dished out sermons filled with prophecy, hell and brimstone, and accounts of his own healing powers, Annie and Nannie Penguin moved through the crowded aisles, their flowing dresses virginally white, pleading with the sinners to go forward and receive their own spiritual gifts. The twice-passed collection plates overflowed.

Boston Blazer leaned against a tree and drank Styrofoam-cupped coffee across the road from the Elgin Motel where Brother Solomon had a room. Apparently, the furor of sermons increased his needs, because Annie Penguin left the comforts of the BASRR van and visited him at night as well as morning. Boston watched as Annie left the preacher's room, hair disheveled, wiping tears from her eyes. He thought about the needs of the hungry lion and subconsciously, a plan flickered to life.

≈≈≈

Four days after Hazel Farron's death, Boolaburg collapsed back into its former state of a sleepy, backwoods town. Two events brought the panic of unknown bacteria to a standstill.

The EIS, EPO, EHL, NCEH, CDCP in Atlanta, the ceds in Nashville, and the Vanderbilt University School of Medicine studied water and air samples gathered from the Boolaburg High School campus. Similar samples went to the University of Chicago and the Health Science Center at Houston.

The reports from these facilities were consistent: No bacteria, no viruses, no fungi, no parasites, no protozoa, no toxic gases, no chemicals—nothing dangerous.

The second and most telling event was the emergence of brothers Bob and Eli Stanford from the high school cafeteria. For three nights, heavily armed hazmat-clad SWAT teams wearing infrared glasses searched the cafeteria and gym for the source of strange lights and even stranger thumping sounds. Turned out that the thumping noises were blind Eli dribbling a basketball in the dark recesses of the gym, and the strange lights were Bob and his flashlight searching storage facilities in the cafeteria for 'nanners.

≈≈≈

Mayor Alice Linden scheduled a press conference in the Boolaburg Gymnasium. One hundred and fifty chairs were arrayed in two concentric semicircles facing the platform that would be occupied by the medical team. To her great relief, Mayor Linden would not be able to attend since this was the day that unemployment and Medicaid checks arrived. Walgreens would be swamped with customers demanding instant filling of prescriptions for painkilling drugs. Sudafed, lithium batteries, and acetone were also big sellers on these days.

Twenty chairs would have been adequate. Gone were CNN, Fox, major network satellite trucks, and newspaper reporters. WCAV's Charlie Colson sat in the middle of the front section of chairs, a door-to-door, Bible-selling midget on either side. Clipper Duncan and Tommy Heitz hung a back in an hour sign on the barbershop door and now sat on the second row behind Charlie and the midgets. Deputy Sheriff Juno Lang and Chairman of the Fair Board, Willie Johnson, stood arms akimbo by the speaker's platform. Boolaburg High principal Bashette sat uncomfortably in a folding chair at the side of the gym, arm in a plaster cast. Aviator sunglasses shielding his blind eyes, Eli Stanford sat with a basketball in his lap on an end chair. His brother, Bob, baseball cap askew and still wearing his plastic heart-shaped sunglasses, stood behind him. The red-haired Warren twins stood in the partially opened men's restroom door at the rear of the gym, cigarettes in cupped hands behind their backs.

Boolaburg Chief of Police, Herky Payne, read from a yellow legal pad the names of the seven medical personnel sharing the stage with him. It was not easy. Most of the doctors' names ended with *ski* or *vich,* or were a hyphenated mixture of Spanish or some type of Hindu word that contained at least eighteen letters.

The doctors discussed the earlier happenings in a panel format. They used words like mass psychogenic illness, epidemic hysteria, and situational disturbances. To those gathered in the gym, the doctors might as well have conversed in Sanskrit. After fifteen minutes, the medical team opened the conversation up for questions. Not surprising, there were none.

Chief Payne, menacing in a black uniform with a pistol, handcuffs, Mace, telescoping baton, and three two-way radios hanging from his belt, walked to the microphone and put his hands in his pockets. "What the doctors have said in a nice way is that all this panic and puking was just a lot of hooey. Hazel died of a heart attack. Oscar Simpson got damned near scared to death because he'd never touched a dead person. Mr. Bashette tried his best, but he added to all this crap by dismissing classes and telling the students to stay away from the water fountains. Then, them Warren twins really stirred the pot. All them sick football players, hell, they just didn't want to go back to class. Cheerleaders. Never saw one that had sense to pour pi—water outta a boot. That teacher, Ms. Felder, she just got too hot running across the football field. Ain't no telling how much money and manpower was wasted. And in the end, this whole damn business was just a crock of shit."

Epilogue

Millie from Autry's Barber and Beauty Shop stopped by and styled Hazel's hair. She added a bit more of blue rinse than usual and tamed Hazel's cowlick. "There," she said and tucked an unruly wisp above her ear. "Toned down that yellow and made it a graceful gray." She stepped away and admired her handiwork. "Everyone will be absolutely charmed. And envious."

Hazel's suit was a powder blue with enough polyester to add body to the wool. Her white blouse had a frilly front, ending with a mass of lace at the neck. Her favorite American flag pin and her husband's silver UMWA pin sat above her left breast, contrasting beautifully against the blueness.

Evelyn from Chic's Salon tapered the nails perfectly and identically. The Revlon Deep Red polish was applied carefully—no bubbles, no ridges, none on the cuticles. Since they would not show, the toenails were left natural.

The narrow gold band Hazel had worn her entire married life was her only jewelry. It had been polished, given the same attention to detail as her attire.

Ralston Four, a name Moody Rushing had bestowed upon himself last year, from Jolene's Salon of Satisfaction, spent almost two hours on Hazel's makeup. To offset the artificial lighting, he applied a foundation layer with a latex sponge; it was a shade darker than Hazel usually wore. He was especially careful to work the creases around the eyes. A soft brush helped set the foundation over the eyelids. Powder to the rest of Hazel's face assured that the foundation stabilized properly. He brushed the eyebrows to dislodge any trapped foundation, then used an eyebrow pencil to define their shape. Black liquid eyeliner was applied, one sweep to the outer corner of each eye. A touch of blush outlined Hazel's bone structure. He primed her lips with balm before adding a bold color.

Ralston Four reduced the intensity of the overhead lights and turned the exhaust fan off. He unlocked the door, opened it, and stood admiring his work. Perfect, if he did say so himself.

Hazel was the most beautiful corpse he had ever seen emerge from the double side doors of William's Mortuary. No, that is not right; she was *the* most beautiful corpse he had ever seen.

≈≈≈

Hazel's two sons were upstanding businessmen. "Took after their mother and daddy," former Boola County Chief of Police Herky Payne said at their memorial service. "Wouldn't have expected anything else."

They died on a medical mission trip. Their plane crashed outside the Kathmandu Valley of central Nepal, and their bodies never recovered. A monument fashioned into the profile of the Himalayas was erected beside the gravestone of their parents in the Boolaburg City Cemetery.

≈≈≈

Clipper Duncan opened a worm ranch and sold Clipper's Cuts to Charlie Colson, the former radio guy from WCAV.

The barbershop is now known as Charlie Colson's Clipper's Cuts and gives a silkscreened T-shirt with the name of the business on the back to the first customer each month.

≈≈≈

Tommy Heitz retired from the barber business and lives in a converted school bus in his mother's back yard.

He raises fighting roosters and digs ginseng roots the last four months of the year.

≈≈≈

Oscar Simpson, the first-year chemistry teacher who was in the principal's office when Hazel collapsed, moved to Chattanooga.

He lives under the Norfolk Southern Railway bridge and raises hamsters that he sells at the farmer's market.

≈≈≈

The Boolaburg Mercenaries lost the final seven games of their season. The Patton kid, Juky, who was a shoo-in for a football scholarship at the University of Tennessee broke his leg with six games left.

He did not get any scholarship offers and manages a combination coin-operated laundry and used-shoe store in Harlan, Kentucky

≈≈≈

Mr. Bashette retired at the end of the school year. He wrote two self-illustrated poetry books.

He is now a state senator representing the plateau region.

≈≈≈

Deputy Sheriff Juno Lang attended a four-hour-per-night truck-driving school for two consecutive months. He recently completed a quarter-million accident-free miles for Titan's Turbo Truck Transfer.

His wife became lonely because of his frequent nights away from home. She ran off with a sewing machine mechanic and now lives near St. Louis.

≈≈≈

The red-haired Warren twins hijacked a truck that was supposedly carrying high-end silk shirts and dresses. Instead, the cargo was a million and fifty-thousand sanitary napkins.

Presently, the twins share a cell in the Bledsoe County Correctional Complex in Pikeville, Tennessee.

≈≈≈

Chairman of the Fair Board, Willie Johnson, married Ms. Felder, the humanities teacher, and adopted her five children.

Mr. and Mrs. Johnson manage the flea market in Nashville.

≈≈≈

Former Boolaburg Mayor, Alice Linden, had a nervous breakdown. Walgreens dismissed her after she dispensed four thousand hydrocodone pills to an illiterate goat breeder who had asked for a bottle of Vitamin D pills.

The two married and live in Piggott, Arkansas. They manufacture goat cheese and soap in an abandoned chicken house and peddle the products at county fairs.

≈≈≈

On weekdays, Bob and Eli Stanford still ride the bus to the boola county senior development facility.

They are required to sit at the front of the bus and to exit immediately after the driver.

≈≈≈

Former Chief of Police Herky Payne lives outside of Nashville on a houseboat at Old Hickory Lake Marina. He is the spokesperson for the Tennessee Bureau of Investigation and known for his bluntness in media interviews.

He has a single tomato plant in a Jack Daniel's barrel on the stern of his boat. "Keeping it simple," he says.

≈≈≈

One mystery remains even to this day in Boolaburg. After preaching his final sermon on the night basrr was to leave town, Brother Aaron Solomon disappeared. He didn't take the van, any clothing, or any personal possessions. He just vanished.

Three recent converts speculated that the Reverend was taken up into Heaven. They had not seen his ascension, but he'd told them he had that power. Their account was heavily discounted when an investigation revealed the three were addicted to animal tranquilizers.

≈≈≈

Even after the mysterious nighttime disappearance of Brother Aaron Solomon, Annie and Nannie Penguin continued with the basrr. The two midget-door-to-door Bible salesmen joined the movement and preach in tandem from a three-foot-high stage. Business has never been better.

Nannie Penguin is expecting a baby near the end of the year—hopefully on Christmas Day.

≈≈≈

Boston Blazer—christened Gerald Grey Grubbs by his Massachusetts Catholic parents—disbanded the carnival, dismantled the ferris wheel, and sold it for scrap metal. He lives in Andytown, Florida, where he manages a roadside animal menagerie at the State Highway 27 and I-75 exit.

The Blazer Brothers' lion also lives there. Normally calm and docile, the lion becomes agitated by red clothing. Agitated might be too strong a word. Perhaps excited—licking his lips and roaring—might be more appropriate. Boston has a pet name for the big cat—Disposall.

SINCE FRANKLIN

Catherine Moore

I hated you, Harpeth River. I tried to rise above you
   in the warm swell that unusual November afternoon
   as you brimmed with fodder from cannons and canons,
   a spate of deathly sermons from muskets.

   And those who were not left compost for your banks
   enjoyed the embrace of four pinewood planks to coffin
   a fallen tide, to sojourn with the Widow of the South.

THE TWEET

Suzanne Webb Brunson

"Kids, let's show our moms how we blow bubbles. While you are hanging onto the side of the pool, you can put your face down, your mouth in the water, and blow out. It makes bubbles! Now, close your eyes, then try putting your face in the water. Go ahead. You can do it! If you want us to help you, just raise your hand, but keep the other one on the side of the pool until we get to you.

"Want to know how to keep your feet up on top of the water?

"Yes Danny, and your legs, too. Try holding onto the side of the pool like this. Put your right hand on the edge of the cement, yes, where you always hold onto the top side of the pool. Now put your left hand on the side, under the water. Yes, turn it around like this so your fingers point to the bottom of the pool. That's right, one hand on top and one on the side, you are holding the pool together. Yay! No, it's not going to split open, Jerry. It's called irony. No, not the metal. I know, that's a big word. It's me being silly. Yes, I can

"Roll your head sideways. Breathe. Roll your head into the water and look at the bottom of the pool, if you want. All right, blow. Okay, then just try blowing bubbles. Right. You got it. Now, turn your head sideways, breathe, put your face in the water, blow, turn your head sideways, breathe, put your face in the water, blow.

"No, don't stop, I didn't blow the whistle yet. You did ten? Okay, kids,

Buddy says we did it more than ten times, which is not a bad thing. That's right, Minnie. I know. You and Buddy can both count to ten.

"Cathy, just keep your eyes closed. You can remember to close your eyes, right? Let's try it again. Breathe. Close your eyes if you want. Roll your face down and blow bubbles. Cathy, I know you can't see them. You closed your eyes. Can you feel the bubbles? No? Then don't put your eyes and nose in the water when you roll. Put your mouth in, blow, and watch the bubbles. Or try this. Just look at the top of the water and blow. Can you make the water ripple or move? Hey, everyone, try blowing the top of the water and watch it move. No, Greg, no spitting, and no, you can't hock a loogie. Lucy, you can go ahead and climb out. Ask your mother if she has a Kleenex you can blow into, all right? No, you aren't in trouble. We'll wait. We'll just look at the water and blow. Oh, no running.

Tweet!

"Wait, kids, no, don't get out yet. That tweet was for Kathy so she would stop running. It's a different tweet, but that's okay. Now, everyone, get back in, down by the steps, and we'll line up along the side of the pool.

"Roll your head sideways. Breathe. Roll your head into the water and look at the bottom of the pool if you want. All right, blow. Okay, let's just try blowing bubbles. Right. You got it. Now, breathe, blow, breathe, blow.

"Lucy, you're back. That was fast. No, you can't make Joseph move so you can be by Sally. Just hold on down at the end. No, honey, you are our anchor. Right. Thank you.

"No, Greg, you can be the anchor tomorrow.

"Yes, I won't forget.

"He did what? Ricky, did you just go to the bathroom on Rose?

"Don't cry, Ricky. I'm sorry, Ricky. What? Come here and whisper in my ear.

"What?

Tweet!

"Everyone out of the pool. No, Dan, we don't need the rescue net. Ricky wasn't sure. It might be a false alarm but it's time to end class, anyway.

"Okay, class is over early. Please check with Coach Rand about your next class. No, Buddy, we don't have to drain the pool. Come here, and let me see. Did you know this was bleeding? All right, good to know. I'll make sure Coach knows you've had your tetanus shot. Follow me, and we'll get the first-aid kit. You did what? Didn't pulling the thread out hurt? All seven? No wonder you're bleeding. I thought you were counting our breathing and blowing.

"Don't cry, boys. You all can start in the new class in a week. Right?

"You're signed up for t-ball? I thought your moms knew this was a two-week class. Okay. Well, classes run every two weeks, so I'll be here all summer.

"Uh oh, it starts next week? Well, we'll ask your mom if you all can come back the next week, *after the pool is cleaned*. I'll give you your very own private class, on one condition. Well, two. You get a waterproof bandage on that cut, and everyone goes to the bathroom before class.

"No! Greg, don't jump! That's the deep end."

Tweet.

≈≈≈

"Everyone, did you see my lifeguard-jump where my head stayed above water? Greg is fine. Greg's mom is getting him a Coast Guard-approved life vest. Isn't that cool?

"Barry, please put the net back over on the rack, and the life buoy goes on the lifeguard stand. Yes. That's right. Please, stop crying. I really do appreciate that you wanted to help, but let's learn the rules, okay?

"Yes, it's okay to hug the lifeguard. Your mom is right over there, sweetheart. What? Oh, I'm too old to be your girlfriend. Maybe when you get in high school, we can be friends.

"Okay, middle school. I'm not allowed to go on car dates yet, anyway. You don't have a car? Maybe you could get a job and save up and buy one in high school.

"Okay, middle school.

"The end of this summer? You let me know what your mom says."

DRINK IN THE DESERT

Tom Wood

From the day we met nearly a decade ago, Wally and I forged an instant bond. We were both fifteen, though I'd matured relatively faster. That youthful naïveté was part of the charm that drew me to him. It was the summer of 1970, and Wally was recovering at his Nashville, Tennessee, home when we met.

He'd spent two weeks at Baptist Hospital, suffering from what doctors called "a moderate case" of rheumatic fever. He later told me it started as a sore throat that he picked up on a church mission trip to Haiti with his father and ten other volunteers. By the time the youth group returned to Nashville, Wally was running a slight fever and had achy joints. His parents took him to the doctor the next day, and Wally was diagnosed with strep throat. But his fatigue worsened, and when a body rash broke out, his parents rushed Wally to the emergency room.

Following the antibiotic treatment at Baptist, Wally was allowed to go home with orders to get plenty of aspirin, rest, and water. But he was still weak, and his overly cautious mom would not allow school chums to visit.

Wally pleaded that he *reeeally* needed a friend, and a month later his mom finally relented. She found me one Saturday—a runaway wandering the streets. That's for another story, but she took me in and fed me, gave me shelter, and I'll be forever grateful.

Anyway, after lunch, she opened the door to Wally's bedroom and introduced me to the sickly teenager who was watching Curt Gowdy call the

NBC baseball game of the week. Wally's face immediately brightened, and he said, "How ya doing, buddy?" I responded, and when he called me Ralph, I flashed an ear-to-ear grin toward my new best friend.

About a week later, I overheard his worried mother on the telephone.

"I'm glad you called," Mom said. "I've been so worried about Wally. The medicine's finally kicking in, but he was coughing up a lot of phlegm. The doctors warned that he might need heart valve replacement surgery someday."

Wally's mom hacked a harsh bark herself. "No, no, I'm fine. These damn cigarettes," she said. "The doctor told me Wally's no longer contagious, but I'm not taking any chances. School starts back next month, but if he's not well, I'm keeping him home. Even if he has to repeat his sophomore year, that's what he'll do."

I couldn't tell Wally what I'd overheard. I'd just be there to support him through his recovery. Mom broke the news of her decision an hour later.

Wally was disappointed because he liked school. His favorite class was English, and he confided to me that it started because of a crush on his teacher, Miss Fox. "At first, it was the way she read the words, but I started listening to the *stories* themselves, and it was like watching a movie in my head," Wally said. "We'd talk about them, kinda like we're doing, and that's when I really got into reading. Now I can't stop."

So in that respect, confinement to the bed couldn't keep him sidelined for long because the books were taking him to other times and places—and I liked making those exciting journeys with him. Wally's preferences ranged from the hard-boiled detective noir of Mickey Spillane and to the Doc Savage serial pulps and Tarzan's jungle adventures, from the early science fiction of Verne and Wells to modern masters like Heinlein, Asimov, and Bradbury.

But his favorite genre was Westerns, another love he'd picked up from his father. We'd all sit around the TV and watch *Bonanza* and *Gunsmoke* together.

When I first met Wally, he was working through a stack of Zane Grey novels. I'd never heard of Zane Grey, but Wally told me all about him, saying that fella sure could spin a yarn. Wally was in the middle of *The Her-*

itage of the Desert, and he started reading aloud so I could follow along. At first, I would close my eyes and listen, his melodic voice painting mental pictures before I'd drift off.

But the more he read, the more I looked forward to hearing the stories. With excitement in his voice, Wally would say, "Let's go, Ralph." I'd respond with similar eagerness, and we were off on another wild Western adventure. Sometimes I'd pretend I was the bad guy, but usually I day-dreamed about being the good guy, saving the ranch, getting the girl, and finding the hidden gold.

≈ ≈ ≈

Wally returned to school that October, made up classwork, and still managed to graduate from Overton High with the Class of '73. During that span, his parents—Mom especially—hovered with concerns about his health. Wally did seem more susceptible to common colds and tiredness, but his mother made sure he had regular checkups. He enrolled at Middle Tennessee State University that fall, and we were roommates in off-campus housing.

Wally majored in English and landed a job on the student radio station WMOT. He started in production but soon hosted his own show called *Book It*, focusing on weekly reviews and author interviews. He got to meet a lot of his favorite writers that way. Sometimes, I met them, too!

Three years of summer classes helped Wally obtain his college degree in December '76, a semester earlier than scheduled. And that hard work earned Wally a surprise graduation/early Christmas gift from his parents—a '67 blue Dodge station wagon with 80,000 miles. It had belonged to a neighbor who'd bought himself a candy apple red Camaro SS.

Wally appreciated the wheels, but told me he'd wished for the Camaro. He spent most of January and part of February mulling his future, uncertain what direction his life should take. He was going west.

≈ ≈ ≈

I'd never seen Wally's parents so angry as when he told them of his plan—to tour the Old West, to see it through the eyes of his favorite Western author, Zane Grey. Mom said it was "downright dangerous, you're going to get yourself axe-murdered by some drugged-out hippie," and Dad called it "friggin' foolhardy."

Wally stood his ground that day. He and his father often argued over sports, politics, movies, and had other generation-gap arguments in the past, but never a blowup like this one.

"You don't get it, Dad. I'm doing this," Wally finally said. "It's not like I'm going off to join a commune. I'm going sightseeing. And to spring training. It starts next week."

His father started to speak, but Wally kept talking.

"I've got some money saved, and I'm going to be working the rest of my life. Think of it as a senior trip, a graduation gift I'm giving myself. And besides, I won't be going alone—Zane Grey and Ralph will be with me."

≈≈≈

Wally spent two days planning his trip and another half a day explaining it to his parents. He seemed certain they would never understand, but I got the idea that they were secretly proud of him . . . and maybe a little envious.

"If I don't do it now, I might never get the chance," Wally said, running his finger along the Route 66 map to Holbrook, Arizona. "From there, it's straight to Phoenix. I'm coming home through Tucson to El Paso all the way to Dallas. From there back to Fort Smith, then to Memphis, and I'm home. Voila!"

Dad had been nodding as he followed Wally's finger-tracing. "And how long you reckon this'll take?"

"Not sure. Maybe a couple of months."

"Two months," Mom gasped. "Now, Wally—"

"Maybe more," Wally interjected. "It depends on how many side trips I make—and how long my money holds out. I want to see as much as I can, not just the big cities and the historic sites, but the parks and the culture. A lot of side trips—and a lot of camping trips."

An excited wave swept over Wally as he pointed to the map again. "First stop is the cowboy museum in Oklahoma City. When I get to Amarillo, I'm going to drive down to Palo Duro Canyon for a couple of days and see for myself the colors and hues on the rocks and canyon walls—and to be able to say I hunted for the lost gold. Albuquerque looks cool, so I'll probably stay there a couple of days, go on a Western trail ride past the piñon pines and cottonwoods to the Rio Grande—"

"Wally, you've never ridden a horse," Mom chided, shaking her head.

"They'll teach me. I'm going to camp out in the desert under the stars. I want to climb a mesa and stare out over the cactus and sagebrush. I'll visit an old ghost town, not just one of the tourist traps. After Phoenix and Tucson, I'm heading to Tombstone to see where Wyatt—"

"Slow down, hoss," Dad said. "When are you leaving?"

"Probably next week."

≈≈≈

The car was packed, and we were ready to go, me already inside riding shotgun, anxious to hit the road. Wally had stuffed the station wagon like we were going to be gone for a year instead of two months, and had even tied down his three-speed bicycle to the roof. With Dad at his side, Wally walked around the wagon and pointed out camping gear; emergency equipment, including a flashlight, flares, a medical kit, and batteries; clothes for every weather condition; a harmonica that Wally couldn't yet play; and the list rolled on. Finally, Wally pointed to a box on the back floorboard.

"And my Zane Grey paperbacks to read by the campfire."

"Well, you won't get bored, that's for sure," Dad said, reaching into his back pocket for folded bills. "Here, take this."

Wally's hands shook as he counted off the fifties. "Dad, this is five hundred dollars. You and Mom didn't have to—"

"Half of it's from Grandma and Grandpa," Dad said. "They said to tell you it's an extra graduation gift. You should write them a note from out there—or at least send postcards."

"Will do."

"And I learned something," Dad added. "Apparently, we've got family out that way, maybe in the Phoenix area. Grandma's third cousin, or something like that. They're going to try to track down a phone number, and I'll let you know when you call . . . every third day, right?"

"Don't fence me in," Wally said, smiling. "Every third day, if I can. They don't have phone booths in the desert."

"How do you know? You haven't been there yet," Dad said. "And call collect. It'll keep your mother from having a nervous breakdown." He shook his head. "Speaking of," Dad said, pointing, "I guess she wanted one last hug from the wanderer."

Mom hurried down the walkway carrying two shopping bags which she handed to Wally. "You can't go out West without these," she said. Inside one was a cowboy hat and pair of boots. The other contained an Oakland A's baseball cap and a new glove. Wally squeezed the air out of his mother before getting in the driver's seat and rolling down the window to wave goodbye.

Dad leaned on the side of the door and looked past Wally to me.

"Take care of him, Ralph."

I smiled, and we were off.

≈≈≈

We visited a lot of places in those first ten days, but my favorite was Palo Duro Canyon in the Texas Panhandle. Wally said a lot of people called it the "Grand Canyon of Texas." Staring across the vast expanse, I could only imagine.

"Look at the Spanish skirts. That's what they call 'em," Wally said of the rock formations. "Remember the frilly dress of that pretty senorita we saw dancing across the floor at the cantina? That's what they look like." I didn't disagree, but all I saw were huge cliffs.

We checked into our cabin, then spent the day exploring and looking for the supposed lost treasure the rest of that day and the next. If it was there, we didn't find it. I spotted the tracks of what might have been either a coyote or bobcat, and warned Wally. We moved on to another area to search. That night, after supper, Wally and I had a great time howling at the full moon. Wally's lonesome harmonica playing was getting better.

I napped a lot while Wally drove west, half-listening to him talk about the sites he'd seen. The national parks and great outdoors places we visited were always my favorite. Days were mostly sunny and warm as we drove through New Mexico, but nights were still chilly, so we didn't do as much outdoor camping as Wally wanted. My coat was warmer than his, I guess.

It was raining when we arrived in Phoenix, but the weekend was warm and beautiful. We visited different ballparks during the day, and then after dinner, Wally would hit the town while I stayed in the room and rested. When he got in, he'd read a couple of chapters from a book before turning out the lights.

One of my favorite stories was how the hero was chased into the arid desert and survived by relying on his wits and knowledge. He knew how and where to find water.

≈≈≈

After three days of watching the A's at their minor league camp, Wally said he had "a hankering" to go prospecting and see the desert up close. He called and reserved a campsite for "at least" the next couple of nights at Lost Dutchman State Park, about forty miles east of Phoenix at the foot of the Superstition Mountains.

"It's you and me, Ralph. If we strike gold," Wally said, "we'll be set for life. You sniff it out, and I'll dig it out." I didn't say anything, but golden sunsets were all I expected. That, and Wally reading a story by the fire-light.

Wally set up our campsite before noon. We had lunch and then hiked the nearest trailhead. I can't find the words to describe what all we saw, but the view was fantastic as we climbed a slope. We'd been out on the trail about an hour when I heard some animal scurrying noise and took off running to see what it was. Wally tried to keep up with me, but surely lost sight of me once I went through a cut in the rocks.

I'm embarrassed to say I'd forgotten all about Wally; my focus was all on the fast-moving animal up ahead, and I kept pushing forward, deeper into the Superstition Mountains. The more I climbed, the harder it was to breathe, and I finally gave up the chase. I looked around, and didn't see Wally.

The winds picked up, and a wave of panic flowed over me. I had no idea where I was or how far I'd traveled. The lonely desert below was dotted with cactus and scrub brush under the stoic scrutiny of towering walls of red or gray.

I tried backtracking, hoping I could spot Wally, but when I got to the last place I remembered, he was nowhere to be found. I came across two sets of shoeprints, but could tell that neither one belonged to Wally. Then I spotted fresh animal tracks going in the same route, and followed both around an outcropping. The setting sun made tracking difficult, but I have pretty good night vision and was able to keep pursuit.

The trail led to a sheer cliff, and that's where the two sets of footprints went in opposite trails. I heard a screeching behind a rock to the left that made the hair on my neck stand, and I got on my belly so I could sneak in for a closer look.

Somewhere in the distance, the wind played symphony with either a coyote howl, or maybe a lonesome harmonica. Then the wind shifted, and I heard nothing else. The star-filled sky lit a faint path that I followed through the brush.

I stayed on that bearing, upward, twisting and turning, until I was more lost than ever. Tired, I sat down and stared in every direction. The campground was out there somewhere, but where?

It was about then that I realized how hungry I was. And thirsty. And the temperature was dropping. What now?

≈ ≈ ≈

The first thing was to not panic. Wally was probably somewhere out there looking for me, I told myself. But what if he, too, was lost? He'd had the canteen with him, but the sun had been mighty hot, and he was probably out of water by now. If that was the case . . . I yelled in despair, and the only answer was a mournful echo of my howling.

I plopped down, closed my eyes, and tried to think about my situation. After several minutes of silence, I heard Wally's voice—in my head. And he was reading a passage from a Zane Grey story about desert survival.

"You can do this, Ralph, but first you gotta get down this slope. Watch your step, because if you lose your footing, it could be bad," Wally's voice warned me.

"A rabbit would make for a tasty dinner if you can catch one. Or maybe a lizard. They're supposed to taste like chicken," Wally's voice said with a laugh.

"But if you're gonna make it outta here, you gotta find water. Look for an overhang as you descend—someplace that will block the wind and keep you safe," Wally's voice cautioned me. "It was raining when we got to Phoenix, so look near the cliff face to see if any small pools of water collected. Save your strength and rest up tonight because you're going to need it tomorrow. When you wake up, head back down the rest of the mountain and dig near the cactus. They need water to survive the desert. The water's there. You just have to get to it."

I did as Wally's voice instructed and carefully made my way down, staying close to the rock wall to check for water or shelter—or both. Once, I misstepped, and a stream of loose rocks cascaded down the grade.

Feeling my way along the slant, I found a spot I liked, a ragged nook in the cliff face that might be a good place to shelter. The recess was deep enough to provide protection, but I still needed water. Lost in my thoughts, I didn't hear the first drip. Or the second drop. But the third one got my attention. It came from the back of the shallow cave, and I followed the sound.

Without light, it was almost impossible to find my way, so I relied on my ears and other senses to lead me to whatever water might be there. I scooted to the back of the niche, which got smaller and narrower, so much so that I had to resort to crawling. When I thought I was at the back, I felt a small burst of wind and kept going toward another droplet noise. I felt along the stone, and it was damp. I'd found water, and I lapped it off my hand! I kept reaching and pawing until my thirst was sated. Hunger gnawed at my stomach, but I curled into a ball and managed to fall asleep.

≈≈≈

I woke at sunup, gathered myself, and set out in the morning cool. I remembered what Zane, er, Wally's voice said about finding water in the desert and how to forage for food.

The sun rising over the mountains would've been spectacular any other time, but I didn't see it like that. For me, it was pointing the way back to the campground.

Probably an hour elapsed before I recognized a familiar landmark. When we passed it the first time, Wally had said the giant saguaro cactus looked like it was saluting. I knew where I was. If only Wally was there. I took off running.

When I got back to the campsite, Wally was squatting over the fire stirring up a bunch of eggs and frying some bacon. I was so happy, I almost tackled him.

"There you are, Ralph," he said, tousling my head. "You had me a little worried when you disappeared like that. But I reckoned you'd be fine. Good fella."

"Rowf," I answered.

Wally knew I was hungry and sat the plate on the ground, then stopped and stared. His eyes lit up like the golden flecks that glittered on the paw I'd used to feel for water. He bent close to my paw, and it sparkled in the sunshine.

"Eat up, Ralph, and then show me where you spent the night." I cleaned the plate in three bites, and we hit the trail.

≈≈≈

We didn't find gold that day, nor in the week afterward. But what Wally had seen convinced him that the Legend of the Lost Dutchman's Mine was true. The next morning, Wally decided to skip Tombstone and drove straight to Dallas. We stayed the night, and then got on back to Nashville.

Last year, Wally got a job in Phoenix, and we spend most weekends exploring the Superstition Mountains. That gold's out there, and someday I'll find it again for Wally. But whether we do or don't, it doesn't really matter to me. I'll always treasure that trip of a lifetime and the night an old dog survived a night in the desert, thanks to Wally and Zane.

SANGRIA MORNING

Sandy Ward Bell

What I miss most about Atlanta is the abundance of sunshine, and of course, Harold. We created a lovely life together there until ten years ago, when he left me. No, it wasn't for another woman; instead, it was a disease, the kind that steals the mind. Simply, my husband's time on this world ran out. The next step was easy. I needed to be closer to family. Ta-da! Here I am in Pittsburgh where there are some nice bright days, but they don't last long. Waking this September morning to eighty-six degrees, a brilliant sun, and a spicy fragrance emanating from the mums tempts me to soak my feet in the plastic kiddie pool. My granddaughters play in it often, but now it will get some adult use.

My neighbors, Cynthia and Virginia, should arrive any minute with sangria and gossip. The dessert was made last night so now I'm in the backyard, using the hose to rinse out mud from the pool. When the cartoon fish that decorate the bottom are clearly seen, it will be officially clean.

The big birthmark near the knuckles of my right hand is shaped exactly like a map of Australia including a gap for the Bass Strait that separates the mainland from Tasmania. I can't help but look at it every day whether I'm combing my hair, cooking, or clicking the remote. When I was younger, I assumed the mark was a sign, a message from the beyond telling me it was my homeland. Three attempts were made over the years to visit the Land Down Under, and not one had been successful. Tragedies kept happening as if someone cast a weird spell on me. First, my dad lost an arm in a car accident, then my honeymoon was canceled due to inefficient funds, and my last try was fifteen years ago. Harold and I were packing for the big trip when we got the call that Mother died. My birthmark must be cursed or God doesn't want me to travel to that continent. I already have doubts about my fourth attempt. My sister and I bought our plane tickets for next month, and she just texted that her husband is back in the hospital with a bad case of the shingles. Should I travel alone? I rub my birthmark as if it were a genie's lamp, attempting to make my wish come true.

"Hello. Hello. We let ourselves in." Cynthia crosses the patio carrying her giant purse, which is always bigger than her head. She's an emergency room nurse working seven days on and then seven off. I believe that schedule is causing the circles under her eyes to become darker.

Virginia closes the sliding door while lugging a mini cooler. "I brought little umbrellas for our sangria." Her smile is brighter than the sun.

We chat about the weather while setting up three black and gold short-legged beach chairs around the kiddie pool. Cynthia sits in the middle. One by one, we slip off sandals and plop our feet into the cool water. We devour our fancy drinks and peanut butter brownies without taking a breath as if cheating on a diet.

I raise my red Solo cup and announce, "This is the best lunch I ever had."

"Sorry, Jane." Cynthia adds, "I got grass in your clean pool."

"No worries. Happens all the time with the girls. As the day goes on, it'll fill with leaves and dirt and whatever other crap is flying around."

Sporting white sunglasses, Virginia seems to focus on the shimmering water. "Jane, how are your grandbabies? Wasn't there a birthday?"

"Mandy turned five last weekend. A Barbie party. We did each other's hair and makeup. Mandy was thrilled that the two-year-old slept through most of it. Did you see the photo I posted on Facebook?"

"Adorable." Cynthia finishes her drink as if it were a shot of tequila. "Hey, is Australia still a go?"

"As of this minute, not sure. My sister's husband is ill."

They both moan, "Oh, no."

I continue, "May have to buck it up and travel alone. I'm debating with myself, which is never a good idea."

"I'd go with you if I could," Virginia says.

"What's stopping ya?" Cynthia pours herself another.

"Gill would burn the house down."

I lick chocolate off my fingers. "Really? He seems competent enough."

"He puts on a good show. Don't get me wrong, he can build you a brilliant piece of furniture, but once that TV goes on, forget about it. He'll warm up SpaghettiOs on the stove and only think about them when the smoke detector goes off. He's banned from the kitchen."

"Like having another kid." I sigh as Harold takes center stage in my brain. He loved to make me bacon pancakes with blueberry syrup, and that prideful smile he had as he set them down on the kitchen table is the same grin keeping me awake at night.

"William is a grill master. Hell, you all know that. You've had his chicken." Cynthia leans back, closing her eyes to the glaring sun. "If it once had a beating heart, he'll grill it."

I add, "He needs to bottle that sauce of his."

She bolts upright. "No. Don't ever tell him that. He just might do it." She gulps down her drink and leans back again.

Virginia scoops out an apple slice from her cup. "Did you hear about the O'Brians?" She nibbles on the fermented fruit.

"Everybody's heard." Cynthia dabs sweat off her chin. "She put that flyer in all the mailboxes. The entire neighborhood."

"Wow, I thought it was just our street." I shake my head. "Telling the world her husband is a cheat and a fraud is not going to help her in the divorce."

"That woman is mad. Crazy angry, like cut-off-his-penis pissed off." Cynthia adds, "Never liked her. She has soulless eyes."

Virginia says, "But it's not her fault he strayed."

"Sure, he was and always will be an ass-hat, but he married a nutcase. That's on him." Cynthia pours herself another sangria. "Anyone need one?" She holds up the pitcher.

After cups are full, we sit back, soaking up the sunshine just like the fruit steeping the alcohol in our drinks.

Virginia giggles. "It's that house."

"What do you mean?"

She can't stop laughing. "It's the divorce house. Think about it. I've been here twenty years and four families have lived there. All divorced."

Cynthia adds, "It's not funny."

"Yes, it is." Virginia smiles.

I sense Cynthia's looking for a fight. I announce, "Ladies, let's get manis and pedis together before I leave on my trip. Maybe schedule a day next week."

They agree, and then we fall into a routine discussion about how the Millers need to chop down the dead tree in their front yard, the Kents should close their curtains, and that the Arnolds' should bury their dilapidated shed two feet underground with all thirty of their garden gnomes.

Virginia gives us a case of the giggles as she describes what each gnome would say as the dirt covered their face. "And the one with the black glasses would yell in a deep voice, 'I'll be back.'"

I wipe away a tear. "You're the best."

My words put an exclamation mark on our discussion. We pause, recline, watch the water caress our ankles, and listen to the birds sing.

"Polly's pregnant." Cynthia stares at her soaking feet.

"What?" I'm completely caught off guard.

"Sixteen and pregnant. There. I said it out loud." She pours herself another drink.

Virginia whispers, "Jesus, Mary, and Joseph."

"How far along?" My heart is heavy. Cynthia's strong, but this might break her.

"Four months. An abortion was off the table from the start. She's leaning toward adoption. Yet some days she's looking up prices for cribs, and then, she's planning a March trip to the Bahamas for spring break. She's all over the place."

I pull out a torn Kleenex from my pocket and before I can hand it to Cynthia, she has dug through her giant purse for a fresh one.

She holds the white tissue over her eyes. "I can't take care of a baby. I'm too old."

"Nonsense." My mind is racing. I can't think of anything helpful to say. "You're a spring chicken compared to me."

"Jane, how old are you?" Virginia shakes her cup at me and grins. "My sangria wants to know."

"Sixty-two and proud of every wrinkle and gray hair." I lift my straw hat, showing off the brittle color, and plop it back into place.

"Bless your heart." Virginia finishes her drink. "Good for you. When I hit sixty, I'm going to stop dyeing my hair. Yah, six more years or is it seven? Fill me up. It will help me remember."

"We're off track yet again." My head is swimming. I grab the plastic pitcher. "Cynthia, what can we do to make your life easier?"

"You could tell my husband. He still doesn't know." She nods at her filled cup while holding the tissue under her nose.

"He's not a monster. He'll understand." Virginia stuffs another brownie in her mouth.

"You don't know my William. I'm afraid he'll kill Peter–like run him down with his car."

"Peter's the father? Does he know?"

"Yes, and he's acting squirrely."

I return my feet to the cool water, adding more grass to the dirt buildup. "Squirrely, how?"

"He's a teenage boy putting on this fake manly persona." Her fingers create air quotes. "Like look what my sperm did." She picks up her cup and rolls her eyes. "And then he ignores my daughter when she says anything about keeping the child. Money is all the support he'll ever give."

"That's better than nothing." Virginia's smile is contagious.

And the more I stare at her face, the more I think it is chemically induced. "Virginia, love, did you have a bong party without us?"

Her smile is glorious. "Small one. Helps my tennis elbow."

"When was the last time you played tennis?" Cynthia's blinking is unusually slow.

"A while ago. Stopped cuz of my bum elbow."

As Virginia smirks, Cynthia asks, "How do I help my daughter without being a new parent all over again?"

"Well, I'm sure we can come up with a plan." The alcohol has made me a bit fuzzy. "If we don't eat some real food soon, we'll go downhill real fast. A cheese platter. That's what we need. I'll be back." I stand, wiping my feet on the grass.

The girls lift their cups in agreement and say, "I'll be back–like Arnold. I'll be back." They giggle at their impression while I shake my head and think we need carbs, stat.

Walking toward the house, I overhear Virginia say, "Shopping for baby stuff is the best."

I enter the kitchen as my buzzing head intensifies. I drank too quickly. Clumsily, I fill a tray with different deli meats, sharp cheeses, pickles, and grapes. With a box of crackers under my arm, I lift the tray as the doorbell rings. Paranoia sets in as I set it down. I am embarrassed for being slightly drunk before noon on a Tuesday. I stuff an Altoid in my mouth and open the door.

"Hi, Jane, is my mom here?" Virginia's daughter, Lizzy, is standing on my porch with a stroller that is cradling her napping son.

"Yes, we're out back. Come on in." I help lift the stroller into the hallway.

Without a word, she rolls her son to the sliding door and waits for me to assist her out onto the patio. As she pushes the buggy to the edge of the concrete, I say, "Ladies, guess who I found at my front door?"

As they turn toward us, Lizzy says, "Hey, Mom, Cynthia. I've got hot yoga in half an hour. Their childcare room's being remodeled so you have to watch Horizon. Back in a few hours. Text me if you're home by then." She's closing the sliding door behind her. "Diaper bag's on the bottom rack." She's gone.

With hands on hips, I stare at Horizon and pray he doesn't wake up. "Maybe she didn't see that we were drinking."

Virginia stands next to me. "No, doesn't matter. She knows I'll say yes." My friend's smile has disappeared.

Carrying a cup and a tissue, Cynthia leans over the stroller. "They're cute at that age."

I add, "Until they wake-up and don't get what they want."

Cynthia holds the Kleenex over her mouth. "Oh, God, I can't do all that work . . . again." Her whimpering reminds me of a sick animal.

"You won't have to." With a frown, Virginia places her hands on the handle. "I'll stroll him home."

"Cynthia is upset over her own daughter's situation." I pat her hand. "And no, you're staying here. You're not in any shape to babysit alone. Three drunks are better than one."

"That doesn't sound like a good idea." Cynthia wipes her moist eyes.

I add, "It's not like we're wasted."

"Speak for yourself." Cynthia finishes her drink.

"Well, I guess I'm the most sober. I only had two or was it two and a half?"

Virginia raises her hand. "Three and some weed."

"That was number four for me." Cynthia reaches for her purse and almost falls over.

"Okay, the sangria is going in the fridge and I'm making coffee."

"Jane, no!" Cynthia pours herself another. "We've every right to enjoy ourselves to-this-day. Virginia, call that daughter of yours and get her back here—like now. We're not babysitting." She falls back into her chair and drops her feet into the pool. "You let that girl walk all over ya. Just say no."

Virginia shouts, "Huh, seems to me that Polly needs to learn the word no."

Horizon is rolling around. I whisper, "Shit."

"Nice shot. But you missed." Cynthia's arms are crossed over her chest. "I already know my daughter is free lovin' . . . and she's lovely and kind."

"Ladies. Let's nip this in the bud." I move the stroller back and forth. "It's not about us anymore. There's a kid we have to take care of."

"Wrong." Cynthia splashes the water with her feet. "Virginia's job. Not mine."

"I'll just take him home."

"Hell, no!" My shouting wakes the baby. "Damn. Virginia, I'm sorry, but I agree with Cynthia. You need to call Lizzy."

"I can't. She'll be upset and it's not worth all the . . . you know." She holds Horizon and sways. He stops crying.

"Have you ever said you can't watch him?" I gently rub the baby's back. She shrugs. "I like being useful. Helpful. Needed."

"Sure, but how many times have you had to cancel your plans because of her?"

"Not many."

"Bull." Cynthia digs through her purse. "You missed my Downton Abbey lunch and our Fourth of July party cuz of Lizzy's wants and demands. You always cancel last minute." She pulls out a tube of sunscreen. And then in one smooth motion, she takes off her shirt revealing a red bra. She lathers up her arms.

I ask, "Is that a new swimsuit?"

"Close enough. Nothin's showing." Her face tells me she's experiencing freedom.

I remember that same exact moment when responsibility for kids and parents dwindled down to just me and Harold, and there was a surprising realization that I had been holding my breath for years.

Virginia sets her grandson into the stroller. "I don't think I brought my phone."

"Lizzy's in my contacts." I hand her my cell. "We'll back you. Be strong."

"Tell her we charge fifty bucks an hour." Laughing, Cynthia spreads lotion on her flat stomach.

I hold my friend's hand while she shows the depth of her nervousness by chewing her lower lip. "Lizzy. Honey. It's Mom . . . no, nothing. Um. Well, we, I mean I'm not able. You see-"

Cynthia jumps up and grabs the cell away from Virginia. "Lizzy. Hey. Cynthia here. What your mom's trying to say is we be wasted. We been partying all morning. In no shape to take care of your kid. Best you get back here and do your job instead of making the rest of us do it for you."

Virginia tries to pull the phone away from Cynthia, but is only successful after the harm is done. She wipes lotion off the cell. With it at her ear, she whispers, "Lizzy. Honey."

We can hear bits and pieces of her daughter's angry voice. She is yelling at her mother, "You're so selfish!"

The sangria has given me courage. I steal the phone. "Lizzy. Lizzy. Calm down. Horizon is fine. If you had asked instead of assuming, we wouldn't be in this mess . . . no . . . no. You listen to me. Your responsibilities are yours and yours alone. Your mother is not your slave. She has a life outside of being your mother. You must turn around and pick up your boy. Now. Discussion over." I tap the phone and put it back in my pocket.

My hands are shaking while Virginia is looking at me teary-eyed. She hugs me. "Sorry. And thank you." Her smile returns under moist cheeks.

Cynthia is sunbathing with another drink in her hand. "Jane, I might just send Polly over here for a talking to." She scoops pieces of grass out of the pool.

By the time Lizzy returns, we've refilled the pool and convinced Cynthia to put her top back on; she promises not to say anything.

The silence is eerie, and I am assuming Lizzy's coldness is intended to break Virginia. The girl has been practicing this mood for as long as I've known her. There is a good chance Lizzy will deny her mother access to Horizon, highlighting the consequences for doing what is right for one-self, but in the end, the resentment will disappear, hopefully. Lizzy looks down her nose, refusing help as she lugs the stroller over the sliding door threshold. She allows me to hold the front door for her, and she does not look me in the eye. I suppose I deserve her bitterness. The child has done nothing wrong. I say, softly, "Goodbye, Horizon." Closing the door, I do not feel regret. My heart and mind feel light.

Rejuvenated, I stand at the patio table with a big grin. I set down the Steeler tray of real-food treats, and then I pick up the grandkids' little yellow plastic bench. Walking toward my friends, I announce, "Cynthia, trade seats with me. I'll put the bench in front of the middle seat. Easy access to our snack. And with you in my seat, you can still have your feet in the water while we feast." She follows my direction. The tray is on top of the bench, and without a word, we nibble and sip.

"Virginia, you okay? How are you feeling about all this?" I pop a grape into my mouth.

She grins. "Surprisingly, I'm relieved. There's going to be a big blowout, but maybe . . . yes, maybe that's all right. We needed a shift of sorts." She washes her hand in the pool water and then shakes them at us.

We all laugh, but the silliness of earlier is gone; tension is the replacement.

My cell rings, it is my sister. "I better take this." While standing, my heart pounds because I assume it will be bad news. I sprint to the kitchen.

"Hey, my crazy husband just read me the riot act. He said if I don't go to Australia with you, he'd divorce me. Do you hear me? Jane, pack your bags. We'll be on the plane two weeks from today."

My excitement causes tears, happy ones. "This is really happening." We talk for a few more minutes and end the conversation with plans to speak tonight.

I step out into the backyard to find both of my friends with their shirts off, sun tanning in their bras. After sitting, I realize Cynthia has lost the bra and is using salami to cover each nipple. My laugh fills me with joy.

Smiling, Virginia hands me a full Solo cup. "Today is our day."

I explain the great news and add, "Their son'll move in for three weeks to make sure his dad takes his meds. Suppose it won't really hit me until the plane lands in Sydney. Boy, my dream. I . . . I'm going to walk and talk and breathe Australian air."

After they share in my excitement, Cynthia says, "Screw it. I'm getting all in." She takes off her shorts revealing red underwear and steps into the pool. She rearranges herself allowing her torso to be covered by the cloudy water while her legs and head hang over opposite sides. The salami is floating and swirling next to grass and a dead bug.

Jokes are made and the laughter is explosive and absent of restraint. They attempt to convince me to take my top off. The world is thankful for my refusal.

Later, when napping becomes our new focus, my friends hug longer than usual. They leave happier than when they arrived which is always the goal of a good hostess. I smile at the meat floating in the water. Well, I must clean up before lying down. Harold often said, 'A tidy home before rest makes living the best.' Even though I haven't heard it from his lips for years, I can't help but follow the rule.

Rinsing out the pool, I realize my birthmark will never again fill me with regret. The water pulsing from the hose pushes the grass out of the pool and back onto the ground. The bright eyes on the fish are clear. Leaning the pool against the fence to dry, I think about how tomorrow it will get dirty all over again. Some days are cleaner than others.

Lake

DOCTOR MIDNIGHT

MEETS PRINCESS

SILVER LAKE

Michael J. Tucker

The Summer of Love hit San Francisco in 1967, and Timothy Leary was telling thirty thousand hippies to "Turn On, Tune In, Drop Out," but like most things in West Texas, we were late to the psychedelic dance by two years. We were starting to catch up. Fast.

It happened in 1969, sometime after Woodstock but before Altamont. I was bookin' on a starlit night somewhere west of Abilene an easy 130 miles per hour on my custom Shovelhead. An open throttle, wind in my hair, the lion-like roar of the bike, the motor's vibration pulsing through my loins and into my gut—a rush better than my drugs.

Every five miles or so, I'd slow down and sometimes downright stop to wait for Fitzgerald. He took the fun out of cruising on Hogs. His bike was stock H-D Street 500, off the showroom floor, a beginner's ride. He was something of a misfit with my friends and me. He had a Buddy Holly look to him, but not the coolness. Money was the only reason we let him hang with us— or rather his family's money, which he freely spent trying to buy our friendship. Tonight, the tables were turned. He was leading me to meet some of his college buddies. They were interested in my pharmaceuticals. You see, I was Doctor Midnight—the local drug dealer. My practice was to wait until parties hit their peak midnight, the witching hour, when alcohol clouded my clients' judgment, and when money was easily made.

I pulled over to wait for Fitz. His bike puttered as he decelerated and pulled up next to me. "What took you so long?" I asked.

"Wait till I get my next bike, Doc. It'll be bigger than yours. Blow the doors off your Harley—if it had doors." He laughed at his little joke.

"Fitzy, you get you a big bike, who's gonna help ya pick it up when it falls over while you're sittin' at a stop sign? Sides, it's liable to give you a dirt nap. You lead the way from here. I think I know the cove you're talking about, but it could be a different one."

"OK, follow me, Doc." He revved his motor. It still sounded like a kitten purring next to my lion's growl.

I was edgy riding into Fitzgerald's posse. Back in town, I was the alpha dog, but these were Fitz's people. Not that I thought he'd be their alpha. Still, there was a queasy feeling in my stomach. I didn't know these dudes, but I knew they'd be exactly like him. Unlike my regulars who checked coin returns on soda machines for money, these guys were rich, smart, and spoiled. Maybe the best way to describe my feeling is to compare it to crashing a party at someone's house that you don't know. You wouldn't go in the front door, say hi, and then go help yourself to whatever is in their refrigerator. I couldn't very well do that to Fitz's friends, at least not right away. I knew that before the night was over, I'd not only get in their refrigerator, I'd own the damn thing.

We turned into the parking lot where the trailhead led to the cove and rode past their Porsches, Mercedes, Cadillacs, and Lincolns. We steered our bikes down the trail to the beach and rolled into the cove with motors revving. They had a campfire burning. Even with that I couldn't tell how many people were there. A dozen that I could see, and many more in the shadows. We were greeted with hoots and hollers and whoops.

"Yo, Fitzgerald's here."

"Way to go, Fitz."

"Where's the doctor?"

Fitz stepped off his bike, raised his arms to the sky like the geek he was, and shouted, "Ladies and gentlemen, boys and girls, I give you, Doctor Midnight!"

Of course, they already knew that. They screamed as if they were fans at a rock concert and came running toward me like I was *the* rock star. They circled me, a hunger in their eyes and smiles on their faces like children on Christmas anxious to open their presents, wanting to know what I had.

I flashed open my denim vest and displayed the dozen small pockets I'd sewn on each side, every pocket stuffed with my sweetest samplings of non-medical pharmaceuticals north of Mexico. "What do I got? I got uppers, downers, sidewayers. And for you trippers, I got acid. Whatever you need, I got. And if you don't know what you need, the Doctor will prescribe something for you. Gather 'round, gather 'round." Their circle pressed into me.

Fitzgerald's people were just like I expected. They smelled of money, which they pushed into my hands in exchange for my drugs and hashish. Sales were brisk. I was replenishing my supply from the saddlebags on the Harley, when out of the darkness, a goddess appeared. The fire's reflection danced in her eyes, silky black ringlets fell to her shoulder, a buttoned chambray shirt stirred my imagination.

In a sultry voice, she said, "Do you have any snow?"

This woman had just given me two more reasons to like her. I pulled out an envelope and a straw, laid out the coke on the seat of my Harley, and we both took a hit.

"Wanna go for a swim?" she asked in a fetching tone. When I said yes, she unbuttoned her shirt and let it fall to the ground, showing nothing but smooth skin on a perfect body. She ran laughing toward the lake. My only choice was to rip off my clothes and chase her. We swam out a ways until she let me catch her. In neck-deep water, we embraced our naked bodies and kissed, until our passion led to nature's usual course, sex.

We came ashore and stretched out in a patch of grass ten feet from the fire where Fitz and his friends were dancing to a throbbing beat from someone's boom box. They all still wore their swimsuits, cutoffs, and bikinis. Bodies flickered around the fire, alternating from silhouettes to contorted faces reflecting the fire's orange glow, like *National Geographic* footage from the Serengeti or the Outback. They were their own tribe, with their own chemically enhanced rituals.

The girl and I found our perfect world outside the ring of dancers. She pushed me over onto my back and then lay on top of me. Her fingertips danced lightly across my face, gently exploring—forehead, eyebrows, mustache, nose—like a blind person seeing with her hands.

Oblivious to the others around the fire, we started the deed again. Our moans faded into the shouts and chants of the rhythmically gyrating fire worshippers.

My stamina was fading, so I said, "How 'bout a toke of Acapulco gold?"

"That's cool."

At the bike, I pulled out the marijuana, paper, and a lighter. I also picked up a bag of Quaaludes and a bottle of Jack Daniels. When I returned, I rolled the doobie, fired it up, took a deep breath, and passed it to the girl. She knew what to do with it.

"Wanna lude?" I asked.

She smiled and opened her mouth. I placed the Quaalude on her tongue and gave her the JD as a chaser. I did the same. Then I stretched out on my back on soft grass. She pressed her body against my side and ran her fingernail through my thick, dark chest hair.

"Have you ever watched Spaghetti Westerns?" she asked.

"You're not talkin' about food, are you?"

"No! You know, the movies at the drive-in, withwhat's his name?"

"I don't know who that is."

She laughed. "You'd know him if you saw him. Clint Eastwood. That's it!" She was slapping my arm with excitement. Cute, I thought. "I'd watch his movies every Friday and Saturday night. And I wasn't neckkin' either. I watched the movie. Handsome. I had such a crush."

Neither of us said anything for several minutes. She just kept drawing figure eights on my chest with that fingernail, and chills were running up and down my spine. "So what about this guy?"

"What guy?"

"The guy you had the crush on."

"Who are you talking about?"

"Clint, whoever, from the spaghetti movies."

Her eyes squinted as though a migraine had suddenly smacked her in the head, and then she started laughing again. I loved the laugh. It was soft and quiet, as though joy was escaping her body. "Oh, yeah. Him. That's what I wanted to tell you. Your hair is darker, but other than that, you look just like him. Muscular, hairy chest, a scruffy beard, and the beginning of a mustache that brackets your lips. Yes, those lips." Then she kissed me.

"You make me happy," I said.

"I think it's your Acapulco gold that's making you happy."

"Yeah, that too. But seriously, you're the coolest chick I've ever been with." I didn't want to tell her she was also the best-looking one. That could spoil everything by giving her an ego trip.

"Look," she said, pointing toward the lake. "The moon's broken out from the clouds."

The full moon's light reflected onto the lake and lit it up like a runway, a path of silver from the middle of the lake to our shore. It was like we were sitting in front of a gigantic painting.

I held her chin, turned her head, and saw the glow of the fire on her face. "God, you rev my engine, babe. And you know what?"

"What?"

"I got something that will light up that lake like fireworks. Are you ready to take a trip? I got some tabs."

"I dig you too, Big Guy, but I don't know your name, and I don't take trips with strangers."

"I'm Doctor Midnight."

She laughed again, covering her mouth, and said, "Oh, that's right. I forgot."

"What's your name?"

"Well, if you're Doctor Midnight, then I'm Princess Silver Lake."

I laughed and kissed her pouty lips. I'd never used the "L" word with a girl before. I bit my tongue to keep from saying it to her. Love at first sight was something I never believed in, but she was making me think about it. Think hard. I decided to hold back. There would be tomorrow. Or even next week, or next month. There would be time.

≈≈≈

Birds were chirping, and I felt cold and damp. When I opened my eyes, I saw dew on blades of grass. I sat up and realized I was still naked. It was that time of the morning when night slowly yields to day, the sun still below the horizon, but the sky getting lighter. A whiff of smoke in the air, bits of charcoal, and a charred log were all that remained of last night's fire. I was alone except for Fitzgerald, who was sleeping with his back against a tree. I saw a jumbled pile of denim that was my clothes, put them on, and walked over to my bike. The saddlebags were empty, except for the cash. A lot of cash. Tens, twenties, and Benjamins. His friends were generous, if sketchily honest.

I nudged Fitz's leg with my foot. He grunted and looked up at me with bloodshot eyes.

"Where's everyone?" I asked.

"They cut out."

"I can see that. What about the chick?"

"What chick?"

"That righteous chick I was . . . makin' it with. The one I went swimming with. The one that curled up with me and fell asleep in my arms." I walked over to the matted grass that had been our bed. "Right here, Fitz. We were sleeping right here in this spot."

"Doc, I don't know what you're talking about."

"Did you see a girl—a female, dipshit—with curly, black hair? Did you see her leave?"

"I don't know. All the chicks piled into cars with the guys and left."

"How can I find those yahoos?"

"They're from all around, man. Some from Abilene, some Odessa, and a couple came all the way from Waco. Why?"

"I gotta find that chick."

"What's her name? Maybe I know her."

"Princess . . . ah, never mind."

≈≈≈

Over the next couple of years, I continued to look for Princess Silver Lake. I visited every town in a hundred-mile radius and hung out at diners, bars, college campuses, anywhere young people would be looking for a good time, and often I returned to the lake, but I never again saw her. Occasionally, I would doubt what happened that night, thinking it was a dream, or maybe a hallucination from the drugs. Each time, I would shake off the thought. Nothing that blissful could be a dream or delirium. No. Princess Silver Lake was real.

AQUAPHOBIA

Micki Fuhrman

With one arm vise-gripping a weathered square post and my toes curled tightly around the worn-smooth edge of the dock, I ponder the dark, rippling surface of the lake. *It's not even over your head, they said. You could stand up and walk right out to the shore.* I'd just watched three cousins, clomp-clomping down the dock, bare toes splayed, leaping into balletic cannonballs. The last one, Andy, pushed my brother backward off the end. I see him bobbing up, shaking droplets from his dark hair, laughing in croaky adolescent barks. *Come on, Marcy. The water's fiiiiine.*

Dad's minnow bucket bumps every few seconds against the post where it is tied. The galvanized rim breaks the surface, then dips back under black-green water. For some reason, the bumping makes my throat tighten.

Inside the cabin, my aunts and mom are washing up the lunch dishes. The men, wearing khaki pants and aviator sunglasses, are stretched out in lawn chairs talking lazy man-gossip. They look out over the lake, without really seeing it.

No one can tell I'm holding my breath, just thinking about the water. What the cousins don't say—maybe don't know—is that there's no breathing down there. No seeing or hearing, unless you count the subwoofer sound of shapeshifting bubbles and the lake gushing into your ears. No living down there. Not for long. I back up a step.

≈≈≈

The summer I turned seven, my mother gave me a choice, and I took the swimming lessons over the tap dance classes. Chorine stinging my nostrils, I followed the instructor's every command, her voice bouncing in funny echoes over the clear water and off the sides of the concrete pool. When it was my turn to freestyle to the opposite side, I was surprised by my forward motion. My scooping hands and madly fluttering legs were actually propelling me. Except . . . when my fingertips finally touched the rough blue wall, I realized I'd swum a distance of twenty yards, but lost four feet in altitude. Clawing up to the tiled edge, I wondered how long my classmates had been laughing at my steady, sinking submarine descent to the bottom.

The instructor was a sunburned teenager with yellow pigtails. "Only one more lesson after today," she urged. "You need to relax, Marcy. Then you'll stay on top of the water." But I never did either of those things.

≈ ≈ ≈

"You won't even know you're on a boat. Trust me, this vessel is a lot bigger and a hundred times classier than anything I boarded in the Navy." My husband, the retired lieutenant commander, carefully hangs his tropical shirts, still in dry-cleaner plastic. His loafers and deck shoes, stuffed with cedar shoe trees, are lined up on the floor, and his toiletries are already stowed neatly in the bathroom, which he immediately begins referring to as "the head."

Our mammoth cruise ship will be underway in half an hour. I've already found the ship's navigation channel on TV, and I'm perched on the corner of the bed, noting wave heights and wind speed.

My husband surprised me with Caribbean cruise tickets for our tenth anniversary. *How could he not know?*

≈ ≈ ≈

In four days we've docked at three islands with names that roll off our margarita-relaxed tongues. We've learned how to say "Excuse me" in a few dialects and that all island gift shops sell essentially the same trinkets, made in Vietnam or China. The wind has picked up, and to my husband's aggravation, I've just caught news of a potential hurricane stewing four hundred miles away. Again, I'm planted in front of the ship's nav channel, eyes glued to the changing weather and bearing stats. "We're heading northwest! That's not the way to St. Martin! Look, the waves are at eight feet."

My husband is reading on the balcony. "Eight feet is nothing."

Half an hour later, the captain announces that we are rerouting and will not dock in St. Martin. He apologizes and assures us we will all enjoy St. Croix. At dinner, our smiling server holds a silver tray shoulder high. There is a motion I still can't define. Not so much a sway as a gentle pulling of everything around me toward one side of the room, then pushing back the other way. I feel a stomach flutter. The server swings her arm around, quickly recovering control of the tray. "Even I felt that one," she jokes, and begins distributing champagne flutes.

I can't wait to get back to the stateroom TV. "Twelve-foot swells!" I tap frantically on my cell phone. *Three-dollar-a-minute international roaming charges, be damned.* "It has a name! Igor! And it's skimming the Virgin Islands . . . only three hundred fifty miles to the northwest."

"No need to worry, hon. Why, this one time on the South China Sea, we had waves coming over the—"

"This is not a good time for Navy stories. You're not making me feel better."

"Well, what is it exactly that you're afraid of? Capsizing? Sinking? We have lifeboats, you know. Remember the drill?"

"Like I said, you are not making me feel better. Don't put those visuals in my mind. I was terrified at the drill, remember?"

My husband settles into a club chair with a Clancy paperback. "I don't get why you're so afraid of a ship."

"Not the ship. Just all that, that . . . everything under it. Like you being afraid of heights. I'm afraid of . . . depths. Depths of water, to be specific."

"Well, I'm sorry I brought you on a cruise. I hoped you'd enjoy it."

"Oh, I *have* enjoyed parts of it. The islands were amazing. I mean, the people were friendly, and the mountains were cool. The flowers! You know how I love flowers. Don't be sorry. I . . . I'm the one who should apologize."

With great intent, I turn off the TV and pick up a magazine. I flip through the pages, reading none of them.

≈ ≈ ≈

Of course, I know how it started. I was five years old, spending time at the lake with those same cousins, aunts, and uncles. Jackie, a cousin ten years older than me, picked me up and waded out into waist-deep water. She was slightly built. I could feel her boniness as she propped me on her hip. Maybe I was slippery from the splashing of my surrounding cousins. Maybe Jackie had taken on more than she could manage. I slipped from her arms and fell backward into the water. She immediately scooped me up.

But then, she dropped me again. This time, I fell backward and sank to the bottom. I remember looking up and seeing Jackie's distorted face. She took longer to react than before. My memory is one of air, water, and light. Bubbles streaming upward, the low swoosh of water in my ears, sunlight fractals shimmering at the surface.

Jackie pulled me up by my arms and carried me ashore. I felt limp and tired. My mother laid me on the sofa and covered me with a blanket.

That's when the fear began. What I don't understand is the other feeling I have when I think of deep water. It doesn't make sense. The closest I can come to explaining it is *guilt.*

≈ ≈ ≈

I lie awake in the stateroom. The low hum of the engines is more noticeable at night. My husband is blissfully sleeping. Through the balcony door, I see stars, brighter and more plentiful than I can see back in civilization. I watch them until I finally fall asleep.

I'm in a boat. My father and his best friend, Ron, are at each end, holding oars. My little brother and I are on the middle seat of the jon boat, wearing life jackets. Did he jump in or fall? I can't tell. I only see dark water, and no sign of my brother. Ron is about to go in after him. My dad, like me, is a non-swimmer. Then, we hear a bump, bump at the bottom of the hull—like the sound of Dad's minnow bucket. "He's under the boat," says Ron. "Just try to keep it still and I'll go in after him." Suddenly, it's surreally quiet. My dad works the oar to keep the boat from moving. As Ron is about to bail into the lake, my brother's head bobs up alongside us. Ron drags him aboard.

My brother is surprisingly calm. When giving his account later, he swears that he was breathing underwater and that he feels fine. An illusion of his? A miracle, maybe? All I know is that I wanted to go save him, but I knew I couldn't. I flashed back to air, water, and light. I might have lost my brother, all because I was afraid of the depths. Under the rippled waves of my subconscious, the guilt still gnaws.

≈≈≈

Back on dry land. As promised, St. Croix was a lovely, if unplanned, stop. Now that I've survived my first cruise, and some years have passed, I am entertaining the thought of another cruise with my husband. We just so happened to be at sea when a major hurricane blew through. What are the chances of that happening again?

When your anniversary falls in September—high season for hurricanes—the chances might be pretty good.

HIDING IN THE CYPRESS KNEES

Suzanne Webb Brunson

A shaggy, black bear roared as it climbed out of dark, murky swamp water onto solid ground. It squeezed between jutting stumps of wood growing upright in a ragged circle. Its roar morphed to a low growl. The animal clawed the thick trunk of a mammoth bald cypress. No longer growling, it walked around the tree, rubbing and scratching, and repeatedly licked one of its rear paws.

Three people sat on large cypress tree limbs, one above the other, close, each leaning back against the tree trunk. Rags that had secured them during the night were now loosened and blending with the Spanish moss.

The woman tapped the man directly under her. She motioned for him to look at her left leg. Then she pointed at the bear and mouthed the words, "It's been cut."

Once, the bear pulled up some plants to chew, but it did not seem aware of the three humans. It finally extended its forepaws, leaning against the bark. It stretched at least eight or nine feet tall. It looked up at them, then down at the bloody, wet paw. The three could see that the gash went up the leg and the full length of the animal's torso. The wounded bear quietly pushed away from the tree and waddled back into the water. The layers of peat moss trembled. All three stopped breathing until the bear disappeared.

"Could it climb this high?" It was Emmanuel, one of the men, whispering. The woman above patted him, and he quit talking. Then he said, "Working them fields makes my bones ache. I'm sore the same way in this here tree."

"Finding sleep is just as bad, too," John said.

Emmanuel nodded down toward John, agreeing. Even though all were strong, they would strain muscles clinging to branches, wrapping their arms and legs around the wood. The woman, Esther, slept on the highest branch. She would extend a hand or leg and tap one of the two men below when they began to roll too far to one side or the other. None of them wanted to fall onto lower branches, crashing through to the ground, breaking bones, or worse. Esther rarely slept.

"You think we're safe now from that bear?" Esther looked at a mosquito crawling on her arm. "There hasn't been a human soul to pass us." She flicked the mosquito away.

John, sitting at the lowest point, wiped his bug-infested branch with a wad of moss, while still holding onto the trunk with his other arm. Although older by one year, he was modest, a quiet man who often deferred to his brother.

Esther fanned her arm at more swarming mosquitoes. Her husband, Emmanuel, sat on the thick branch below her, the branch above John.

"No, we aren't safe until we get moving outta this swamp." Emmanuel shoved his rags into his pockets. "I don't want those bounty hunters trapping us up this tree. We been resting, but I believe they haven't sat down once. They have to be heading south, just like us."

"Yeah, most runners head to Savannah, or north. Here, we have to hide in this." Esther hadn't smiled in a long time.

"Maybe that bear will slow them down. Wonder what tore him up like that?" Emmanuel threw his leg over the branch, hanging onto it while he felt for a lower foothold. He hugged the tree, stepped past John, and began inching his way down, stretching until his foot reached the soft ground. He reached for the top of one of the tree roots that grew around the base. "If I die tomorrow, I'll know I touched the strangest thing ever—this here hump of wood. I've never seen anything reach up out of the water and sit there like a fence post. They are all be the same, a big ole mound of wood. Lookin' like lumps of cypress roots. They stand guard round the base."

"Yes sir, brother, a mighty fortress." John leaned back in a gentle slide down the rough-ridged bark toward the mossy ground. "If I was to sit in the shallow water, my knee be sticking up the same way as this cypress wood. You are right; knees around the trees. Never heard of such. It be a new tree growin'? Tree roots?" He shook his head and inched downward.

Esther began her descent.

"Maybe we'll come across one o' them hammock islands I heard about. Got a stand of trees. Remember old Hamilton came south from Virginia. Master Carter bought him when he was young, maybe eight, but not any of his family, just him. He be big and strong even then," Emmanuel said.

John reached down for a hand from Emmanuel, who kept talking. "He told a couple of the older guys about islands in the Dismal Swamps where he came from. Said he was sold before he could run."

"Eight not too young to run." Esther was still coming down the tree.

"Land ought to be higher than this water, but it's not," Emmanuel said.

The brothers waited for Esther.

"All right, all right, girl, come on. I'm right here. We both are. Yes, he said that there are the same kinds of places in the Okefenokee. We have to believe that." Emmanuel nodded.

"I bet he run here like us. He's been gone a good while." John took hold of Esther around the waist, easing her onto what little ground there was next to the tree trunk.

"Old man Carter probably run out of slaves to beat, and then he'll start whippin' his own son, what with more than one of us running into this marsh." Emmanuel hated his owner. They all did. "His son even hates him. Snuck around with me all the time. We figured out how to swim one time when we both be drowning. We was down in that old hidden pond. That woulda been something to see. Master Carter finding his son and one of his darkies floatin' away, dead." Emmanuel leaned on the trunk, still talking. "He wouldn't o' cared. I figure his God know he a sinner. Stop him from getting saved. He try God's patience ever which way."

"Yes sir, and he'll keep on whippin' cause he likes it." On this, John agreed with his brother. Their master was cruel.

Esther's anger included Virgil, the overseer, and the worthless round-abouts who helped him beat the field hands. "Thought he got him a man to keep us down. Not anymore." Esther spat at the ground.

"We live in evil times." Esther was tying up her skirt. None of them had ever said this much—not in their whole lives.

A thin mist floated around the massive trunk, rolling through the surrounding emerald marsh. The air filled with birds chirping, the taps of woodpeckers, and an occasional shrieking panther. The jungle teemed with noisy animals and colorful flocks of birds sweeping overhead—except for the humans. They whispered.

"We did one thing right." Emmanuel looked out across the swath of water and trees, some with few branches to climb, so sparse, the trio could be easily spotted. In another month, some of the cypress needles and hardwood leaves would begin to fall. The heat would be a bit more bearable, but not this day. "No one has seen us yet, or we'd be hanging from a branch instead of hugging those tree trunks."

"I still can't believe those roundabouts didn't catch me. I slammed the door open when I went in the barn. I be grabbing the flint box and running back out. Those fools were passed out from corn liquor, while everyone else rushing around, trying not to get killed. The crazy overseer deserved to die. Yes sir, we left that hell behind," John muttered. "But this place is trying my soul."

"The Lord be watchin' us since we left. He put them woods there behind the cotton field so we could hide. Those awful men couldn't see us even if they weren't corned up. That has to be a sure sign he's looking down on us. I believe that." Esther was trying to be brave.

"We did something else right. Look at all this. Its big water, the place where dogs aren't able to track us." Emmanuel crouched against the tree trunk. "Least ways, if they make it out alive, it's not always with four legs."

"If they are lucky, but there ain't never gonna be too much marshland between us and them bounty hunters." John stepped into the water and the earth shook. He took another and then stopped.

"All those stories are true. Did you feel that? Hamilton said the ground shivers. It does."

"There must be a drop-off here." John realized he was sinking. He began to take another step but sunk a bit deeper, water lapping at his legs.

"Think I might be stuck."

"I'm right behind you." Emanuel moved, and again, the swamp floor shook. The same happened with Esther. Both were reaching for John.

"The swamp is shifting." John had his brother's arm. "Is it gonna suck me down?"

Esther clutched the back of Emmanuel's shirt. Both pulled and all three ended up flat in the water. Emmanuel went under and grabbed his brother by the ankles. It worked. He shoved him forward a few feet and they all began paddling.

"The mud wobbles 'cause there be too much of it, everywhere. It goes deep." John was crying, happy to be alive. Emmanuel tried crawling and waved for them to stand again, "Come on. We can walk now toward that next cypress tree."

"That is how come this place got its name. Hamilton say something about the Creek tribes. Like it means 'water-shaking.'"

"Come on. We've done good this far. You jumped on a loose pile. We're in a swamp, and it's tremblin' and shiftin'. Hush now," Esther's eyes were also welling up, and her lips quivered

This was the third day of their trek through the swamp. It was the first time any of them admitted they were afraid of being pulled down into the mud.

≈≈≈

All night and into the dawn, when the sun poked through the leaves, leaving golden spots floating along the ground, the riotous noise never subsided. There was no wind. The air was still and heavy.

"We were so busy clearin' the land. Not much to see except cotton. This is like blankets of birds and bugs, trees, bushes, and ferns. Are those ferns?" Emmanuel was encouraged that this was the morning of their fourth day and that it was in his mind, therefore, a day to be hopeful.

"Yes, and flowers that eat the bugs." Esther gave a slow smile.

Fragrant bay trees were plentiful, and each time they passed one, Esther broke off a branch or grabbed some leaves. She carried them inside her shirt, and even as the three splashed along, the bay leaves would begin to shrivel, and that was when she'd crush a few and sprinkle them on herself and whoever was close by.

"Creek tribes been running down here way before us. A lot of 'em Seminoles now, did ya know that? Think we'll see any, or did they all get run out west? White masters been cruel to a whole lot of folks. Red baby. Black baby. They ain't never give a damn." Emmanuel wiped his hands on his pants and sighed. It was wasted energy to get worked up about anything but staying alive right this minute.

Floating peat mats released a bitter, acrid smell that never went away. Swamp lilies dotted the water, abundant enough in some places to choke out other plants. While it might mean shallow water to plod through, it also meant breaking through stems, roots, and always, the snakes. There were occasional purple irises, swamp orchids, flowers they'd never seen before. Green plants pushed and shoved each other for room to grow, like green snow. They'd never seen snow, but the green seemed to cover everything.

"This water feels like the devil keeps grabbing my legs, like it wants me to stoop down on my knees." John was now a whispering storyteller. "I can feel snakes and fish swimming around my legs, even through my pants. They never stop. There's always more, and yet we still have a hard time catching one to eat."

Emmanuel stopped walking and held up his hand. "Wait. Look over there at that turtle. Over there on that log. It's huge. Let's catch that, instead." As quickly as he started walking, he stopped cold with Esther and John running into him. Right behind the turtle, on the same log, was an alligator.

"That thing has to be as long as you are. Let's get away. Got to be a gator hole somewhere close." John didn't even try to pretend he wasn't afraid of everything.

Then they heard it, a caterwauling in the thick bush.

"I know what that noise is. It's a panther." Emanuel was watching the alligator and turtle. "I heard that scream back at the farm."

In that moment, they saw a brown panther creeping toward the log. The alligator slipped into the water, moved down the water's edge several yards, and then began crawling onto the muddy shore. The brown panther moved as though the air had stopped being heavy and gave the stalker a path. It walked low, paws padding lightly. Then it lunged, pouncing on the alligator. Clenched it by the neck. Dragged the giant remnant of another era long gone back into the jungle.

"That there alligator be bigger. How'd that happen? Which way do we go to get away from all this?" Esther said. This was the first panther they'd seen. Alligators sunned all along muddy banks, but rarely moved.

"Sweetie, we are going straight for that log. Turtle still be sittin' there."

≈≈≈

At last, after another two days, they found an island. It was covered with bottomland hardwood and bordered by pines.

"Hamilton was right. This is what he talked about. Might be small, but I bet there's bigger ones."

≈≈≈

John spotted an osprey nest perched high in a tree and began waving his arms and pointing. "We might be near some prairie land now," he whispered. "Those sticks are thick and solid. Make a fine nest. It so big, we oughta be climbin' up there tonight. That is the biggest bird nest I ever did see."

The three scavenged for roots and berries. They ate raw fish and insects, afraid to start a fire. At sunset, they sometimes trudged farther, past more cypress knees. They continued sleeping on any sturdy branch, while one tried to stay awake to beat off snakes.

Esther gasped when a motionless egret suddenly lifted off a nearby stump. Its feathers brushed her nose and cheek as it swooped past her. Then it moved down, diving into the water. Without hesitating, it lifted right back up. The only thing sticking out of its beak was a fish head. The rest was already in the bird's beak.

She fell backwards into the water. "Lord, you ever see a bird do that?"

"Can't say I have, not in my face, anyway." Emmanuel said, and he and John both smiled. Esther did not and was still miffed with both of them as they began slogging along again.

"It's not funny. Hmmf!"

Sand cranes sounded like woodpeckers. Snakes brushed past in musky water, which was about two feet deep. Sometimes it drifted away bottomless and unfathomable. Emmanuel taught them how to paddle when this happened. Some days they saw so many lizards and creeping fish that they would stop. They'd climb a tree and sit for a few minutes. This was when they'd tried not to weep for the dangerous, strange animals and the lifetime of brutal sorrow.

≈≈≈

Tilda, now fourteen, watched all three running toward the back of the plantation, John following Emmanuel and Esther. Earlier, the violent overseer had barged through the door, drunk and waving a shotgun. She had darted out of the women's cabin. When the men heard the yelling, they ran up the hill to help. She ran and hid behind the plantation owner's favorite magnolia. That was when she saw the three sprint out of the cabin. Emmanuel waved a long knife. John ran to the barn for a minute, and then they were gone. There was no gunfire, so she didn't know what happened, but Virgil didn't follow. Neither did the roundabouts.

"They be running!" That was all Tilda knew. Her mother had grabbed Tilda's baby when the fight started and the women's shack emptied. They were still hiding, but Tilda couldn't find either.

Tilda told herself, "I'll come back one day and find you both, but I have to leave now. I can't stay here anymore. They will hang one of us tomorrow."

It would be dawn soon, but Tilda ran across the last cotton field and into the stand of trees that bordered the property. She ran south toward the swamp water.

≈≈≈

Every day, she tried to catch up but she was weary, exhausted, sleepless. The first nights, she'd climbed any tree she could find, once a scratchy pine, then slept lightly, expecting each branch to break. That first night, no cover in sight, she ran across cotton fields toward the next stand of trees. She'd wait, then dart across a field toward more cover. She'd dropped to the ground once, afraid the field hand had seen her. She didn't have time to tell her story. When the land morphed into marsh, she rested in a cypress, her feet on a cypress knee and her arms tied at the wrist with a rag torn from her skirt. Frightened she might slip away, Tilda tried to be brave. She would feel fish brush her legs and walk faster or climb a tree. She'd sit on the highest branch she could touch and stare at the sky. If it rained, she climbed a tree. If the birds chirped, she climbed a tree. When she feared she couldn't climb at all, she began whispering to herself as she trudged through the water.

She saw a small fire on the sixth night, while leaning on a cypress, her feet on a hump, but waited until daylight to move, not sure if it were her friends or bounty hunters. She was tired all the time.

≈ ≈ ≈

"Hold it right there. What are you doing here?"

Tilda turned and fainted. The man gathered her up from the shallow water and walked. When he reached camp, he loosened his grip and released her on Esther's skirt.

"I found our first bounty hunter," John said.

Esther leaned close to her. "Wake up, baby, wake up. What do you think you are doing?"

Tilda moaned and whispered. "I've been running, just like y'all. No never mind I can't swim. Y'all like to drown me way back more times than I can say—even yesterday. I never been through as much peat moss and mud. What was Godamighty thinking when he come up with all this?" Then she cried, pulled up into a ball of legs and arms, hiding her head.

"We've been thinking much the same. It's not the master's cotton field, it's the Lord's gift of everything that water brings. It's liquid gold in a world we've never seen. Some of it is beautiful and some very strange. Darkness is what scares us all." Esther looked away, pretending to wipe her forehead. Her sweat and tears melted into one liquid permeated with every fragile moment of the days they survived, each one unique. It was now Esther who needed to talk."

"All right, let's get back to taking care of our sister. You eaten at all?"

"No ma'am. Well, one bug, yesterday, but couldn't keep it down. I've just tried to catch up with you all, but I was guessing about following your trail. Well, no, there's not a trail to follow. I just tell myself, 'Tilda, this is the right way.' When the rain came and I couldn't be sure which way was south, I'd climb a tree. Yesterday, I pretty much gave up. Like I was waiting to be caught, or to die."

Tilda squirmed, and Esther shook her head. "No worry. We are thankful we found you.. Look at you, and you always were skinny as a rail."

Emmanuel was already motioning to John. "Come on, brother, let's find us some dinner for Tilda. Keep that fire small as you can until we get back."

"What happened after we left?" Esther asked.

"I don't know. I left my baby," Tilda simpered. "I couldn't find him or my mama, but I knew she had him, and she'd take care of him. I took off before the master found out. I didn't hear no guns, so I figured it was my time to run."

"Well, then, it has been 'we' the whole time?"

"Yes ma'am. What are we gonna do?"

"We will keep running," Esther said. "Oh, there weren't any guns fired. There was a pitchfork with blood."

Tilda looked at Esther and frowned. "Was Virgil comin' after you again?"

Esther looked away. "Yes." It was still too soon for her to talk about what Virgil had done and then what Emmanuel had done. "You know what? I been crying a lot. I gonna stop that. You, too. We are free, little girl, free. I just know it."

When the rain started, the women scooped dirt on the fire, then walked back toward the water, looking for the men.

John and Emmanuel had moved cautiously back into the jungle, hoping to gig at least a pig frog, any kind of frog, or a cooter. The afternoon rain brought the one thing they wanted most, sky water. They held up two makeshift pouches, looking for breaks in the canopy of trees. The rain came harder and then, what they didn't want to happen, thunder.

The rain pushed the women to follow the men. The men had stopped for fear of deep water and lightning. "No climbing a tree right now." They found a heavy growth of bushy plants and hid. "If the lightning hit one of these things, we won't be breaking our back falling, right?"

"You got it." Emmanuel lay down. John crouched, always wary.

≈≈

The rain stopped, but the clouds stayed dark. It would rain more. "What's that noise?" Both John and Emmanuel crouched behind a thicket of palmettos. The dry land had disappeared, again. "It's not a sand crane, that's for sure."

"No, not a bird at all." Emmanuel pointed toward the strange sound.

Click. Click Click. Whatever it was, it was headed their way. It was at that moment that John saw a huge water moccasin about to drop from a tree limb onto them. He grabbed Emmanuel by the shirt, jerking him toward the shallow water. Emmanuel saw it at the same time and was already pulling out his knife, slashing at the snake as it fell. They tried to scramble back onto nearby stumps and grabbed the cypress roots for leverage. John ripped a tree limb and used it to beat on the snake. Emmanuel kept stabbing and finally caught it at the right angle and cut it in half, without being bitten. There was a miracle.

"It's all right now, brother. Just leave it be and let's get away from it." John was already running to the next cypress, slogging, shaking the ground as his feet pounded the peat.   Emmanuel followed, but kept looking back, when he saw an alligator snap both pieces of snake that he'd dismembered, before any bird could snatch it.

"Lord, help us," moaned Emmanuel. They figured it was only a matter of time before they'd have to get away from a hungry one.

Click. Click. Click. Both turned to look toward the noise and saw an enormous wild boar in the distance, running straight for them. Its horns kept striking trees, clicking as it did, but the tapping didn't slow it down. Then the animal let out a huge groan and began writhing on the sliver of land it had tracked. It rolled and began splashing in the water.

John gasped. "It's a swamp pig."

Emmanuel stayed in the water as the boar moaned. "I think it's dying, but I'm not touching him." He was whispering and motioned for John to be quiet.

"Come on, we need to hide. Somebody else killed it, but I can't tell how. A hatchet, a knife? Didn't hear no shot." As they backed away from the boar, the women whistled, and they moved toward each other.

"We changed our minds," whispered Esther. "I believe they are getting closer."

John murmured, "That was a hatchet what killed that thing. I saw it sticking out of its neck."

≈≈≈

"We got him. They must've kept on running. Can we eat this thing? I can't eat no more lizards."

Both men were old, with gray hair and scruffy beards.

"Not so fast. Hush your big mouth and help me. I heard one of these pigs can kill you if you eat it." This man had a red bandana around his neck.

They wore regular clothes, ragged from their own trip. They had been searching for the runaways the whole time, hoping they'd head for the High Trail, but the slaves were doggedly heading into the middle of the jungle. The men lost their horses when they started rearing, struggling, and bucking, and would no longer walk or swim in the swamp. One caught his harness in the thick jungle, and nothing worked. They couldn't untangle it from the limbs. It writhed and pawed at the ground and tried once more to bolt and broke its neck. The other one disappeared into the wall of greenery. They'd pulled the saddle bags from the dead horse, considered eating it, and cut its throat and belly. They pulled out the innards, grabbing the heart and liver. The red bandana held both pieces, and they put it in the saddle bag.

"We need to get out of here before the gators eat us. You sure that bag'll hide the smell?"

"Long enough for us to git gone from here."

They grabbed their rifle and gear after hanging the saddle in a cypress branch. They continued their trek into the swamp, unwilling to give up the hunt. They, too, knew dry land was close by, and they still had their rifles.

The taller one, Gus, pulled a hatchet from the pig and carried it, as well.

"Wonder where them slaves got a hatchet?"

Wilbur, the shorter, scrawny one, followed.

≈ ≈ ≈

Esther froze when someone clasped a hand over her mouth. It was a stranger. She quit struggling, and he held up one finger to her lips. Two more men appeared. They stopped each runaway the same way.

"We are here to help you. Follow us. We know a safe place."

John and his brother looked at each other, then Emmanuel raised his arms in peace. "How do we know you won't kill us? What tribe?"

"Seminole." And he held out his arm, the palm of his hand, turned down.

"You will not be harmed. See this?" and he pointed to two bloody clumps of flesh and hair secured to his breechcloth. "You are safe for now. Come with us. We know where to hide. There are many looking for you, but we can help. There are more of us, and we have an island no one can find. We have crops and a few goats."

"Who are you? Why are you here?"

The men all had straight, black hair, narrow eyes, and wore no shirts. The tall one looked at the two women. "They are not our friends, either. We are hiding. We, too, sleep in the trees sometimes. You don't have to run anymore."

John grinned. "Well, I'll be. That was your hatchet."

They nodded.

Emmanuel stood for a minute or two and then said, "Did you see a big, black bear? We thought it was going to climb right up our tree a ways back."

The quiet Seminole stepped forward and lifted his necklace of bear claws. "You do not have to worry about that bear. Swamp screamer got in a fight with it, ripped a hole in it, then ran away. Bear stood up, roared, and ran into the jungle. He came on our path, and I saw him first. Two arrows, and he dead." The bear—no longer a threat, an enemy, as once, when it came inside the circled fortress of cypress knees and stood up against the base of their tree.

KITES IN LIFE

Michael J. Tucker

A funeral stretches across Baltimore,
Cars thread though Harbor Tunnel
Like popcorn on a string;
I go from under the Chesapeake
To the slate surface of Michigan's lake
Where the night is a song and
The twinkle of lights connect in the sky
Like a tail of a kite.
You were there for the dirge,
You were there for the purge
On horses in rain forests,
Pink beaches by the sea;
You are my creamsicle,
You are my dreamsicle,
Forever I will be
The tail of your kite.

DESTINY'S EVENING

Michael J. Tucker

On that eve the sky reflected a deepness of blue that would have
   made one think they were looking up at the ocean, except for the white
   puffs of cotton that moved across the horizon with a sense of urgency.
   It was early September and the heavy weight of summer heat that was
August
   could scarcely be remembered. The air had a fresh smell of a new season
coming.

For you in your naïve unsuspecting way, it was to be an evening round
of golf,
   one void of serious links practitioners, no hurried foursomes, no big
bets, just
   leisurely singles and casual couples. But for me it was an evening of con-
trivance,
   a plan thought out, logistics in place. It would be a night that would control our destiny.

Knowing my fate would be decided within the hour, my nerves awoke.
   My hands quivered as I gripped my club, worms moved in my stomach
as I swung at the ball.
   How did I strike it? How did it manage to fly?

Moving with you to your tee, my knees weakened as I slung my bag with its precious

contents over my shoulder.

Careful, don't break anything, not the contents, not the mood, let fate be unbridled.

You were innocent as you set to play, for you had no knowledge of my secrets.

Your graceful swing sent the ball arching across the lake's placid black surface

that reflected the instant changes for its inhabitants. A mated pair of Canada geese

create a wake, martins dart through cattails snatching dinner from the air.

Water splashes as a fish leaps to eat an unseen meal.

Tonight I will ask you to be my bride.

Forever so long, you have been with me and no other; how can I live life without you?

When my path was cluttered, you cleared a way. When my life was dark, you lit candles.

When my time was of sorrow, you brought in joy. You give so much, you ask so little.

How can I live life without you?

My plan is to get you to a special place, where golf will stop.

Where under a canopy of bark and branch and leaf and upon an emerald carpet

I will stretch out a linen cloth, pour red wine into crystal, toast ourselves and

present to you a faceted jewel worthy of your faith in me, and ask you to forever

be mine, and I yours.

But I will not challenge destiny, I will not attempt to control fate; what will be will be.

As we cross knolls of grass, patches of sand, billiard smooth greens, the shadows grow and you become weary.

A breeze moves your strawberry hair across your forehead and I see a frown on your brow.

The game's frustration has turned you sour and you plead to turn back, and we've not yet reached that special place.

My heart sinks, worms return to my stomach. It is an omen. It's not to be.

For I am determined that tonight is the night, the only night.

If we don't reach that special place together tonight, then our destiny is to never be.

Could my love for you be false, a fool's gold of comfort and lust?

I gently suggest, one more hole, and through the valley across the creek and over the knoll

you agree to go.

To my nervous joy we reach that special place.
To your surprise, out of my bag comes
the linen cloth to cover the emerald carpet,
and under the canopy of bark and branch and leaf
I pour red wine into crystal and toast ourselves.

Then the birds grow silent; the crickets stop their chatter and the leaves stand at ease. The universe goes quiet to hear my question.

Will you marry me?

Your yes is the climax of my life. Together the birds and crickets sing with joy

as the trees raise their branches and shout hallelujah.

Our fate is decided; destiny has her way.

Rain

RAIN-DANCE AND MOON-EYED MAE

Catherine Moore

The cottage stood nearly an acre into Ruby Mae's farmland, which by the looks of the fields was permanently fallow. The former driveway lay overrun with weeds, so Grace left her Mercedes parked at the road and traipsed her way up, moving with caution through thick underbrush that smelled musky. The cottage fence was wrapped in chicken wire, and the top of its pickets included a barbed-wire header—getting through the gate required tricky maneuvering. This new fortification meant that Ruby Mae's peafowl had become more aggressive since Grace's last visit. If visitors thought the elaborate fencing was to keep the birds away from the house, they'd be surprised to find it was her way of keeping them close.

Grace kept an eye out for the birds as she crossed to the front porch. The stair railing wobbled in her hands, and the steps groaned underfoot. She wondered when the last time Aldrid had been out to check on his mama. *This property's a disgrace, even if Ruby Mae preferred living in a fifty-year time warp.*

Daylight was considerably dim on the porch crammed with every stick of furniture that Ruby Mae had inherited but had no use for—a dining set complete with chairs, five dressers, a couple of wardrobe cabinets, several bed headboards, and at least three pie safes.

"Ruby Mae," Grace called. Her voice echoed between the furniture piles on the encaverned porch and disturbed its occupants. She felt feather and wing atop her head. Heard loud squawking. A peahen's sturdy body fell in clumsy flight to land behind her on the steps. There was a low clucking of other unseen hens in the porch clutter, then the honking of a peacock running to check on his shawl-colored harem.

Grace opened the front door and helped herself inside before Errol showed up. The peacock looked confused when he hopped to the porch, peering left and right for the supposed rival. He waddled up to the screen door and poked his head at the netting as if to warn her. *Or to pick up her scent.* Grace wondered whether he could smell fear. It certainly coursed through her veins, given the size of this bird. "Folks should not be able to look fowl directly in the eye," she said aloud.

"Who's that?" Ruby Mae called from the back bedroom.

"It's Grace Johnson," she answered and could tell by the shuffling that Ruby Mae was trying to red up for company. "I'm just here to drop off a package for you. Please don't feel like you have to entertain me." Grace placed a shipping envelope on Mae's crowded dining room table between a party of peacock statues and a pile of unopened bills. The table top was strewn with miscellany and open photo albums. "I'll be on my way as soon as Errol's not blocking the doorway."

She heard more shuffling, and Ruby Mae appeared from her bedroom, dressed in a house smock, with gray hair sprung wildly out of a cattywampus bun.

"Oh, Errol," Ruby Mae said, her wrinkled face softening with the warm smile she gave the peacock. "Won't hurt a soul, now would you?" she said, still addressing the bird. The large fowl, named after the movie star Errol Flynn, lifted his feathers and waved them as if to answer. "My prince!"

"Charming," Grace said as the peacock dropped guano on the porch floor before departing.

"What's this package, dear?" Ruby Mae asked while fumbling to put on her glasses.

"I dunno—it was being held for you at the mercantile. You haven't been in Burnt Springs for a while, so I thought I'd bring it out to you. You been feeling alright, Ruby Mae?"

"Dandy. Just getting old, that's all. My bones hurt so bad it makes a body not want to move," she said and made her way to the table. Grace pulled out a chair for her.

"I hope this ain't from the Indians." Ruby Mae placed her pale hand on the envelope. Her fair Anglo complexion belied the shape of her features, which looked Native American. Exotic even, with crescent moon-shaped eyes, one colored a woodland green and the other sky blue. Ruby Mae, as she once confided to Grace, had a Cherokee grandmother. This, she wanted to keep secret. Down off the highlands in the heart of Muskogee territory, old prejudices remained, and Ruby Mae told anyone who questioned her lineage that she came from "Welsh Indian." She certainly would not respond to the Alabama Indian Affairs Board with their Creek leadership. Unfortunately, Ruby Mae's obstinate secrecy led to more speculation in the Burnt Springs community. Folks believed "Welsh Indian" was code for "witch," and their children had taken to calling her Moon-eyed Mae.

"Maybe something you ordered?" When Grace handed her a pair of scissors located from a miscellaneous pile on a sofa pillow, she noticed the return address was Oklahoma and winced.

"Figured," Ruby Mae said as she opened the packet and pulled out a stack of papers. "G'damn. They're thieves! They didn't send a dime and kept my things."

"What? What did they keep?"

"Oh, Aldrid sent them some of my old things. Tribal things I have no use for. Don't you think they'd want them in a museum? And they could send me a little damn money?"

Ruby Mae's son Aldrid was a rascal in Grace's mind, but she knew better than speaking about him with the older woman.

"They probably don't have much in the way of funds, Ruby Mae. Speaking of money, if you're in need, there's the Indian Affairs—"

"I'm not dealing with the likes of them. Their blood percentages. Their councilmen. My DNA is staying right here, thank you. And I'm not taking money from the government neither—walk out of the house to cash THAT check, and they'll shoot you dead."

"Ruby Mae, that's not true."

"I know. But rednecks that'll be doing the shooting don't. And it might be partly true. I have a TV, and I seen them killing the darkies. I know you don't call them that anymore," she added.

Grace shook her head and indicated toward the paperwork as asking do-you-mind. Ruby Mae nodded.

"Shake your head all you like, but half-Indians like me, we know—partly white don't make you white. Mostly white ain't white enough."

"They're wanting authentication on the items you sent and include forms to fill out," Grace said, summarizing the letter out loud.

"I'm not completing any paperwork." Ruby Mae rubbed at the corners of her wrinkled eyes. "Did they mention money?"

"No. Oh, and it has to be notarized."

"Ha, see! They're just looking to track me down."

"Ruby Mae, what are you talking about?"

"I'm talking about the people who want to kill non-whites like me. Haven't you been listening?"

Grace dropped into a deep knee-bend where she could look directly into her friend's eyes. "You need to stop being so afraid," she said and reached for Ruby Mae's hand.

"Yes, Lord, I'm afraid. Afraid of them all. Because I don't know who the bad guys are anymore. I see a guy's picture on TV, and I wonder, Italian or Arab? I can't tell them apart either. How are folks supposed to know who is coming to shoot them? How—?" Ruby Mae's lip quivered to the point of speechlessness. Her hand involuntarily moved to a photo in an open album. It was a picture of Ethel, Ruby Mae's youngest, and darkest, child. Kneeling at the edge of the Burnt Springs sink, the girl's expression, sadder than a ten-year-old's should be, was sunlit by a rare beam that fell between tree branches in the Burnt. Almost angelic. The photo looked to have been taken about a year before she disappeared. Five years ago, Ethel's remains were pulled from the murky waters at Whiskey Bay over in Baton Rouge.

"Let's get you out of here."

≈≈≈

Ruby Mae wore a winter slicker despite the autumn warmth and an unusual dry spell. She grabbed a cane at the top of the porch steps, using it not to walk down but to swish through the overgrowth below. As they moved across the yard, she hit upon abandoned farm implements buried in grass.

"Do you want to go for a drive?" Grace asked.

"No, I do enough sitting. It feels good to walk some."

When they got close to the barn, Grace saw there were dents down the side of Ruby Mae's abandoned seventies-era car—once rust-colored, now just rusted out.

"What on earth happened here?"

"Oh, that was Tom Jones. I can't stop him when he's incensed. Peacocks, you know, are so full up on ego, they can't even stand their own reflections. There he pecked, believing he was much more handsome than the other cock, destroying my car in the process. Come see Tom; he's a dandy."

On the far side of the barn, there was a separate fenced area and within, what looked to be a younger, thinner version of Errol. The peacock pushed itself past Ruby Mae as she opened the gate, and Tom Jones ran to face Errol Flynn. Throats palpitating, with trumpet-blast war cries, they flew at each other, nearly colliding. They landed, swiveled around, their train feathers swirling like bejeweled cloaks, and repeated the process. Eventually, the smaller Tom gave up and was chased ignominiously away.

"Wahoo, Errol's still got it." Ruby Mae smiled.

"I'm surprised you keep another cock around here," Grace said. Ruby Mae had once told her that she separated and sold the males as quickly as possible. Most of the peafowl were sold to a specialty meat distributor, and her birds were served at the finest restaurants in Birmingham.

She shrugged. "It's time. Errol is getting up there in years," Ruby Mae whispered.

From this vantage point, Grace could count the peafowl tails nesting on the cottage porch. She was fortunate to not have been attacked at first entry.

As if on cue with her thoughts, a peahen nudged Grace from behind and marched past, crest atop head bobbing, and her four chicks trundling behind. The peafowl pecked their way through the garden's wild brush by instinct, but not by need since they shared a diet from their caretaker's pantry.

"Ah, honey, look, they're such social creatures," Ruby Mae said.

They smiled at each other as they watched the hen cluck and corral her little ones together.

"We're having a barbecue after church on Sunday. I can come out and carry you in to the Burnt if you'd like."

"Nah. I might run into Aldrid."

"That would be good since you miss him."

"I don't anymore. He has become—surly. Thinks he's too good for my ways. That new wife of his has made Aldrid ashamed to acknowledge his mother." While she spoke, she collected the off-colored eggs hidden in the tall grasses around the fence posts, placing them in a nearby basket.

Ruby Mae gifted a couple of warm eggs into Grace's hands. "Here, for you."

"Don't you want them?"

"I have dozens in the house. Please," she waved, "they're the best. Take them."

Grace tucked the eggs in her sweater pockets. She would enjoy eating them in omelets tomorrow. She'd never tasted the bird's meat, though, despite the number of times Ruby Mae had invited her to taste a dish. Grace had some jerky once that she thought might be close. It was delicious, so she didn't ask too many questions.

In a first movement for leaving, Grace stepped back toward the cottage. She pointed overhead. Dark rainclouds gathered on the horizon to a slow beat of thunder. Mellow light rays pierced through chinks in the cloud cover.

Raindrops fell just as they reached the porch, first one by one on the sun-parched trees, then in number on Ruby Mae's pride of splendid peafowl who had left their nests and were dancing under the gray skies. Errol unfurled his train with a dazzling shudder as the rain came down. Tom followed suit.

May-yew, may-yew, may-yew! The peacocks hollered.

"Make a wish, Grace."

Grace closed her eyes and listened to the sound of singing birds in the rain. She wished this sort of rural melody would last and last. When she opened her eyes, she smiled at her older companion. "Ruby Mae, tell me what you wish."

"I wish it would rain every day so the peafowl would dance for me." She frowned a little, then added, "I wish life held the bliss it once did. I wish the children would come around looking for that witch Moon-eyed Mae." She ended with a smile.

"But didn't they throw rocks at the house?"

"Yes, roadway pebbles. Bah! That's all they ever threw. Least someone would come see me."

Grace took the old woman's hand, and they watched the peacocks dance in a rain hued with sunlight breaking through the clouds. Charmed by an iridescent prism of feathers and droplets, the tired, brown yard became resplendent in all conceivable colors.

They stood together until Ruby Mae said it was time to go back inside.

Previously published in *American Writers Review*

Shortlisted for the Faulkner–Wisdom Competition

SMITH ISLAND

Michael J. Tucker

As soon as I saw Jesse Morland's Neanderthal brow and boot-shaped jaw enter McDonalds, I turned my back to him, hoping he wouldn't see me. Like me, he was an ex-con, and the kind of man who would try to weasel his way into my life and ruin my plans for a new beginning. I'd been clean for three months since my release from the Eastern Correctional Institute, and wanted to keep it that way. Mixing with other ex-felons was one sure way of going back to jail.

"Deuce! That you?"

He was coming toward me doing the prison shuffle, more of a waddle, mimicking a con wearing leg irons. He had a big grin that told me he was happy as a fat tick on a dog to see me, and that couldn't be good.

There was no handshake or fist bump. Badasses didn't do that gentle-manly stuff. He slid in opposite me in the booth, one leg stretched on the seat, his back pressed toward the wall. One might think he was just making himself at home, but it was an animalistic survival tactic from his prison experience. Limit the paths a person can take to attack you; protect your back.

"When'd you get out?" I asked.

"Last week."

"Got a job yet?"

"Ha! You kiddin'? Naw, parole officer says she's gonna line me up with some stuff this week, but I ain't gonna work. Not me. What 'bout you?"

"Been working at the rendering plant. Killing chickens and shoveling guts."

"Good God, man. Don't you got no pride?"

His bloodshot eyes drilled into me like I'd turned into a sleazy organism. His reddish-blond stubble suggested he hadn't shaved since the first day of his release. His head was nothing but thick bone. If I hit him in the face, I'd do more damage to my hand.

"I'm straight. Not going back to jail again. Not ever," I said.

He leaned halfway across the table, getting his big head as close to me as he could. "Yeah? Well, guess what? I ain't goin' back either, and I ain't gonna be killin' no chickens." Then he glanced around the room and lowered his voice. "I got somethin' in the works. Somethin' big." His eyes widened as he stretched out both hands. "And it's low risk, but I need another person. I could use you if'n you're up to it. Mean no more shoveling chicken guts."

"Forget it." I got up to leave. "I want a new life. An honest life where I don't have to be looking over my shoulder all the time."

"But, Deuce—"

"Stop it! My name is William Charles. Call me Bill or William, or even Billy, but not Deuce. We're not in ECI anymore."

"Buddy, you got two first names." He held up two fingers. "What is it, William or Charles?" And rocked his head from shoulder to shoulder. "Either way, they're dumb and boring. But because you got two, that make you the Deuce, the coolest guy around."

What was the point of arguing with a low-life scumbag, an unsuccessful burglar that'd been caught and locked up a half-dozen times? I turned to walk out.

"Deuce! Hear me out. It's the opportunity of a lifetime."

Without looking back, I gave him the finger.

≈≈≈

Not having a car, I walked the two miles to the trailer park where I lived in a cheap rented truck camper resting on cinder blocks. The town is called Eden, like the garden of, on Maryland's Eastern Shore. It was the first week of fall, but summer really hadn't gone away yet. Temperatures were in the nineties, and the humidity numbers weren't far behind. Making matters worse, the camper was at the back of the park next to a farmer's field. His tractor kicked up small dust storms that invaded my camper even when the louvered windows were closed. It left a fine coating of what looked like brown talcum powder on everything.

My neighbors were another issue. Most fell into narrowly defined categories: alcoholics, doobie users, and opioid addicts. Six black-leather-jacket motorcyclists, who enjoyed all three vices simultaneously, inhabited one of the trailers. Three days ago I woke to the sound of sirens at two in the morning. Some woman had stabbed her boyfriend. The cops cuffed her and took her away, while an ambulance carted him to the hospital. The next evening they both were sitting in lawn chairs next to their trailer, sharing a six-pack. All was forgiven. Such was life at my new home.

The day after I saw Jesse at McDonald's, I came home to him sitting on the cinder-block steps to my camper with a six-pack of Coors at his feet. He was already working on his second can. I could feel the anger boiling up, but knew I had to control my temper, and still get the message across that I didn't want him in my life.

"What the hell are you doing here?"

"Hey, hey, take it easy. Just stopped by to socialize. Have a beer."

He tossed one that I caught. "How'd you know this was mine?"

His face wrinkled up like I'd asked him to come up with some algebraic formula.

"Well, 'cause I got mine in my hand, and yours was the next one in line. You want a different one? They all taste the same."

"Not the beer, dumbass—the camper. How'd you know this is where I stay?"

"Oh, yeah. That. Your neighbors told me."

"Which neighbors? Nobody knows who I am."

Jesse's raised eyebrows yielded a snide grin. "Oh, yeah, they do. Those boys in the leather jackets make it a point to know who's who. And they know you as the murderer that served his time and got out."

≈≈≈

Murderer! That word. That accusation. That night changed my life forever. I was never sure why the place was called Red's Deep Dive Bar. It may have been because Red was once a deep-sea diver, the kind that wore steel helmets connected to a hose that pumped oxygen. He had once been an underwater welder working on bridges and ship hulls when an accident ended his career. Or maybe it meant that the place, formerly a gas station, was a dive bar that had a very bad reputation. The place reeked of cigarettes, sweat, and spilled beer.

The bar's nautical theme consisted of lobsters, blue crabs, one mounted swordfish, and netting hung from the ceiling. The only semblance of realism was Red's actual dive suit and helmet displayed behind the bar.

I'd been dating a girl named Julie for about a month. Her lips seemed to be in a perpetual pucker, as though inviting a kiss, and she had brown eyes that looked like she'd either just woke up or was about to go to sleep. Sexy to the nth degree. Her straight black hair was shoulder-length, and her body vibrated with every move. We seemed to be getting serious, if spending a couple of nights together is defined as serious. For whatever reason, she liked Red's. The place was always packed on Saturday nights because there was a DJ. This was the third Saturday night in a row that we'd gone. We'd spend most of our time dancing. We were really putting energy into "Crocodile Rock." We both knew the lyrics and sang as we danced, except I would change the girl's name from Suzie to Julie, and I swear she inserted a rhyming word on 'the biggest kick I ever got.'"

When the song finished, I went to the bathroom, and Julie went to the bar to get us more beer. On the way back, I saw Julie turn away from the bar. As she did, a guy behind her reached around and slipped his hand down her low-cut top. She turned and jerked away from him as I pushed my way through the crowd. When I got to them, she was yelling something I couldn't hear over the din of the music. He was three inches taller and twenty pounds heavier, but that didn't matter. I got his attention by pushing his right shoulder with my left hand and followed through with a roundhouse right to his jaw. His head snapped back, and I knew his jaw was broken. He was unconscious before he hit the floor. I heard the crack of his skull on the concrete.

Julie would be the last woman he ever assaulted. He never regained consciousness. It turned out he was an eighteen-year-old football star that had just graduated from high school with a scholarship to the University of Maryland. I was convicted of involuntary manslaughter and served all of a six-year sentence. When I heard Julie got married, my mind flashed to the character, Suzie, in the Elton John song. Just like her, Julie left for some foreign guy.

≈≈≈

"Deuce, did you hear me?"

"I'm not a murderer."

"Well, you were known at ECI as the mean-ass bastard that killed a man with your bare hands. And that was good enough that Crips and Bloods left you alone. The Aryan Brotherhood never messed with you. Prison word travels faster than a text message, and these here leather-clad neighbors probably got the word before you even moved in. But, good for you. The same rules apply outside. Nobody gonna mess with you here either."

In prison I had to be a mean-ass to survive. My boxing skills probably saved my life. Going in the ring at ECI showed everybody I wasn't to be messed with.

"Hey, you know what those motor heads said when I asked for you by name?"

"You mean William Charles or Deuce?"

"Ha, yeah. No, I just asked for Bill Charles. And you know what they said?"

"You're gonna tell me, aren't you?"

"*El gringo con manos de piedra.*" He laughed and said, "Yeah, that's what they called you, the gringo with hands of stone. Guess they have a Mexican connection at ECI. Probably running drugs for them."

"What do you want?"

"Deuce. Why do you think I'd be wantin' somethin'? Can't buddies just hang out and have a beer together? Huh? Talk about old times. You know."

"We don't have any old times together, Jesse. There's nothing to talk about."

"Yeah we do. We got the ECI boxing matches." He tossed his empty beer can, jumped up and started shadowboxing, shuffling his feet, and throwing jabs. It was a pathetic scene. He'd throw a left jab and *hupf*, then a right cross and *hupf*. His feet were too close together and out of sync with his punches. He dropped his hands, smiled, breathing like he'd run a marathon, and said, "You were the hundred-and-eighty-pound champ the entire time you were in the house. You fought on the outside, didn't you? Were you a pro?"

"Golden Gloves."

"I knew it. You had training. You were no street fighter like the rest of them. You was up there in the ring, a-bobbin' and a-weavin' like you was Muhammad Ali. You'd get in close, and then *bap, bap, bap*." Jesse again shadowboxed, moving his head left and right, then following with the jabs. He lost his balance and staggered, looked up, and continued. "Those other guys would step back, drop their guard, for just the tiniest second, and you'd swing that looping right." His right swung in a high arc hitting air. "And bam! Down they would go. Yes sir, hands of stone. *Manos de piedra*."

"Time for you to go, Howard Cosell. I gotta take a shower."

"You do that Deuce, 'cause you smell like chicken shit."

The next morning on the way to work, I kept thinking about Jesse saying I smelled like chicken shit. He was right. I did. I started to gag thinking about it. When I got to the plant, I found out my boss had something planned for me that would make my life even worse.

It was late afternoon, and I was sitting on my cinder-block step draining my fourth beer, thinking about what I was going to do with my sorry life, when a rust-bucket '89 Toyota Corolla stopped in front of my camper. The sun's glare on the windshield kept me from seeing who was in the car. When the passenger door opened, Jesse stepped out and shouted, "What you doin' here?"

"Don't you remember? I live here, dumbass."

His response was a *hee-hee* laugh, then, "Yeah, right, but you ain't usually home for another hour or so." As he was talking, the driver crawled out of the car. A woman.

"So, what were you planning to do, break in and rob me of all my valuable possessions? Master burglar that you are."

He spit out another obnoxious *hee hee*. "Naw, thought you needed some cheerin' up, so brought a friend and figured we could have a little par-tay. You know what I'm sayin'?"

I let my eyes settle on the woman and estimated her to be maybe mid-forties, but she might've been older. She was the kind that had spent her life in rough bars with rougher men, and had a face that once, a long time ago, might have been pretty. She wore a strapless top that covered breasts that were too large for her too-thin body. Her top was cut short, exposing a tattoo of a rose encompassing her navel, the stem of the flower disappearing into denim short shorts.

"So does your friend have a name?"

"José." Jesse was still leaning on the passenger door, smirking.

"José? You mean Josie?"

"No, José." He reached onto the passenger seat and pulled out a bottle. "Deuce, meet our friend for tonight, José Cuervo."

"Jesse, I think he mighta meant me." She gave me a gap-tooth smile and said, "Didn't cha, hun? Hi, I'm Dorrie." She put a hand to her mouth and coughed a smoker's cough, phlegm rattling her chest. Her face was a motley tan, complexion rough as sandpaper, and dark blonde hair with black roots. The sound of her voice reminded me of a cement truck downshifting to second gear as it goes up a steep hill. Smoke drifted off a cigarette she held in one hand, while she extended the other. I thought she wanted to shake my hand, but she held my hand, examining it like a ring referee looking for a cheat. By this time Jesse had joined us. She looked at him and smiled. "You were right. He has hands of stone." She was still holding my hand when she nodded toward Jesse. "He says you're a tough guy, and you got the hands for it, but you got the eyes of a kind man. And I know 'cause I seen the eyes of mean men and kind men, but mostly mean men."

"Ok, you love birds. Break it up now. Time for some serious drinkin'. Get us some glasses, Deuce." Jesse pushed past me, holding the tequila bottle in front of him as though it was a candle leading his path into my camper and saying in a sing-song voice, "We be daytime drinkin', daytime drinkin'." Dorrie brushed alongside me and followed him.

I was starting to get a bad feeling about how this was going to turn out. But I had enough beer in me that I didn't care. Sometimes a man gets so low that he can't see any up. And that was my view of things now. It no longer mattered what Jesse was or what it was that he was planning.

We'd finished our second shots of Cuervo Gold when Jesse asked why I was home early. I'd had enough beer and tequila to have that warm glow, loose tongue, and what-the-hell attitude, so I opened up.

"I quit."

"You quit, just like that?" He snapped his fingers.

"Yeah. Pretty much."

"Come on, there's more to it than that, good buddy." He pushed against my shoulder like a long-lost friend. "What's the deal?"

"Ok, soon as I got to the chicken plant this morning, boss says they needed me over to the pig plant."

"Pig plant?" Dorrie inquired, brow furrowed.

"Rendering plant for hogs. It's where your bacon comes from."

"What you mean?"

"Just that. It's where they kill the pigs, butcher them into different products—ham, pork, bacon, chitlins, all that. And let me tell you . . . it's awful. I'm never gonna eat bacon again."

Dorrie interrupted with a cough. "I can give up a lot of things, but I ain't never gonna give up my cigarettes or my bacon." As if to demonstrate her will power, she lit another cigarette.

"Yeah, I bet you can add sex to that 'cause you ain't never gonna give that up either."

"Shut up, you mister know-it-all, Jesse. I might start givin' that up tonight. See how you like that."

"You didn't give up eggs when you was killin' chickens," Jesse said to me. "What was so bad about the pigs?"

"Well, first of all, it starts outside when they pull up in these trucks with trailers that are three levels tall. Looks like condominiums on wheels. There's this squealing that sounds like screaming. It's ear piercing. The pigs are all packed in together, and you can see them through the rails in the trailers. Their little beady eyes are terrorized. They know. These animals aren't dumb. Somehow they know they are going to be slaughtered, and they're screaming and jumping over each other trying to escape. It's pure panic. They run them through a chute and get them to an area where they're stunned before slaughter."

"What'd ya mean 'stunned'?" Dorrie asked.

"I was told there are different kinds, but here they use percussive stunning with something called a captive bolt pistol. Basically, it looks a little bit like a gun, but instead of a bullet, a bolt punches the head, making the pig unconscious. Sometimes."

"Sometimes?" she said.

"Yeah. That's when it got really ugly. One of the pigs was clearly still aware of what was going on. He was squealing, wiggling, trying to get up and get away from his murderers. They just snatched him with a hook and dragged him along the floor to the scalding tub. He's dragged alive and dumped into the boiling water."

"Ew! That's awful." Dorrie was cringing at this point.

Jesse poured another round of tequila.

"You think that's bad, Dorrie. Think about this. What does a pig look like? He doesn't have feathers like chickens, doesn't have fur like cattle."

"Cows don't have fur," said Jesse.

"Yes they do. Now shut up. Think about this. A pig basically looks like a big fat man with its hairless white skin. And now we're torturing these smart animals, boiling them alive, so we can eat them. And they look like people." They both gave me a doubtful look. "Yeah, you've seen people that when you look at them, you say, 'Hey, he looks like a pig.'"

Jesse shook his head. "Name one."

"Ok, George Clooney."

Both of them burst out laughing.

"I'm serious. Look at a picture of him when he's not smiling. Bill Cosby, too. You'll see."

"All this talk of pork is makin' me hungry. Give me your keys, babe, I'll get us a pizza, and it looks like we're gonna need more José. You got some bucks to chip in on this, Deuce?"

I pulled out a ten and gave it to him. He looked at it, then back at me. "This ain't gonna cut it, my man. Come on, cough up another Hamilton." I pulled out two fives and handed them to him.

"You want pepperoni and bacon on your pizza?"

On his way out the door, I said, "Just extra cheese, and you know I'm unemployed now."

"Yeah, I ain't never been employed. Never stopped me."

Dorrie poured drinks for us, her expression sad, almost verging on tears. "What's wrong?"

"I was right 'bout when I said you was a kind man." Her words slurred. She wrapped her free arm around me while holding her glass in the other hand and nuzzled her face on my neck. "You quit your job 'cause the people were cruel to piggies."

We sat on the edge of the bed, which also served as a sofa in the tiny camper. She was still hanging on to me, and I could smell her cigarette breath. I started worrying about Jesse's attitude about this. Was she his girlfriend? Would he be mad if he walked in and saw us like this? Would he even give a damn? At this point I started thinking I didn't give a damn what he thought.

"Jesse says you were a big-time boxer, that you won a gold glove. Is that something like what Michael Jackson had?" She cleared her throat with a raspy cough.

"No, no. It's amateur boxing. You don't get paid. It's called Golden Gloves. That's all."

"How old?"

She was getting harder to understand, and her head was now resting on my chest. I expected her to pass out. But I started thinking back to how it all began.

≈≈≈

Bigger boys were always picking on me. I'd come home from school with bloody noses, bruises, and black eyes, until my mother had enough of it. The year I turned ten, she sent me to Baltimore to live with my uncle and his family for the summer. She told him to toughen me up. I stayed two years. As a father of three daughters and no sons, he was happy to have me. He'd boxed as a pro for five years with a record of losses more than wins. For his boxing career, he received a misshaped nose and cauli-flower ears.

His basement was a full-blown boxing gym—everything but the ring. He had a heavy bag hanging from a rafter, an uppercut bag, a speed bag, a strike bag that, if I wasn't careful would snap back and bop me in the face. And there was more that I can't remember. He lowered all the equipment to fit my height. We'd get up at five in the morning and run. Started with a half mile and then he'd increase it by a quarter mile a week until we were running six miles. And then there was the diet. No candy, cake, or ice cream. It was protein heavy. I didn't like it at first, but I was getting bigger and stronger, which I did like. All of that, and sparring, too.

It went on for six months before he ever took me to a boxing gym with a real ring and real boxers, even kids my age and older. I started sparring with others my size, then some that were taller or heavier. I was scared to death the first time in the ring, thinking about times getting beat up by the kids back home. But my uncle had done a good job, training took over, and it kept getting easier, and I kept getting better. Three months later, it was time to register for my first Golden Gloves competition.

I won my first match, and the next, and the next, and kept winning until I got to the regional finals where I lost to a long-armed kid who kept me off him by jabbing at my headgear. He wasn't fighting, just keeping me away from him. I couldn't land any punches. I fought him again the next year in the regionals. This time I got under his big gloves and pounded his ribs. He didn't come out after the second round.

When I got back to my mother's, no one messed with me anymore.

≈≈≈

Dorrie was asleep, her head still on my chest, so I couldn't move, a wheezing sound coming with each breath. The Corolla rattled to a stop, and Jesse fumbled with the trailer door while juggling with two pizza boxes and another bottle of Cuervo.

"Can I get a little help?"

"I would but as you can see . . . someone's asleep."

With that, Dorrie jerked her head up. "What? I wasn't asleep."

Jesse put the pizza on my small table and pulled out plastic plates. Dorrie started a coughing fit that had the gurgling sound of boiling water. I wondered if she had lung cancer. I caught Jesse's eye and nodded toward

Dorrie, as if I was asking what was wrong with her. All I got was a shoulder shrug.

Once she got control of herself, Jesse said, "Who wants a slice of the bacon and pepperoni pizza?"

After that, the drinking got pretty heavy. At some point, Jesse put Quaaludes on the table. I don't remember if I took any, but I probably did.

When I woke up the following morning, I was naked with Dorrie beside me, naked. Jesse was asleep in my only comfortable chair, a recliner. He was also free of clothing.

I dressed and put on a pot of coffee, went to the bathroom and popped a couple aspirin, and chased them with a tall glass of water. When I emerged, Dorrie and Jesse were putting their clothes on. No one mentioned the previous night, and I wasn't going to ask. Last thing I remembered was finishing the pizza, and that was all I wanted to remember.

Dorrie said she had to be at work by noon. Before passing out, I'd learned she was a waitress and sometimes bartender at a seedy bar on the other side of town. I asked if it was East of Eden, but neither of them got the joke. Jesse said he'd catch her later. I didn't like that at all. He was up to something, probably some illegal scheme, but whatever it was would smell of rotten fish.

I suggested we go to a nearby diner and have breakfast. It was a half-mile walk from my place. The oppressive heat of earlier in the week was gone, the air now fresh and breezy with low humidity and a clear blue sky.

Jesse was unusually quiet as we walked. I figured he was working on getting the words just right on what he wanted to say. Finally, he opened up.

"Remember that deal I told you about the other day at McDonald's? Now that you're not workin' and all, I was thinkin' maybe you'd be more interested. It's a big haul, and it'd be the easiest money you've ever earned. With your share you could get out of here, start a new life for yourself. Go west maybe. Texas. California. Hell, even Mexico. Wherever you wanna go!"

"How much money are you talking about?" No sooner were the words out of my mouth than I felt like kicking myself. I couldn't take them back.

And yet I wouldn't have asked unless, out of desperation, there was something deep inside of me that was willing to do something I never thought I'd do.

"Ah . . . half a mil, total. So I've been told. We'd split it even."

A bell over the door jingled as we entered the diner. The morning rush, if there was any, was over, and the only remaining customers were four men in their seventies or eighties sitting at a round table nursing cups of coffee. They looked at us like they knew we were ex-cons.

"Howdy, boys," Jesse said with a sloppy salute. They continued staring at us.

We took a booth at the far end of the diner. The waitress brought us coffee. Jesse ordered pancakes. I asked for two eggs over and a double side of scrapple. I needed the protein for my hangover.

"Who's your source, Jesse? How do you know about this?"

"Yeah, that's the best part. Makes it solid. You remember Higgy?"

"No."

"Higginbottom?"

I shook my head.

"My cellmate."

I never talked to Jesse on the inside. I only knew him to see him. How would I know his cellmate? My response was a cold stare.

"He must have come in after you got released." He lowered his voice. "Anyway, he's all pissed off at his uncle, that's our mark, and the old man has all this money in cash stashed in his house."

The waitress brought us our order, and Jesse covered his pancakes in syrup and continued to talk in a hushed tone. "The old man is like eighty or something, lived his whole life on Smith Island. He oystered and crabbed till he couldn't do it no more."

I knew Smith Island was a small, inhabited isle in the Chesapeake Bay, but I'd never been there.

"Just sold his boat. Got a lot of money for it. Higgy says they never spent a dime. So tight their asses squeak when they walk."

"They?"

With a mouthful of food he said, "Wife."

"How does Higgy know all this?"

"He lived there till he dropped outta school. He still talks like he never left the island. Fact is, you didn't know, you'd think he just got off the boat from England. One night the cellblock was real quiet. Kinda spooky. And Higgy says to me, 'Mighty cam tonight.' And I said, 'What?' That was how he said calm. It was cam. And then when he was tellin' me about his uncle's house, he kept callin' it 'haise,' and when he wanted to walk around the prison yard was 'rayund' instead of round. Told me the island was set-tled three hundred years ago by the English. Islanders didn't have much to do with the mainland—no television, no movies—so they just kept talkin' like their ancestors."

We finished our breakfast and were working on a refill of coffee when I asked, "How are we gonna do this if the old guy's there?"

"He ain't. Higgy says they're up in Delaware visiting grandchildren."

"How do you know the money's there?"

"Hell, there's less than two hundred people livin' in the damn place. Ain't got no bank. If you're visitin' and you buy somethin' in the little store or restaurant, you can't even pay with a credit card. Higgy says everything's cash. And the old uncle ain't carryin' cash to Delaware."

We paid our bill and were walking back to my place. The cellmate had given Jesse all the details, including a map to find his uncle's house, with the expectation that the stolen money would be split with him. But Jesse had other ideas. He didn't think Higginbottom would survive his ten-year sentence. He was sure Higgy would piss off someone and get a shiv in his back. He wouldn't need the money.

This was not something I ever would have considered yesterday, but that was yesterday, and this is today. I'm stuck in a nothing town with no job, and no chance of getting a decent job. I need a new start.

I didn't like the thought of stealing the old couple's life savings, but the way Jesse described their lifestyle, and the island life, they didn't need the money. What the hell, their social security checks would be more than enough for them. For me, that cash would mean a new life. There was no need for me to stick around here. I had served my full sentence, so I didn't have to report to a parole officer. I could get a bus ticket to anywhere, and never look back.

By the time we arrived at my place, I'd made up my mind. It seemed to be my only way out of this life. I got myself a beer and handed one to Jesse and said, "No guns?"

"No guns."

"What about security system or safe? You bringing your burglar tools? Whatever it is you use?"

"You don't understand, Deuce. Everybody knows everybody. Hell, they don't never lock their doors. Higgy says there ain't a lock on any door on the whole damn island. Trusting sort of people, ain't they?"

"And you're sure the house is empty?"

"Got it straight from the horse's mouth." Jesse made this sound as simple as picking money up off the street.

"When do we do this?"

"Tonight. Sooner the better. Gotta do it at night 'cause everybody knows everybody. Someone sees us go to that house, they'd know somethin' was wrong."

"How do we get there?"

"Dorrie'll let us use her car. We drive down to Crisfield, take a boat from there out to the island."

"Someone's gonna let you borrow a boat?"

He tilted his beer can for a swallow, then raised his eyebrows and nodded.

"How far out is the island?"

"Oh, I don't know, ten, maybe twelve miles."

≈≈≈

The sun had just set when we arrived at the Crisfield dock. There was still a twilight sky with rose color reflecting off a tall thunderhead to the south, the water flat and calm, the only ripples from the few boats preparing to dock.

Jesse said, "We'll stay in the car about an hour. It'll be good and dark by then. That's when I'll get our boat."

I got out, leaned against the front of the car, and took in the sunset along with the saltwater smell of the Chesapeake. When it was dark enough, Jesse told me to go down to the dock and walk out to the end of a pier that looked to be a hundred yards long. He'd come around with the boat to pick me up. I was out there waiting for him, when I heard a weak puttering sound and in the darkness saw a wooden flat-bottomed boat with a blunt bow moving slowly toward me. The front end banged into the piling. In a stage whisper, Jesse said, "Quick! Jump in."

It was a three-foot leap into the boat. On landing, I fell backward and felt myself sitting in an inch of water. Jesse opened up the throttle and steered west into the darkness. The motor was a small outboard with a high-pitch whine. We didn't seem to be moving very fast for the sound it was making.

"There's water in here," I said.

"Well, start bailing."

"With what?"

"With your hands, Deuce. We ain't got anything else."

"What about life preservers?"

"Didn't see any."

"What the hell kinda boat is this? Who loaned it to you?"

"It's the kind that's easiest to steal."

More like a stolen piece of driftwood. I was hoping the rickety boat would hold together long enough to get there and back.

Off in the distance lightning danced around the thunderhead and a wind was starting to kick up. After some time passed, I couldn't tell how long, lights twinkled in the distance. "There it is, Deuce. Smith Island. Not long now."

The lights got brighter as we got closer. Then Jesse spotted a beacon on a tower. "There . . . see that? That's where we're headed." He cut back the throttle as we glided through marshes. He steered the boat into some soft mud, then got out his map and a Maglite. I looked over his shoulder. The crude map didn't give me any confidence that we were at the right location.

"Yep, this is it." He pointed to a darkened single-story house. "That's the place."

We climbed out of the boat and sunk up to our ankles in the muck. We trudged through the marsh to a sucking sound with each step. We got to the front door, and Jesse turned the doorknob, and the door swung open. "See? Told ya."

"What do we do now?" I whispered.

"Why you whispering?" he said in his normal tone. "Nobody's here. We'll start tearin' apart this room and work our way through the house. You get the other side of the room. I'll start here."

I had taken five steps across the room when an overhead light went on, and I heard, "You son of a bitch." I saw the dull, metallic gray barrel of a shotgun extended from the hallway and pointed at Jesse, and then the sickening loud *click* of the gun being cocked. I lunged for the barrel, grabbed it, and heard a deafening explosion. Next thing I knew, I was lying face down, ears ringing, and my hands on the warm barrel of the shotgun. I felt the gun move, then turned and saw beefy hands and arms pulling it away from me. I knew if he got the gun, I'd be dead. We began a tug of war for my life. He was an old dude but outweighed me by more than a hundred pounds. His hands were on the stock, but his finger was not on the trigger. Yet. He pulled me to my feet as I held onto the barrel. I could feel my hands slipping. Letting go and pushing the shotgun aside, I clocked him in the face with a quick combination. I was off balance, and it wasn't my best shot. He was stunned but still had hold of the gun. I shifted my feet and threw another solid combo. This time the gun fell, but he was still standing. The old man was tough; I'll give him that. My hard left broke his nose, and I stepped into him with a right hand that shattered his orbital socket.

As he fell to the floor, I heard a screaming banshee and felt a pecking at my back. I turned to see an old lady flogging me with her fists. It felt like I was getting lashed with wet spaghetti noodles. I heard two quick pops and felt blood splash my face before the woman dropped.

Jesse was standing three feet away, a revolver in his right hand, his left arm bloody and spots on his chest from the shotgun's pellet spray. The old man groaned. Jesse walked over and emptied the gun into the guy with four shots.

"I thought we said no guns."

"Higgy never said nothin' 'bout the old man havin' a shotgun."

"I meant *us*! We weren't supposed to have guns. Didn't need them, you said. No one home, you said."

He nodded, still looking at the man he'd just put four bullets in and said, "Yeah, well, never can tell when you might need one."

"You think anybody heard anything?"

"Don't know, but turn out the lights. Use your Maglite to see if you can find something to stop this bleeding, then go find the money and let's get outta here."

I got Jesse into a windowless bathroom where I could turn on a light and see what I was doing. There was antiseptic to clean the wounds, and I tore up a bed sheet to wrap up his arm. The sheet around his bicep quickly turned crimson. I was worried about blood loss and him going into shock. "Are you ok?"

"Yeah. I can show you some scars that make this look like nothin'. Now quit bull shittin' and go find the money."

I proceeded to ransack the darkened house. While mindlessly ripping things apart, my thoughts went to Jesse's gun. Why did he bring it? He expected this to be an easy job. He thought no one would be home. The only possible reason was he planned to use it on *me*. He was going to keep all the money. I never thought he had it in him to be a killer. Wrong about that, obviously.

After cutting into cushions, mattress, prying up floorboards, and emptying every drawer, I went into the bathroom where I'd left Jesse. He was asleep, propped against the bathtub, his legs splayed apart. I thought about leaving him, but he'd likely turn rat and implicate me. Probably tell them I did the killing; after all, I was the murderer. I kicked his right foot. "Wake up."

"What?"

"Here's our take. One hundred and twenty-three dollars in cash that I found in a combination of mister's wallet and the missus's purse, and there's an undetermined amount of money in coins in a huge glass jar. Apparently, they saved their loose change."

"Did we hit the wrong house?"

"Don't think so, unless there's more than one Higginbottom on the island. I found his driver's license, but not hers. Maybe she didn't drive. Contrary to Higgy's impression, they believed in banking. Got their debit card, and here is their last bank statement showing $4,329.52, and they have a savings account with some $32,000 in it. So, we're in the right house."

"The half mil's gotta be hiding somewhere in this shithole."

"I looked everywhere. Kicked at loose boards, turned dressers and closets inside out. This is all we got."

"Shit."

"Yeah. And I think that's something your buddy, Higgy, is full off. Where's your gun?"

"My pocket. I'll toss it overboard when we get into open water."

"You have any bullets?"

"Left them in the car."

"Thought you'd only need one, huh?"

"What're you trying to say, Deuce?"

"Nothing. Let's get the hell out of here. I heard thunder."

I couldn't leave him behind. He'd say I was the killer, and the cops would believe him. My only choice was to help him into the boat. It did occur to me that I could push him into the water after we got out from the shore, but I'm not a murderer. He is. I'm not.

There was a light rain when we stepped out of the house. I helped Jesse get to the boat. The tide had gone out while we were inside, leaving the boat aground. I had to drag it into knee-deep water. Jesse got into the front of the boat, no longer in shape to steer us back to Crisfield. I started the motor with some priming and several yanks of the cord, then guided us through the marsh and into open water. The sky was crackling with lightning, rain began pelting us, and the wind was stirring up whitecaps. I had little knowledge of water and boats, but I knew enough that I had to steer into the oncoming waves or risk capsizing. Some time passed riding into waves before I became uncertain of our direction. Were we still going toward Crisfield, or toward Virginia, which I knew to be much, much farther? Or worse, could we be headed south to the Atlantic? It was black as ink, and the rain was so heavy I could barely see Jesse only three feet from me, the boat filling with rain and seawater, Jesse unable to bail.

Then the one thing sure to doom us happened. The motor stopped. I shook the gas tank. Nothing.

"Jesse! There another gas can somewhere?" I shouted over the waves, wind, and rain.

"You don't see one, do ya, 'cause there ain't one."

Drifting, we were pushed sideways and into a trough. A wave hit us broadside, and we went over.

When I surfaced, the bow was the last part of the boat I saw before the sea also swallowed it up. I called for Jesse, but there was no answer. With one arm he had no chance of surviving.

I started to swim, but had no idea of which direction to go in. I threw my arms forward, right, left, right, left, just like boxing, but now my opponent was the sea. Right, left, I'm not a murderer, right, left. The sea fought back by slapping my face with wave after wave and filling my mouth with saltwater when I tried to breathe. My training told me to keep going. Right, left, I'm not a murderer. Keep punching until the final bell.

Epilogue

Delmarva Peninsula Today Online

Body found on Tangier Island identified and linked to double murder

Maryland State Police has confirmed the body that washed ashore on Tangier Island last week has been identified as Jesse Moreland of Eden, Md. Personal effects were found on Moreland's body that initially linked him to the murders of John and Elizabeth Higginbottom, longtime residents of Smith Island. Police spokesperson Amanda Brown confirmed today that evidence found in the Higginbottom residence places Moreland at the scene of the crime.

Ms. Brown also stated the MSP are looking for William Charles, 28. Charles is a person of interest in the Higginbottom murders.

The MSP would not tell reporters why Charles is a person of interest, but a review of court records reveals that Charles was previously convicted of manslaughter and served his prison sentence at Eastern Correctional Institute during the same period that Moreland served a sentence for burglary.

OLD TIME DROUGHT

SOLUTIONS

Catherine Moore

bathe a cat in sulfur water
to make it rain
O sisters, O daughters
& gift him flea-less mane.
cross two matches, sprinkle salt
light a fiery chain

under smoky assault
"*aguamenti*" chant
above dry cistern vaults.

O conjuring rants,
refilling charms,
make rain in dance—
no harm
in burning yarrow
to free our farm

from a dry tomorrow.
there's time to atone

a pagan borrow:
boiled hog bone
& fennel soup
sieved onto stone,

circle the coop
with a hen's wet feather,
an hour's whistle loop.
if nothing is better
then there is eve, O
eve to mourn the weather.

HER STORY

Sandy Ward Bell

The crunch of gravel on Great Aunt Mary's long driveway reminds me how she refused to have it blacktopped. She believed most would become confused, thinking her place was an extension of Henders Street. Pulling up to the white farmhouse, I notice the shutters have been freshly painted blue and the hedges recently trimmed. When I was a kid, the large porch seemed like a giant bow wrapped around the home as if the walls and roof were a gift. Did I imagine at age ten that this day would arrive?

I whisper, "It's all mine now." The knot in my stomach grows. "And all the responsibility that goes along with it." The seven-hour drive from Nashville to Bluffport, Georgia, put a kink in my back. After closing the car door, I raise my arms, attempting to loosen muscles, as the sweet scent of peaches brings on a smile.

Months ago, a lawyer read the will of my ninety-nine-year-old Great Aunt Mary, and then he handed me the keys. Even though she once mentioned that I would inherit, I always assumed the two-story house with several acres of land and untamed woods would go to Mother. My life is with my husband in Tennessee, not here. Of course, this river town has its charms with fruit and vegetable stands at every corner, but they also believe Wi-Fi is a stereo system.

Maybe she picked me because of all the summers we shared in this house. Mary made me feel loved, safe, and wanted; she kept me sane. We bonded over books by Georgette Heyer and old TV shows like *Mission*

Impossible. I miss her. I miss those days, those moments when life was simple as we wiggled our toes in the tall grass while licking watermelon juice off our hands.

I haven't spent a summer here in almost twelve years, using "busy" as an excuse. Just a little lie because I couldn't tell Aunt Mary the truth, visiting her became a chore. Summers should be relaxing, giving me a chance to reenergize my passion for fifth graders. Reading romantic novels and swimming should be the only things on my to-do list. No. Instead, I'll be working, dusting, organizing, and trying to figure out what to do with this place. "I'm exhausted already." As I grab the box of cleaning supplies off the passenger seat, a crisp breeze flutters around me while a chill runs down my spine.

Ah, company. A new playmate. No. I know her. She's been here before when she was younger. Maybe she's come to look for the old mother because I haven't seen her poking about for a while now. I wish I could control where I float and wander. The universe is in charge and they don't tell me anything. I've been guessing for over fifty years. Dates are known to me because of the old mother's calendar hanging in the kitchen.

What should I do to this one? Nice long blonde hair. If I concentrate hard enough, she will feel me tying her locks. She'll think it's the wind. I want to laugh as I did when I walked alongside them all; the noise coming out of me sounds like ringing church bells instead of jubilation.

I'm too late. She's entering the house. With all my might, I picture myself next to the fireplace in the living room. My soul floats upward. Here I go.

Damn. I'm in the lonely woods next to the ancient barn, the center of it all, an anchor I've been bound to in this new life. And here it comes, the sensation that makes me feel like I'm under a cold burst of rain. Sometimes it lasts for seconds, other times days. I look around for an animal to fluster. Nothing. I'm ever so bored.

As I enter the farmhouse, I remember how Mother said she might join me, fly up from Florida, but that's just talk. The community in Orlando pampers her, and she knows I'll be too busy to shower her with cool drinks and compliments. I don't know why she hates this place. Bluffport is her hometown; she lived two streets over and spent most of her time in this house with her Aunt Mary. All I know is something happened when Mother was eighteen. She packed up everything she owned, headed to Nashville, and never looked back. When I came along, Mother dropped me off here in June and picked me up in August. She would stay for one meal, and then she was gone; maybe she was running away from me or Tetty.

Tetty is my great aunt's only child and she has been missing for six decades. Alive and lost or dead and hidden–no one knows. Mary had always said Tetty would come home someday. And if she does surprisingly reappear, I have to turn the estate over to her, which is fine with me. Yet, I doubt a seventy-eight-year-old woman would suddenly appear on the front stoop.

I shift the box from one hand to the other while staring at Tetty's shrine. Aunt Mary never moved it from this spot in the entrance hall. She wanted her daughter to see how much we all cared. The tiny wooden table is draped with an off-white doily. In the middle, rests a white pillar candle able to burn for three days straight. Mary believed that if she kept the flame alive, so would be her daughter, and if it went out, that meant she wasn't coming home. Often a battery-powered candle has saved the day. A real one is lit. Toby is keeping his promise to Mary. The waiting game continues. A framed photograph also sits on the table. I've examined that picture hundreds of times: high, blonde ponytail, red lipstick, blue eyes, tight cheerleader sweater, and her expression that reveals a glimmer of naughtiness. Aunt Mary called it her glow of goodness. The picture was taken in 1950, a year before nineteen-year-old Tetty went missing.

The box of cleaning supplies is heavy, so I step into the living room and set it down next to the fireplace. The scent of vanilla was a constant; it used to be infused into the rug and curtains. Now, with Mary gone, sadly, a dusty moldiness has taken over.

"Sage!" Toby walks through the dining room carrying a plate. He's the one who keeps the outside pristine. Ten years ago, Mary gave him the title of property manager because she felt a fifty-year-old shouldn't be called a lawn-man. "Perfect timing. These here are your auntie's lemon bars. Still a mountain of 'um in the basement freezer." He sets them on the living room coffee table.

"She wanted there to be some around for when I had grandkids."

"I'd say that's a possibility."

We laugh, sigh, and then stare at the treats, lost in thought. Breaking the spell, I say, "Toby," and spread my arms, looking for a hug.

We embrace. "Ah, baby girl. Good to see ya. Is Jake with ya?"

Stepping apart, yet still holding hands, I answer, "No, a last-minute big deal is brewing. He promised to come in July."

"That boy works too hard." His cheerful face is leathery-red because he believes sunblock is for babies.

"You're right . . . well. With no Wi-Fi, he can't work in this house. It's on our to-do list, right?"

"Number two, I believe." He points to the floral sofa that needs a good cleaning. "Sit a spell. Ya had a long drive." As he rests in the wooden rocker, it creaks. "I made iced tea." He springs up. "Where's my head? Be back directly." He dashes to the kitchen.

Unpacking the car should be my first chore, but I'd rather hang out with Toby. With a gooey snack in my hand, I plop onto the couch and cross my legs. I don't believe I can eat a lemon bar without thinking of Great Aunt Mary. "Grandma Mary" would have been more emotionally accurate, but Mother wouldn't allow such things–too disrespectful. I never met my real grandmother, Mary's sister; she died before I was born. Happily for me, Mary stepped in with sloppy kisses and advice, that is conduct befitting a gracious, good-mannered Southern lady like any good grammy.

Toby returns with two glasses of tea. I say, "This is my favorite room." My eyes go to the crocheted doilies on all the flat surfaces. "Aunt Mary is everywhere."

"This was her spot. I'd have-ta run the mower over one of her tomato plants to git her outside to yell at me."

"That's right. Remember when you had me pretend to get stuck in the big tree by the driveway?"

"Once we got her outside, gloominess disappeared, and she'd find this and that to do in the sunshine."

"Do you think she knew we were tricking her?"

"Just last year your auntie said, 'Toby, if ya going to break the clothes-line, could ya do it before lunch?'" He rubbed his stubbly beard. "She spent the entire mornin' in that chair by the garden, readin' an old book."

Toby is a gem. He is more than an employee. He is family. At sixteen, he started mowing the two acres of lawn and by the time he graduated high school, he was my great-aunt's handyman, chauffeur, and get-it-for-me fellow. After his divorce, she let him move into the fourth bedroom. He has been here ever since. Mary treated Toby like a grandson, a best friend, a confidant. The sixty-year age difference never seemed to matter. And I've come to think of him as an uncle.

"How's your mama doin'?" Toby grins.

"Fine. Still in Florida. She may come up next month, but I wouldn't hold your breath."

"It'd be nice to see her." He sits up straighter. "We danced once you know."

I nod.

"Senior year, it was. We swayed to "The Dock of the Bay." She was the prettiest girl in the gym. Made the football team jealous. Was fixin' to take her to the drive-in, but she left for Nashville soon after. Then I met Ashley. Well, you know how that got all tore up." He shrugs. "Ah, I reckon I told ya that one already."

"I love it when you talk about Mother as a teenager. It helps me attempt to understand her."

Mother was born in April of the same year Tetty went missing. An emptiness, a void, was filled. Aunt Mary's extra attention created a spoiled child who now lives with her latest boyfriend in a retirement community. Mother is a healthy fifty-nine-year-old, and my face heats up with anger every time I think about her lounging in a handicap pool. I slowly sip my tea hoping it'll soothe my frustration.

"Well, I best git goin'." Toby stands. "Ma's frying up chicken for supper. You're still invited. She'd love to see ya."

"Thanks, but no. I should settle in. And Toby, you don't need to move out while I'm here. It'll always be your home, forever."

"I know, but Ma gave me the dos and don'ts in this here situation. The cot on Ma's sleeping porch suits me just fine."

"I'm glad you agreed to stay on as the property manager."

"Sure thing. Wouldn't want to be anywhere else. Know every corner, every tree. Well, I've got mowin' to do tomorrow, and if you make up a list, I can git your groceries."

"Sounds like a plan."

"See ya in the mornin'. And Tetty's candle should last two more days."

"Got it. Give your mother my best."

"Will do. Call if you need me." He bends down and kisses the top of my head like he did when I was little. He goes through the dining room and kitchen, and I know he's gone when the heavy back door slams shut.

With that door closing, all my senses seem heightened. Being alone in Aunt Mary's house is unsettling. The ceiling fan hum sounds more like a moan, and there's a shadow in the dark dining room that resembles a wolf. An overwhelming feeling of anxiety makes my hands sweat. I wish Jake were here or even Mother. I lie still and picture my aunt with her intense blue eyes and thin, tall frame swaying in the rocking chair, comforting me with stories about Tetty. I can almost hear Aunt Mary's strong voice.

"Sage, did I ever tell you how much this here town loved my Tetty? How could they not? Her smile made you feel like nothing bad would ever happen. So positive. Don't believe she ever said a bad word about anyone." She'd pat my knee, making sure I paid attention and didn't pick at my cuticles. "Tetty was not pretty. No. She was beautiful! There was some jealousy." She shook her head. "Hm, hm, hm, my girl just killed them with kindness. She was homecoming queen, student body secretary, president of the Homemakers of America. And the boyfriends, well, she had the pick of the litter."

I asked in my teenager squeak, "Did you have a favorite?"

"Oh . . .Wendell was handsome, but he only had one oar in the water. Now, Perry, he was good looking and smart. Had a way of keeping all his lies straight like politicians do. He's a mayor or congressmen up yonder in Charlotte. They went steady for a spell, had his class ring, and she sometimes wore it around her neck on a chain."

Well, isn't this keen. I'm in the living room. It's been a long time. The universe is saying I belong here. I'm tired of seeking answers, asking why. Let's have some fun. First things first, the candle must be extinguished. My reach is halted. Damn, the hallway is off limits again. The blonde on the couch is sleeping. She must be wakened. I push the cardboard box of bottles to the hallway, and with all my might, I shove them toward the little table. Even with all my concentration and force the box only taps the table; nothing falls.

Here I go. Floating. I predict my destination is the crappy barn. Of course. Damn. And here it comes, the wet, cold sensation that makes me feel like I'm under a shower.

A loud clunk sound wakes me. I'm staring at the ceiling fan with a chill in my bones. Sitting up, I rub my face. The house is quiet. How long was I out? It's still nighttime. My phone says 7:07, so a few hours. Something is not where it's supposed to be. My cleaning supply box? It's not by the fireplace. I stand at the threshold of the hallway, scratching my head. "Maybe Toby set it there or someone is telling me to clean up this Tetty mess." I laugh it off and shake my head. "Time to unload the car before it gets dark."

≈≈≈

I roll over onto my left side in Great Aunt Mary's queen-size bed as the sun filters through the sheer curtains. She often said that early morning light was nature's alarm clock. Last night's strangeness lingers in my brain like the crusties do in sleepy eyes. When I was in the bathroom, getting ready for bed, weird unreliable shadows popped into the mirror, reminding me that I was alone with no place to hide but my car. Lying in bed was even worse with the creaky footsteps on the stairs. My head buried under the covers was the only solution. Exhaustion became my lullaby.

Often I felt as if Mary's daughter was still lingering, attempting to stop her mother from waiting. Maybe that is why I didn't use the guest bedroom upstairs. I've been telling myself I want to stay on the first floor, closer to Mary.

Fluffing a pillow behind my head, I sit up and realize the room looks fresh even though the night before it seemed stale. Nothing has changed since I was a kid. It's as if Tetty's disappearance froze Mary in the fifties. The vanity table with its cotton fabric base and glass top is my favorite. As a kid, I'd sit on the floor and pretend to pick the roses off the cloth while

Mary removed her pin curls and brushed out her hair. And I would ask questions about the man in the photograph who had his foot resting on the bumper of a Ford Deuce. Great Uncle Bob died in a sawmill accident when Tetty was five, and with the settlement money, Mary bought this house and land debt-free.

On the nightstand to my left sits the infamous blue binder. It holds everything about Tetty's disappearance. The book is about four inches thick with yellowed clippings, trying to escape. Mary carried it from room to room, never letting it leave the house. I drop it onto my lap. "When did I last read this?"

On the first page is Mary's handwriting with its beautiful wide loops and delicate curves. My finger traces a few words before reading her story, again.

My one and only priority is finding my daughter, Tetty. She will not be forgotten. If you know me, you will also know her. Every conversation with grocery clerks or church friends or neighbors will include a tale about Tetty. I will be vigilant.

March 20, 1951.

This is what I know. Friday, March 9th, 1951 started out as a delightful day. It had rained for two days straight, so it was a blessing to see the sunshine. Tetty and I have a well-oiled routine for our breakfast meal. I make the coffee, toast, and soft-boiled eggs while she squeezes the oranges for juice, and then, I wash the dishes while she prepares for her lunch shift at the Feed Me Diner. She waitresses five days a week and takes painting and typing classes in the afternoons. She's resolved to be independent like me. I hate to see her work so hard, yet her determination puts a spring in her step. The lightly starched, pastel blue uniform with the white apron looks smart on my Tetty. Blue is her color.

Her day is unknown to me because we didn't eat dinner together, even though I made baked potatoes and ham hock green beans. She said she wasn't hungry and needed time to dress for the Spring Fling dance. It's an annual event for all ages and held in the high school gym. Two boys asked her to accompany them, but she declined, wanting to be free to dance with whomever she pleased. She had broken up with Perry weeks ago, and this was going to be a night out with just her friends. Tetty wore her new navy-blue rayon dress that had a fitted bodice, three-quarter-length sleeves, and off-the-shoulder neckline. She looked stunning as usual. I insisted she wear a proper hat and gloves. She called me a goof, unhip. She won the argument, leaving with naked fingers and no headpiece. Her best friend, Betsy, picked her up in the Fleetmaster "Woodie" Wagon and off they went. I waved goodbye from the porch, not knowing that was the last time I would ever see my precious girl.

A knock on the bedroom door startles me. Toby shouts, "Should I put the coffee on?"

"Yes. Thanks." I return the binder to the nightstand. I'll leave it for another day.

≈≈≈

Where has the week gone? I feel like a slacker, only one checkmark on the to-do list. We now have Wi-Fi. The easiest job was supposed to be the guest bedroom; I attempted to start there first. Instead of cleaning, I've been reading Aunt Mary's old cozy mysteries. Yesterday, Toby caught me sleeping in the recliner by the upstairs front window with a Lilian Jackson Braun novel on my chest. The look on his face told me he knew I hadn't showered for two days. This house, the responsibility, it weighs heavy on me. Maybe I'm depressed. Toby is the best, but I feel alone. I need someone next to me, holding my hand, and telling me I am doing everything perfectly.

I miss Jake. We text throughout the day and speak at night. My two best friends would be up for the task of diving into this mess, but they are busy with babies and ill parents, and I refuse to add my burden to their pile.

A hot afternoon sun spills onto the pages of Anne Perry's *The Cater Street Hangman*. I close the book and push down the footrest. Stretching my arm over my head reveals an odor, reminding me that showering is a must today. At least I'm not sweaty-smelly. Thank you, Aunt Mary, for installing air conditioning throughout the house. It was the one modern improvement she ever made. "First things first. Sweet tea and lemon bars. Yes, more than one. Aunt Mary would insist."

At the bottom of the stairs, I check Tetty's candle. Toby and I decided to only use the battery ones from now on and this one should last until July. As I pass through the living room, I hear the door slam. "Toby, you back already?" I step into the kitchen and my stomach turns into a giant knot.

"Surprise!"

"Mom! Wow. Um."

Her arms are wide and inviting, "Bring it in."

We hug. As she squeezes, I melt like burnt marshmallow and chocolate on a graham cracker. I guess Mother is my cure. Tears pour out of me, working me into hiccups.

"Sweetheart, I had no idea you were so overwrought." She rubs my shoulder while handing me a tissue, which is uncharacteristic behavior. She continues, "See, you get it now. This place is a morgue. All that waiting for nothing. And that damn chill. That one that sneaks up on ya, and seeps into your bones." She looks around with wide eyes. "It hasn't hit me yet. I just have to wait a moment. It always comes."

"Mom, I'm glad you're here." Breathing normally again, I step away, and pat my cheeks dry. "You're here to help?"

"No. No heavy lifting for this old gal." She sighs. "Truth is George got mad. Said I flirted with his friends. Kicked me out. He'll be begging for me to return soon enough. Give him a few days. You'll see. I'm always right. Now, let me look at you." She holds my shoulders at arms length. "Well rested. Good. Need to lose a few pounds. Too many of those lemon bars." She taps my nose.

"Mom. Stop!"

"Right." She licks her lips in that nervous way when she wants to apologize but won't. "What a trip. I just need the two bags from the front seat, and I sure could use a cup of coffee."

I step toward the back door and halt. My recent laziness has given me an unusual iron will. "No. Um, I'm going to have tea and a lemon bar. You can join me if you wish."

"Sage, I will not be disrespected."

"No disrespect. I'm creating boundaries."

"What the hell does that mean?"

"I'm not your maid."

"This rebellious thing, again. I thought you grew out of that."

"Mom, a please and a thank you goes a long way."

"We'll just talk in circles, like always. Toby'll be nice and respectful. I'll wait for him." She turns toward the bathroom. "Save me a lemon bar. Don't eat'em all."

Anger takes over my body. I run outside to the chair by the garden. After kicking the legs a few times, I scream at the hunk of wood. It saddens me, knowing I want that chair to be Mother. "I'm a teacher for God's sake. Keep it together." Returning to the kitchen, I find Mother making coffee. I smile.

"You'll have to move your things upstairs to the guest room." She plugs in the percolator.

Closing my eyes, my smile fades. "No. Um, no thank you. I'll stay in Aunt Mary's room which is mine now because I own this house."

She laughs. "No, according to Aunt Mary's declaration of war, this is Tetty's house. You're just the caretaker until she shows up."

"No. This is my house."

"Whatever helps you sleep at night." She leans against the kitchen counter and slides a strand of hair behind her ear. Aging hasn't touched her beauty. Even at fifty-nine, her smooth, bright face and trim body could be found on any magazine cover. She continues, "I need to be close to the bathroom. My knees can't take going up and down those stairs."

"Bullshit. You run twenty miles a week. Your knees are fine. You want the bigger bed and the bigger room."

"So . . . I deserve it."

"Just because you're older than me?"

"Here we go again. Circles." She collapses into a chair by the table. "Let's not fight. How's Jake? When's he coming down?"

I don't know why she causes me such angst. When she's around, I change into a teenager fighting for my right to exist. We work best when I let her be a narcissist, receiving everything she demands. If I give in, she won't jab me with passive-aggressive comments. Besides, she won't last long here anyway. I'm taking the gloves off. I sit next to her, apologize, and we talk about nothing important. And I make a point of not retrieving her bags from the car.

I wake in the guest room, determined to knock out my to-do list with or without Mother's assistance. Dressed in my bathrobe, I pass Tetty's shrine and overhear Mother and Toby talking in the kitchen. She sure had him blushing last night. Passing through the dining room, I notice the blue binder on the oak table. In the kitchen, I say, "Morning."

"Mornin', Sage. Toby is delightful. He's telling me about your lost sneaker in the back pond."

I pour myself coffee. "That shoe was supposed to be a boat. I'm sure I told you that one before."

"Maybe, but Toby has a talent for storytelling." She caresses his hand.

"Too kind, Christy. Too kind." The affection he has for Mother is written on his broad smile.

"How old was I?" I join them at the table.

"That was eighty-eight when Mary decided to stop refillin' it."

"Nine, then."

"Built that pond in the late sixties. My fault. Bad location. Became a swamp."

"That pond was eerie, scary. My shoe was like a sacrificial offering." My stomach growls as I reach for a muffin.

Mom nods, "One is plenty."

I grab a second muffin from the tin and set it in front of me. With a you're-not-the-boss-of-me smirk, I say, "And that pond smelled like dead things. It's been years since I was back there."

"Nothin' to see. It's part of the untamed portion now." Toby takes a swig of coffee.

"Playing in those woods was magical. The best. I was Snow White, and there was that barn with three walls. That's where the dwarfs lived." The muffin is beyond delicious. "Oooh, your ma made these, didn't she, Toby?"

"This is when peaches go in everythin'."

"Thank her. These're awesome." I take another bite. Toby refills our mugs while I ask, "Why is Mary's binder in the dining room?"

Mother stirs sugar into her coffee. "I can't sleep in the same room with that thing. Just burn it."

"Mom, don't say such things. It's the key to finding Tetty."

"Finding her? Don't be silly. She'll never be found. It's best to move forward and live with the living. Waiting's for idiots."

"That, that collection of questions and answers meant so much to Great Aunt Mary."

Toby has never liked to see womenfolk arguing. A wrinkle forms on his forehead as he stands. "I'm fixin' to head to the grocery." He places an Atlanta Braves ball cap on his head.

"But, Toby, you were there yesterday."

Mother adds, "He's picking up some things for me."

"Like what?"

"What do you care? It's none of your business."

"It is when I pay the bill." I can feel my face reddening. Mother and Mary argued about money often, so it's my turn now?

We talk over each other and only stop when we hear the back door slam.

She says, "Look what you did! You frightened Toby away."

I shake my head and devour the second muffin.

"Tetty's dead and gone. Just leave it."

"How do you know? Maybe she's lost and needs our help."

"You're as delusional as Aunt Mary."

"I like being like her."

"Then you'll also die alone."

"She didn't die alone. She had us. Me and Toby and–"

"Two people, that's it. That's alone and all that money not being spent."

"Money will make you lonely."

She laughs, "Nice try. Money can buy you friends and happiness. Don't let anyone tell ya any different." She finishes her coffee. "Aunt Mary lost all her family and friends because of her obsession. I gave her you, for the summers, hoping your youth and spirit would bring her back to reality. Didn't work."

Mother's wrong, and Mary's right, and I'm going to prove it. Instead of cleaning, I'll play detective. I never looked at this tragedy with adult eyes before. Who knows? Maybe I can make something good happen. Or maybe I've been reading too many mysteries.

Mom says, "I'm going for a run."

"Well, I'm going to solve Tetty's disappearance."

She steps toward her bedroom. "Whatever. Aunt Mary brainwashed you. I should've never exposed your delicate mind to her kind of crazy. Good luck. You'll need it." She attempts to make a point by closing the broken door hard, but it barely shuts. She mutters, "For Christ's sake."

I spend the rest of the day in my bathrobe sitting at the dining room table attempting to read every single fragile page in the blue binder. And I have about a third yet to get through. There are articles of Tetty's disappearance as recently as ten years ago. She has copies of police reports and witness statements. Lord knows how she got them. An entire section is dedicated to Mary's own personal interviews with Tetty's friends and people who were at the dance. As I'm reading the statement Betsy gave to the police, a hand lands on my shoulder. I shout.

Toby whispers, "Sorry to disturb." He places a chicken salad sandwich on the table next to my arm. "Ma's leftovers."

"Thanks." I rub my neck and glance at my phone. "Wow, I've been at it for almost six hours." Thirsty, I head to the kitchen. "Will you join me? Want some tea, water?"

"Reckon I could sit a spell."

I return to the table with drinks, two forks, and a pan of peach cobbler. "We should be finishing up those lemon bars, but who can resist your ma's cooking?" Feeling a bit embarrassed and not meeting Toby's eyes, I ask, "Did my mom say goodbye to you?"

"Sure did. Don't git why she needs to go to Augusta all-a-sudden."

"She has friends there who will give her the coddling she requires." Feeling defeated, I add, "It's my fault. When we fight, she runs away."

As we eat, the lack of conversation makes me anxious so I say, "Before she left, she patted me on the head and told me I was wasting everyone's time. I sure know how to make mother disappear."

"The two of ya love each other so much ya can't be in the same room."

Chuckling, I ask, "What does that mean?"

"Your love–hate line is dashes instead of solid."

My head rests on his shoulder. "Wish it was that simple."

We talk about Aunt Mary and finish up the cobbler. He sets down his fork and grins, "Best be gettin' to Ma's. She's fixin' biscuits and sawmill gravy for supper."

"Right, that was just your appetizer." Laughing, I add, "Thanks for everything, Toby." I straighten my robe. "Before you go, what can you tell me about Betsy Miller, Tetty's friend?"

"Mary got mad at her 'bout, what was it . . . maybe twenty years ago cuz Betsy said she'd had enough."

"Is she still in town?"

"Lives with her son . . . off Main."

"She's seventy-eight now like Tetty would be, right?"

"I reckon."

"Do you think she'd talk with me?"

"Don't know. Her address and such are in the back." He points to the book. "Mary worked hard on gettin' current numbers on anyone related to it all. She had to know where they were just in case she had a question."

I lift the last tab in the binder. "Wow. Updated a year ago. Toby, your mother's in here."

"Sure, she served refreshments at the dance. I was in her tummy so you could say I was there too."

"Right. That makes sense now. Mary said something about how you could have heard Tetty's voice. Crazy!" What did I get myself into? After clearing my throat, I add, "I haven't read your mother's interview yet."

"She fills up a few of those papers."

I run my thumb over the last pages. "God, there's a ton to go through."

"You'll be busy for a while yet. See ya in the mornin'."

As Toby's truck engine rumble fads, a chill runs down my spine. I shiver. "A shower will clear my head." I close Mary's binder.

The dining room? Okay, this is new. Usually, I'm in the kitchen. The blonde girl ran away before we could play. Ah, the Tetty book. The old woman cradled this blue thing like a child. What does the universe want me to see? I wave my hand as the pages turn. It stops on a picture of me. Yes, I was lovely. Way more attractive than Tetty. Perry knew I was keen, a true beauty, but she had a hold on him. The bitch. Damn! I made them mad.

Here I go. Returning to the ancient barn, and the cold water-dripping sensation.

The shower isn't as refreshing as I hoped. And my phone call with Jake is cut short because he agrees with Mother, meaning I should just clean the house and forget about Tetty. I said some mean things before hanging up. He's wrong. I can find Tetty and I will show them both how right I am. Where was my mindfulness to look for her sooner? This is stupid; I'm arguing with myself.

Too tired to read, I lie on Aunt Mary's bed and notice a transistor radio sitting on a high dresser. Melodies will sooth me. After turning it on, big band music fills the room. The dials move up and down, yet nothing happens; it's stuck on one station.

I'm stuck. My courage and ambition only exist when people are around, but as soon as they leave, procrastination takes over. A trumpet's solo pulses my ears. Lying down, I close my eyes as a dream takes flight.

For some reason, Toby let me sleep-in; no knock on the door. The lawn mower is humming out back as the aroma of fresh coffee lures me into the kitchen. Ah, another tin from Toby's mom. This morning, it's peach cookies. Seems like a good breakfast to me.

In the dining room, I sit before the blue book while wiping a cookie crumb off my cheek. That's odd. I don't remember seeing this page before. Maybe Toby had a look at it this morning. There, in front of me, are two five-by-seven photographs; one is a group of people posing for the picture and the other is an action shot of them dancing. They aren't the best quality, a little fuzzy. What should I expect; it's from 1951? Who are they? I turn the page and read Aunt Mary's handwriting. A few of the names look familiar. On my legal pad, I jot them all down and then look for them in the final section of the book to see if they are still living around here. Were they the last to see Tetty?

Perry died a few years ago. And Wendell, well, he's down the street. And here's Betsy. Looks as if Sue, Roselyn, Marcy, and Ken passed away. Hmm, four more moved out of town and no idea where they went. Should I start here, with these pictures?

The doorbell rings. "Shit. I'm still in my pajamas. What time is it?" My cell says 10:10. The visitor is knocking loudly. "Crap." I grab one of Mary's old sweaters, throw it on, and hurry to the front door. The scent of her lilac perfume is still nestled into the cardigan. Everything will be fine. My blood pressure seems to return to normal. When I see an old woman on the front porch, it spikes up again. No. It can't be Tetty. Can it? I open the door.

"Hello. You're Sage. We met briefly at Mary's funeral."

"Um."

"I'm Betsy. A friend of Tetty and Mary."

"Right. Sorry. Come in."

"I should've called first, but didn't want to give myself a chance to back out of talking with ya."

I'm surprised at the spry skip in her step.

She continues, "Got my nine holes in before it hits ninety and then thought it best to just haul my ass over here." She picks up the shrine photo of Tetty. "Don't know why you're keeping up this charade. Mary can't hurt you now. Great one of Tetty though. Such a beauty." She returns it to the table and walks into the living room.

"Please sit . . . I'll return with refreshments."

"Water would be fine. That caffeine will kill ya."

In the kitchen, as I pour water into tumblers and set some peach cookies on a plate, my mind swirls with questions. This is all too weird. How did she know I wanted to talk with her? Do wishes come true in this house? I wish Jake was here. Looking at the back door, I whisper, "No such luck."

In the living room, I set the food and drink on the coffee table. "How did you know I was here?"

"Toby called me last night. Well, it was more of his ma's doin'." She takes a big gulp of water. "Thanks. Anyway, he said you're trying to find Tetty or at least attempting to put this ridiculous case to bed. And, well, I tried to tell Mary a thing or two twenty years ago. Needed to free myself. Long story short, she thought I was a liar, and she kicked me out."

"You know where Tetty is?"

"God, no. I was a sheep, followed the pack. A coward. It eats me up every day." As she wrings her hands, I notice how they seem more old, bent, and wrinkled than her personality.

"You're upset. Um. I don't want to cause any–"

"No. It's not you. Here's the deal. I lied."

"I see."

"It just snowballed. We were young and you know what I mean."

"Sure. But–"

"Here's what I came to say. Tetty did not leave the dance by herself to walk home like we all said. What really happened, well, she was with us when we all piled into my folks' Woodie and drove to Cliffton to get more booze. I tried to explain this to Mary, but she wouldn't hear it. Her girl didn't drink or smoke or have sex." She shakes her head.

"Well. Okay." It is time to play detective. "Um, who was in your car?"

"Me of course, then Tetty, Perry, Wendell, the Lander brothers." She counts the rest out on her other hand. "Let's see . . . Roselyn, Sue and Marcy. We doubled up. Lots of girls on boys' laps."

"What happened?"

"It was a normal night out. We'd drink, smoke, snog, watch the submarine races, that sort of thing."

"Submarine races?"

"Obviously there weren't any, an excuse to make out, kiss. It was a thing."

"Did you stay in Cliffton? Is that where Tetty went missing?"

"We ended up at the barn. You know, the one at the corner of your land and the Landers' farm."

"The one with three walls?"

"It had four then." She removes her glasses and rubs her eyes. "By telling the truth, I was hoping for some relief . . . let me get the entire story out." She attempts to stop her tears. "All right. The barn was hidden, our secret place. And we loved it even though it was falling down and smelled rancid. We claimed it as our own until Tetty disappeared."

Betsy went on to explain how they were there for a few hours drinking and smoking. Then they paired off. The Lander brothers escorted Sue and

Marcy to their family garage. They bragged about having the biggest back seats. Wendell and Betsy went to her car parked in the lane near the Landers' garage. Roselyn walked home while Perry and Tetty stayed at the barn.

She added, "I was sure they got back together. Perry put his class ring onto Tetty's pointer finger. Without fail, they were extra friendly at parties, but in the daytime, they fought like Joe Louis and Sugar Ray Robinson.

"Anyway, the next morning Perry was at my door. He told me how Mary's looking for Tetty. And he insisted that when he left Tetty last night, she was fine. And what he said rang true. She always wanted another smoke before going in for the night. Then Perry went on and on about some internship in Washington DC, and how he couldn't mess it up with folks making the wrong assumptions. Once again, what he said made sense. The way this town gossips, we all knew Perry'd be in jail because he was the last to see her, even without a bit of evidence saying he did anything."

"You all lied to help Perry."

"Not really. At first I said no way. I knew lying would get us in more trouble, and if my friend were missing, being truthful would help find her. But, Perry had a hold on me. Hell, he had a hold on everyone. He collected secret information like someone would collect coins."

"Blackmailer?"

"Exactly . . . I had an abortion." Her voice is very matter-of-fact. "I know it's not a big deal today, but it was then. Illegal. If I didn't say she walked home alone, he would tell the world about what I did and he had proof."

"So sorry."

"Bottom line. The abortion, well, I did the right thing. It had to be done. I would have drowned being tied to Wendell."

"Do you think Perry hurt Tetty?"

"That's the funny thing about it. No. He wasn't a violent person, just sneaky. He cared about himself more than anyone else in this universe, but he loved her. He couldn't harm Tetty."

"I still don't understand why he wanted you all to lie."

"The internship meant more to him than Tetty. He, like the rest of us, assumed she ran off to have a life without Mary. He kept saying that there was no harm in letting Tetty escape in peace."

"Mary wouldn't allow peace?"

"She was a pushy broad, and the cops didn't do a thing to look for her daughter." Betsy's talking faster like she's racing to a finish line. "About twenty years ago, I couldn't take it any more. Mary was still searching. Insane! It had to stop. I tracked Perry down in North Carolina. We had a cordial talk. It was kind of nice catchin' up and remembering old times. He said he and Tetty were in a good place. Had relations, laughed, and she was excited about visiting him in DC. They didn't fight at all that night. He didn't walk Tetty home because she wanted to do one of her 'big thinks,' the kind she did alone with a pack of cigarettes. He got a Lander brother to take him home." She leans back on the couch, puffs out her cheeks, and exhales loudly. "He still loved her even after all these years. Tetty had a way of pulling you in close, in return you admired her, honored her." She rubs a tear away.

"Can I get you more water?"

She shakes her head. "I've got to get this all out . . . With Tetty's car gone, I was certain she went to Mississippi. I even checked the barn. No sign of a struggle. I cleaned up, took away our bottles and cigarette butts. She finally did it! She ran away from Mary's strong grip. Tetty was really drunk that night, enough so to have that kind of courage."

"Why Mississippi?"

"Tetty'd been talking about this Art Colony near Jackson. Mary would've flipped her lid. I kept my mouth shut. At first I thought I was protecting my dear friend. I knew I'd hear from her. After a year went by, I contacted that Art Colony. She wasn't there. Too late to change what I said. Easier to lie. Life just went on. And went on without my best friend." She rubs her forehead and stands. "And damn it! Mary wouldn't listen. I tried to tell her." Betsy steps to the fireplace and removes a framed picture of five-year-old Tetty holding her father's hand.

"What do you think happened to her?"

"I believe something evil snatched her up on the way to Mississippi."

With a sigh, she returns the photograph to the mantle, and whispers, "I would of gone with her if she asked."

Betsy and I fall into a rhythm. My questions are answered with a faint smile. About twenty minutes pass, and she finally stops wringing her hands. The release of her secret burden has lightened her eyes. Yet, sadness lingers because her friend is still missing.

We hug on the front porch. I add, "I'll keep you updated."

She holds my face with her palms. "You have Tetty's look. There, in your eyes. Tell me again. You believe me?"

"Yes, Betsy, I believe you. Don't worry about it anymore. You're free."

She closes her eyes. "Thank you. Thank you." She pushes up her glasses. "Bye for now." And off she scoots to her car.

As I wave, an ominous black cloud hovers in the sky. I want to get to the ancient barn before it rains. Racing upstairs to change my clothes, I hear thunder above and lightning flashes outside the window. "Damn." I sit on the top step and wrap Mary's sweater closer to my heart. What do I do next?

So, dear, sweet Tetty likes to party . . . like Mother. And Great Aunt Mary raised them both. Interesting. I feel weird, out of sync. I never saw Mary as the enemy or Tetty as a rule breaker. Am I wrong about everybody? Rubbing my head I convince myself not to go down that rabbit hole.

What's next? Tetty's old bedroom seems like the logical next step. On my summer visits through the years, Mary had me search her daughter's space. Mary felt by using my teenage instincts, we'd find a secret that only a kid would know. What was I searching for? Maybe Mary's approval.

Toby yells from the kitchen, "Sage, you there?"

"On the stairs."

Out of breath, he stands by Tetty's shrine. "Got to git to Ma's. She havin' window troubles and with the storm and all–"

"Go. See you tomorrow."

"Good talk with Betsy?"

"Yes. And thank you for pushing her my way. I'll fill you in later. Go to your ma."

He nods and his warm smile makes me grin.

I wait to hear his truck rumble away before stepping into Tetty's room. The door's rusty hinges greet me with a creak. The familiar odor of dust and staleness slaps me in the face. Mary never let the maids touch this room. She always took care of it herself. My best guess is that she hadn't been in here for a couple of years. My sneeze echoes throughout the house. I'll have to clean before I dig for clues. An enormous task. Not now. No energy. Storms make me sleepy. I close the door.

Lying on Mary's bed, I listen to the rain tapping on the windows and the thunder yelling while imagining Tetty in Mississippi creating paintings and sipping wine.

"Hey."

Screaming, I jump out of bed. With a hand over my thumping heart, I catch my breath. "What the hell, Mom. You scared me to death."

"Don't say that. Bad luck." She does the sign of the cross and makes a spitting sound.

Shaking my head, I ask, "What happened? Why aren't you in Augusta?"

"Don't want to talk about it." She drops her purse on the floor and crawls into Mary's bed next to me.

"What's going on? Are you okay?"

"No."

She wants me to pry it out of her. I don't have the energy to ignore her. I say softly, "Did George make the breakup official?"

"How'd you know?"

"You always get this way even when you're the dumper."

"I was halfway to Augusta when he called. He wanted to know where to send my things and to let me know the storage unit bill is due next week. If I don't pay, I will lose everything I own."

"Do you have the money?"

"Yes, of course I do. I pretend to be poor so I don't have to use my own money. I've told you that a million times." She rolls over and stares at the ceiling. "Promise me you still have a separate account from Jake?"

"Yes, but he knows all about it." Copying my mother, I turn over and look at the popcorn ceiling. "You've been gone some twenty-four hours . . . what did you do?"

"Nothing. No revenge. No, this one hit me hard. I had to pull over. I couldn't stop crying. Then found a hotel with a bar . . . well."

"What's his name?"

"I don't know. That's why I snuck out of his bed and came back here. I'm tired."

"You really liked George."

"A nice man. Sweet and kind and funny. And I messed it up."

This is always the point where I have no idea what to say to Mother. I really want to make her feel better. Shifting gears, I tell her about Betsy's visit. She acts interested, asking questions and adding her opinions.

"I knew she wasn't a saint." She sits up in bed full of spirit as if she just drank an espresso. "Let's go to the barn."

"We can't. The storm."

"It's almost over." She pops out of bed. "Come on. It's the last place she was seen, not the dance like we all thought."

"What got into you? You hate everything to do with Tetty."

"This is new information. Aunt Mary had been rehashing the same old lies for sixty years."

"And that's my point. For sixty years, any clues or whatever had been washed away. One more day won't matter."

"Think about it. Where's the one place Mary wouldn't snoop. Tetty knew not to leave anything in her room or her car, and now we know the barn was her safe place."

"But Betsy said she was there the following day cleaning up. No sign of Tetty."

"Shit. That's right." She sits on the bed deflated.

Being next to mother, my ever-present heavy feeling of dread lightens a bit and floats. The weight, the depression is still there, but not as bulky. I'm not alone. She's here to help, to connect. "Did you hang out in the barn as a kid?"

"I knew it existed. Never been a nature girl."

An image flashes in my mind. "Tetty's painting in the guest room." I sprint away and soon return with the framed picture. Catching my breath, I show it to Mother.

"What am I looking at?"

"The barn. It's the barn."

"How do you know?"

"When I played in there, it had three walls, but it's the same one. I'm sure of it."

Mom chuckles, "And Tetty gives Mary a painting of her secret place. I'm liking Tetty more and more."

We take off the frame and remove the cardboard backing, hoping to find a clue. I flop onto the bed. "I guess that only happens in the movies."

She holds up Tetty's artwork. The composition is beautiful, like a Renoir. The sun is gingerly sweeping over the walls and peeking through the open door and onto a dusty floor. I lean in closer to the painting. "What's that inside?"

"Where?"

I hold it upright while she grabs reading glasses from her purse.

"There, by the wall."

Mom breathes onto the paint. "Looks like a handle on the floor." She slips the cheaters onto the top of her head. "Everyone would see the handle and lift it up, so not a secret place."

"But maybe it's a decoy."

"What?"

"Never mind. Stupid idea."

She gives me a little squeeze. "Let's check out the decoy."

As we are layering ourselves with Mary's rain gear, we laugh at each other's white plastic head coverings.

"Jake would say we're nuts."

"Nothing wrong with a bit of crazy in your life." She grabs two flashlights from a kitchen drawer. "Even though it's four o'clock, it looks like midnight out there."

We tap our flashlights together as if they are celebratory drinks and then head outside. We forgo umbrellas because of the chance of lightning. The rain has slowed to a drizzly mist. Before treading through the untamed woods, we take a hammer and a trowel from Toby's shed and place them in my backpack.

"The old path started around here somewhere." I light the ground near the overgrown boarder. "Mary had Toby stop mowing a path to the pond and barn when my summer visits ended. Wait. We need breadcrumbs."

"Breadcrumbs?"

I return with three wooden spoons and three giant balls of yarn.

"What ya going to do, knit a lawn mower?"

Laughing, I say, "Great idea, but no. Did this with my students. It helps them understand distances and measurements." I tie the end of one yarn ball around a spoon and stick it into the ground, and as we walk forward, I leave a trail of red and blue.

"I bet you're a great teacher."

I halt. She has never said anything nice about my job before. "Um, thanks."

"If I was your student, I'd be in the corner all day. Always in trouble." She grabs the yarn. "I'll do this. You've got the backpack."

As we walk, I add, "Growing up as your daughter helped me to be patient during chaos which is a necessity for teachers."

"Glad I could help. So . . . without me, who knows where you would've ended up."

Shaking my head, I don't feel the usual hot anger; instead, I'm just pleasantly annoyed. Her selfishness seems more of a joke now. Maybe that had always been her intent.

Trudging through the weeds and bramble surrounded by the smell of wet dog, I think of Tetty walking this path. Was she happy or frightened? A chill causes me to shiver. I don't believe she made it to Mississippi. A warm sensation fills my chest as if to say my belief is true. As I attempt to sort my bizarre feelings, ten minutes pass, and then the mist turns into a downpour. Quickening our pace, I stumble and fall flat on my face.

"Good God, you okay?" Mother helps me to my feet.

"Fine." Wiping my eyes, I add, "My underwear was the only thing dry. Not anymore."

We laugh as we march forward.

Ahead, peaking through the space between some thin, dark trees, sits a gray mass. "That's it."

We scurry into a hurdling run like Dorothy finding Oz. We duck inside the building. It's much smaller than I remembered. The roof is solid, considering its condition. The rain is still soaking us sideways because one long wall is in a crumpled heap on the ground. We huddle in the corner, catching our breath.

"Shit. I dropped the ball of yarn when we ran."

"That's okay. We'll find it."

"Well, nothing here except that tree trunk and it's covering the trap door handle."

"The tree was here when I was a kid. All the dwarfs slept on it."

"Cute, but, well, our tools can't move it."

Thunk. Tap. Thunk.

"Hear that?"

"Yes. I think it's under our feet."

A chill makes us shudder.

Ah, visitors. How nice. It's the blonde all grown up and ready to play with her imaginary friends. And the other one, older, yes, but she was never here before. Who is she? I remember now. It hardly took any effort to frighten her at the house. So long ago. Funny how they're as wet as I feel. What should I do to them?

We shine our flashlights around our feet.

Tap. Thunk. Tap.

I squat. The floor planks have eroded, creating big gaps exposing the space underneath. My light shows a swell of water under the barn. "God, it's a pit full of water and mud. It's maxed out, overflowing. And as the water swells, it's pushing something against the barn floor."

No! No one is allowed down there. I attempt to push them. My hand passes through their bodies. Damn it! I must concentrate. With all my might, I heave myself into them. My touch is gone. I've passed through the crappy barn and I'm floating outside.

"Did you feel that chill? Went right to my bones."

I nod.

Mom stands and with hands on hips, looks at the tree trunk at the other end of the building. "With a cellar under the entire barn . . . I suppose this could be the hiding place. Maybe Tetty's suitcase is making all that noise."

"Oh, God." My butt lands on the floor with my back against the wall. "No. It's a skull. I saw the jaw."

Thunder bellows above.

Damn it! You found her, the bitch who stole my man. I loved Perry more than she did. She used him. Would you like to know how I killed Tetty?

"Mom, what if that's Tetty?"

"It could be an animal."

No, it's Tetty. She only wanted Perry when someone else wanted him, and she knew how I felt. She didn't care about anybody but herself. I pretended to walk home, but I stayed to watch them have sex. She was a mess. I'm a much better lover. Perry even told me so, several times. After Perry left, I decided Tetty had to disappear. She was so drunk she didn't see me coming. She dropped her cigarette as I held her head under the water in the full rain barrel. She struggled, but not for long.

"What should we do, Mom?"

"We can remove these rotted boards to get to it easier. The hammer should work."

Tap. Thunk. Tap.

Everybody knew about the hidey-hole under the barn. Rumor was they stowed booze in there during prohibition. I'm very intelligent. I know how to hide a body. I pushed her all the way into the corner, and with mud, stone, and twigs, I covered her so well, Tetty looked like she was the back wall.

Mother is holding a human skull. She lovingly sets it on the floor. "The poor thing." She makes a sign of the cross over her chest.

"When did you get all religious?"

"I went to mass with George every Sunday."

"Is it Tetty?"

I had Tetty's purse. Her car had to disappear too. That night I drove it straight to Savannah to my cousin's place. He sold it for parts. Two days later, when my bus arrived in Bluffport, Perry asked me to lie about Tetty's whereabouts. My sides hurt from laughing so hard. Yet, even with Tetty out of the way, Perry never came back to me. Her death didn't change anything. Then he moved away. He never said goodbye. But I still loved him. It messed me up. Savannah became my new home. A year later, I drowned in my neighbor's pool. I was too drunk to save myself.

"Should we call the police?" I pull the plastic hat on top of my head as the rain pounds the barn floor.

"Did you bring your phone?"

"No."

"Me neither."

Lightning flashes. A shiny object catches my eye. It's just inside the opening we created when we removed the skull. Passing my flashlight over the area, it glitters again. Something is stuck in the muddy wall under mother's feet. "Mom, hold your light over there."

"Here?"

"See it?"

"No."

With my finger, I dig it out. As I'm wiping away the dirt, Mom hands me a tissue. Rubbing, I expose a man's class ring.

That damn ring. I forgot to take it off her finger. Miles from Savannah I remembered. There wasn't time to go back. This never would have happened if he gave his ring to me. Perry and Roselyn sounds perfect together, musical. A swirl of air pushes me upward. What the hell? This feels different. The wind pushes and tugs. I'm dangling over the old pond. A driving force pounds me into the earth. Blackness. Nothingness.

As I palm the ring, I'm overcome with emotions. Tetty was here with me when I played alone in this barn. The tears flow slowly, blending with my rain-sodden face. Mother sits next to me and holds her hand in mine, and together we protect the ring from the storm.

"Mom, do you think Great Aunt Mary knows?"

"Oh, sure, she helped us find her daughter."

"We were supposed to do this together." I notice the rain easing.

"That's a nice thought."

"Look, a rainbow."

We watch the sun gradually brighten the sky.

"Sage, we should take advantage of this break in the storm."

"You go ahead. I'll stay with Tetty. She's been alone long enough."

"I'll bring your phone so you can call Jake."

"Thanks, Mom."

She hugs me and kisses my cheek. After walking toward the woods, she bends down, and then rises, waving a small ball of yarn. She lets it fall to the ground, and she disappears behind a tree. The setting sun gracefully paints the gray barn floor as beautifully as Tetty's painting.

MORNING SIDEWALK
STORY

Catherine Moore

Every day this week
I've happened on a different page
of *Goodnight Moon*
strewn along my walkway.
In water-frayed edges and stained faces
the pages stare up at me
each gray dawn
on the abandoned street.

First, the great green room beckons
as the good night ends,
and I have to lean in close to see
its dark and quiet phone.
Oh no, pair of mittens weather bitten.
Oh no, little toy house soused in rain.
Oh yes, red balloon,
there is something about littl' rabbit mama
rocking and knitting,
that reminds me of Nana Jane's *hush.*

But it's *Goodnight mush* sticking in my mind.
that child-size bowl and simple spoon
now barely stained on faded paper
left to asphalt and tire tracks.
I try to remember— Goodnight owl?
Goodnight song? No, that's wrong.
The worn-eyed wind tells me
to go home. Read it again.

Which is how I lost an afternoon—
tossing through boxes
Goodnight fable?
Goodnight mantra?
No, *Goodnight nobody,*
this sad and strange tale I find,
Goodnight air,
in a sacred text of babyhood.
Hush, still we tuck in the little ones each night,
Goodnight noises everywhere.

Ocean

JONAH AND THE

WHALE

Bill Woods

Jonah blinks at the darkness, unsure if he is awakening from sleep or death. He struggles out of the chaise lounge and holds onto the balcony rail for equilibrium as he floats amid the Milky Way. Between Ursa Major and its quivering reflection on the placid bay, a strand of minuscule Christmas lights twinkle, the shoreline of Anguilla twenty miles away. The beacon at the airport swishes bright and then fades as it rotates.

The outline of Anguilla materializes as the gray twilight separates from the blacker ocean. When the lip of the sun emerges, fringes of the purple clouds floating above catch fire, and Anguilla turns the green of its namesake lizard. Jonah's world is created this way each sunrise and then dissolves in reverse order at sunset. Always the same, yet always different.

Below, in Margot Harbor, something seems out of place. Their red jon boat, usually tied to a mooring directly in front of their cottage, is missing. He spots it out in the harbor, twisting and bucking as the ebb tide pulls it further from shore. Ropes must have worked free during the night. If it reaches the reef a hundred meters out while the tide is still low, it will be splintered and sink.

Underneath the balcony, he hears his uncle loading fishing gear into his wheelbarrow. If he were to yell down about the dinghy being loose, Tonton would immediately dive in and swim after it. He wouldn't think that it is drifting away faster than he can swim. Even if he were able to catch up, he wouldn't know what to do next. He could put the painter in his mouth and swim it back to shore, but he wouldn't think of that. He would heave himself over the stern and without paddles just sit there in confusion until the boat crashed onto the reef. The old boat isn't worth that risk.

His uncle uses the tethered boat as a weather vane, so he will see it is missing in a few minutes anyway. By then, it will be too far away to reach by swimming. Jonah sinks back onto the chaise lounge to wait.

"Whoop!" his uncle yells up to him.

Jonah struggles back to the handrail looking in the direction his uncle is pointing. He covers his face with his hands, appearing to cry. When Tonton moves his arms as if swimming, Jonah holds up crossed pointer fingers and shakes his head. They both quietly watch the boat until Tonton becomes resigned to it being lost and begins to fish from shore.

Tonton sails a slice of stale loaf bread just beyond where the surf begins to curl. He collapses into a squat with his buttocks resting against his heels, his forearms propped between his knees and jaw. This transition into a crouch is as natural for him as a gull folding its wings after landing. His canvas trousers are a lighter shade of the same color as his sunbaked chest. Except for the gentle lap of the waves, the beach is quiet and deserted. Tonton waits as patiently as the blue boulders protruding from the sand beside him. His tongue darts in and out of his toothless mouth, tasting the air like an iguana.

The bread begins to twitch as if coming alive. Little by little, the slice dwindles to crumbs as the water swirls. He breaks apart another slice into stamp-size pieces and throws these to the same spot. Immediately, the water churns. The water is as clear as from the tap, but Jonah cannot see anything except the bread.

His uncle stands and gathers his nylon throw-net onto his arm, carefully adjusting the tiny edge weights to dangle uniformly. With arms and legs perfectly coordinated, he pirouettes like a ballet dancer ending in an arabesque. The net spirals open into a perfect circle as it hits the water. With short jerks, he cinches the net before pulling it onto the beach.

Dozens of finger-size baitfish flash silver as they flop in the mesh. Three of the right species and size are sorted into a pickle jar of water and the rest flicked to the waiting gulls swarming overhead. His only fishing gear is a coil of thin wire with a weight and hook clipped to the end. The wire whines as it is twirled like a shepherd's sling. When released, the line arcs out beyond the breakers. Tonton tightens the line so he can feel a bite and again waits in his crouch.

The first morning breeze cools Jonah's sweaty forehead as he watches. The sand bottom seems to undulate as the waves swell over. Tentacles of sea grass stretch first toward shore and then, as a wave ebbs, out to the ocean, as if unsure to which world they belong. One of these dark patches keeps Jonah's attention, and he doesn't immediately know why. But then it definitely moves, slowly like the shadow of a cloud passing over. With it lying still again, the shark cannot be distinguished among the rocks and seaweed.

Jonah's legs feel rubbery, and he lies back on the daybed and pulls a patchwork quilt up to his neck. The front door slams. The floorboards creak, and a shiver stiffens his body as Brad approaches from behind.

"Are you having a chill?"

Jonah doesn't look at him or answer. Brad reaches to Jonah's forehead to feel for a fever, but Jonah shrinks away from his hand.

"Stop that. I can't catch AIDS from just touching you." Brad goes to the rail and watches Tonton below folded into his squat with the wire taut between his fingers.

"Tell me," Jonah says.

"No. The fever will pass in a moment and it will be too late. I'll fix coffee."

"Tell me." Jonah insists. He waits quietly while Brad decides.

"Snow is like—"

"No. Start with the river. Start with the fishing."

"I'll make coffee first," Brad says. "I could use a cup myself. Give me a minute."

The coffee pot and cups clink from behind. The breeze is pushing the boat faster now toward the white froth of the reef.

Brad returns with two pottery cups. Jonah uncovers his arms and cradles his cup in trembling hands. Brad goes back for another blanket to cover Jonah and a kitchen chair to sit beside him.

Brad watches the gulls circle above as he reorients himself in time and place to tell the story Jonah always asks for when the fever gives him chills. "The Hiawassee River is like liquid ice in the winter. It runs too fast to freeze, but the rocks along the shoreline shimmer with glaze. Behind the rocks are the steep cliffs of the gorge with tall white pines and cedars on top. Against the snowy sky, the cedars are like black dinghies with their bows pointed up to heaven."

"Tell about the other trees––the ones with no leaves."

"And there are oaks and maples that lose all their leaves in the winter and look like skeletons. But they are still alive, down below ground in their roots, and in the spring they put on leaves and become beautiful again."

"Deciduous. They're called deciduous."

"That's right. And I thought you didn't really listen."

"We don't have that kind of tree here. It's a miracle, don't you think?"

Brad looks out to Anguilla. "Yes, I guess it is. I've never thought about it, but if I'd never seen it before, it would be a miracle."

"Tell about the water––how the water feels."

"The only reason to get in the water is to fish for trout. My dad took me once when it was still snowing and made me wade out so he could teach me to cast. Even in the insulated waders, my feet began to throb and then went numb. It's stupid to go through all that for tiny fish."

"I wish I could do it. I've never been cold before. When I get the chills, I think I know what it would feel like. Is it like that, do you think?"

"Yes, it makes you shake and your teeth chatter. It feels just the same."

"Tell about the snow now."

"You've already heard everything about snow. Don't make me tell it again."

They are quiet watching the old man below crouching like a bird.

"Did you see that?" Brad jumps to the rail and points down at the water.

"Yes, I saw it earlier. It's a baby whale shark. Keep your voice down and stop pointing or you'll kill it."

Brad turns with a puzzled face.

"If Uncle Tonton sees you pointing, he'll stand up and see it too. He'll wade out, sit on its back, and stab it to death with his knife. It will just lie there and let him do it. Whale sharks are too big and dumb to be afraid of anything."

"He wouldn't do that."

"Call to him then. It will be quite a show. But in the end, the fish will die."

"Would he eat it?"

"That's not why he would kill it. I don't think he would know why either, but he would do it."

They watch, waiting for the shape to move again. When Tonton looks up at them, Brad turns his head away and sits back down.

"Whoop!" Tonton yells.

Brad jumps back to the rail in panic.

Tonton is pulling the wire hand over hand as it jerks. "Whoop," he yells again as he glances at the balcony to see if they are watching. A glistening tube the size of Tonton's arm is pulled onto the sand. Its body doubles back on itself as it flops. Tonton kicks sand on it to make it easier to grip before picking it up and breaking its spine across his knee. The limp fish is held above his head for them to see before being washed in the surf.

"*Beau poisson*," Jonah yells down to him through the handrail balusters.

Tonton's toothless mouth gaps wide as he laughs. His arms wave about, and his hands bounce off each other.

"It's a needlefish, and he wants to cook it right now for breakfast," Jonah says."

"He said all that?"

Jonah smiles for the first time. "Yes, and more. The fish fought bravely and the wire cut his hands." Jonah chuckles. "You've never seen him talk before, have you? Only my grandmother and I can understand him. *Grand-mère* is a deaf-mute, and Uncle Tonton is simpleminded, so I guess they kept to themselves when he was growing up. Uncle Tonton never learned to talk like other kids. Those two worked out their own sign language. When I was twelve, when mother found out I was different, she brought me here for *Grand-mère* to raise. I learned how to read their signs."

Tonton dumps the rest of the baitfish on the sand. They sparkle as they flip around. Gulls circle above waiting for him to leave before swarming in. Tonton disappears under the deck, and they listen to him cleaning the fish.

"Does he know how to cook?"

"Of course. He will cut it into steaks, rub on his special seasoning, and pan-fry it. You're in for a treat."

"Is your chill over? Can I get you anything?

Jonah turns his head on the pillow and frowns up at Brad. "You shouldn't stay. I'm not so helpless that Tonton and *Grand-mère* can't care for me. I don't want you here at the end."

"You're getting better, don't you think? We'll go to the States together--to the mountains. We'll go this winter when the snow—"

"*Merde*! Stop it!" Jonah throws back the covers and reaches for the balcony rail to pull himself to his feet. The sudden exertion makes him swimmy-headed, so he holds tight to the rail to keep from swaying. "I'm not a child. You should leave."

Brad stands at the rail beside him, his face toward Anguilla. "I won't go."

"There is nothing you can do here. Your visa is expired. The *gendarmes* will come looking for you. You have to go. What we had together is over."

"Is that what you expect from me--just catch a plane and bail out? Well, it's not over for me, Jonah."

"Why do you have to be such an . . ." Jonah tries to recall the English word, "*imbécile*? Don't you understand I don't want you here anymore? When I see pity in your eyes, it hurts double. If this were turned around, would you want me to watch? I wouldn't do it, you know. If I had any place to go, I'd leave you and never look back."

Jonah follows Brad's gaze into the turquoise water below. If the shark is there, it is resting on the bottom. "The whale is safe now," Jonah says. "I saw it swimming out."

"You're lying." Brad turns a scowl to Jonah. "You'd stay."

"No, I wouldn't. How do you know what I would do?"

"You're right, I don't know--and you don't know either, so stop all this bluster."

They stand together at the rail, watching the gulls dive at the entrails Tonton throws into the water, neither wanting to talk more. Jonah searches out the red dot bobbing at the horizon. "Whoop!" he yells down. When Tonton walks out from under the deck, Jonah points. Tonton shields his eyes with a hand as he looks out to sea.

When Tonton turns, his arms wave above his head and his legs dance wildly. "Whoop," he yells back jubilantly. His tongue darts around in his laughing mouth. Somehow their boat had made it through the reef. Soon it would be out of sight and gone forever. The boat might drift into the open ocean or wind up against Anguilla's rocky shore, but for now it is safe.

A NIGHT AT THE BEACH

Tom Wood

Solutions to all the world's myriad problems were a twelve-pack away. Operating on a remedy-by-the-beer approach, I figured we'd settle at least half of them. It was a warm, early August night, but gusts blowing off the Atlantic Ocean made it feel fifteen degrees cooler. I was glad I'd worn a windbreaker as we trudged barefoot through granulated-sugar sand, carrying beach chairs and a cooler between us.

We kept walking on this clear, moonless evening until residual light from nearby condominiums, vacation rentals, and motels had been left far behind. In the distance ahead, hazy pier lights stretched into the sea. Much farther beyond, on the other side of Charleston Harbor, the Sullivan's Island Lighthouse beam flared with monotonous rhythm. Blackness masked two glowing smiles.

"X marks the spot," my uncle Reagan's baritone voice said.

"Drop anchor!"

We released the cooler handles at the same time, unfolded our lounge chairs, and settled into a nocturnal serenity. So many stars, their twinkling lit the sky.

My face tingled, and salty breezes provided a soul-cleansing moment from the inside out. "Ahhh," I deeply exhaled. The only sounds we heard were breaking surf in the dimness, followed by waves rushing up the sand before petering out, and the whooshing wind—then the sound of a can top being popped.

"Have a beer," Reagan said.

I reached out, and the cold aluminum can found its way into my hand. Absolutely perfect.

Any other midnight, we'd be at the condo waging a winner-take-all backgammon game. But the lure of a celestial light show was too great to pass up. The Perseids meteor shower was supposed to peak around two.

≈≈≈

My uncle had invited me to stay at his Folly Island beach condo while I was in the Charleston area for three job interviews at newspapers of various circulation sizes. I'd graduated earlier in the spring from Middle Tennessee State University, then sent writing and editing samples to papers throughout Tennessee and in my home state, South Carolina. I'd arrived early at Reagan's seaside retreat to relax and enjoy his company before going job hunting.

Six years had passed since our last get-together, and we had a lot of catching up to do. I got a glimpse of us in the hall mirror and was struck by how much we'd both changed in that span. I'd gone from skinny, geeky teenager to a slightly overweight, long-haired, bearded college grad, while my uncle had transitioned from sandy-brown buzz cut to a head of more-salt-than-pepper, wavy hair. He also wore glasses and carried a few extra pounds. It made me think that I was seeing my future, what I'd look like at his age.

But it was great just to hang out with Reagan again. We'd always had a cool connection, aside from splashing in the same gene pool. We shared the same world view on many things, even though we were politically opposed, and both wanted answers to the hows-and-whys of the way things were. Our sojourns always made for stimulating conversation.

Topics over several days included family, politics, the economy, the latest jokes about Washington and the Russians, new movies we'd seen, and who'd make it to the World Series. One particular exchange focused on the media's role in a red-state/blue-state stalemate, the future of print journalism, a shrinking job market—the whole shebang.

"Don't worry, something will open up," my uncle said, commiserating with my frustration. "Somebody will recognize your talent."

"It's a bad time for the industry, but a newspaper job is all I've ever wanted. Maybe I should join the Army and write for *Stars and Stripes*."

That good-natured jab rankled Reagan as I knew it would. Not that I would or wouldn't work for the all-service military newspaper, but that I'd consider joining the Army. He was a retired Marine colonel and wouldn't abide kin serving in another military branch.

"I'll be your obstacle course on that one. Aim high, not low," he said.

Was he joking? I couldn't tell, but his voice had a harder edge than anything he'd directed at me before. Laughing, I responded, "Go Navy," which he answered with an expletive.

My uncle spent the bulk of his career at the Marine Corps Air Station in Beaufort, about two hours from where he'd settled on Folly Island. I knew very little about his duties there; I'd inquired once and got a terse "Don't ask." That meant something important, probably classified.

≈ ≈ ≈

I claimed the Grand Strand as home, but we lived closer to Murrell's Inlet than Myrtle Beach. Dad's company transferred him to Nashville when I was ten. After high school I enrolled at MTSU so I could pay in-state tuition, but the ocean's call and laid-back coastal lifestyle beckoned. Nashville's a great city, everything a country music fan like me could ask for, but Music City is too landlocked. It was as simple as that. Instead of blood, my veins coursed with a fifty-fifty mix of ink and sea water. I wanted, no, *needed* this job.

But that was for another day. Right then, it was all about enjoying the night's light show and Reagan's company. Memories flowed like the beer, and every drop was savored under the starry canopy as sea foam inched closer. I handed my uncle another beer before opening mine.

About that time, ocean breezes picked up, and an unusually tall cloud bank moved in from the south, making me think a storm was brewing.

Our conversation shifted from politics to religion and philosophical questions—subjects avoided by many families, but not ours. Reagan had always been a deep thinker with innate curiosity about what makes us tick, and he'd studied many convictions and beliefs as he traveled the world. My side of the family was mostly Methodist and Presbyterian, but the times, the liberal college atmosphere, and the culture of the era made me mostly agnostic. I had more questions than faith at that stage of my life—open-minded to heaven, while praying there wasn't a hell—and he supplied answers that I could digest and understand.

The meaning of life, the purpose of God's plan . . . whether God existed, the complexity of nature versus nurture, man's inhumanities, heredity versus environment, reality and perception—nearly every issue came under scrutiny, and it got deep. I'll never forget one point he stressed—that in his view, all the world's great religions were promoting basically the same underlying message of peace, love, and brotherhood, and that political leaders throughout time had twisted those messages to their own ends. We talked about cultish televangelists and their starry-eyed followers, then the chatter drifted toward grand design, mysticism, and the paranormal. Alcohol fueled what I laughingly referred to as "our harmonic convergence," and I meditated on his way of thinking.

I sipped at the beer, stared into the glowing heavens, and brought up a familiar and favorite topic. I loved science-fiction television, books, and movies, and was fascinated by flying saucers. Reagan was more grounded, even though he'd flown airplanes and commanded an air base.

"Do you think we're alone in the universe?"

"It would make for an awfully lonely place." His arm swept the expanse. "All those stars out there . . . millions more you can't see. And billions of worlds around all of 'em."

I laughed, thinking of Captain Kirk, Mr. Spock, and the Klingons. "So the question isn't if we're alone in the universe, but whether the others are good or evil."

Another sharp retort was expected, but he said nothing.

≈ ≈ ≈

As we talked and drank the night away, I relaxed and yawned. Reagan was just the opposite, becoming more animated. I remembered him as convivial and funny—though my dad referred to him as "a hard-assed know-it-all growing up," which was the only qualification he needed to excel as a Marine.

Though the edge of the cloud bank moved steadily closer until stars in the eastern sky were hidden, we were still able to watch the Perseids.

As the peak hour approached, meteor streaks grew in number, and talking ceased. We were awed like kids watching a cosmic pyrotechnics spectacle with the fireballs crisscrossing the sky before fading out almost as quickly as they appeared.

"Ooh," I said as one cut across the horizon. "Over there! Aaah." I pointed as another streaked north to south. "Oooooh," I exaggerated as three flickered in rapid succession, hoping Reagan would follow my lead.

"Hand me another beer," was his response, followed by an "ooooh"-popping top, long gulping sounds, a belch, an even longer "aaaaaaaaah," and the crumpling of a beer can. Maybe it was because of the beer, but I laughed so hard I almost rolled off my lounger.

We settled into silence again as shooting stars continued ripping the horizon. As cloud cover moved closer, I noticed faint sparkles of heat lightning, not bright enough to detract from the stellar light show above. Eventually, I dozed off.

≈ ≈ ≈

Sometime later, my uncle stirred me. "You should see this."

Sitting up, I shook my head and lifted my eyes. An elongated series of clouds, dark and dangerous, had silently moved in, and much of the sky above us was blacked out by them. It reminded me of the scene in *Close Encounters of the Third Kind*, when the billowing mists surrounded Devil's Tower right before alien spacecraft appeared. I didn't want to get caught in a thunderstorm and told Reagan we should head toward his condo before we got soaked.

"No rain's coming," he said. "Just sit still and watch."

I did as told, and we witnessed an amazing display of heat lightning.

From one end of the clouds to the other, flashes and flickers of light, some stronger than others. The soundless electrical discharges conjured images of pirate ships firing cannonballs across the bow. Then, as the Perseids continued to dart in, around, and through the clouds, I realized I was thinking in the wrong era. Not nautical pirates, but space pirates. More like *Star Wars* blaster fire. I felt like I had a front-row view to the latest science-fiction mega-hit. Only things missing were the sound effects and powerful theme music. "Use the Force, Luke!"

Heat lightning trundled for several minutes, sometimes mimicking a Fourth of July fireworks show. In the pitch black sky, the bursts of light made a stupendous display. We were the only two people on the beach at this hour, and I wondered if anybody else witnessed the weather phenomenon.

And the Perseids continued to blast across the sky.

≈ ≈ ≈

It was hypnotic, watching the heat lightning in soundless short and long bursts to the left that reminded me of Morse code, and I supplied accompanying sound effects—*Zzit Zzit Zzah* answered by a series of laser flashes to the right *Zzit Zzit Zzah Zzit* and one final long roll of *Zzah Zzah Zzah*. The heat lightning surges that had begun at each end of the cloud bank drew closer to the middle like magnetic attraction. Lambent glowing continued at a staccato pace as the intensity rose and fell and rose again.

Just when it seemed as if there must be a nova-like explosion of energy, the sky suddenly went dark. Then the clouds dissipated, and the stars reappeared. And the Perseids raced across the heavens, only at longer intervals between streaks.

"Show's over," Reagan said. "Grab a handle."

We folded our lounge chairs, lifted the cooler, and trekked to the condo, each lost in thought.

≈ ≈ ≈

The next afternoon, following many hours of alcohol-induced sleep, we drank Screwdrivers and resumed our winner-take-all backgammon game.

Reagan shook his dice cup and rolled a six-four combination. He covered two blots on his home board and looked up soberly. "So what'd you think about last night?"

"Very cool. Never seen anything like it." I rolled doubles and hit one of his men. "Better than when they turn on the Christmas lights at Opryland Hotel. Why?"

He didn't answer as our backgammon game continued. Double sixes! He was off the board and running. Then instead of answering my question, he asked about my job search. I had an interview the next day with the *Post and Record* in Charleston before heading back to Nashville. We talked about various newspapers and other media, then he posed what seemed like an odd question.

"So what do you think of the tabloids?" He hit one of my men.

"You mean the *New York Post* and *Daily News*? Great papers."

He rolled snake eyes—sort of like the glare he was shooting me—and shook his head as he started bearing off checkers. "Naw, supermarket tabloids. Like the *National Enquirer* and *The Sun*. All those. Bet you could land a job there."

I snorted as I rolled the dice. A four and a five. I couldn't get off the bar. "Not to be taken seriously."

"I've heard they pay well," he said. "If you don't latch on to one of the regular newspapers, check 'em out. A job's a job."

"Thanks, but no thanks. Journalism isn't a job; it's a calling."

A six and a four. Reagan celebrated another backgammon championship.

"If nobody calls, don't write them off," he said. "They break news stories nobody else has."

"All the news that's not fit to print," I said derisively.

That ended the exchange. We cleaned up and left for either a late lunch or early dinner.

The next day, I had a great interview but no job offer. After a farewell lunch with Reagan, I returned to Tennessee and soon landed a job in Shelbyville, about ninety minutes south of Nashville. The South Carolina contacts paid off, though, and a year later the Charleston editor called to ask if I was still interested in a desk job.

≈≈≈

As my career took off, contact with my uncle became less frequent, even though we were in the same city. It was nice having a relative nearby if something went wrong. We'd go to lunch occasionally, maybe dinner, and see each other if my parents came to town. Not having a family of his own (he always said he was married to the Marines), Reagan rode to Nashville with me a couple of times for Thanksgiving and Christmas.

I figured I'd remain single myself, then met a woman with dark hair and sultry eyes who changed my life for the better. We bought a home in North Charleston, joined the church, started a family, and enjoyed life. We spent nearly every weekend on the water, either fishing or at the beach. Jan and I also got involved with the city's night life, joining a Shag Preservation club, an ode to South Carolina's contribution to the American music dance scene. Meanwhile, I lost touch with my uncle. Years and holidays passed with only occasional phone calls. Nothing bad occurred. We just drifted apart. I imagine it happens in lots of extended families as we age, seeing each other only at weddings and funerals—it's just the way life goes.

≈ ≈ ≈

Three weeks ago, not long after taking an early retirement from the paper, I got a telephone call. My uncle was in the VA hospital in Columbia, South Carolina, and wanted to see me. The nurse said I'd better hurry.

As I ran for the car, I called my wife. Jan said to go on, that she'd pick up our daughter after work, pack overnight bags, and they'd see me at the hospital. I called my elderly parents while driving, and Dad said they were on their way.

Traffic was terrible, and I got there ten minutes too late. My parents had just reached Knoxville when I phoned them with the bad news. They were upset, but decided to stop in Asheville instead of driving straight through. Nothing they could do but pray for him. We didn't know how ill he'd been, and that thought pained me. My uncle had become very reclusive and not talked to our family for months.

After the duty nurse told me of his death, she handed me a yellowed manila envelope stamped LAST WILL and TESTAMENT. Clipped to it was a white stationery envelope with LAST NOTE and TESTAMONIAL scrawled on the front. Reagan's sense of humor showed till the very end.

"He brought these with him and said to make sure you got them," she said before departing.

I went to the chapel and looked over the notarized legal document. Then I read my uncle's handwritten letter, eyes welling. He recalled my visit to the beach, watching the meteor shower while getting drunk, but most of all our conversations of those days—remembering details I'd long forgotten. The note closed with him appointing me executor of his will. It also was witnessed and notarized. After the funeral, Mom stayed a week to help get his affairs in order, then flew to Nashville.

≈≈≈

I unlocked the door to my uncle's condo, and the first thing I saw was a reflection of myself—and Reagan—in the hall mirror. It was the first time I realized the depth of our family resemblances, how much I now looked like my uncle had thirty years ago on that particular night at the beach. One difference: my hairline receded like ocean waves, but the ruddy features were similar.

My wife wrinkled her nose at the condo's musty smell, and we began the emotional task of sifting through his belongings, packing things to sell, things to keep, other things to . . . I felt overwhelmed by the whole process.

"Hon, come look at this," she said, staring into the carton she'd opened.

It was a large black scrapbook, with my name on the front and marked personal. Inches thick, it smelled of smoke.

"Take your time," my wife said. "You can look through it now or tomorrow, next week or next year. Whenever you're ready. I'm going to tackle the bedroom boxes."

Wondering what the contents might reveal, I opened the memory album. It was full of yellowed newspaper articles, an interview he gave as class valedictorian, more about military battles he'd fought, a few clips about my dad's high school sports exploits, but many more about mine. My appointment as city editor, our marriage announcement, the birth of our daughter. Stories and headlines I'd written.

I flipped to the center spread, and the first words to catch my eye, in faded red ink, were *A World Star Exclusive.* Below that, a bold headline with inch-high block letters. I stared for several moments, then studied details of the artist's rendering and read the story. My God!

SPACE CORPS REPELS
ALIEN INVASION!
Moon station destroyed, but Earth is saved

CHARLESTON, South Carolina—It was almost the end of the world, but thanks to a joint military effort—and the heroic sacrifice of a United

States Marine battalion led by an as yet unidentified female colonel—the Earth has been saved from total destruction by an alien armada, one possibly from the Alpha Centauri triple-star system.

Details are still hush-hush, but the *World Star* has it on good authority that the unnamed colonel, who was based out of the Marine Corps Air Station in Beaufort, South Carolina, ended the siege a mere 10,000 miles from Earth when she managed to blow up the aliens' mothership at the expense of her own life and others under her command.

For perspective, 10,000 miles is about the distance from here to Adelaide, Australia. The intense space battle was mostly blocked from Earthview by a cloud cover that blanketed most of the East Coast. Some cloud banks had to be artificially induced so as to prevent widespread panic, according to our military source.

"We expected to send the aliens back with their tails tucked— literally—between their legs. Therefore we needed plausible deniability so as not to alarm the public," our military source said. "Of course, if we'd lost, it wouldn't have mattered because there wouldn't have been anyone left to care. We had to win."

The invaders were first detected more than four years ago as they entered the solar system, and the newly established U.S. Space Corps built a first line of defense base on the Moon. When that command fell in

CONTINUED ON PAGE 6

I flipped pages and scanned the rest of the article. The *World Star* had it all. Every detail of how Earth was almost lost. The rest of the aliens' crippled fleet fell quickly after destruction of the mothership. One disabled starship surrendered, with its crew being held at Area 51.

It was either Pulitzer-worthy or one of the greatest journalistic fabrications ever perpetrated. If *The New York Times* or *Washington Post*—or our paper—had reported this, most people would be inclined to believe a "trusted" news source. But the *World Star*? Just another "crackpot" exposé ¹ike Bigfoot, vampires, zombies, and the Loch Ness Monster that only their ˙lers and conspiracy theorists would accept as gospel.

˙ I looked at the date on the article—two weeks after the Perseids meteor shower and that awesome heat lightning display. Setting aside the paper, I shuffled through more clips about UFO sightings. One that grabbed my attention: a *Washington Post* story about the deaths of Marine Colonel Jane Oregan and a dozen members of her platoon in a helicopter training accident. It was dated several months after my beach trip. Following that were obituaries of military personnel from all the branches who had died one way or another during that same year.

Did it really happen the way the *World Star* reported? We'll likely never know the whole story, and I might have laughed it off except for one final piece of evidence courtesy of my uncle—a stack of government documents.

Those files were discovered in a separate box—they had been obtained through the Freedom of Information Act and heavily redacted. Nothing indicated who requested the FOI files or how they came to be in Reagan's possession.

But it sure convinced me. I know what *I saw* that night. In darkness, truth shines—like heat lightning.

MAN ADRIFT

Bill Woods

Arriving midmorning off the coast of Belize, Blake pulls the sails of *Carpe Diem* before reaching the reef and motors his thirty-five-foot Beneteau through the dark coral heads sprouting under the azure water. Ahead, a plank of driftwood bobs. Then he sees the fabric attached, and it becomes a body floating face up. He cuts the engine alongside the corpse. It drifts at the same speed as the boat. Shoulder length black hair wafts to and fro around the young man's head—in his twenties, Blake thinks. Judging from skin color, still pinkish, he has been dead only a few hours.

Climbing onto the foredeck, Blake scours the horizon for another boat, then the deserted beach a quarter-mile away. He spits overboard and watches the current sweep the spittle toward open water. In another hour, a cloud of small fish will form under the shadow of the man, and by noon, saltwater crocs will check out the commotion. By nightfall, the body will be gone.

If left on the beach, someone will find him. At least his family will know he is dead. Blake unlashes the two-man rubber tender from behind the helm chair, lowers it to the water, and ties it along the port side. With the gaff, he snags the man's trouser pocket and pulls him into the dinghy.

He cranks the diesel again and parallels the beach in water a few feet deeper than his five-foot draft, looking for a good anchorage. Ahead, a pier materializes and then the thatch roofs of a village rising above the palm thicket edging the shore. Arriving at a village with a dead man might be trouble. Reverse course? Dump the corpse? By the time he decides, people are watching from shore.

Blake drops anchor off the end of the pier and lowers himself into the dinghy, stepping over the crumpled body to the aft seat to run the outboard. When he grounds on the beach, two boys who had been diving off the pier rush toward him, gawking first at his cargo and then suspiciously at him. The youngsters, their features a mixture of Indian, Spanish, and Negro, jabber among themselves, then dash into the palmetto surrounding the village. They return following a barefoot, shirtless old man in ragged khaki pants, massaging his gray-whiskered chin with one hand and gripping a machete beside his knee in the other. The old man kneels beside the dinghy and twists the head of the corpse. A gap opens in the neck where it had been hacked to the vertebra. He brushes the hair aside to see the face clearly.

"Aah . . . no," the old man says to the corpse before crossing himself and slumping onto his butt beside the dinghy. The boys remain quiet and still behind him out of respect.

"*¿Hablas español?*" the man asks.

"*No. Francés o holandés o inglés.*"

"*Inglés, un poco.*"

"I found him. I did not do this."

The man looks from Blake to the body, and then into Blake's eyes again.

"*¿Comprende?*" Blake asks.

"*Yo creo.* I believe. I believe, or I kill you already."

A girl, thick-bodied, no taller than the boys, but older, elbows past the old man. When she sees the dead man, her hands jerk to her face. Her shriek sends a chill through Blake.

"My son," the old man says and then points to the girl. "His wife."

"I'm sorry."

The old man turns to the boys. "*Llévarla lejos.*"

The boys take the girl's elbows and try to turn her away. She jerks free but then acquiesces to being led back toward the village.

"*Contrabandistas*," the old man says. "Kill her also. Tonight, I think."

"No. Smugglers would not do that."

"My son steal from smugglers. They kill her . . . example . . . to others."

The old man seems sure of it. Blake does not know how to respond.

The man gets to his feet, glances once more at the body, and then leads Blake up the path the boys had used to a one-room concrete-block house. Smoke seeps out the open doorway. The girl sits on a flat rock beside a fire pit in the center of the dirt floor, weeping into her hands.

"Eat?" The old man points to a stack of tortillas in an enamel pan beside the fire.

"*No. Gracias.*"

"*Lolita, viertes un poco de café al hombre.*"

The girl wipes her eyes and nose on the hem of her skirt, snarls at Blake, and then spits words at the old man fast and sharp as snakebites. The old man does not even look at her, and she finally gets a cup and pours coffee from an aluminum pot beside the fire.

"Thank you," Blake says, "I'm sorry about your husband."

"*El ofrece simpatía,*" the old man tells her; she nods and sits on the rock again. "I tell her. She no talk *inglés.*" The old man points to a wooden bench, and they sit side by side. "*Vas ahora.*" He looks away, searching for the English words. "You go now. The smugglers . . . *ellos volverán.* They will return. Kill you." He walks to the doorway looking out toward the pier and the sailboat at the end. "Take son." The old man looks back, and Blake sees how hard this is for him to say. "Take to ocean."

"No. This is not my business. You should bury him."

"*Mi hijo fue asesinado.* Son murdered. You know. I know. *Pueblo* . . . the village know. They kill all who know. It better he never found. Nobody know."

Blake's face must show he does not believe the smugglers would kill a whole village. The old man nods his head to assure him it is true. "My son *estúpido.* The smugglers *estúpido.* If you as much *estúpido,* we die tonight."

Blake stands, looks down at the man's pleading face, then to the girl watching them. "No. I'll go now." He strides down to the beach, eager to dump the body and get back on his sailboat. The boys are still there and stand aside.

The old man follows, pulling the girl by her hand. "Save *la niña*; you take."

The girl, her face a rage, bends into the inflatable to close her husband's eyes. Blake sits on the nose of the dinghy with his palms pressed to the sides of his head. All this is coming too fast. He can't think.

The old man grabs the two boys by their arms. *"No viste nada."* He looks each boy in the face. *"No viste nada. ¿Entiendes?"* He waits for each of them to nod. *"Ustedes chicos huyen!"*

The boys scamper away without looking back.

The old man rushes to the girl, who is still leaning over the dinghy, and jerks her to her feet. *"Lolita, te escapas con el hombre."* He twists her toward the house and pushes her along while talking urgently in her ear in Spanish. Before they enter the palm thicket, the old man turns and calls back, *"Un momento por favor,"* and vanishes before Blake can answer.

The old man returns with a black garbage bag over his shoulder, pulling the girl by the hand. She compliantly stumbles behind, looking at her feet as if in a daze.

"I pay you. All I have . . . in bag." He tosses the bag on top of his son's body, then guides the girl onto the middle seat. "Get in. Go. Go," he urges Blake.

Blake wants to stop this, but he cannot think of the words to protest in Spanish or what else to do. He climbs in the back and lowers the outboard's foot into the water as the old man pushes them away.

When Blake cuts the motor at the yacht, he hears a groan from shore. The old man is on his knees at the water's edge, hands stretched to the sky, head tilted back in an anguished lament. The old man has finally given in to his pain. The memory of this horrendous day will dim over time, Blake thinks, but the cry of the broken old man will return to wake him from sleep.

≈≈≈

Past the reef, Blake pulls the throttle back and sets the autopilot on a heading away from shore. He goes aft and hand over hand pulls in the dinghy. As he lifts the nose of the inflatable boat onto the transom, the corpse rolls out, sinking at first, and then bobbing up in the wake.

Blake hesitates before pulling the dinghy on deck and looks to the sky. The wind has changed to blow from the north—both good and bad. Two days and nights with the wind at his back would get him back to Curaçao. If he sets sail, the dinghy should be aboard. But a north wind also means a storm. Already the clouds are building and turning dark. Best to get back inside the reef and find a sheltered anchorage. After the tie line plays out through his hands, the dinghy jerks and then skips along as before.

Back at the helm, he sets *Carpe Diem* into a sweeping turn. Through the cabin doorway, Lolita lies face down on the bench against the starboard bulkhead, only her filthy bare feet visible hanging off the end of the cushion. An undocumented passenger would be trouble in any port. The sooner he puts her ashore, the better.

≈≈≈

The girl comes up when she hears the anchor chain playing out. She ignores Blake and studies the shoreline.

"No," she shouts to him and motions for him to move farther down the coast.

Blake reverses the transmission and backs *Carpe Diem* to set the anchor. When she rushes to grab his arm, he roughly pushes her onto the stern bench. Jumping back to her feet, she squalls a protest in rapid-fire Spanish. When Blake turns, hand raised to backhand her across the face, she sits down and draws a thumb across her throat as she points to the shore. Blake studies the coast. The beach is undisturbed; the jungle behind it like the rest he had passed. *What does she want?* Like him, he finally decides, she wants to live through the night.

As Blake winches up the anchor, she climbs onto the foredeck and holds onto the mast, her arm outstretched, pointing the way. For another half hour, they motor inside the reef until the overcast sky begins to darken at sunset. In another fifteen minutes, it will be too dark to spot the coral heads. Just as Blake makes the decision to anchor and take his chances, Lolita points to a dip in the jungle canopy. A darker blue streak in the water indicates a channel leading to an opening in the lush green palmetto. He studies the girl, looking for doubt or fear. She adamantly urges him on.

Blake anchors in the middle of a lagoon the size of a soccer field, as the shoreline fades into darkness. After the engine dies, he hops onto the fore-deck. The moorage is ideal to wait out the coming storm—if he does not get boarded in the night. Already he cannot see the shore, but there are only the undisturbed sounds of the jungle and no flicker of a campfire.

The faint form of Lolita gropes through the companionway into the cabin. Blake follows and flicks on the cabin lights just long enough to see her stretched on the bench behind the table again. His night vision is ruined, but he knows the cabin like an extension of his own body. He pulls the bed cover from the aft berth and tosses it at Lolita before going up to the cockpit.

From a side compartment, Blake retrieves a bottle of DEET and the Luger. If trouble comes, he won't be able to run. Even if he cut away the anchor, he would never find the lagoon opening in the dark. *Carpe Diem* would be a white plastic duck puttering around in a barrel, an easy tar-get. He stretches onto the aft bench with the pistol on the deck beside him. No one can board without shaking the boat or making noise, he convinces himself. But if the bandits are as stupid as the old man said, they might try it.

≈ ≈ ≈

At first light, Blake wakes to the roar of the dinghy motor. When he jumps to the rail, Lolita is speeding to shore—not looking back when he yells. She pulls the rubber dinghy beside a wooden skiff half-hidden under overhanging bushes and then vanishes into the jungle. This is why they are here, Blake thinks. She knows someone within walking distance, and this is where she wants to be left. It is then, when he turns to put the Luger away, he sees the gun is missing.

The storm starts with a downpour. *Carpe Diem* lurches at the anchor line like a frightened animal. Blake watches out the porthole to see if the dinghy blows away. At dusk, the nose of the yacht rotates about the anchor to face the south, and the rain slacks. Blake goes onto the foredeck and searches the shore. He could swim in to retrieve the dinghy, but with-out the Luger, he would be at the mercy of anyone waiting. The dinghy is a small price to pay to get rid of the girl and leave Belize alive.

As he goes back below, his toe catches the black garbage bag Lolita had thrown under the table. Her clothes. Why would she leave without her clothes? He dumps the bag onto the table and sifts through Lolita's wadded dresses until he finds a zippered banker's pouch—inside, dozens of Ziploc sandwich bags of white powder. The old man's payment. Probably why his son had been killed.

"Damn," he whispers between his teeth when he realizes Lolita is going for the police. A murdered man, a kidnapped girl, and now drug smuggling. He scampers up on deck and looks at where Lolita had disappeared. "Damn you," he yells, and it echoes back from the far end of the lagoon.

If he can only make it through the night. A faint gibbous moon shines through the clouds. By morning the sea will be calm again, and he will run as fast as *Carpe Diem* will carry him out into the Gulf, put all this behind. If he can just make it through the night.

With only a fillet knife as a weapon, there is no point standing guard, so Blake sleeps fitfully in the bunk below. In the gray half-light of morning, he is opening his last can of fruit cocktail when he hears an outboard motor. Through the rain-streaked cabin porthole, he watches Lolita, ochre hair matted around her face by the drizzle, cotton dress clinging to her stocky body, maneuver the dinghy toward the swimming platform at the stern. He goes topside to catch the tie line. She hands up a woven wicker basket mounded with food. On top is the Luger.

While Lolita showers in the head and changes into dry clothes from the garbage bag, Blake checks the contents of the basket—cans, cellophane pouches of beans, a moldy slab of bacon. When he sees the magazine of the Luger is empty, his eyes jerk to the head door, cracked open enough to see a sliver of her torso reflected in the vanity mirror. What happened in the jungle? Every scenario he thinks of ends in death—maybe deaths. The man adrift has been avenged.

DÉJÀ VOYAGE

Catherine Moore

I opened the front door to find a mermaid standing on my stoop, her carved body painted an aged teal green like the haint color used on the thresholds of Caribbean cottages. Under the protruding scales on her tail, paint had mottled away, and wood grain showed through. The same soft fading dimmed her face. I could not tell if her expression was happy or sad. I could not make out if her spotted cheeks were stains or tears. She stood wooden and weathered. As if to remind me of my own tide's arrival. "I buried you six years ago," I said, but invited her inside so the neighbors wouldn't watch.

≈≈≈

Despite my effort in watercress sandwiches and her taste of soundless tête-à-têtes, our perfect conversation was hampered by a rolling fog and its belching horn. Still, she was mute, like inaudible hope. I missed her in the mist. Sensed her lifeless breath, her dumb state. Reached through the brume to trace my fingers along her face, and I knew it is time to leave.

≈≈≈

I applied dark lint for lashes,
crushed pimentos along her pout line,
wiped WD-40 across her decollate
then noticed a deep and worn crevice
where her left breast used to be.
The edge of wood cuts had gone silvery

soft except for bitsy paint flecks
folded down like a naughty reveal.

≈≈≈

She looked like every other petrified burlesque queen sitting in the convertible next to me. I nearly doffed her in my red wig since she'd gone
paint bald, but I loved how the skeleton of her hair still flowed in sculpted
waves. It turned heads as we sped into town. The teak, her cheek, a tease.
She carved a swath of admiration down Main Street. The butcher swore
she adorned a scrimshaw he inherited from his mother. The baker embell-
ished our crossed-buns with salty fins. We passed by the candlemaker
when she saw his cat drooling door-side. In each eye her upright held,
some discerned only mer, some caught maiden-poised. This grace was her
gospel. I'm not sure why I had not seen this before. Hers was an incised
beauty that fooled time into thinking it mattered.

≈≈≈

Hallelujah for the haze of time, a maid's lament, a matron's rapture. This
mermaid turned mer-woman, she confounded an idle beauty. Immortal.
Though six years since her corpse was buried in shipyard rubble, I asked
why she returned. I stared at this siren of candor. Coaxing her to share.
And the fog returned. The blasted horns. Now, the significant revelation.
How, she was eyeful of the authentic. A glory in simplicity.

≈≈≈

I left her where she asked, where she always
begged the winds to take her, and she curled back
into the sea as cylindrical as a golden nautilus
each spiral another rung in her charmed age
the light and dark of crevices, like a pit of fruit
jagged and delightful despite its flesh torn away,
I saw she was both mortal earth and water spirit.

≈≈≈

At rest was the birthing of a goddess.

SUGARBIRDS IN A FIRE TREE

Bill Woods

The male hops sideways, fans his tail, puffs out his handsome yellow breast, and chirps an invitation. Facing him a meter away, the female matches his dance exactly, quick flamenco stutter steps with rigid pauses so he can admire her statuesque pose. When the male responds with a new step, she plays hard to get and flies up into the flame tree. The male prances in circles, squeaking for her to come back.

"Paco," Webb calls out the open doorway. "This new girlfriend is a flirt. She will break your heart, Paco. Don't be a fool."

Webb sits at the kitchen table watching the sugarbird mating dance—the first sign of the coming dry season. Next, the bare flame tree overhanging the patio will burst into fire-like blooms, and then it will be time to fish seriously. The billfish will be herding the ballyhoo out of the Puerto Rico Trench onto the Anguilla coastline where he can reach them in *The Little Lady*.

When the hen sugarbird drops back in front of Paco, she flutters her feathers and crouches onto her stomach to steady herself. He can't resist. Mating takes only a second and then Paco flaps up into the tree to sing to the other males about his conquest. The hen flutters again, calling him back. He's hooked.

Paco's carefree bachelor days are over. She'll want a nest in the flowering flame tree. Webb will get to watch their progress over the next week. Only the best materials will do. If Paco tries to pass off a stick as good enough, she will jerk it from his beak and drop it to the ground, squeaking her irritation like a rusty hinge.

He will feed her for two weeks while she broods the clutch and then regurgitate most of what he eats into the gaping mouths of the hatchlings for three weeks after that. With the breeding cycle ended, his mate and off-spring will fly off, leaving the poop-stained nest as his only reward.

Webb's eyes glance at the broom behind the door. He should shoo Paco away, break the trance cast by the hen. Of course, this wouldn't save him. There's only one thing going through his pea-sized brain right now, and it won't be denied. A couple of weeks after this first family leaves, he'll be back strutting around the patio, none the wiser, calling out to every female that flies by, ready for his next servitude.

≈≈≈

The email had been from EPWorthy with a British domain suffix. A full-day charter. It was the slow season, and he needed the money. His reply confirmed the date, just a week away. He had told EPWorthy that fish-ing was picking up and lied about all the fish he had caught yesterday. He asked who recommended him. There was no answer, but a few days later, a deposit arrived in his PayPal account.

≈≈≈

A woman wearing a loose-fitting blue jumpsuit and canvas deck shoes stepped out of a cab in front of the pier. A pink sun hat, brim held to the sides of her head with a ribbon tied under her chin, shaded her face. Rose-tinted sunglasses turned to the beach bar where Webb sat with his cousins. After she waved and he waved back, she walked straight to *The Little Lady* tied at the pier, lowered herself in, and sat in the fighting chair. Some-thing—the gait of her walk maybe—seemed familiar; the nurse flashed in his memory, and then he dismissed it as impossible.

His cousins, horny bachelors, smirked at Webb. He took a last sip of cof-fee and grinned back.

She kept her head tilted down as he climbed aboard and greeted her.

"Good morning." He was about to go through his usual disclaimers: *if you'd gotten here earlier . . . a front's moving in—*

"Hello, Webb."

He froze, one leg on the pier and one leg in the boat, the cast line he had been uncoiling from a cleat limp in his hands.

"How have you been?"

His head jerked around, his mouth open and his mind blank.

She took off the sunglasses and smiled, the cheery smile he remembered when he thought of her.

Webb finished pushing off from the pier, then sat on a cooler staring at her while the boat drifted. So many questions, each crowding to come out first. "Twenty years," he stammered.

"Aren't you glad to see me?"

"Yes, yes." He jumped up to hug her.

She stood, turned her back, propped her arms on the chrome rail atop the gunwale, looking out at the island in the harbor entrance. "Are we going to drift in the harbor all day?"

"But—"

"I want you to take me to Petit Cove."

"But—"

"I've hired this boat for the day—and the captain, as well. I want to go to Petit Cove. If you want to hug me, it should be there."

Webb stored the bumpers and prepared the boat for the run. As he maneuvered through the rocks between the reef and shore, she stripped down to a bikini, throwing her fishing clothes through the doorway to the cabin under the foredeck. When he gunned through the outlet at Shoal Bay, she stood beside him, holding onto the top of the windscreen, letting the air stream her long auburn hair behind. She was still beautiful.

≈≈≈

Webb idled behind the boulders into the little cove and pointed the bow at the tiny beach, still half shaded by the overhanging cliff. "Hop to the beach when I nose in."

"No, let's anchor out. We can swim ashore later. I've got something to discuss with you first."

Webb threw a bow anchor onto the beach, then idled back and dropped an aft anchor so they would be suspended in the flat water in the middle of the cove. After he cut the motor, he searched her eyes, trying to guess what this was about. His eyes fell to her ample cleavage, the nipples reading through the thin white halter. When he felt his shorts began to bulge, he turned to adjust the aft anchor.

"I see you missed me, too."

The nurse pulled off her bikini, slowly, hanging each part separately on the two throttle control levers. Walking around to face the fighting chair, she grasped the arms and leaned forward, bracing her legs wide. "I have something to tell you, but I need your attention."

"You've got my attention."

"No, not until after. You will be able to listen after."

Webb remained frozen, trying not to stare, staring anyway. "I won't do it this way."

She turned her head to grin over her shoulder. "Yes, you will. Unless you've changed, there is nothing that can stop you."

Dropping his shorts eased the throb. The breeze made him uneasy. "You think you can make me do anything, don't you?"

"Please, stop thinking about it. I want to feel you. I want this badly, too."

And he did—stop thinking. The beach, the ocean, everything except her became a blur in the background. The sun blotted out. A tsunami jolted him to his knees. Little bursts of fireworks flashed in the corners of his vision as he slumped to the deck, panting to make up for not breathing.

The water splashed when she dove in. He crawled to the side of the boat, pulled himself to his feet in time to see her lie back on the sand. He slouched into the captain's chair, watching her stretched out, eyes closed, contentment hinted at the corners of her lips. He waited for her to look his way, call to him, but she seemed to be napping.

Webb dog-paddled ashore, holding towels above his head. Even when he stood over her shaking his wet hair like a dog, she still didn't open her eyes. Unfolding one of the towels, he lay down beside her, covering his eyes with an arm.

"Andrew's dead," she said.

Andrew? It took a moment before the face of a snarly seven-year-old flashed into his mind. Their son. He had visited Webb once during a school holiday—fifteen years ago.

"I'm sorry. I didn't really know him."

"He died just last month. Do you want to hear about it?"

He didn't. "Of course."

She turned her head to look at his face. She walked to the water to rinse off the sand, dried herself with the towel, and folded it to sit beside him. "I need to tell you anyway." She sat cross-legged, looking down at the sand in front of her legs. Her smile was gone.

"The boy you remember from the visit didn't change much as he got older. He was never happy, never content. Something about him, chemicals in the brain maybe, made him depressed. At least that's what I tell myself to excuse for my failure as a mother.

"When Andrew was a toddler, I knew everything about raising kids. I read all the books, knew all the answers. He would go to the best schools, have all the opportunities England could offer. I daydreamed how successful he would become—a doctor maybe, how much he would adore me."

Her face contorted with agony as if she might scream. She put her hands over her face, took a deep breath, and resumed.

"Anyway, the older he got, the dumber I seemed to get. He rebelled at whatever I suggested. Every day was a fight. Everything I tried seemed to drive him further away. I was working long hours at the hospital, mostly at night. I should have seen it coming, but I didn't.

"He fell in with the punk scene at school. Things got worse from there. I found out about the drugs when he was expelled from high school, but it had been going on for years. We did the rehab thing—several times. Counseling. Antidepressants. Nothing helped. He overdosed in a flophouse. I didn't know until a constable came to my apartment looking for someone to bury him."

"Damn."

Her head jerked to face him as if she had forgotten he was there. The agony in her eyes sent a tremble through him.

"I'm sorry, Webb." She reached over to touch his arm. "You didn't need to know, except . . . " Her eyes closed again. "There's a baby—with a girl at the flophouse, another heroin addict. She brought it to me after he died, before she went to prison for theft. They'd both been caught several times. Anything for a fix. You know how that story goes. After the baby, they got into prostitution, as well. Andrew was pimping her, she told me."

Webb got up, walked to the water's edge, looked out at *The Little Lady*, imagined idling out of the cove before the nurse could say more.

"William. That's the baby's name. I had the DNA tested; it's his."

He could feel her eyes on his back, waiting for him to respond, ask a question, something. He couldn't face her.

"Do you understand? William is your grandson."

"I've got a couple of thousand US dollars I've been saving up for a motor overhaul. High season's coming, and I could send maybe a hundred—"

"Webb, come here and talk with me." When he turned, she was waving for him to sit beside her. "Yeah, I've come back to ask for something, but it's not money. I make more in a month than you'll make all year."

He felt naked for the first time. Inadequate.

"I'm moving back to Anguilla. I'll be teaching nursing at Saint James. It's been in the back of my mind ever since I left. I should have come back to have Andrew here. Things might have been different."

"You'll bring the baby here?"

"He's here now. I left him with your mother before I came this morning. I told her about Andrew, and William, and everything else." She paused and a faint smile crept onto her face. "I told her what I want from you."

"I've got *The Little Lady* and a tin-roof shack. Not much has changed. What did you tell Mother?"

"I wanted to see if you could still make my toes curl. That was the most important thing. Second, I wanted to see if I could still make you snort like a pig."

"You didn't tell her that."

"No, I didn't."

"I don't snort like a pig."

"Third, if one and two were a go, I want you to take me back."

"Just like that? Me and you?"

"And William."

"What makes you think I'd be such a good grandfather or husband?"

"Husband? I'm not proposing marriage, if that's what you're thinking. I want you as a lover again. Your mother told me you never married, but you've had a string of live-in girlfriends. That's all I'm asking."

"You didn't think I was such a good prospect twenty years ago, and I'm still the same guy."

"You are a good man, Webb, but I was a scared little girl. We wouldn't have lasted a year. It's me that's changed. That's why it will work this time."

"I'm too set in my ways."

"If this arrangement turns out bad—for either of us, William and I will move to The Quarters, closer to my work, and you can have your life back, no strings attached."

Webb looked out at *The Little Lady*, bow nodding in the gentle waves. "Let me think about it."

She walked to the end of the beach, leaned back against a granite boulder, and looked out the cove entrance at the ocean. He followed.

"Back in England, on rainy weekends, I'd daydream about this beach—the sun, the rumble of the waves against these rocks, the breeze on my skin while we . . . I'd try to block it out of my mind, but my body remembered. A woman's body remembers her first lover like he's chiseled into her skin." The dreaminess on her face faded, and she looked up at the cliff. "The fantasy got me through some bleak days."

She finger-combed her drying hair behind her ears, stepped forward and kissed him lightly on the lips. "Today is real, Webb, don't you see? This can be our second chance. Maybe I don't deserve it, but I'm asking anyway. Give me a second chance."

His body reacted to her closeness. He couldn't remember what she said.

"You think with your dick, so I'm appealing to your dick. I'll fuck you to exhaustion. You won't have the energy to chase other women. Your cousins will have to carry you to the boat in a wheelchair when you have a charter."

≈≈≈

The mating dance. Webb watches.

He picks out an over-ripe banana from the fruit basket on his kitchen table and lays it on the sill of the open window. When the hen is through with Paco, he'll need to eat—build up his strength.

Through the window, Webb sees movement behind the flame tree. A little rump sticks out from behind one side of the trunk and half a head peeps around the other. A hand reaches to the rear pocket of the rump. Webb charges out just as William is taking aim with his slingshot at the distracted sugarbird pair.

"Hold up there, Will."

"Pops, you scared 'em off. I could have got one for sure."

"Maybe, or maybe the window glass. We done talked about you shooting that thing around the house. Besides, those birds are my pets. Don't you see me feeding them?"

"Sorry, Pops, I forgot."

"Maybe leaving that thing on the kitchen table for a few days will help you remember."

Will shuffles forward, his head bent down, his arm outstretched with the slingshot. Even when Webb holds out his palms that he isn't going to take the slingshot after all, Will still looks glum.

"Why not . . . " Webb is about to suggest Will go down to the harbor, shoot at the gulls, then thinks about all the boats, the busted windscreens. If only there were other kids to play with. In his mind, he searches the neighborhood, mostly retired older couples who keep to themselves. The only people out in the heat of the day would be his cousins, gruff old bachelors hanging around the dock. Nursey has already warned William to stay away from the dock. He thinks back to Andrew's visit, and then further back to when he was growing up. The neighborhood was boring then—and now, as well. Even the charter fishing he has done for thirty years has become mundane work, the fun gone out of it. Just a job.

"Hey, I've got a pair of skis here somewhere. Bet I could teach you how to ski."

Will's face lights up.

"We'll have to fuel up first, but if we start right now, we can be back by dark."

They grin at each other.

"You go check in the tool shed; see if the skis are there. I'll leave Nursey a note. No need her worrying if she gets home and we're not here."

Webb cannot help but chuckle at Will scampering out the door. He thinks back to when he was Will's age, how he had lain awake at night thinking about the next day's adventure with his father. So much he can teach Will—driving the boat, fishing. Teaching the boy will be like doing it all again for the first time.

Outside on the patio, the sugarbirds are still at it. They haven't even taken a break for the banana on the windowsill. Paco hops jauntily from limp to limb in the flame tree, singing his heart out, as if losing his freedom is something to celebrate.

River

SWEPT AWAY

Catherine Riddle Caffey

My heartbeats quicken at journey's end, twelve hundred miles from home. A cormorant calls *welcome, welcome back.* Inky purple plumage skims River Road's edge. Swept away by anticipation, another summer—sweet bliss.

Behind dark shades, my eyes open wide to drink in the view. Lungs drink too, salt stung air—like baby's first. Sandaled feet silent, stir old Indian souls. I kiss the wild thyme—woody perfume releases with each eager step. Straw hat perched above this pale face, smile spreads to embrace sun-kissed freckles. Swept away by shoreline majesty—storybook hamlet hemmed by Atlantic beauty.

Screen doors slam, dogs yip, babies squeal, cradled in the arms of shingle-clad cottages—dark brown beginnings honed to shimmering silver by wind-swept caresses. Gas lamps flicker on historic homes, inscriptions spotlight passages, sensational storms—badges of courage. Unfurled flags of red, white, and blue twist in the sun. Stone stacked fence rows dot the landscape, bring tranquil order to the wildness of the place.

Boiled in a white enamel relic—Mama serves lobster clarified—now swimming in shallow butter-yellow bowls. Crack, crack the delicate spines. Spear with tiny forks, placed for tonight. Whisper close, diamond shards shimmer across black velvet sky. Wee hour beach frolics, feet bare in wet sand—I shiver, as he clasps my hand. Shadows dance in the arms of

215

broad boulder clefts, chaperoned by pearly sphere. Waves crash, crash, as spirits entwine.

Bright, bright, Westport blue day rises before us—stretching after sleep of the dead. Lulled by waves lap, lapping, all the night through. Rooster-capped weathervane rotating with ease, shifting and spinning in heavenly breeze. Blackberry brambles sharp, plump, and wild—tart-sweet against eager tongue. Seagulls trumpet *come play, come play*, gliding overhead on their way to the sea.

Slathered with lotion, paler than pale. Short walk to water—sand, hot, hot, on shoeless feet. Raked beach, overnight seaweed strands forgotten in heap. Diapered babies, plump round bellies, tethered to guiding hands—pull, pull. Flat on their bottoms—angry, hot tears roll down cherubic cheeks. Reach up, ready again. Red suited lifeguards, blow a warning trill—mind the watery beast! On the horizon, masts glitter and sway, exclamation marks to accentuate sailors' delight. I roll over, turn the page, swept away by a best-selling read.

Kitchen window's daybreak view, I spy mama fox trot down the drive, full red coat, head held high. Close to the burrow brown baby bunnies nibble tender clover. Well-weathered pine-perch on fledgling day—robins' flap, flap in first feeble flight. Mourning dove couples coo from lines high above. Inside warm galley, bathrobe cinched tight. Breasts heavy for new-born in arms. First time mother swept away, by cobalt blue orbs, reflecting generations back at me.

Through the cherry trees, in my patriot's dream, they appear. Founding fathers lofted on stilts start the procession. Festooned floats ferry costumed revelers. Harmonious ensemble, bows glide across strings, wheeled in fisherman's boat. Freedom followers join the parade—starred and striped from head to toe. Adorned trikes, bikes. Strollers and scooters. Woody-waggoneers, vintage tractors besides. Sweets rain down from cloudless skies. On leads, crossbreeds and goldens move with the crowd. Star-stenciled ponies clop, clop with spangled flourish. Pass Elephant Rock—in twinkling sea—rippling red, white, and free. Gather round as Old Glory rises. Lady Liberty live on her lawn. Snow-satin gown, radiating crown. Amplified torch in her hand—the opera singer intones, "God bless

America, land that I love . . . ." Fireworks of sentiment—bursts of applause. Celebrators united in spirit—swept away by endless liberty.

≈≈≈

Oooooga, oooooga, the Model-T driver taps twice rounding the bend. Next door, weekend beach goers scamper right in, regulars at old Harbor Inn. Mrs. Ogden; postmistress, secrets keeper, inn proprietress—welcomes them all. Thriving retreat for ankle-length bathing suited gals drawn like moths to dapper lot, down by the shore—swept away by summers romance.

≈≈≈

Sax peals against the warm night—*Indian Summer* rises. Perch Rock Road Casino alight, pulsing jazz combo, parquet floors aglow. Gloved flappers lift bubbly from silver trays, fueling the Charleston, Fox Trot, and Tango . . . longed to dance for days. Servers on their toes with requests, swept away cake crumbs from iron-pressed cloths.

≈≈≈

Mild fall day, immigrant gardener drops shears, "Big blow, me go." Year-round resident in '38 shakes his head with disdain, pulled fresh from shipping crate—new barometer's forecast—hurricane. Lone police car crackling door-to-door warning. Cottage-lined seashore, sixty in all, scooped up like wallflowers, hesitant to dance. Ripped from roots, splintered into space—dog asleep on spare bed surfed inland—completely unaware. Second story window thrust open wide, maid to her charge, "Swim like the dickens, use all your might. Hush, child," with hasty embrace, "I know you . . . ." Twenty-two souls swept away, swept away that salient day.

≈≈≈

"Ahoy, who goes there?" Captain Kidd, keen eye, stout skiff. Westport, his harbor hideaway. Out on watery blue tracking secluded shoreline, clever fellow, slips silently into the bay. Only pirates hold the illusionist's key. Red-coated British Captain, flummoxed, unable to see. Fired a shot off his bow—all he could muster. Back to deep waters, swept away by defeat.

≈≈≈

Wampum, wampum strung on tanned hide. Wigwams pitched, Wampanoags' line in the sand. Acoaxet, claimed by the great

Chief—moons before Pilgrims take land. She squats, papoosed babe on back, scrapes oysters from ocean cooled rocks. Drums beat, beat, warm every heart, 'round fire-lit ring. Shell bracelets jangle with pounding feet. Embers crackle, crackle, snap in the night. Tribe swept away by bountiful gifts from *nippe*, Wôpanâak for water.

≈ ≈ ≈

Echoes of lost summers sting my closed eyes. Cold metal cottage keys pressed in warm hand . . . words catch deep in my throat, "Be a good steward, adore this old land." Rising on currents, I crane to make out, Indian spirits chant, "Acoaxet is heaven . . . you'll always be near." My heartbeats slow, one last time to be—swept away, swept away by eternal tides.

SINKHOLE CLOSED, NOTHIN' TO DO

Catherine Moore

By the first of September, the algae count in Burnt Springs, Alabama, was at levels such that state officials from Montgomery posted cease-and-desist signage along the water's edge:

NO ENTRY. NO SWIMMING. NO FISHING. (MEANS NO DRINKING, Y'ALL.)

For most of the Continental US, this particular month meant the advent of fall weather, but deep in the South, September was a purgatory between seasons. A holding space for all the summer projects one had failed to complete and would not be finished in the continuing heat. And a time for seeking distraction from fevered ennui.

Fletcher Norris attempted to stay cool while sitting under the carport by his garage. He played with cleaning out a carburetor from an old Chevy Suburban that served as his albatross project. A rusted metal fan stood two feet away from his workbench, roaring its artificial breeze on high spin. He'd rather be inside his air-conditioned triple-wide, but the kids, who were usually swimming at this time of day, had spent their lunch hour bellyaching "nothin' to do's" and then taken over the family room in a Sponge Bob marathon. And Emmalee had left for the afternoon to attend an emergency meeting of the town's festival committee, so there was no noise patrol happening inside the Norris home.

The Burnt Springs Mermaid Festival committee now faced a crisis with the closing of their waters. The entire festival centered on a theme of the mythic Burnt Mermaid, and any plan to move it away from the springs would ruin the atmosphere. "Not to mention the diving contest, dunking games, inner tube races, and the extra dollars for mermaid hunting cruises," Emmalee said before leaving him alone with the rug rats.

Just as well I didn't go with the wife to the meeting, Fletcher thought while mopping his forehead of sweat. *Though the refrigeration of The Lodge would have been nice, I couldn't stand the bunch of wet hens running the festival.* Fletcher spent another forty minutes pseudo-working on the carburetor, then decided to get out of the mounting heat. He walked down his driveway and across to his neighbor's yard.

Kelley Bergeron had crawled up into the Burnt from Louisiana bayou country about a year back. Crawled was the apt description of Bergeron's monstrous RV when it navigated the overgrown dirt road with a Harley trailer in tow. He had parked the beast of a diesel home next to the Smith's old shack and hooked his RV to electricity by running a drop line through their broken window. The former camp became shelter for birds and snakes, but Bergeron managed to keep the raccoons out—"There's only room for one coon-ass around here." He shot anything as big and cunning as a squirrel and lived meanwhile off the ground "as God meant it to be" over the expanse of rubber tires and riveted steel frame. His RV sported a picture of a gator chomping Uncle Sam and the words "*Rebel Kell!*" painted across the back end.

Fletcher liked his neighbor's ne'er-do attitude. He could do without Bergeron's damn purple flag tied to a PVC pole at the end of his drive, but the local Roll-tide crowd would take care of that ugly LSU blemish come later in the football season, Fletcher thought with some satisfaction.

"Kell!" Fletcher called out while pounding the storm door on the RV.

He yelled the name twice more before getting a "who's dat?" in response. If Bergeron wasn't answering the door, it meant he was having a "shorts day." Sure enough, when Fletcher entered the den, the host was

in his boxers, sprawled on a lazy-lounger. Shirtless and tan, Kelley Bergeron was one of those fellows who magically looked fit with little effort.
If Bergeron made good time with the ladies, it wouldn't surprise Fletcher
none. He wasn't one to ask about those kinds of stories, though; Fletcher
was a married man. Biblically married, not just the legal kind. And in his
mind, it made no sense courting temptation in sex talk.

"Hey padna, get yourself a cool one. You look twice-cooked in da devil's
furnace." Kelley tipped his beer to point at the kitchen. Beads of condensa-
tion dropped off the bottom of his bottle onto his bare thigh. It might still
be afternoon, but the overheated Fletcher was up to partaking.

The television was running, another heatwave oddity since Kelley
prided himself on being the reading sort who despised daytime TV. On
screen, a couple of guys balanced in a shaky boat, one explaining to
another how they'd use a fifty-five-gallon drum to float a log up, then haul
it off in their Gheenoe.

"What's going on?" Fletcher asked, opening a bottle of Dixie Beer.

"Claim to be swampers," Kelley said, "trying to haul up some sinker
wood."

The two guys on TV were wearing near-matching flannel shirts, as if
provided by the show's sponsors. The taller one in blue flannel walked
across a submerged tree, holding a long wooden handle with an end-hook
to pick and push the log around.

"Get back in," said the smaller flannel TV fellow, gunning the engine,
hoping to pull the encabled log on shore. The log twisted under the force
and dipped further creekside.

"T'ain't grabbin good!" The taller blue yelled, pulling back the cant
hook.

"We'll end tong that deadhead," small flannel said. He brought out a pair
of big tongs—rusted old ice block clamps like Fletcher's great-grandpar-
ents had lying around their barn. After the tall flannel affixed the antique
clamp to the log end closest to shore, the small flannel hopped in the water
with the end of the cable, wrapped it under the tong arm, then carried the
cable length ashore and tied it to the back of a pickup truck.

"Yeah no!" Kelley burst out laughing. His dimples deepened with mirth.

Fletcher had a couple reasons why he befriended Bergeron, the first being the man's face. He took one look at this guy last year and decided he'd make nice with him before his wife Emmalee did. Keep your enemy close, as they say. But despite his cajun ways, Bergeron had uncommon sense and didn't mind talking intellectual things, unlike the rest of the Burnt. The friendship that started by way of a surveillance impulse turned out much better. There was nothing intellectual about this show, though, especially when the guys on TV pulled out revolvers to shoot into the water since their sonar "was broked."

"What in the hell?" Fletcher said; they both looked at each other and laughed again.

"I don't know how these *coo-yons* get a show—out there with a cant hook and an underpowered boat. My cousin would make for better watching. Now, Teet's a real swamp logger."

"Teet?"

"Dat's short for *petite*, like Petite Jean, his daddy being Grand Jean. Teet's always been able to sniff out anything in da swamp—chanterelle 'shrooms, little beaver, gators. Nowadays, sinker wood's where da money's at." Kelley took a swig. "He's got a nose like a fox, dat Teet."

"So, there's real money in this?"

"*Mais*, yeah! A virgin deadhead haul brings in thousands. I saw one show, a professional now, and he was selling a slab o' bald cypress for ten grand." Kelley flashed a splayed palm at Fletcher twice for emphasis.

"Southern rivers could be loaded with sinker wood." Fletcher ran a hand through his wispy hair thoughtfully.

"True dat, Fletch." Kelley pointed his finger pistol-style.

"Could be, we got us some deadheads in the Burnt." Fletcher stared blankly at the TV screen.

"Go on. I've been telling Teet to come up and check out da Burnt water. Man, its beautiful tea color, its tannin—preserves wood, ya know. Oxygen depletion and all." He swigged again. "Bet it's a mess of treasure under dat black waterline."

"Maybe this is worth consideration, Kell." Fletcher addressed Bergeron.

"Trouble is, permits and dat." Kelley waved his hand dismissively, then stood up, adjusted himself, and strutted to the fridge for another beer.

≈≈≈

Emmalee was back home and cooking up Hamburger Helper. Fletcher regretted not taking the previously offered bowl of spiced gumbo at his friend's place.

"You've been over at Kell's," she said after Fletcher planted a beer-breathed kiss on her cheek.

He tried on his sweetest smile and took up a kitchen chair, prepared to hear her out.

"It was decided to put the festival off until the end of the month. Folks think it may be too cold to wait for October, but shoot, I don't know where they've been living these years. October can be just as warm as September."

"Warmer some years," Fletcher agreed.

"Grace insisted that the last day of the month was as far out as it could be rescheduled, and you know she calls the shots around here." Emmalee slammed down a head of lettuce and grabbed some tomatoes.

"Don't know why the date matters so much to you, hon."

"It don't, really. I'd just like to see the day when everything doesn't go the way the Johnsons decree. And it would be a heck of a lot easier to change 9/8 to 10/8 on the festival signage."

Fletcher chose to highlight her latter point. "Very sensible."

"Sensible doesn't seem to rule this town." Seeing Fletcher nod his head, she continued. "But rescheduling is the right call. The man from Montgomery was there, and by his report the springs are a cesspool of problems—on top of high algae counts, that are toxic by the way, the water tested positive for a 'PFOA,' and the 'Chromium-6' levels are unacceptable. Not sure that even October would bring safer water yet."

"They're just trying to scare the daylights out of us until the algae blooms go away."

"Well, if the algae don't make you sick, then this other stuff gives you cancer. I don't think my kids should be swimming in there."

"Look, the Burnt is one giant sinkhole—the springs—they dry up and then they come back. Nothing lasts forever. It's nature's way of flushing."

"It's okay for the children to be swimming in a toilet bowl? I hope that ain't what you're saying, Fletcher Norris." Emmalee aimed her knife in Fletcher's general direction.

"I'm saying you and I swam Burnt Springs as kids and we never died, so—"

"This is different. The sheriff's department is going to be out riding with the marine patrol, that's how dire it is. They'll be arresting trespassers. I don't want the kids, or you, going near that water this month."

"Can't wait to break the news to them." Fletcher headed toward the family room.

"By the way, Hazel left a voicemail for you. Don't get no ideas about secret fishing expeditions with him, Fletch. They sounded serious with this enforcement stuff."

≈≈≈

Later that evening, Fletcher stepped out on the deck to call Hazel in private.

"Hazel Wallace," the voice on the line responded after a couple of rings. He was all business like that, Fletcher thought, and answered in kind, "Fletcher Norris."

"Hey, I wanted to catch up on the campaign. Spoke yesterday with the manager at WALA. I'd still like to do those radio spots, Fletch, but as you know, campaign contributors have been scarcer than hen's teeth. Sheriff Boone has all the money flowing his direction right now."

Fletcher nodded, letting silence act as his answer. He noticed Bergeron flick off the floodlights over at his place. "Hey, remember when I said I might could come up with a financial plan? Well, I got one."

"Tell me."

"You ever heard of sinker wood?"

"Yeah, Georgina picked up a coffee table made of some in Atlanta, and it set me back eight hundred dollars."

"Shit, Hazel, you could have just pulled one out of the Burnt."

"Yeah . . . you saying there's profitable logs down there?"

"Loads of them, down the deep-water creeks, near the river end. Loads. And the best kind, too, naturally stained in that beautiful Burnt water. Leastways, that's what my crazy cajun neighbor thinks."

"Huh."

"Crazy being a term of endearment. He's alright, even if he's acting the coon-ass."

"Have any experience logging?"

"Some. Mostly it's his cousin that's got the rig and the know-how."

"Always a cousin." Fletcher could hear Hazel's smile even over the phone.

"Yup. But Kell says we're looking at ten grand on this here venture, and that seems worthwhile."

"Ten grand in?"

"Nope, profit."

"Ten grand is an awfully large cash donation for a county campaign, Fletch."

"Best I can figure it, the campaign corporation has to dissolve after the election even if we are flush with funds. So we shouldn't worry about how much we put in the coffers. And you decide what to do with the money, Hazel. Though usually divided among the principles. Spoils of the game as it were."

"Seems too fishy to fly. Undetected."

"How do you think Sheriff Boone's wife gets a new Cadillac every year? No one's looking at the damn accounting in this county."

"You could be right about that, Fletch, but there may be a better way of padding the campaign coffer. I mean, what's the river regs here—this kind of salvage requires a license, don't it?"

Fletcher bent his head against the doorframe and rolled his eyes—*these damn law school grads and their regs.* "We're talking about trees that've fallen by an act of God, not by an axe. We can haul out the naturals all day long."

There was an extended pause on the line, and Fletcher couldn't tell if Hazel was along for the ride or not. "Look, Boone's the one who operates outside the law. He's the trespasser. Think about your campaign slogan—You are the native son. Who better to inherit the native woods?"

"I *am* the native son." There was another pause. "Okay, just do it. Carefully."

"Yup. I'll see to it."

≈ ≈ ≈

Although Norris told his wife he'd be at Bergeron's watching late night boxing matches, the two were in Fletcher's Suburban headed to their swamp logging *rendez-vous*. It was only about a week since they first talked over the scheme, but Kelley's cousin understood the significance of having solitary access to the waters and made time to drive up with his "li'l rig." They were meeting him at the springs for a quick in-n-out heist.

"Why are you interested in the damn festival?" Fletcher asked after Kelley inquired on an update.

"I told Emmalee I'd be up for some alligator wrestling. People would pay to see dat, won't they?"

Fletcher gave a shrug.

"But she said over her dead body, far too dangerous. Dat *chere*, she's sweet on me." Kelley wore a cocky smile, but he could see his charm failed. Fletcher was about to tear into him, so he said, "Naw, I know my commandments, Fletch; don't pay my talk any mind. My mamma raised me right."

"You're just full of wind."

"*C'est tout.*" Kelley agreed.

"Just don't blow any in my wife's direction, you hear?"

Bergeron saluted his assent and fell silent for the rest of the ride.

Fletcher was relieved to see what Bergeron referred to as Teet's "li'l rig" was a full-size catamaran pontoon equipped with what looked to be a large mechanical winch in the middle. Even in the dark, Fletcher could see a mangy man figure arranging orange floater buoys and some dive gear on the tube decks. The engine stuttered quietly across the water, and Kelley refrained from calling out a greeting in his usual style. He spoke only after they had approached the boat, *Stump Knocker* painted along its side.

"Fletch, come see, dis here is my cousin, Teet. He's da swamp fox I've been telling you about."

Teet's face was covered in a reddish-brown beard, and his features were pinched and pointy, including his distended nose. He offered his hand to Fletcher, and a wide smile broke under the facial fur. They shook hands rigorously.

"*ça va!* Coosin Kell's padna is ma padna."

The insects at the shoreline were so loud they sounded like a den of rattlers in an electrical storm. Even with that static, Fletcher could tell Teet spoke in the kind of dialect that would be subtitled on TV.

"Good. I'm good," Fletcher said, emphasizing the guttural sound of his English.

"*Bien,*" Kelley said, "we're all good, except dis water, p-yew!" The air was foul in pestilence and toxins; they hopped aboard in order to get moving.

"Catch me dat line, ya?" Teet asked, pointing at the dock rope. Fletcher untied the boat, coiled the rope, and waited for a signal to push off. Kelley positioned himself under the small canopy at the wheel. Teet nodded.

"Before I get to talkin', I've got something to say," Kelley said with his hand hovering on the boat throttle.

Fletcher hid a smirk. *Lord, this was going to be a long night.*

Kelley removed his cap and rested it chest-side in front of his heart. "If we was to go down in the swamp tonight, I can't think of better padnas, nor a better view of da moon."

The three men looked up at the night sky; a ten-day old moon shone through the overhead trees, cascading over massive branches draped with Spanish moss and bromeliads. The haze of surrounding light created a lavender ring around its circumference, like a lunar crown. Three silent prayers were said, and then they launched, lights low, running as quiet as possible over the top of the main springs and past the bordering homes. Kelley opened the throttle a bit when they entered one of the tributaries that was unpopulated. Fletcher pointed him to the upper springs area.

"Good of your cousin to come all this way and help," Fletcher said. "What's his take?"

"Go on now, Teet's happier than a coon in the Friday night trash.

Lookey." Teet was standing on the bow with his hands folded across his chest, hair blowing backward, and his nose up in the air.

"*Allons-y*, find us a deadhead." Teet waved for more speed to his makeshift crew.

"He'll be mostly signaling, dat quiet one. Feeling da water depth and sensing changes," Kelley said.

They weren't too far into the springs when Fletcher heard an incessant buzzing sound, at first thinking it was an insect swarm, and then at Teet's hand signal, realized it was another boat. Kelley switched the engine to troll, and they drifted toward the shoreline. Along with the engine drone, there echoed sounds of a woman's voice on top of the water, like a song playing. Around the bend, an airboat came flying past with the lyrics of "Crazy" trailing behind it, the voice of Patsy Cline lingering after the boat went out of sight again. Fletcher recognized the AirRanger and reckless driver, Aldrid Hagan. The kind of person who thought himself above the law. *Of course he'd be out here.*

"Night time swamp running—dat's what it's all about, ain't it, Teet?"

Teet responded with a grin and looked back across the water as they began moving again.

"Something in da world had it in for Patsy, poor *chere*." Kelley shook his head, as they could still make out the fading song. "Speaking of the dead, did I tell ya Teet's a walking one? Been bit by every swamp snake known to mankind."

Teet nodded his head. "*Mais* talk about."

"Remember dat moccasin who ate through your damn boot to take you out?" Kelley laughed and turned to Fletcher. "*Pee-o* he was dead for about three days till he finally came back to life, bless my soul. Family gathered around bedside burning da incense like it was a holy holiday, weeping and praying, then Teet opens his eyes, looks at the priest, and says, 'Sweet Jesus.'"

Fletcher surveyed Teet who still stood on the pontoon's bow, now with his hands raised out over the water to sense its depth. Fletch knew it weren't time for the second coming, or he'd have to consider this fellow to a greater extent.

"Yassuh, just about everyone who's lived on da bayou long enough is going to need a little resurrection now and again." Kelley finished up the story before moving on to his next.

It had been a while since Fletcher boated on the Burnt after nightfall. He loved the strange beauty of trees dipping toward a waterline that curled mist back up into their branches, a fecund embrace between sea and land.

"*Garh la*," Teet said, pointing to a darkened branch rising from the water. "Kell!"

"Tu-wee, let's make a pass at dat!" Kelley replied and steered the boat along Teet's directions. They moved slow, Kelley zagging around, "a lot of knees in this spot, Teet, hope it's worth da time."

Kelley trolled and reversed through near impassable shallows. Fletcher had to credit him on steering a boat as well as he did an RV. Finally at the stump in question, Teet grabbed an exposed limb, swung himself across the wet, and walked on the sunken tree. In this stillness the water algae breathed of malaria and smelled like methane. It stung at their eyes.

"What it look like?" Kelley asked.

"Like wood." Teet grinned. "Pine. Look like a big heart, too."

"Dat'll be a couple thousand." Kelley squinted at Fletch through a haze of gnats.

"Didn't you say an old sinker cypress brought in ten g's?"

Kelley nodded.

"Let's go for something better," Fletcher decided.

Teet re-boarded and toweled the scum off himself. He rummaged through a wet locker and pulled out a square black box. He connected the device to the console and set it on the bench beside Fletcher, saying, "Densest wood sink to da bottom." Teet smelled like the rotting vegetation he just came out of. He quickly took his position at the bow of the boat away from the others.

"We going for deeper water?" Kelley asked his cousin, who nodded while stroking his beard, wild-eyed. The gesture sort of reminded Fletcher of Hazel. This was the right call, holding out for a cypress, having nearly promised ten thousand he needed to deliver payday. Fletcher turned on the sonar.

Kelley started the engine and wove back in the channel. "You know how to use dat?" he threw the question to Fletcher.

"It's a fish finder." Fletcher shrugged his shoulders.

"Just be looking for da long shadows."

Fletcher nodded and watched Teet with curiosity. He appeared to be sniffing the swamp as they rode through the final branch of the creek into the Burnt River. He guessed it must have been about fifty minutes time, and he began wondering if they'd hit empty. Second guessing that maybe they should go back for the heart of pine. Kelley, who had succumbed to the meditation of moonlight on dark water, must have had the same thought—he slowed the pontoon for a turn around.

"Scout da other side," he called to Teet. They ran halfway back to the creek when Teet threw his arms straight up and signaled to circle.

"*La*! Got it!" he said excitedly.

"He's da best." Kelley lifted his eyebrows and smiled at Fletcher as he spun the pontoon. Fletcher doubted the science of that claim. At the designated spot, he looked at the sonar. It registered only darkness until the display went gray, like sand. That was a big tree trunk down there.

"Yup, we're on it," Fletcher said.

Teet showed them that the winch no longer had a working button but how touching two live electrical wires together controlled the cable movement—green to red was for up, and the green wire meets black for down. Fletcher was used to swimming the springs, so he passed on the task involving an electrical experiment and opted for the dive. He began suiting up, and Teet shook his head over the swim fins. "Dem for a pool."

"Teet can tell you the difference between pine, cypress, oak with just his feet," Kelley said. Teet wiggled his gloved feet in emphasis.

"Why?" Fletcher asked.

"'Cuz you can't see under, in fine deadhead waters." Kelley laughed.

After Fletcher dove in, he saw what Bergeron meant. The underwater lamp in his hand cast a russet light through the murky water, making the sunken world barely visible. He had never tried this at night, when the river's tannin water was so dark one couldn't tell which way was up. Within the heavy silence, he sensed surface only by the movement of current, slowly sideways. It was a panicking feeling. A brief flash of light came and went above him. *Was it the pontoon?* A return to complete darkness indicated not—something had moved away. Then the white lightness came again and brushed close to him, like a large fin.

Fletcher rose up quickly. He ripped off his gear and hung on the pontoon side, breathing hard. "Mermaid," he whispered unexpectedly.

"What?" Kelley asked and shook him. "Fletch? Man?"

A burp of trapped air broke surface; Teet emerged from the water after Fletcher. "*Sa*, okay?"

"He's okay, just disorientated. Found one?"

They got a thumbs-up signal from Teet before he took the harness end of the cable that Kelley lowered, and submerged again. Fletcher watched the amber color of Teet's lamp turn to a darker orange as he dropped.

As soon as they started the winch, the first of the coyotes howled.

"Rougarou?" Teet asked, jerking his head right and left, scanning the tree lines quickly.

"Naw, ain't none of those here, Teet. Got themselves a mermaid in dis spring, though. Right, Fletch?"

"That's what the widows and the fools tell me."

"*Couyon*, eh?" Teet said.

"Exactly. Coo-yon." Fletcher said warming up to the cajun word. Since meeting Bergeron and adding to his vocabulary, he found it a handy way of calling people idiots without them knowing.

"Or *fifollet*."

"Fool's fire. Swamp lights," Kelley answered to Fletcher's puzzled expression. He looked at the murky water that kept everything below view, both dangerous and benign, and added, "Souls of the unbaptized." A nearly unrecognizable scream came from the trees, which was the beginning of some owls screeching back and forth.

"*Garh la*," Teet said as the cypress appeared at the waterline. Mud and river flushed up along the sides, but the trunk stopped rising because a stub of a limb was caught under the pontoon tube. The winch started a high-pitched squeal like a piston under strain.

"Halt!" Teet threw down his dive gear on the deck.

"Don't get like me now." Kelley stopped the winch.

"Catch me dat long sonnaf-a-gun," Teet said as he touched the wires together and lowered the tree trunk a bit.

Kelley handed him a four-foot-long chainsaw.

"Let's think about this for a sec," Fletcher said.

Teet didn't hear him over the sound of the saw, his lanky frame wielding it into the flesh of the water-logged tree. With the branch cut free, the main trunk of the cypress was easily lifted by the winch and rested in its cable hammock between the two tube decks.

"Every log has its day. Ain't that right, Teet?"

Fletcher rubbed his hand down the side of the large slimy deadhead. Cleaned up and cut, this sunken tree was pure treasure.

"It's a beaut," Kelley agreed.

"Whoa, there it is again," Fletcher said pointing at the water.

Teet dove into the river yippeying, "Mermaid!" He caught hold of her tail and yanked with the strength of a man twice his size. Out of the water popped the white head of an albino alligator.

"Damn!" both men on the boat said.

The ghostly gator spun sideways toward the pontoon, pale jaw gaping, making a hissing sound. Teet hopped on the gator's back near the front shoulders. His knees squeezed the animal's flanks and his hands held on the alligator right behind its jaws and front legs. Between the animal's thrash forward and Teet's push, the alligator found its front body pinned against the boat. There was a moment of human amazed stupor at the reptilian pearly white scales and piercing blue eyes before they were shaken alert by the rancid breath of a gator. While Kelley worked the boat's engine to keep it pressed against the gator's jaw, both of Teet's hands gripped the alligator's neck.

"Grab da snare pole while Teet calms it down," Kelley shouted at Fletcher.

Teet slid an arm forward down the middle of the alligator's head to cover its eyes. The gator went still but then began to shake violently.

"Dem tail, can't . . ."

Fletcher had the snare cable near over the gator's jaw when it rolled left and slipped through the noose. Teet lost one handhold and immediately grabbed the pontoon. The gator continued its spinning roll to turn back on Teet who was halfway up, and the right side of its jaw came down on Teet's dangling leg.

"'im nostrils!" Teet yelled.

Fletcher spun the handle on the pole around and punched the gator's nostrils. Its jaw reflexed open, and the animal floated briefly, stunned by the turn of events, then waved its tail eerily mermaid-like and dipped back into the murky water. Teet was shaking with either laughter or shock as Fletcher wrapped his bloody leg with a towel. There was enough flesh gnashed that it would take stitches to pull the skin flaps back down.

"Pee-o, can't keep you out of emergency rooms, Teet," Kelley said, cracking up along with his cousin.

"Guess dat's Burnt Springs's mermaid," Teet said in between laughs.

"And about a hundred thousand dollars of da pearly alligator leather."

Fletcher sat staring into the water in disbelief. He was past ready to head home.

Previously published in *The Corvus Review*

REMEMBRANCES

Tom Wood

Dipping into the fountain of youthful memories, I realize how many of my favorite ones involved water. Like listening to the roaring waves and praying for an ocean breeze to flow through the open windows of our un-air-conditioned beach cottage on hot summer nights during our family's annual trip to Myrtle Beach. Or learning to bait a fishhook on the rod and reel Dad got me one Christmas. Or "moonfish" jumping out of the water as we camped for days on an Intracoastal Waterway beach near Cape Kennedy to watch the moon launch of Apollo 11 in 1969. Experiencing the eerie calm of the hurricane eye passing over our home in Largo, Florida. Getting soaked on the Log Jamboree flume ride at Six Flags Over Georgia and later on the Grizzly River Rampage at Opryland USA. Watching the fun of my little sisters' first trip to the wave pool after we moved to Nashville. Or like the first time Dad let me steer the new speedboat on Percy Priest Lake, wind whipping my already receding hairline.

Here's another memory about Dad—this one from my Uncle Bill, whose heartfelt tribute flows in the accompanying poem. In April of 1986, my dad, Tom Sr., was facing surgery—and his mortality—when his brother, Dr. William Wood, traveled from North Carolina to offer support and spend time with our family. It was the brothers' final visit together, a cherished week. Dad passed two weeks later.

Before leaving Nashville, my uncle penned a poem for Dad, an insightful childhood reflection from a simpler time with his brothers at the family farm (about 1938 or '39, my uncle recalled). I get choked up every time I read it. Thank you, Bill, for allowing me to share your words in this water-themed anthology. And as you lovingly told Dad before departing, "Thumbs up, Podner!"

A Summer Walk in the Pasture

We walked along, Pete, Tom and I, without
purpose, beside the pasture creek that day.
Willow poles, tobacco twine, and hook in hand,
and Tom said, "Billy, did you ever wonder
what makes it this way?"
Green grass, lush and soft in the meadow with
wild grape hyacinth growing there, the
brook's fresh water over smooth stone,
and blue endless sky with sweet clean air.
Pete had stopped to tease a crawfish
only to be diverted by a trout near a stone.
Tom and I, with attention to other things
as I puzzled over his words, continued walking on.
"Yeah," I finally replied, "...I guess sometimes I might."
But underneath, deep down so this older, wiser
brother wouldn't see my doubt, I was not
sure the answer I had given was right.
As if sensing my uncertain ease, read
from apparent confusion on my face,
Tom looked all about and with no further
word drew closer as he slowed our pace.

"I mean..." he then began, "how it all fits together;
we are all a part of God's plan to be kept."
And we talked as friends and brothers can.
That night, with a sense of belonging, I slept.

William Wood
April, 1986

WATERMARK

Catherine Moore

The
merge into one flow
requires no holding back;
this is a river's fluency,
always choosing—adherence,
anarchy.
In dark folds on its surface,
separating under and above,
liminal swell that ripples warning
or readies itself for the making
of
high-water markings.
Within more gentle eddies
some confuse calm and serenity, love and pity,
marooned stirrings that cast no shadow.
Water
is only bound to reflect time,
climates that cloud across its plane,
the faces of children contemplating
a river's conveniences: how its current
spurns
boundaries, how it gifts

great height in its scaffolded bridges,
both a thresh-way between
existence and essence. In running,
the
river leaves its own inscriptions
like the lace biographies a wave
leaves on sandy shores.
It carves a scar into the earthly
notion
of loyalty and kin,
and endears false tithings
to unsolid ground. A few souls know wading
through nights that toss cruelly,
of
days X'ed aside, they braid an expanse
in everyday hazards survived,
make barge of the chaos left behind.
If the wounded float, they sing and
shape
artless river tales, in verses
under pens or along guitar strings.
To hint at the terrible stains
that never lift.

FAKE WATER

Suzanne Webb Brunson

Janey stood in front of a full-length mirror, grimacing. "A walking disaster, that's what I am."

She leaned in to check her makeup and to see if any new creases were visible on her dry skin.

"There it is, the Grand Canyon, right in the middle of my forehead."

"Here, drink this." A bottle of water rolled under the dressing room door, and Janey could see her mother's brown shoes. They were high heels, but not too high for standing up all day—sensible. "Drink it. I bet you're dehydrated. You're always dehydrated. Cokes won't replace the fluid in your body."

The adult daughter, who now felt like a dressing room hostage, looked at the bottle. "You've got to be kidding. How many bottles do you carry at any given time?" She unlocked and opened the dressing room door, and her mother stood there smiling. Her plastic employee badge reflected light from the bright lamp, the kind that hung in all the dressing rooms.

She was dehydrated, and her mom was smiling. "Mom, you know you are grinning at me."

"I know. You look cute in that, but stand up straight. How many bottles of water? I brought a couple to work and picked up an extra at lunch."

"So, you are sufficiently hydrated, which helps you maintain good posture, right?"

"No need to be hostile." She was still smiling. "Quit frowning in the mirror, and please pick it up, and drink some. You know I'll pull my back out if I bend over in heels. And, yes, I'll say it again, just to irritate you, stand up straight."

Janey's mom did not understand that it was moments like this that lowered her chances of shopping with her daughter again. Ever. *Stand up straight?*

"Here it comes, Mom—my eye-roll expression. You know you love it." She turned a bit to see how the back of the dress looked. There it was—the not-quite-bad posture that ensured no one would ever mistake her for a prima ballerina. Her mother was right on that point.

"You're thinking Anna Pavlova, right?"

"Who?" Janey turned back around.

"All those dance lessons, and you don't know who was the most famous Russian ballerina ever?"

"Mom, you used the word *was*, so I'm good. I'll look it up later, and I got the bad posture from Aunt Linny; she doesn't stand up straight either. You're the lucky one. It skipped you. You could be a poster girl in the military for good posture. They'd let you be the first woman ever to march in front of Buckingham Palace in those red uniforms from, well, the sixteenth century. See, I know some history. I can just picture you in one of those furry, black, conehead hat things."

"I'm going home and looking that one up. Oh, darlin', don't worry about it. That outfit looks so nice. It hides the rolls and everything."

Janey had been listening to her mother's go-around-the-barn-to-say-what-you-mean compliments all her life. "I know, I've kind of quit working out lately. Yes, there are rolls, one big one when sitting, two when I lean over, or three, if I count my stomach. That's what I've been checking in the mirror."

Janey's mother leered over her shoulder. "Honey, this is beautiful. You've got a lot of sweaters, but I'd go ahead and splurge for blue. You look great in blue. Jackets are coming back in, but maybe not for this dress. We have the perfect sweater, very light and summery. It's not on the floor yet. I'll run get it from the back."

"Hey, it's not summer anymore," Janey said, "but climate change, weather change, whatever, is a consideration for getting a lightweight sweater during autumn because it sure isn't cool outside, yet."

≈ ≈ ≈

Her mother, Iris, now worked at her favorite store, part of a national chain. It was the one that charged at least twelve dollars for postage and handling if a customer was foolish enough to order from their computer, while enjoying the comfort of home in a brown recliner, which Iris had. Janey thought maybe the store purposely maintained a sparse inventory, specifically in whatever size Janey was currently wearing, thus ensuring shoppers' anxiety. Now that her mom worked here, she could pull Janey's size from the stockroom. Iris would either buy it herself, put it on hold, or tell Janey to hot-foot it to the mall. Crowds hadn't been a problem in recent years, as pedestrian mall traffic declined. Janey thought they ought to consider converting some of the surplus stores upstairs into condominiums for seniors. Her parents, Marvin and Iris Winkelman, would love it.

"Honey, I promise, no one is holding out on you. The store depends on demographics and sales numbers to maintain stock."

≈ ≈ ≈

Janey sipped some water and then looked at the label on the bottle. Iris walked back into the dressing room with a deep royal blue cardigan. "Mom, where do you suppose this water came from? Is it actual spring water or what?"

"Lean over so you don't spill any on the merchandise."

"I did."

"Okay, where do they get the water? I don't know, mountain creeks?"

"Next time I'll fill a bottle with gin or vodka and bring it with me. Think your boss would mind?" Iris, leaning against the wall, gave her daughter the eye roll.

"I know I need to drink more water. Then I think about all the plastic bottles that are thrown away every day. They are not biodegradable and sit in landfills that no one wants to live near." Janey put on the sweater. "That's when I spend twenty minutes looking for my bubba cup."

She studied herself in the mirror.

"Mom, you have done an exemplary job. I'll take the dress and sweater."

Here, put it on my credit card. I would kill for your employee discount, but not enough to get you fired."

"I knew I raised you right." Iris hugged her daughter. "See you Sunday?"

Iris later found a necklace and bracelet that would look great with Janey's new dress. She'd give it to her over the weekend.

≈≈≈

Janey stopped at the big box store on the way home. Her mother was right. She did need to drink more water and so it was on her shopping list. This big box was the one where she had once asked for help reaching merchandise on the top shelf. The female clerk had just looked at her, scowled, and said, "I'm as short as you."

Hopeful that she could find water on her own and that it wouldn't be on the top shelf, she gave the store a second chance to treat her right. It was like maybe they'd be waiting for her to return to make up for any inconvenience or wisecrack from the last shopping trip.

And there it all was, in the back of the store—water, cases, six packs, and individual bottles at four times the price of a case. On the other hand, the bottles in the case would collapse and were so cheap they made crackling noises when she tried to drink. She always got at least a teaspoon of overflow on whatever shirt she'd decided to sacrifice for the cause, thus her mother's cautionary moment back at the store. She'd quit letting the kids drink from the cheap bottles and caved on the non-crackle, maybe biodegradable brand. They had outgrown sippy cups and Janey's ability to tell them what to do. She couldn't reach them from the front seat anymore, so it was a tie. They didn't get a nudge from Mom and so, drank the good stuff. Janey made them say thank you for every bottle and yes, they'd take the bottles inside with them when they got home, to recycle.

"Mom, can I have a bubba cup that keeps stuff cold but doesn't spill if it gets knocked over?"

"Sure honey, when you quit losing your lunch bag, Tupperware, and sweaters."

She soon caved and got them all one to make sure they didn't drink from the water fountains at school. Metro Nashville water had been tested for lead that summer, and results were positive. Janey didn't think the water was cleaned up in a satisfactory length of time, like it took being outed to get any action in the first place.

≈≈≈

Hanging onto the cart, which the aerobics instructor, and recently the physical therapist, both said defeated the purpose of walking the long aisles, she examined a liter bottle. It was solid as a plastic cup, or even glass. Her mother told her the vitamin water she'd been so proud to drink had additives, fake sugar. She'd read the label with a magnifying glass and found out it wasn't spring water.

Fake? Fake water? Janey wanted to know more. What was the chemistry, beyond H2O? From what so-called mountain spring did the water come? Had it been stolen from a local farmer so that the food conglomerate could sell it as the elixir of life? She particularly wanted to know the specific mountain spring location, not some vague paradise.

Clean water was the new rum runners' product. There was no need to build a still on the other side of the mountain for water, just siphon it up. Craft beer? Make wine in the bathtub and sell it as an artisanal beverage? That was a whole new word Janey never heard of until she was trying to look up artesian well and got sidetracked. Another added plus was the now-legal and highly advertised change that made it possible to buy a beer and drink it while at the grocery store. Open carry took on a whole new meaning to local shoppers at the grocery chain. Iris told her she'd tried sitting at the bar—yes, they had an actual bar—and ordering some wine, but it was just too tacky. She told the guy she wanted a bottle of chardonnay, and moved on to the health food aisle.

"Now there's a wonderland of 'do you even have a clue what's in the food one aisle over?'" Iris said. "I ditched the wine bottle on a shelf with some sparkling water bottles. Tell me I don't think of you often!"

≈≈≈

When the local news dropped the story about lead levels in the water, Janey bought purifiers for the kitchen faucet and the refrigerator. She also grabbed a purifier pitcher to keep in the refrigerator. Last ditch effort was when she went to the Sears scratch-and-dent outlet and bought a refrigerator. She considered a new one, but remembered Marvin and Iris telling their story of nearly being mugged while trying to buy their own refrigerator. They'd gone ahead and bought one, off the floor, but highly recommended scratch and dent.

"Who would believe I was excited to get a major appliance for a birthday gift?" Janey said.

She never found a dent, but there were two horizontal scratches on one side like someone dragged it too close to a counter or while loading or unloading it out of the box.

≈≈≈

The local government assured citizens they'd taken extra steps to clean up the river that was the fountain of water for everyone in the metropolitan area.

They told the people in Flint, Michigan, the same thing.

Bottled water was the new moneymaker.

Janey loaded her cart with three cases of the least expensive of the expensive stuff and then went off to find new totable water bottles. The kids had already left two at school, and she hadn't had time to search the huge lost-and-found boxes in the school hallway. She vaguely knew they were located somewhere near the cafeteria.

"I swear, is there anything easy about having kids and drinking water?" Janey loved being a mother, most of the time.

"Wait a minute, if this water is the cheapest of the best, is it the cleanest or is the bottle what's better about it?" She walked back and pulled a bottle of the best/best stuff off the shelf and compared sources. "Good grief, will I have to do a geographical survey to make sure I'm not drinking from a toilet?" There was not a lot of information on the bottle. She later found out, unlike food, bottled water is not awesomely regulated.

She stopped reading labels and considered buying a cart full of individual bottles, each a different brand, so at least one or two might be good. She finally got out her phone, took pictures of all the bottles, left the cases in the buggy, and walked out.

When Janey got home, she grabbed a caffeine-free Diet Coke from the refrigerator. She had seen the pictures of what that stuff was doing to her and didn't care.

"Rot gut in college did the same thing." She was talking to an empty house.

She poured the drink into her bubba cup and then hit the ice lever. She let it fill and then had to get out a knife to break up the iceberg so she could use a straw. She had hidden the ice pick, until the kids got bigger, and now, had no clue where she'd put it.

"Janey, you will get wrinkles around your mouth if you keep using a straw," she told herself. "Just use the kid's old toddler cups. No, wait, you have to suck from those cups, too, don't you?"

≈ ≈ ≈

Janey got online and started reading sites, and they all said that half of all bottled water was tap water. *Go ahead and buy that spring water, and all its impurities. Take a chance on the one that claims to have stuff in it to make you strong and healthy and in all ways, hydrated.*

She'd stick with the pretend spring-fed water she'd already wasted good money on, while waiting for soft drinks to be marked down. She had divided the number of cans in each carton and come up with something hovering around thirty cents a can.

She felt like she was panning for gold in mountain creeks like those tourists in north Georgia. They paid landowners to be prospectors for a day, buying or renting pans and tramping up and down stream beds. One Saturday afternoon, Janey's son turned on some random internet post about a guy staking out some land to mine. He was scraping and digging with a bulldozer or backhoe and hit gold. One year he made more than a million dollars. The last scene had him handing his bag of gold over to the guy, who weighed it and made an offer.

Janey thought she'd go pan for gold, but what she'd really be doing was filling up her bubba cups and jugs with spring water. There was the gold.

If there were cattle rustlers and moonshiners, how about faucets? Janey decided she could buy a navy-blue jumpsuit, embroider her initials on the front pocket, and tell people she was a plumber, but she'd really just keep running the water outside into her big, honker tank and take it to the local bottler. Being an actual bottler would require an investment. Being a plumber would require a second jumpsuit for her father, who happened to be an excellent plumber, and painting the word plumber on his pickup truck. Heck, she thought, they could go camping and siphon creek water just as easy and have more fun. No one would care if she didn't stand up straight because she'd be crouching by the water. It would be a stealthy operation, a *Thunder Road* kind of business with an old Ford, vintage nineteen fifties rigged up just like that of Robert Mitchum, who also had a liquid business.

WASIOTO

Catherine Moore

I am the river flowing west from Appalachia to converge with the great Ohio. My movement is steady, mostly below reed line. Marshes are the first to know—the wandering look of dark water in twilight, its natural call to a fury path. Brethren of river, creek, or stream, we are always at a flood stage.

Watershed (April 28, 2010)
In early Chinese maps there exist images of sea monsters.
They mark the wisdom, "there be dragons out there."
These symbols swam on maps of seafaring peoples,
But what of the warnings in river waters?
Of the great beast hidden between their banks?

Along the limestone bluffs of the Mississippi
Native Americans etched the *Piasa* in cautionary murals—
Fevered red eyes, horn-headed, calf-sized bodies
Covered with scales, ending in a long winding fish tail—
This dragon-bird warned travelers of the river's evil spirit.
Even in a long dry spring . . . when only the trickling reminds
What once receded will rise.

Daddy lifts a final shovel into the last sandbag, which he tosses into the back of his pickup, destined for grandma's place. Sand-full plastic bags

in a magical wall already surround our house. After he drives off, I play
with the spade on the sand pile, loving its rustle of metal against the small
grains. It sounds like the work Daddy does—heaving and wise.

Bankfull (April 30—10:38 a.m.)
"Watch for the avian cloud.
When all the birds of the woods,
The meadows, and high mountains
Form a cloud flying North to South,
That will be the sign. Birds move first.
I tell you, follow the animal's path away
For they know when land will disappear."

A levee's tipping point is reached in a flash. One fast moment snaps
off the television as the power cuts out. Completely. Not just her house
but all the homes around. Neighbors come outside looking at cloudy skies,
wondering what is happening. A police patrol weaves through the hollow,
telling everyone to go to higher ground. My son said that yesterday, she
remembers. There is no phone line for calling.

Minor (May 1—12:39 p.m.)
Native names advise on a river's temperament—
Chicopee means "violent river,"
Wewoka, "barking water"
And Susquehanna "swift river from the mountains."
When you dwell riverside to the Cumberland,
Its name gives no counsel.

The light acts strange when I open the basement door, as if being
reflected. "Yes, like a halo on water," I tell Mama. Then odds and bits like
paper boxes, my toys. She cries out my Daddy's name. I cry out for my rag
doll—her swollen face floating in the dark water. "Overwash," Daddy con-
firms. He wades in slowly to gather items not yet taken by water. "How?"
Mama repeats. We carry up the Christmas ornaments before floodwa-

ters swallow the basement. "Water deepens where it has to wait," Daddy replies, over and over.

Moderate (May 2—9:30 a.m.)
When waters covered the earth
And kept rising, the trees lost their branches
In the drowning. Every useless limb swept away.
The voice was heard again: "I shall send a web-toed creature
At home on land and in water,
With light and dark,
Through conscious and unconscious."
Into this purge and purgatory
A turtle entered the water and disappeared.
The sign-seekers waited
Through the uprooting and sinking,
Vigilant for the return.

Mama tells Daddy to move the dog's bed upstairs. From their bedroom doorway, I hear the whispers—*waded through chest-high water, currents nearly swept them away, people plucked off the tops of cars.* Mama comes to me for a goodnight kiss. We look out my bedroom window. The only thing we can see is water, pouring in sheets. Our yard surging like ocean waves. "Mama, are we gonna die?"

Major (May 2—4:19 p.m.)
If the dead become rain clouds,
They burst with their own tears.
A gray canopy cries above, beneath
It trembles, as every river desires a cloud.
Lonely wanderer, its winged song in air expires.
Because the heavens are in love with horizons
A cloud once spent will never come back
Like the waters, and the drowned—
We remember with glass teardrops.

Human voices become echoes across floodwaters. She stays put while people leave their homes, tossing random items onto makeshift rafts. When traffic quiets, the current becomes her companion. Along with a dark night, a damp wool blanket, and a loaded gun. She wakes to a series of loud pops—down the rivered street a whole house moves in the current past her place. There are no visible souls, only a swell of objects and secrets floating away in the sudden river. Until she sees a distant figure paddling a canoe. She fires her weapon and the shadow stops. "Do you see me?" A moment. A flashlight. "Yes," he answers. "Help," she cries.

Record (May 3—6:00 p.m.)

We smell it. Everywhere. Dankness. Then as the river forgets the rain, sewage. Everything pushes up without warning. It pools around us. There is always something in the water. "Snakes," Mama warns, "don't touch a thing." Not the debris washed curbside, or the damage Daddy brings up from our basement—carpet, playthings. "Neighbors have it worse," Daddy says. I sit next to the moldy hand of Raggedy Ann and try not to cry. Her terrified face stained with unknown organics. I hear Grandma whisper to herself, "the sky is never so pretty as after a storm." Daddy turns on a portable radio for her favorite music to play.

The land reappeared and its people emerged.
They saw nothing but loss, and they wept.
During the night, green grass sprung wide
And deer came back to graze on it.
The second night while they slept, trees
Sprouted to feed them and to fuel the fires.
After the third eve, came hard-blowing winds
to dry the earth and spread the seeds.
Everything that rises must recede.

Author Notes. Wasioto *"Wah-see-OH-tuh"* was the Native American name for the Cumberland River. While this is a fictitious work, I cite the following for inspiration and sourced materials: *Liquid 615* by Michael

Allison; "In Our Own Words," Nashville Public Library; and Native-Languages.org.

Poem commissioned and previously published by the Metro Nashville Arts through the Bonnaroo Works Fund Grant—written for the public art piece Liquid 615 a remembrance of the Nashville flood of 2010.

Delta

THE MANY NAMES OF

JILLYN

Harpeth River Writers

*The nine writers who brought this collection together decided to also collab-
orate on one story. A setting and a murder victim were chosen, but no one
knew how the mystery would unfold. After one member of the Harpeth River
Writers wrote a section, they passed it on to the next. Here is their creation.*

One Month Before the Reunion

Amherst

Amherst Mayhew arrived at the Red Bottle Café in Palo Alto, CA, selecting
a booth at the back. He felt on top of his game when his caffeine-to-
blood ratio achieved a post-workout feeling, without the morning run. As
Bureau Chief of *Vanity Fair*, he reflected on meeting the "Queen of Silicon
Valley" at last. Maybe the tech maven agreed to be interviewed because
we were only two blocks from Shamrock Systems HQ. He glanced at his
antique Hamilton wristwatch—enough time to get a double espresso.

Jillyn K. Shannon shook the journalist's hand and slipped into the
padded seat across from him. "Never been in *Vanity Fair*, but subscribed
during its 80s resurrection," she said, unpacking her tablet and iPhone.

Amherst slid a latte across the table to Jillyn and said, "Your executive assistant tipped me off about your coffee predilections."

"Don't know what I'd do without Maureen. She's from South Boston. Irish Catholic. And, believe me, no one messes with Miss O'Sullivan. After ten years working with me, Maureen could run the company."

"I could tell. She texted me ten restaurant options for today's interview. Said Red Bottle's your favorite. Thanks for coming. Let's get started, shall we?" Amherst pushed *play* on his phone recorder and began. "Ms. Shannon—"

"Oh, please—it's Jillyn. We're both business veterans. No need to be formal."

"In that case, call me Am." He laughed, feeling his back muscles relax. "My parents saddled me with Amherst—family tradition. That's why I live in California instead of back East. Couldn't handle the over-the-top pretention of going by my full name. Can you imagine? My nod to the men in the family is wearing my grandfather's watch." He lifted his cuff to reveal the timepiece. "Speaking of names, that's a great place to start. Tell me about your middle name, Jillyn K. Shannon."

"K's for Kenmare."

"On Ireland's coast, isn't it?"

"Did your homework, I see," Jillyn said. "Here's my elevator speech."

"Don't rush on my account," Am interjected. "I've blocked out a couple of hours, and Maureen cleared your calendar. The editorial team proposed a JKS retrospective—a cover story."

"Hope they're not considering me for the magazine's International Best-Dressed list." Jillyn glanced at her flats.

"I know Silicon Valley types follow their own dress code. Makes sense. All night programming doesn't call for couture fashions."

"One of my walk-in closets features a color-coded assortment of heels—collecting dust. In elementary school, it was easy to spot me. Front row in class photos. I was the runt until my teenage growth spurt. Didn't get much better over time. Unlike Demi Moore. Remember the sensation—Demi sporting her birthday suit, eight months pregnant? Still riveting twenty years later." Jillyn wrapped her hands around her latte cup. "I caught *Vanity Fair*'s 95th retrospective while working in the LA cloning lab."

"One of my favorites, too. Received more mail—fan and hate—than from any other cover."

"Don't worry. I've ditched all my sweat pants," Jillyn said. "I digress. Want me to go back to your first question?"

With a quick nod from Am, she continued. "You asked about my middle name, Kenmare. It's where my grandparents lived. A two-story stone cottage complete with a thatched roof and widow's walk. I spent summers with them before starting Franklin High. My Gran, may she rest in peace, galvanized the best part of who I am. While I milked her cows, she'd whip up Irish soda bread, pulling it steaming from the oven."

"Never eaten soda bread."

"I'd offer to bake you some, but who am I kidding?" With a wistful look, she added, "You know our twenty-four-hour global world. You're living it, too. We're both in the public eye. I'd prefer to spend more time on the beach."

Am nodded in agreement. "My ideal is the countryside, not the sand. I'd like to be a gentleman sheep farmer."

"You'd fit right in. Most everyone in Ireland keeps sheep. Wouldn't have pegged you as the farming type, though."

"Life is full of unexpected turns," Am said in a taunting tone.

Jillyn twitched and widened her eyes, as though she suspected he might know something he shouldn't, but she clamped her lips shut short of commenting. "One afternoon," she continued, "I followed Gran to the sea rose bushes growing wild by the ocean. Gran'd say, 'mind the thorns' as she snipped off the rosehip fruit. We'd fill baskets to make enough rosehip jam to keep the village jumble sales stocked."

Pausing a beat, Jillyn commented, "I hate it when friends hand me their phone and say, 'Swipe through our summiting Everest shots.'" She trailed off and powered up her iPad. "But since *you* asked, you'll have to deal with it." Her broad smile made it to her eyes, as she held out her device. "Here, meet Gran. And don't let her apron fool you. She's a firecracker."

"You look like her, but I can't imagine you in an apron." Am cocked his head, anticipating her jab.

"I have several, I'll have you know. Pains me to keep them packed away. Only time I'm in my kitchen is to pour a cup of coffee on the way to the office. I regret Gran never got to see how I'm shaping the tech world. Or to know the company's name and logo inspiration came from her Belleek china—decorated with shamrocks."

"You continue to keep Apple and Microsoft on their toes."

"Thanks for stating the obvious," Jillyn said with a wicked grin. "And here's my favorite shot of Grandpa." She gestured to her iPad. "'Don't get smacked by the boom,' he'd bellow from the dock. For the record, I never whacked my head. Is this the kind of material you're looking for, Am?"

"For a 'this is your life' feature, it'll play. Readers enjoy our in-depth coverage, especially the behind-the-scenes view of a female billionaire. Consider yourself in the Oprah and J.K. Rowling camp." Am smiled, revealing a dimple in his right cheek, and continued the interview. "You were by the dock," he prompted.

"Right. I snapped this pic before going aboard. We'd tack along the coast. Before I got too sunburned, he'd drop anchor, and we'd head to a pub for fish and chips. Grandpa loved the local ale. Red Kerry came in garnet bottles with gold Celtic lettering emblazoned on the label. I'd peel the stickers off to press into my scrapbooks.

"Often, I'd slip down to the beach and find sea glass rubies in the wet sand. Over the years, Gran and I filled vases with hundreds of polished pieces. I've wondered if Grandpa rowed out in the night to jettison mounds of broken beer bottles overboard. Quite the trickster, my Grandpa. I'll never know."

"Sounds like ideal childhood summers—until the accident—when you lost your parents," Am said in a sober tone.

Jillyn nodded, then spoke in a rehearsed manner. "Both were killed by a drunk driver on Mulholland Drive. They'd flown out for a law conference during Dad's tenure at Vanderbilt Law School—not long after I dropped out of Cal Tech. The night of the wreck, I'd planned to drive into LA to meet them for dinner at Chez Panisse. Then I got the call about the crash.

I'll never get over losing my parents, but I'm a champion compartmental-izer. It's a necessity—a survival skill." Jillyn glanced down at the floor, then back up at Am. "Can I say something off the record?"

In a fluid motion, Am pressed *pause* and looked at her with intent. "Of course."

Jillyn surveyed the café, noting the thinning lunch crowd. Lowering her voice, she said, "Do you ever wish you could just step out of your life and spin the moon backward? Start over—like shaking an Etch A Sketch clean."

"Most every *damn* day," Am said. "I'm with you."

Jillyn seemed pleased with his honesty. She searched his eyes, as if she wanted, needed, to say more, to reveal an innermost thought. Or maybe a secret.

He turned the recorder back on. He needed to remain on a professional level. "Now, let's get current. Are you seeing anyone? You've been notori-ously silent in the 'who's zooming who' department."

"Not right now," she said with a slight hesitation. "I've been tempted, sure. But it's not high school where you could bumble your way through, experiment, and make throwaway decisions . . . like skinny dipping." Jillyn threw her head back and laughed. "With someone you thought could be *your* one. Remember when you didn't take yourself so damn seriously?"

She changed her mood back to a serious and thoughty one, Am observed. Like something was playing out in her mind.

Jillyn thrummed her fingers on the table. "Next month, I head to Nashville for my twenty-fifth high school reunion. Maybe I *can* turn back time."

The Day Before the Reunion

Joe Lee

Facing a late-June afternoon sun, Stick and I were cruising in on I-40 past Percy Priest Lake, just east of Nashville. A jet swooshed over the top of us—bet it didn't clear us by a hundred feet. Shook my pickup like a heavy wind.

Stick laughed and stretched his neck back to look beyond me so he could see it descend into Nashville International. "Bombardier Global 7000. That baby costs 'bout seventy-five mil. Will haul your rugged ass from New York to Australia without refueling. Cream of the crop."

I never questioned anything Stick said about airplanes. He'd been a contract pilot with Bowen Aero Executive Services out of Smyrna before a redheaded stripper and two kilos of Santa Marta's Columbian Gold hidden in his flight bag made him persona non grata. "If it's got wings, I can fly it," he used to brag. Now he just rides around with me in my pickup.

"Reckon who owns it?" I asked.

"Bet your boots whoever flies in that thing is a heavy hitter. Got a quick look at the logo painted on the fuselage. Looked like a four-leaf clover settin' on a thumb drive."

Dodging potholes and lost tourists, I took the 440 loop around Nashville.

Stick jabbed away at his Samsung Galaxy 9 like a man playing an African thumb piano. "Got it. That is the logo of a major Silicon Valley software company. Shamrock Systems. Been hearing about them. They are scaring the pants off Microsoft." He continued stabbing the phone's keyboard. "Whoa. The brain behind the company is a Nashvillian."

"Bet it's a Vandy grad. Asian, more than likely. What's his name?"

Stick glanced at me and grinned. "It's a she. Jillyn K. Shannon."

"Really! I graduated high school with a girl with that same name. Franklin High School. Class of '93."

"Y'all ever date?"

"Couple of times. She was nearsighted. Sandy-haired. Freckles. Geeky. Flat-chested. I worried she was a drag on my reputation. 'Sides, she wasn't much fun."

Stick punched me in the ribs with his thumb. "Bingo, Joe Lee, old buddy. Google lists her as a '93 Franklin High School grad. Missed your chance. You could've been flyin' high in that Bombardier today drinking Dom Perignon something-or-other outta a skinny-neck glass and not knocking around in this ratty truck sucking warm Budweiser from an aluminum can."

"You forgot to say—and with a redneck!"

"Yeah, and with a redneck. But at least, I ain't a drag on your reputation."

≈≈≈

I dropped Stick off at his trailer park. He checked his mailbox, then the ones on either side of his, just in case the mail carrier screwed up.

The sun was half submerged in the timber along the Harpeth River when I got home. I opened my sixth beer of the day and sat on the patio watching night birds skimming across the placid surface of the river.

Damn! Old flat-chested, geeky Jillyn Shannon. Who would have thought it? No one ever saw her crack a book—not a high school book, that is. She kept her nose poked in books written in German with page-long math formulas. Shamrock Systems. Made sense. She had claimed her folks came from Ireland.

Well, dog my cats! She is here for our high school class reunion.

The Reunion

Bayley

First, we ate at the Loveless Cafe. Even with the promise of downhome barbecue for the class reunion picnic, Jillyn said this was an indulgence that had to happen.

"Bayley, I'm so happy you could meet me here before the small-talk festivities set in."

"It was a fantastic idea, because, honestly, I might have played hooky if you hadn't called. And I still go by Bay."

"Sweet! Then I'll be Jilly again."

The waitress dropped off a second basket of golden-topped buttermilk biscuits as a refill.

"I've lifted my gluten restrictions for the weekend. Remember how everything tasted so great as a child?" Jillyn took two biscuits out of the basket. "None of my personal chefs can recreate this taste. West Coast sensibilities," she muttered and dribbled sorghum onto the warm delectables. "Yum," she added, tasting and savoring the sweetness.

"Do you think this is under five hundred milligrams of sodium?" I frowned at the heap of fried chicken on the platter in front of her.

"You only live once." Jillyn picked up a drumstick. "I won't tell your doctor if you don't tell my trainer."

I lifted the other drumstick, and we toasted in agreement.

"For decades, my life's been splashed across *Time* magazine," Jillyn said, "but you—tell me everything about the life of Bay. And don't leave out any juicy details."

≈≈≈

"Thank you, hon." Jillyn affected her old accent while smiling at the waitress who cleared the table. "Bay, I'm sorry if it feels like I'm bolting." She reached over the condiments tray to pick up the check. "But I promised to meet someone before the picnic gets underway." She waved her Apple Pay screen at the waitress, who indicated "no" and hovered, waiting for a credit card.

Someone meaning Micki Gilliatt, I thought. I pictured a thirty-year-older version of the homecoming queen.

"A less important someone," Jillyn added. "Siri, where is my AmEx?" An in-bag flashlight brightened the contents of her envelope-style satchel. I leaned over to see a blue laser dot pointed on a small slit in the purse's suede interior.

"There!" Jillyn drew a plastic card out of the lining with a flourish.

"Whoa." The waitress echoed my astonishment.

≈≈≈

"It really was terrific to see you again, Jilly, and thanks for lunch," I said as we walked to the parking lot.

"Don't say that like it's goodbye. I want to see you later." Jillyn stopped at a low, sleek sports car in the front row—crimson red with a section of its glass-top roof removed.

"Where in Nashville do they rent those?" The word Tesla was under its rear spoiler.

"A rental? No, it's mine. I flew it in with me. I can't live without open air." She slid inside and tossed her hair.

It occurred to me, this car illustrated how far apart Jillyn K. Shannon was from those she'd left behind. Almost a sad thought. "Hey, remember how Jilly Jewel and Luna Bay always wanted to swim under the midnight sky? That secret dip we kept planning, but it always got foiled?"

We shared playful smiles.

"What exactly are you suggesting?" Jillyn's voice was full of mischief.

"The weather will be clear all night."

"Excellent. Though, I assume the park closes at sundown when our party will be escorted out."

"Um, the rest of the party will be outed. My brother, Forrest—you remember him?—he's the ranger there."

"No!"

I gave a slow nod, widening her smile. "He won't break the rules, but occasionally, he'll turn his head and look the other way."

After starting up her convertible, Jillyn turned and stage whispered, "I never leave a wish unfulfilled." She adjusted the rearview mirror. "I'd love to give you a lift, dearest Luna Bay, if only I hadn't made this appointment."

"It's okay. I have an errand to run anyways. So I'll see you there." I tried to keep my tone light as I waved to my old friend. On the amble toward my plain silver Honda, I considered whether to spend the extra hour browsing the stacks of used books at McKay's or heading now to Harpeth River State Park at Hidden Lake. I could check if the unseasonably dry spring left any water in our old mermaid lagoon.

Before pulling onto Highway 100, I saw Jillyn pause over her iPhone. The chime of a text message reached my phone: "mermaids in moonlight—tonight! Jilly Jewel."

≈≈≈

Lily pads dotted the far side, and frogs made themselves known in song. The perfectly smooth surface of its usual dark pewter self had disappeared into a watery reflection of tree branches with a tiny center pool of sky, the mirrored greener and bluer than the things themselves. As I slid my feet in the cool water, it looked like dipping a toe into a Monet—a Monet of our mermaid lagoon. Or, more accurately, the Mermaids at Hidden Lake—our imaginations once wild with the location, its name, and all things Nancy Drew. Most of the people at this reunion didn't know Jillyn all the way back to grade school like I had. Or how we had traded diaries and blood oaths. And people didn't realize how gracefully a naked Jillyn could swim through water. A ballet of flesh gliding across lush water.

≈ ≈ ≈

The mermaid afternoons were the natural consequence of freedom and secrecy. My oldest brother, Forrest, drove us girls to school each morning. On fine weather days, he took us instead to the state park. After picking through our lunch sacks, he'd tell Jilly and me to scram. Forrest spent the day at the pavilion along the Harpeth River—doing what, we didn't know—napping? Getting high? Sometimes he was met by his buddy Gordon and sometimes by his girlfriend of the month. Either way, the teens kept themselves occupied, and Jilly and I were free to roam the woods, which is how we found Hidden Lake. Any lagoon this beautiful called for mermaids—Jilly Jewel and Luna Bay were born.

The first time Jillyn dropped her clothes, she did it with a giggle. "You can't do anything halfway and be good at it," she said with profound fourth-grade wisdom before diving naked into the water. "Remember that!" she added when she rose back up. I removed my clothing and joined Jilly in what we re-named Forbidden Lake.

The mermaid frolics stopped by middle school. In seventh grade, Jilly Jewel was no more. My bestie went back to her full name, started sporting blazers, and joined the Future Business Leaders of America. When we saw each other across the school hallways, I thought Jillyn gave me an ebbing smile that meant she missed the free rein of those wilder times.

≈ ≈ ≈

I texted Jillyn: "the Forbidden is fabulous and waiting!" I sat dangling my legs in Hidden Lake and looking again across the water, where a bright sun turned its surface shimmering. The heat will keep rising, I thought, and scratched at my long-sleeved shirt, the kind of active wear that ladies wore to the gym in cooler months. Its black sleeves helped hide the scarring on my arms, though it made me extra warm on hot summer days like this, so I stayed under tree canopy. The braille of my past sins across my skin embarrassed me, now in a sober state. "Seven years clean," I whispered, then slipped my feet out and into strap sandals.

As I stood, my eye caught movement in a clearing on the other side of the lake. A woman. She looked familiar. A classmate maybe?

I wasn't good with groups—never had been—but the new Bay's voice, unwavering and without anguish, gave me confidence. Not as self-assured as my jet-setting friend Jillyn, but I was ready to get to the party, maybe circulate a couple of times. And the voices in the distance had risen over the last half hour, meaning there must be a substantial crowd gathered over at the party site. *Now or never.* I brushed off my skirt.

Twenty minutes tops, I encouraged myself as I set out. With a loud buzzing in my ears, I wondered if I was getting woozy from overheating already. No, the noise came from above. It was a little early in the summer yet for large swarms of insects, and this had the high-pitched whine of unnatural origins. I looked through the tree branches to see a mottled-gray drone hovering overhead, its whirring sound as ominous as its anonymous presence.

Joe Lee

Twenty-five years. Bet there will be a lot of bald heads, beer bellies, tummy tucks, and broad butts there. The reunion committee decided on an informal mixer at Hidden Lake Park on the day before the big blowout at Old Natchez Country Club. I lived about three miles up the Harpeth from the park, so they figured I was the logical one to be sure the group was adequately provisioned with beer. Heck, if I'd lived on the moon, the committee would've still chosen me to be the beer-tender. High school reputations can be tough to live down.

Jillyn Shannon. Wondered if she was married, and if not, wondered if she'd even remember me.

≈≈≈

At Kroger, I poured a hundred pounds of crushed ice into a coffin-sized Styrofoam cooler. The bag boy brought fifteen cases of beer out to my truck, and we shoved the cans into the ice like eggs in a giant carton. The boy looked at me, grinned, and said, "Gonna drink 'em all today?" I tipped him five dollars. The kid showed promise.

Hidden Lake Park cuddled around a bend in the Harpeth River like a winter-night lover. I turned west off McCrory Lane just past the manicured grounds of the Middle Tennessee Veterans Cemetery and entered the Hidden Lake parking lot. The place is called Hidden Lake for good reason—it's hidden. From the parking lot, you have to hike close to a mile to the lake. They say it's pretty. I wouldn't know.

I drove down the chert road to a grassy clearing where the course looped. Here, a tree line bordered the river, and steep steps went down to the water for canoe and kayak access. There was also an easier, slanted path to a narrow beach spot at the Harpeth's edge. The clearing is where they'd set up some tables for the food caterer, condiments, and coolers for soft drinks. People could mill about the clearing, walk down to the river, or hike the trail up to the lake. Perfect. Except for one thing. The park was state property, and alcohol was not allowed, except with a permit at certain venues, and Hidden Lake was not one of them.

But I had the answer to that problem. The park ranger happened to be the older brother of a classmate. He'd looked out for me when we were on the football team together. We were both linebackers, and he knew I'd inherit his position after he graduated. I tracked him down, told him our plans, and he agreed to swing by, say hello, and help himself to an icy drink. We left some things unsaid, but understood.

Earlier in the week, Stick and I had hauled two porta potties out to the park and set them up a respectable hundred feet from the parking lot and that same distance apart.

Stick spray-painted a large W on one and an M on the other. "Whatta you think, Joe Lee, reckon that's clear enough?"

"For as long as it matters," I said.

I backed the pickup into the shady grove south of the chert road, leaned a couple of oak planks against the tailgate, and slid the beer cooler to the ground. A buddy had painted a sign for me on a sheet of plywood: pre-pre-registration, with a large finger pointing to the woods.

≈≈≈

It was a little after two in the afternoon, and it would be four before the guests started arriving. In the summer, I'm a blue-jean-T-shirt-flip-flop kind of a guy. If the occasion is dressy, I wear a T-shirt with a pocket. I kept my fishing rod case, a pair of throwaway running shoes, and ragged cutoffs behind the seat of my pickup. Figured I'd go down to the river and work some of the deeper holes along the right bank. I'd fish an hour and still have time for a quick dip in the river and a change of clothes before everyone started arriving.

I'd seen three other vehicles in the park today. One was a black Cadillac Escalade parked near the entrance. Big barcode stickers on the windshield, back window, and the passenger-side window, as well as no dealer markings, indicated it was a rental—another bit of knowledge I'd picked up from Stick. The others were a plain, old silver Honda sittin' in the gravel lot and a fancy, red Tesla convertible parked off in the grassy field. I didn't worry about leaving the truck and beer unattended while I fished. Well, maybe a little about the beer. I dropped three cans in a mesh bag and set out along the path toward the river.

I stood waist deep in the Harpeth's blue water and cast a white Bomber downstream near a rock shoal. I waited. And drank. And watched turtles line up on a log. I twitched the rod twice and felt a tug. In the distance, car doors slammed. The soon-to-be revelers were arriving. It was such a peaceful afternoon, and the three beers on an empty stomach were creating a mild buzz. Perhaps I'd be late for the party.

I cranked the reel and whatever I'd caught came gliding under the water toward me. Heck. It was just a large, white cloth. I raised it out of the water. It was a reddish-stained white blouse with a Shamrock logo centered over a fancy three-letter monogram: *JSK.*

Court

This blasted reunion cost me a small fortune. I hoped the price of image would pay off. My law practice was in desperate need of cardiopulmonary resuscitation. If it weren't for the lowlifes that got sent to me as a court-appointed lawyer, I wouldn't have any law practice. You know that line you see on television when a cop arrests the bad guy: "You have the right to an attorney. If you can't afford an attorney, one will be provided for you." Those are the losers I get, and they are all guilty.

My investment for this reunion was four thousand dollars. Fifteen hundred a day for the rented canary yellow Lamborghini. I needed it for two days. Day one is this dumb picnic reception, and day two is tomorrow's fete at the country club. The other thousand is for the bimbo that I could pass off as my trophy wife. And yes, I met her as a client. Helped her beat a prostitution charge. Regardless, she was pretty damn hot. Heads turned when she walked into a room.

I wanted to test the limits of the Lambo but could never get it past ninety for truckers and squatters in the passing lane. Our exit was coming up, and as I downshifted, Bimbo—her name is Cheryl, so I guess I should call her that—asked, "Where are we? This is not the city."

No kidding. She's so freakin' dumb. I hope this doesn't backfire on me. I'll tell her to just smile and not talk.

"No, we are not in the city, Cheryl. We are in the country. But it's still Davidson County." I think. "You worried about the Nashville Vice Squad?"

She gave me a sour look.

The exit sign said Pegram. Pegram! This is a Franklin High School reunion, but we have our reunion all the way out in Pegram. Who's great idea was this? I went a short distance on McCrory Lane when I saw a sign for Hidden Lake. As I pulled into the parking lot, a black SUV nearly hit me, its tire spitting gravel as it sped past. Tinted windows prevented me from seeing the driver. Maybe it was a classmate who realized she wore the wrong dress. Whatever.

The only vehicles in the lot were a silver Honda and a hot-looking, red Tesla convertible. Humph. I think my Lamborghini tops a plug-into-an-electrical-outlet Tesla. I realized I was early, way too early. No grand entrance. I started to worry about stone chips hitting the Lamborghini and decided to park next to the Tesla on a grassy field about five yards out.

We got out of the car, and Cheryl frowned. "Why didn't you park in the parking lot, Mr. Sabastian?"

"Cheryl, I told you, don't call me that. I'm not your lawyer today. I'm your husband. You're my wife. Call me Court."

"I thought I was going to be your wife tonight." She gave me a smile and tilted her body with a hand on her hip.

"Yeah, that too. But for now, you're gonna pretend to be my wife. Remember?"

"Does that mean we argue about something?" Another coquettish smile.

"No. No arguing. You need to be lovey dovey. A lot of touchy-feely stuff. You know, your arm around mine." Arm candy, I thought.

"You mean like arm candy?"

"Well . . . yeah, if you want to call it that. And if anyone asks how we met, just say law school. But mostly, try to avoid conversations. Just smile."

As we walked through the parking lot, Cheryl teetered back and forth on the uneven gravel. Her high-heeled western boots were giving her balance problems. After telling her it was a picnic, she'd said she had just the outfit. When I picked her up, I thought Daisy Duke had made a comeback. She had the straw hat, checkered shirt showing lots of cleavage, and hip-huggin' shorts. I think she used to do a routine in them during her stripper days, before she moved up to a high-priced hooker.

We came to two signs, one pointing to the lake, the other to the river. "Let's try the river first," I said, and we followed the gravel road down to a clearing where a beat-up pickup was parked back at the edge of some woods. A footpath led to put-in stairs to the Harpeth River. The stair treads had been made of four-by-four boards with packed dirt in between the steps. Erosion had washed away much of the dirt, making our short descent treacherous. The overhang of trees blocked much of the river view, but from what I could see, there looked to be someone knee deep in the water wrestling a white alligator.

"Yo! Need some help down there?"

"You could say that. Who you?"

"Sabastian. Court Sabastian."

"Courtney! Yeah, Courtney, come lend me a hand. It's Joe Lee."

"You stay here," I said to Cheryl.

"Don't worry about that. I'm not goin' near no river. I can't swim."

"Here, take the key to the Lamborghini. I don't want it to get wet." A damp electronic key would present all kinds of problems. A tow truck, as well as the cost to replace the key. Probably looking at another thousand dollars by the time it was over.

I started to make my way to the rock shoreline. Joe Lee Whitaker. I always called him Joe Lee Half-Wit. Everyone called me Court, except for Half-Wit. From him it was Courtney, Courtney, in a singsong voice. Always mocking my name.

By the time I got there, he had what first looked like a white alligator, but now I could see it was a naked body. A woman's body. Lying on the stones and dirt at the edge of the water. I looked at Whit, then the body, then Whit again. "What'd you do?"

"I pulled her body outta the water, is what I did."

"No, I mean what happened?" I was flailing my hands and sucking in breaths. "Was this an accident?"

"Well, I don't know for sure, but a good guess would be a no. I'm not one of those SIU guys on TV, but based on those there marks where the skin is split open, I'd say she was stabbed, and that's usually not an accident."

"So, she didn't drown?"

"Sorry, Courtney, I haven't done the autopsy yet. But I think I can tell ya who it is. Does the name Jillyn Shannon ring a bell?" Half-Wit turned and walked away, one hand over his mouth, and the other on his stomach.

Jillyn. No, couldn't be. She was lying on her side. I rolled her onto her back and knelt on one knee so I could see the face. Hadn't seen her since graduation, but it was her, all right. Except she was cold, naked, and dead. Jillyn's name should be on my diploma instead of mine. Every day after school, I'd spend an hour in her bedroom getting tutored in math. She also tutored me on the fine art of kissing a girl. But it was mainly about the math. Algebra, freshman year, geometry as a sophomore, then trigonometry, and finally, calculus. She taught me enough to complete my homework and pass the tests. Since then, I've never used any of it.

I looked up to see Half-Wit standing over us, holding a white blouse. "I came early to get the beer ready and fish a little," he said. "Hooked this blouse instead of a fish. Reckon this here is a bloodstain. And here, this here Shamrock is her company's logo. She's very rich. Owns her own company, in case you didn't know. And this here's her initials." He pointed to her *JSK*.

"That would be her monogram."

"Whatever. You know, I used to date her. Had somethin' goin' for a while. But then I broke it off. Too bad for me that I didn't stick with her. Wouldn't you say?"

Hard to believe Jillyn dated Half-Wit. She never said anything to me about him. Maybe she was too embarrassed. The idea of her lips kissing his lips and then kissing mine made me shiver.

I closed my eyes to think about what I saw, glanced at the river, then looked at Half-Wit, who was staring intensely at me.

"Joe Lee, let me see if I got this right. You and our class billionaire show up in a remote area, where you may or may not have fished before, two hours before the reunion is scheduled to begin. And by the way, whose idea was it to have this affair in Pegram anyway? Wait, don't answer that yet. Let me continue. As fate would have it, you and the deceased previously had a secret romantic relationship that may or may not have ended badly."

"I told you I came to bring the beer, and it didn't end badly—"

"We know for sure it ultimately ended badly for you." I poked his chest with my index finger to let him think the stink of guilt was all over him. "You didn't get to share in her wealth. And then there is this important issue. Two witnesses observe you trying to either pull the victim's body ashore or possibly trying to push it out into the current where it may be washed down river." I knew Cheryl probably didn't see anything, but he didn't know that. "And finally, Joe Lee, could that fishing knife attached to your belt have been the murder weapon?"

Joe Lee stood motionless, eyes bugged, mouth agape.

"At this point, Joe Lee Whitaker, I would say you need a good criminal lawyer. But don't worry. I know just such a person."

Heather

My watch read two o'clock. I had an hour before calling an Uber. I'd been waiting for this day for months, and it finally arrived; yet there was more waiting to do. Wearing my best yellow dress, I sat on the bed, swinging my legs, and thought how sixty minutes equaled two episodes of "Saved by the Bell," my favorite show in high school and today and always. I placed a disc in my DVR.

It's odd. This had never happened to me before. I couldn't concentrate on the screen—too excited about seeing everyone. On Facebook, a lot of people said they were coming to the reunion. And Joe Lee would be there. He wasn't on social media, but he was getting the beer. Joe Lee was my Zack Morris—cute and nice and funny. He didn't pick on me like a lot did. And I had a gift for him. It was a baseball hat with the logo of the brewery where I work. Maybe that'd give him an idea to ask me out on a date. I still dreamed we'd go bowling and he'd kiss me good night. Yes, I can go on dates now. I am independent. I have a job, and I don't live with my mom anymore. Down Syndrome doesn't define who I am or will be. Mom made sure everyone knew that, including me.

Mary banged on my bedroom door. "Heather, you going to the party now? Can I see the yellow dress and the long purple one?"

"Yes." I opened my door to all her oohs and ahhs and added, "The purple dress is pressed, in the closet, and ready for tomorrow night's party. You have to wait."

Mary was one of three other women who lived in this home with me. We're independent. A nurse was always around because Mary needed help in the bathroom, but I don't. I could do everything myself except drive. And Mom still handled my money because I'd get confused sometimes, but she said I would learn it all soon enough.

Three o'clock. Time to text Ms. Stacy. She's an Uber driver who was also a nurse. When I texted her, she would turn her app on, then she'd drive me.

A few minutes later, I climbed into her black car. "Hello, Ms. Stacy."

"Hello, Ms. Heather. You look mighty fine."

"Thank you. I have a present for Joe Lee in this bag."

"That's right. The baseball hat."

"Everyone will be surprised how independent I am. Following my dreams."

"Yes, they will. Everyone is proud of you."

"I can have two beers. And in my purse, I brought my bottled water for later."

"Good. Have you heard from your mom?"

"Yes. She called yesterday. She will be back from the cruise on Tuesday."

"Did you get pictures of yourself in that pretty dress?"

"I took some selfies."

We chatted nonstop until we pulled into the Hidden Lake parking lot. I froze. My stomach ached. I whispered, "I can do this." Breathe in. Breathe out. "I can do this."

A fancy yellow car turned around in front of us. I waved at the pretty lady with the straw hat. She showed us her middle finger.

"Not cool," Ms. Stacy said. "But that's one hell of a nice ride—a Lamborghini. Did you know her?"

"No. She's a stranger."

"Hmm. There's only two cars here. You sure this is the right place?"

"Yes, I'm sure. I wanted to be early to talk to Joe Lee. I knew he'd be early because he's bringing the beer."

"Okay then. Well, I'll wait for your text to pick you up. Have fun. Don't do anything I would do."

I giggled with my hand over my mouth. "Thank you, Ms. Stacy."

Knowing Ms. Stacy, she would pretend to drive away and then sit in her car a few miles away.

I was glad I wore my flat sandals because the gravel wasn't fun to walk on. In front of me was one sign pointing to the lake and one pointing to the river. I chose the river because it had a road going to it.

I got to a grassy field and saw two men coming toward me. They were coming up from the river. One was talking on his phone, and the other was taking off a wet, white T-shirt.

"Joe Lee," I squealed. "It's you." I put my hand over my mouth and ran to him.

"Sorry. But—"

"I have a present for you. Open it." I handed him the gift bag. "I work there now."

"Do I know you?" Joe Lee hung his shirt over the crook of his arm.

"It's me, Heather."

"Right. Yes. What's this for?"

"Just a friend gift. Because we're going to be better friends."

As Joe Lee opened the bag and took out the hat, the other guy stopped talking on his phone and said, "Hey, it's Short-bus. What, nothing for me?" He glanced over my shoulder up the road toward the parking lot. "I'm going to check on Cheryl and my Lambo." He hurried away with his phone back at his ear.

"That's the meany, Court Sabastian. He got old."

"Yep, good old Courtney. Um. Thanks, Heather, for this." He put the hat back into the bag. "Um, there's been a . . . an accident. The cops and ambulance are comin'. You should go home."

"I'm independent now. I can know what's happening."

"I don't want to scare you. But, um, someone was killed. You shouldn't stick around."

"Oh, no! Dead?" I felt my eyes blinking fast. I took a deep breath to slow them down. "That's bad. Do we know who it is? Is it a classmate?"

"Remember Jillyn Shannon?"

"Kay. Yes. Oh, my God!" My breathing felt funny. Tears came to my eyes.

"Kay?"

"She let me call her that." I took more deep breaths.

"Ya alright?"

"Yes." I got my water bottle and took a sip. "I'm okay. I'm a strong woman. Kay's gone? Dead like Daddy? You sure?"

"It's her."

"We're favorite friends."

"You knew her well?"

"We exchanged Christmas cards every year." I pulled a Kleenex out of my purse. "Her address always changes, but she lets me know where she is. Always California. I know where that is. It's by the Pacific Ocean, and

it's pretty there. She wasn't coming to the picnic, just the party tomorrow."
I blew my nose. "We had secrets. Secret names and stuff."

"Secrets?"

Courtney returned and yelled, "That bitch stole my car!"

"Shit! That blows." Joe Lee crossed his arms, while still holding the gift
bag. "Heather here knew Jillyn."

"How? You weren't in any of our normal classes."

"Yes, I was. My mom made sure I was." I wiped my eyes. I wanted to
cry more for Kay, but I couldn't because I was a grown-up now. I stood
straighter. "Kay was in all my art classes."

"Kay? What the hell! You don't even know who we're talking about."

"Shut up, Courtney. Kay's the name she called Jillyn—her middle initial,
duh."

Joe Lee was making me feel strong. "Yeah, Courtney. And my name is
Heather, not Short-bus. And Kay and I were friends with secrets. So there."

"Secrets? What secrets?"

"I can't say. I promised. I never even told my mom."

Joe Lee patted my shoulder. "You'll have to tell the cops, or they'll drag
it out of ya."

"Right," Court said. "Practice on us first, Short—um, Heather, is it?"

I took a step back. "I don't know." By focusing, I would know what to
do. When anyone pressed, my response was always no. "I promised Kay
I'd never tell, so no."

"But if ya know somethin' that would find the killer, you'd be helpin'
Kay—helpin' your friend."

Joe Lee was nice, and he smiled at me, but I couldn't tell on Kay. "No. I
keep my promises."

"Heather, just spill it." Courtney spat when he talked.

"What'd Kay want ya to do?"

Joe Lee's eyes seemed to hypnotize me. After controlling my blinking, I
said, "I think it would be okay to tell you about the pranks. They made her
very happy."

Joe Lee and Court both nodded.

"Well, Kay would use me as a decoy. That's what she called it. She'd pretend to be helping me. Then with strings and wires and buttons and knobs, she'd make things happen."

"Like what?"

"Kid's chairs would fall apart while they sat in them. Windows would open. And something important would break, and the girl next to it would get blamed. That sort of thing. We did one every week senior year."

"Jillyn did all that? What the hell? Thought it was Blotto's doin'." Courtney's phone rang. "Talk to me." He stepped away.

"Heather, that was twenty-five years ago. Doesn't mean anything now."

"She made a lot of people mad, and they never knew it was her." I covered my mouth and cried. "She's going to be mad that I told."

"No, Heather. She'd want you to help, and tellin' will help find who hurt her."

"What do we do now?"

"We need a beer." He walked toward his truck, parked in the grassy field at the edge of the woods.

I followed. "You think Kay would want me to tell all her secrets?"

"Secrets can't help her now." He opened the door, placed my gift bag on the passenger seat, and hung his wet shirt on the truck door.

"Do you watch 'Saved by the Bell' on TV?"

"What?" He picked up a black T-shirt off the truck floor, shook it out, and put it on. "Beer's in the cooler."

I heard cars pull into the gravel parking lot and doors slam, and I heard sirens off in the distance.

Courtney was next to us again, smelling of sweat. "Here comes the class of '93 and the cops. Hand me one of those cold ones."

Tamara

I stepped off the walking trail into the shade of an Osage orange tree. This I would not have known but for a small rustic sign placed near the roots by some fervently nerdy park naturalist. It was farther to the lake than I thought, more than half a mile.

I whipped out my silver compact mirror (a gift from Bill, or was it Tom?)

to inspect the damage—perspiration beads on my upper lip and only a little smudging of eyeliner. Good makeup has its privileges. A few tissue blots and I was back on the trail. I'd taken an Uber out early to do a drive-by of a property I'd been watching near the interstate. The driver, Mike, promised to be back in few hours. He'd be at Starbuck's, he said, working on his latest crime novel.

Twenty-five years. It was hard to believe we were all once that young. I checked for cell service and scrolled through my contacts for "The Two Catherines Catering."

"Hey, I'm just confirming you're on the way with the food and tables. . . . I know, I know. It was short notice. Like I told you yesterday, my classmate Sandy was supposed to take care of all that, but she's in the hospital. Got her appendix yanked out. Poor thing called me from pre-op. Anyway, thanks so much for making this happen. . . . Yes, exit 192. Shoot me an invoice by text, okay?"

Back in the Franklin High days, I would never have dreamed I'd end up as a commercial real estate development moguless. I was really hoping for something better. Funny, it was always Jillyn and me, neck and neck. We were the only two chicks in calculus, the top scorers on the SAT—she beat me by a measly ten points. Being "smart girls," we hung out a lot by default. Jillyn, the gawky, freckled girl who wore huge gold-rimmed glasses, and me, the intense brunette who was a head taller than most of the guys. That Jillyn had a wild side, but never got caught. I played by the rules, which may explain why things turned out the way they did.

She nabbed the scholarship to Cal Tech I was hoping for, so I settled for a free ride at Vanderbilt. Right out of college, I took a summer gig with a commercial real estate maverick in town. The rest is history. John taught me all the tricks to cinching deals and, with my head for numbers, I became the heir apparent when he stepped down.

All the while, though, I kept up with Jillyn through *Forbes*, *Fortune*, *Bloomberg*, all the business rags. She had smarts, opportunities, and a crazy streak. For every million I made, she made fifty. Like they say, play by the rules and you lose.

It had been ten years since I'd seen her. We met for dinner at Moonshadows Malibu while I was on a business trip. The conversation was friendly, but stilted. Jillyn complimented my outfit and my success. But there was a faint, unnerving aura about her. Smugness, maybe.

After I emerged from the woods and hit the trail, I noticed the parking lot—empty when I arrived—was jammed with several cars parked at all angles. I saw a red Tesla in a grassy field. There was the shrill sound of sirens in the distance.

I stopped at the parking lot to catch my breath. A couple that had just arrived was headed down the gravel road toward the river. Another car pulled up.

"Tamara Comstock! Is that really you? I see your signs all over town, girl." A blond woman whose face meant nothing to me got out of a Prius. "It's me, Suzanne. I won the Betty Crocker award at graduation, remember? And here's Ruth, too. Still got her cheerleader figure." A slim woman waved from the other side of the car.

"Oh, yes. Of course. How are you?" I bent over to receive hugs.

We walked together to the river. A crowd was gathered near the canoe launch.

Suzanne's eyes widened. "What's going on over there? Everybody's looking at something. Oh, geez! Is that a body?"

By the time we reached the scene, a man in a black shirt and wet cutoff jeans was spreading a blue tarp over a still form on the ground. That had to be Joe Lee. He hadn't changed a bit, just a little older and scruffier. Behind him was a linen-suited man with slicked-back hair. I remembered Jillyn saying she made out with him when they were supposed to be studying. Kurt. Kirk. No, Court was his name. Courtney.

"Not fancy, but it's all I had in the pickup," Joe Lee said, pointing to the tarp, then he looked up. "Tamara! Lord, you look, you look great. I'm a sight. Got all wet fishing a body out of the river. " Apparently, Joe Lee and Court had carried the body up the bank.

"It's Kay—I mean, Jillyn, under there!" An awkward girl in a bright yellow dress stepped forward and pointed to the tarp. Her bottom lip quivered pitifully. "Your friend, Jillyn."

"Stay back, Heather," said Joe Lee. "Cops are almost here. We all need to stay back."

I leaned over the body and spoke a few words, then stood quickly. The food truck lumbered off McCrory Lane onto the gravel road. Crowding its rear bumper were two police cruisers and an ambulance, pull-over bull-horns blasting. I hurried to direct the food truck into a space. As I left, I heard Court's voice behind me.

"*What* did she just say?"

Heather answered, loudly. "She said 'Nice work.' I heard her."

Then Court again. "Oh, my God . . . ."

Mary Ann

Oh great, I thought. They hired a food truck. Twenty-fifth reunion for Franklin High School, and they have us going down by the river with a rigged-up truck. Nice touch. What could go wrong there? The Franklin version of a hot dog stand. I hit Puckett's restaurant this morning because I knew it would be a long day, one I'd waited for all those years. What was it we always said? Not.

I was hunkered down in the woods up the bank from the river, wait-ing—still one of the odd girls.

Whoever had planned the river thing evidently didn't know what hap-pened there our senior year. I thought everyone knew. Well, a lot of things happened. Several not so high schoolish, either. The last time there was a party here, things did not go well. Those of us who were here then should've skipped this river picnic and waited for the Saturday night party.

Then came the police. I think old Ricky Rice had joined, and the laughter hasn't dimmed in all these years. What a tool, or maybe not so much. He had a uniform and a gun, in Franklin. I thought, "Hey, Ricky, if I do see you, I bet you look fine."

I pulled a bandana from my front pocket and slapped it onto my face like a jellyfish locks onto your feet in the ocean. The rag was good camou-flage, although I doubted that anyone could see me hunched in the brush.

Still, they were passing by, uncomfortably close. The rag was soaked. So was I, inside the waders.

I kept wiping my face, as the police slammed on brakes, relieved when they didn't notice me. There was a growing little cluster of people in the grassy area of the gravel loop near the riverbank, and the police were waving them back. It was at least an hour before the event was to begin. I figured they were the volunteers—doing what, I couldn't imagine. The food truck was parked and setting up, but that was it.

While the onlookers continued to cluster and irritate the police, I was more relieved that I'd gotten a Pro Wader Bag to stash my gear. A discerning fisherman might have appreciated my decision to spend thirty bucks for a Field & Stream product, but I got it at Dick's Sporting Goods, which I guess was politically incorrect. Who knew these days? I had to lean over to drop a few corked test tubes in it, so I grabbed a handful of some kind of bush for balance.

Here was my thought process during all the excitement. I wondered who decided to get rigged up in camouflage for a high school reunion—any kind of reunion. Me. I thought it might stir people up a bit, keep the party lively. With this crew, it wouldn't take much.

There he was, my favorite cop, so I decided to hang back. That's when the ambulance arrived. I was familiar with that kind of transportation. Had a few rides in one of those, only mine was camouflage green.

I was crouching now, but needed to move, so I tried to stand up, but stumbled backwards. My foot was asleep, so I did a graceful half-sit, half-fall into a trench-shaped foxhole. I'd found it earlier in the week and decided it was the perfect place to set up my own little headquarters, kind of a bivouac. Some kids out playing army probably dug it up. All I wanted to do was test the water and find out who was currently dumping what. Yep, while a few ladies in my class were out in the world, cleaning up financially in IT or real estate, I was a local environmental volunteer with the water conservancy. I'm just as smart, but not as eager, or needy. Iraqi veteran at your service. You sell dirt, while I left a leg behind in the sand. Where's the irony there?

I thought maybe I should hike back east up the ravine and get lost in

the woods before anyone spotted me. Oh, for the love of all things private, there was our spokesperson for bad news everywhere. Who would've
thought she'd climb out of Industrial Arts and end up at a television station? Print journalist gone rogue on the local station. Saw her name in *The
Tennessean*, way back when, and then she popped up on TV. Papers no
one read were folding, literally. They were even selling the old newspaper
building down on Broadway. Local television stations were scrapping veteran newscasters and reporters. Things were changing. What's good now
used to be bad, and what's bad now used to be good.

Who ran into the woods when a Franklin High School alum lay still on
the ground? I thought, why not, they were filming extra footage for the
next night's broadcast.

Court was drooling all over Tamara Comstock. Seriously, she should've
been a rocket scientist, not out peddling acres of earth instead of moon
rocks. A loss to humanity if anyone had asked me, although I never was
anything except a most unreliable judge of character or talent.

One thing I did know, I killed some ISIS rebels. IEDs? I wrote the book.
Crappy military equipment? I was available to fill anyone in on that. Black
Sentry or Rock or Guard, whatever that company was. Those folks have
made a bundle, but they have blood on their hands. I thought about it, but
they weren't interested in a vet with less than all her body parts intact.
Dumb people. I've run marathons and learned some mountain climbing
out West. I've seen men with two legs who would have served our country
so much better as desk jockeys.

I thought about all that while people still hovered over Jillyn and realized I was revving up to get angry and then mean. I decided I needed to
make my appearance at that point. I needed to forget the police and ambulance. I worried the paranoia would set in, among other things my therapist has mentioned. I checked out Suzanne, who I knew still had to be as
weird as me. I wondered if the slouch hat was too much. At last, I'd gotten
the boots off, and the waders would drop when I stood up. Short list: check
the water, wear off-kilter outfit, and take care of business—long overdue.
If I could just get the waders all the way off and the army boots on right. I
decided I had to be nervous if two slugs of whiskey made me this clumsy.

Jillyn K. Shannon, third row, second seat in the almost-end-of-the-alphabet homeroom seating chart with Mrs. Mashburn. I did a deep dive on the internet and found where they had lived in Battlewood Estates. I knocked on a few doors until I hit on the door of a widow in the Shannon's old neighborhood who'd lived there forever.

"Oh, such a sweet girl, a real darling and smart as could be, but she was shy, never tried to sell me popcorn for the high school like the other kids did, or Girl Scout cookies," the woman said. "I don't think I ever saw her in any kind of uniform, not soccer or softball. She always had an armload of books, more than the other kids. What's she doing now?"

All that money, and she never offered me a dime. Conned me out of ten thousand dollars for her startup. That was my bonus money for signing on with the United States Marine Corps. Got me all excited. Then walked away, said she lost it. Yeah, Jillyn was a risktaker and made a great robber baron. I'd love to know who gave her more seed money. I will always believe she lived off mine. How can someone so successful get away with it for so long? I planned to grab our TV star at some point, when she wasn't mugging for the camera, and give her some background on the way some people get rich.

I bet no one but me figured out the truth. Being obsessed and maybe having a bit of PTSD were great incentives. Her shamrock company was going belly up—all of it a sham. She was supposed to be in the air before the unforgiving moneylenders realized what happened. Who knows where she would have headed, but I bet it's way south, an island maybe. A Global pilot, and Iraq veteran, would have flown her out sooner than the posted itinerary. Named Nikolas. Seemed like a nice guy. Said he'd keep in touch. Wonder if he'll still take off when she doesn't show. Ah, he'll know what happened by then. Hope he goes anyway.

Her headline won't read, "Jillyn K. Shannon Missing." Her headline will read, "Jillyn K. Shannon Dead."

≈≈≈

I stumbled out of the brush toward Suzanne and Ruth. "Hey, Suzanne, Ruth, it's me, Mary Ann Smith—from home ec. You don't have to salute me, just help me straighten out the pants on the fake leg. Yeah, a lot of years and still mad as hell about everything."

"Aw, Mary Ann, I didn't forget you. I have clippings about you. You're a hero, or heroine. Whatever." Suzanne propped me up so I wouldn't fall. I decided I'd maybe had more than two shots of Black Jack. "Did you see what happened to Jillyn?" Suzanne said. "Someone stabbed her. Isn't it just awful?"

"Yeah, yeah, too bad, but first, can you run back in those woods where I walked out? I stashed my Jack Daniels there. It's with a bag full of fishing boots and stuff."

"I'll get it," yelled Ruth.

We would all need a drink.

Peri

I stared at the nametag with my Franklin High graduation picture and felt nauseated—both at the photo of the naïve, young black girl whose smile hid years of being bullied, and at the prospect of seeing my tormentors again.

"You don't have to go to the reunion," I told myself for the umpteenth time.

"Yes, Peri, you do. Show them you're more than just who they've seen on TV," I told the confident, no-nonsense Channel 11 news reporter staring back from the makeup mirror.

This back-and-forth argument had simmered for nearly two months—why I shouldn't or should go. Curiosity, I suppose, was why I decided to attend the mixer. And to confront the past.

Like every school, our class had its share of cliques—the smart ones, the pretty ones, the jocks, the nerds, and the cool kids. Then there were the weird ones—the goths, the druggies—and a few you knew would, or should, wind up in jail or dead. Like the Mean Girls. Some kids called them Jilly Jewel and Luna Bay, but to me they'll always be Chilly Jilly and her BayBay. God, how I hated them. And *him*.

I was a favorite target of the Mean Girls. Chilly Jilly, especially. On the outside, she was a gawky, freckled girl who wore huge gold-rimmed glasses, but she didn't fool me. I saw her dark side more than once. And now the Queen of Silicon Valley and rolling in dough. Maybe I should do an exposé on her. If the public only knew the real Jillyn. And Bayley.

It started with the day I told BayBay how I got my name—that my mom named me Periwinkle because I was born with Blue Baby Syndrome and needed lifesaving pediatric heart surgery. By lunchtime, nearly everybody was calling me Periwinkle, or Winkie, or Peri-Scope, or Baby Blue, or whatever they thought funny. It was light teasing, but when you're fifteen, skinny, and insecure, there's no such thing as harmless name-calling. And when they saw how hurt I was, their claws came out. And then their lies began.

That settled it. I'd go to the mixer to prove that I'd overcome every obstacle in my life, including them. But I wasn't going to wear that damned graduation nametag. I grabbed my Channel 11 ID and headed for the car.

≈≈≈

It was a beautiful day, driving away from downtown, but a chill ran through my body as I pulled off the interstate at the McCrory Lane exit. I hadn't been out here in years, and the mental image jarred me like I'd sideswiped a deer or run over a possum.

A quarter of a century earlier, on a day much like this one, but closer to sunset, I was running through the thickets, away from the water, horrified by what I'd seen. A low branch swatted my face as I ran for my car in terror. The next day, I was warned—threatened, really—to never tell anyone, and I'm ashamed to say I didn't have the courage to speak up.

At least he won't be there. Don't know if I could handle that.

The image of his face faded before I entered Harpeth River State Park at Hidden Lake. While walking toward the access path to the river, I heard a siren in the distance.

Those hackles that reporters sometimes get when they cover a big story were up, and bells were going off like an alarm clock. Then I realized it sounded more like the buzzing of a swarm of bees and looked up. Was that a drone flying over the trees before disappearing? At that moment, screams broke the silence.

I rushed down the path and saw my classmates near the canoe launch. All older, but still recognizable. Joe Lee, a head above the others. He was surrounded by a cluster of people, all cringing as if in shock.

When I drew closer, I saw a white shirt on the ground. Somebody said it belonged to Joe Lee, but he was wearing a black shirt. They were all staring at a blue tarp with two naked legs sticking out spread-eagled.

The siren sounded closer, as a preoccupied woman looking around in all directions smiled after she recognized me.

"Oh, hey, Periwinkle"—*after all these years*—"glad you made it."

I was glad I'd worn my news badge. I grabbed Tamara's arm and pulled her away from the others to behind a tree. I got out my phone and took a few photos, then put it on video mode.

"Tam, I came out here today as Periwinkle, but right now I'm Peri Holmes, reporter for Channel 11 News. Tell me what's happened here."

Before she could answer, another woman joined us, a once-harassing voice, now a singsong greeting. "Hey girls, it's me, Bayley. What's going on?"

A strange smile crossed Tamara's face as she locked cold fish eyes on Bayley. Maybe it was my imagination because it happened so fast, then was gone. And Tamara delivered the news as matter-of-factly as a seasoned journalist would.

"Jilly's dead."

≈≈≈

I wiped at Bayley's vomit-stained chin as Tamara stood over her, a gleam in her eye. Bayley had dropped to her knees like she'd been gut-punched, and in a way, that's just what Tamara's icy pronouncement had been to her—a body blow.

"Hope you're happy," Bayley said through sniffles as she slowly stood and glared at Tamara. "Y-y-you never wanted . . . I-I-I'm getting out of here. I can't deal with this right now."

She left in one direction, and Tamara drifted off in another. The strange confrontation was over, and the reunion was over for me. I had a job to do.

≈≈≈

Joe Lee wanted to talk about the time we threw up together after mixing Krystal gut bombs and a six-pack one night at Pinkerton Park down by the Harpeth River.

"Not now, Joe Lee. Maybe later, if you're not in jail. Tell me how you found Jilly. And hurry."

I held the phone toward him and began my video interrogation.

"I'm here with Joe Lee Whitaker, who discovered the body of Silicon Valley tech magnate Jillyn K. Shannon. What were you doing when you found her? Can you show us your exact location? Do you have any idea how this happened?"

"Why sure, Periwink—Ms. Holmes. Follow me."

Grrr. I'd have to edit that out. Joe Lee walked toward the river and pointed.

"I was right about here and she was over there. I wanted to do a little fishing and—"

Good Lord, he's pulled out a knife. Zoom in. There's still blood on it! Be cool. That's it . . . Joe Lee's lightbulb was probably the dimmest in a class full of half-wits . . . no, no, no, he must see my shocked look because he's wiping the blade clean on his pants.

"Now hold on, Periwinkle," he said, raising his voice. "Don't you get any ideas—"

"Not at all, Joe Lee. I just saw someone else I wanted to interview. Don't go away. I'll be right back."

I hustled toward Court, who was holding court with the cops. He had a well-earned reputation as one of Nashville's sleaziest lawyers. We'd always had a strange—strained—relationship whenever our paths crossed professionally. The police left him to interview someone else, and I closed in. He was on guard, knowing he was talking to a reporter, not an old classmate.

"You should know that I will likely be representing Joe Lee, should the police charge him," Court said.

"Is that going to happen?"

"No comment."

My phone rang, and I held up an index finger and walked away. It was weekend news anchor, Luis Reyes.

"Peri, we just heard on the police scanner about a murder at a class reunion or something," Luis said. "I'm crossing my fingers that it's yours."

"Yeah, I'm on the scene now," I said, "and the cops just arrived. They won't confirm, but I've talked to a dozen of my old classmates, and—get this—it's Jilly, uh, sorry, Jillyn K. Shannon."

I held the phone from my ear as I heard my news director, Joan McCall, cussing with delight. Luis must have put us on speaker.

"Jilly was the queen of mean in high school, and I heard she got meaner after that. The world owes a debt to whoever offed her," I said.

Joan started cussing again, but I cut her off.

"Don't worry, I'll play nice . . . oh, poor, dear, sweet Jilly, such a treasure. Who, oh who, would want to harm—"

My news director's torrent of cuss words was followed by a warning that I'd better have something ready for the five o'clock newscast.

"Be on the lookout for Greg. He should be there by now," Joan added. "You've been bumped to the lead story."

"He's not here yet. If he doesn't show up soon with his video camera, the only thing we'll see on tonight's news will be my pretty face and an empty parking lot. I'll be in touch," I said and went looking for one of the cops I knew.

≈ ≈ ≈

Hallie, our ditzy cheerleader, had done my job for me. The high school gossip had apparently graduated as valedictorian in social media. By the time I got off the phone with the office, Hallie had talked to most of our classmates, and even a couple of the first responders.

"You will never believe what Heather said. Jilly contacted her last week about—"

"About what?" the booming male voice said. I turned, my eyes first drawn to the state park ranger uniform. Then my eyes met his.

Oh. My. God. What's HE doing here? "Um, hello, Forrest," I said to one of Franklin High's most gifted athletes until a knee injury in the last game of his senior year ended his career and cost him a scholarship. "I didn't know you were a park ranger. When were you notified?"

"About what?" he repeated. "I just got here, and saw you. Lookin' good, Periwinkle. How ya been?"

Twenty-five years hadn't erased the acrimony I felt. I knew I had to rise above it and remain professional. Dammit. Turning on my phone's video camera, I handed it over to Hallie and stepped in close to Forrest so that we would both be in range. Hallie held the camera toward us and mouthed, *Action!*

"This is Peri Holmes, live for Channel 11 from Harpeth River State Park in Pegram. I'm here with Ranger Forrest Greene, a *very close* friend of Silicon Valley tech magnate Jillyn K. Shannon, a Franklin High School graduate who was in Nashville this weekend for a high school reunion."

I glanced sideways at Forrest, who had a slight smirk on his cocky face. Everything about him said he was in command. Then I turned back to the camera.

"Less than two hours ago, Jillyn was the victim of a brutal murder. Police have yet to confirm any details, but at least a dozen high school classmates have identified her, including Joe Lee Whitaker, who fished her body out of the river."

I side-eyed Forrest, whose mouth hung open. He didn't know that I knew about *them*. A small smile crossed my face, but I quickly turned it into a sympathetic frown.

"Ranger Greene . . . Forrest . . . I think I speak for all my classmates when I say we're sorry for your loss."

Pompous ass. I'll show you who's in charge.

Maureen

The elevator dinged on the top floor of Shamrock Systems. Out stepped Maureen O'Sullivan balancing four Starbucks lattés, her Coach tote, and Jillyn's dry cleaning slung across her shoulder. "Never trust the delivery service with my Gran's old cardigan." Maureen could hear Jillyn's voice in her head.

Her heels tapped across the white marble foyer as she mentally reviewed her list of questions for the scheduled call. *Nice the boss is out of town.* Maureen observed the lobby and security desk, wondering why Jillyn kept the original company branding. *It's not improving. No time to rebrand before the shareholders arrive. Can't continue to look like a relic, especially in Palo Alto.*

Maureen touched her Apple watch. "Hi, Jillyn. How's the reunion? Can't wait to hear how ghastly everyone—"

A male voice broke in. "Ma'am. Excuse me. Are you Ms. O'Sullivan?"

"Why are you on Jillyn's phone—we have an urgent call now. Board meeting questions. No time for this!" She spat her words at her wrist speaker.

"Please listen carefully. I'm Sergeant Michael Kingsman from the Metro Nashville Police Department. Confirm your identity. Are you Maureen O'Sullivan?"

She shifted her weight and drew in a breath. "Is Jillyn in some kind of trouble?"

"For the last time, are you the executive assistant to Ms. Shannon, her ICE?"

"Yes, I'm her 'in case of emergency' contact." No Apple watch, Maureen thought. She wouldn't have lost her phone if it were strapped to her wrist.

"Ma'am, I'm afraid it's bad news."

"I told her not to take her Tesla. Was she in a wreck?"

"She's dead, Ms. O'Sullivan. Is there someone—?"

The lattés crashed to the floor, plastic tops popping. A wide brown sea spread across the white marble.

Six Weeks Later

Peri

I waited in line, then placed my usual order—large hot skinny double latte with two Equals—before looking around. I hoped the loony didn't show, but there was a wave from a table in the back. I pulled down my cloche hat to my eyes and headed that way.

"Christ, Periwinkle, is this the most private place you could think of to meet?" she said.

"Calm down, will you, Mary Ann. You look like you're about to blow a gasket."

"I'm giving you the biggest scoop since Watergate, dammit. You don't care if everybody hears?"

"Nobody pays attention at Starbucks. It's all just static in the background."

Mary Ann's beady eyes scanned the customers at the nearby tables. Nobody returned her glare.

"Guess you're right. I bet I could pull off my leg and set it in the middle of the table and no one would notice."

"So what's this scoop?"

"Back to the reunion—"

"Gimme a break. That's so old news. Jillyn's death and the bankruptcy of Shamrock were over a month ago—nobody cares any more. I don't want to hear any more myself."

"Hear me out." Mary Ann planted her elbows on the table and leaned in. "I know who killed her."

"Then why aren't you telling the police? Why pull me into this?"

Mary Ann sat back, walled her eyes to the ceiling, and then leaned across the table again.

"Because I'm not credible, that's why. You know my history. Who's gonna believe a butch just out of a psych ward? Don't want the press—somebody like you—spreading my picture and history across the six o'clock news anyway. I've nothing to gain, but for you—this could be a Pulitzer Prize or something."

I returned Mary Ann's intense stare for a moment, weighing the possibilities.

"Look, let's say you do have some new, wild-eyed theory—"

"No theory. I know how it went down. I've been researching this for a month. I just got back from California. Discovered stuff about Jilly-Poo even the tabloids couldn't find."

I took a sip of latte and casually looked around to see if anyone was watching me sit with this freak. I took a deep breath and let it out slowly before focusing on Mary Ann again.

"Okay, let's have it."

"Did Jillyn look . . . strange to you at the reunion?"

"I only saw her feet sticking out from under a tarp. Nobody *saw her* except Joe Lee and maybe a few others."

"And me. I lifted the tarp and took a good look. Know what I saw?" Mary Ann sat back with a smug smile.

I waited for her to continue. "So this is where I'm supposed to ask *what*?"

"Jillyn, the Jillyn we all knew from high school."

"And what did you expect?"

"Jillyn—eighteen-year-old Jillyn—the same girl we all remembered. Don't you get it?"

"Look, I'm just a poor black gal with a made-for-TV smile. Guess you'll have to spell it out for me."

Mary Ann did a reconnaissance of the room before continuing.

"Jillyn got a scholarship to Cal Tech. Never came home after that. After dropping out of college, her first job was with a biotech startup in LA. Stayed there about five years before starting Shamrock. After that, her picture was everywhere—of when she was ten years younger, of course, or doctored vanity pictures that made her look younger."

"All the celebs do that. So what?"

"So the Jillyn we saw at the reunion is who we expected to see."

"Still not following you."

Mary Ann gave me the dumb-ass glare I had been expecting, and it made me mad. Mary-Contrary had not been the brightest bulb on the tree in high school either.

"Quit with the games, already. Tell me what you know, or I'm outta here," I said.

Mary Ann took this as the putdown I intended and sat erect with her hands on the table.

"Okay. Okay. I'll start from the top then." She again surveyed the room like she expected to spot a sniper.

"It's those five years at that biotech firm that's the key. This is before anybody knew the name Jillyn Shannon. Tech wasn't hot yet. There was no social media tracking everything she did. I had to do the digging on my own. You know what she was working on?"

I gave her my *I'm outta here* grimace.

"Cloning. This was back in the Dolly-the-sheep era. Lots of research on cloning back then. The scientists couldn't let it be known, of course, or the Bible thumpers would come out of the woodwork. But experimentation went on, mostly overseas. The head of Biogene, the startup that hired Jillyn, was a Chinese transplant named Hung Wye. Biogene was out of business five years later—stock swindle of some sort. I found Hung in the federal pen. A real class act. Sent him a cell phone hidden in a box of brownies and he filled me in on the history of Jillyn."

Mary Ann sat back and crossed her arms with a self-satisfied grin.

"And?"

"Hung said he only hired her because she could speak Mandarin. When the hell did Jillyn learn Mandarin? Cal Tech, I guess. Anyway, Hung found out how smart she was and got her up to speed on cloning. She was his Girl Friday on everything. You wouldn't believe all the animals they cloned—mice, rabbits, dogs, chimps. He said they used the Honolulu technique, which made it all simple. They had cloning down pat, don't you see. Jillyn wanted to do humans next, but Hung thought a human patient could expose what they were doing and bring down holy hell on their heads. Jillyn had the solution. She volunteered."

"Volunteered for what?"

"Hung extracted one of Jillyn's eggs and cultured it with her own DNA. They implanted the egg in a surrogate mother recruited online. Voila! A cloned baby girl—Jillyn version 2.0. They raised the baby to age two at the lab, using private nurses. Experiment a success, right? Well, not quite.

Although the child looked just like Jillyn as a baby, it had the mental capacity of a cucumber.

"Biogene went belly up, and Hung went to jail. It was about this time that Jillyn hit me up for a loan to start Shamrock. Said I'd be a millionaire in two years. The bitch. Anyway, Hung never talked with Jillyn after that. He'd followed the skyrocket success of Shamrock, mostly from tabloids in the prison library. One expose claimed Jillyn secreted a severely handi-capped child in her mansion she had born out of wedlock in her wilder days. Nobody believed it, of course, but Hung thought it was Jillyn 2.0. He said it would be dead soon since animals cloned using the Honolulu tech-nique didn't live long after puberty."

"So you speculate Jillyn brought Jillyn 2.0 to the reunion and murdered her?"

"You've got it, Periwinkle."

I propped my elbows on the table, face in hands, staring down at my latte. This couldn't be true . . . could it? I tried to recall the details of the reunion. There must be some obvious flaw to this preposterous story.

"How'd she do it? Bay said she was driving a Tesla when she met her earlier. It was in the parking lot that day. How did she get away?"

"Yep, that's where she rented an SUV. Joe Lee said he saw it before he went fishing. Remember? And Court said he saw a black SUV leaving when he arrived. The bitch must have left when Joe Lee was fishing and drove around to the other side of the river. She videoed the whole thing using one of those drones."

"You saw the drone, too? I thought Channel 2 must have picked up on the story on a police band scanner, and it was their drone."

"I got there early to take some water-quality samples. That's my job. The drone was hovering over the canoe access when everybody started arriv-ing."

"So where is Jillyn now?"

"Good question. I know a private jet took off at 7:35 that evening for Miami. The next day, the pilot filed a flight plan from Miami to LA. No pas-sengers. She must have used a fake identity to board a commercial flight to—who knows where. She's probably on some private island right now, laughing her ass off watching the latest news reports about her murder investigation."

"Why?"

"Simple. She's disposed of a cloning experiment gone bad. She's out from under a corporation she robbed blind and left for the vultures. Knowing Jillyn, she's got several of the best identity papers money can buy, offshore bank accounts worth billions, all the bases covered. But the biggest reason—cute, little, innocent Jilly-Poo couldn't pass up playing one last prank on her old classmates."

I felt my skin crawl. It all added up. "Mary Ann, have you told anybody else?"

"Are you kidding? It would be a trip back to the loony bin for me. I won't even tell my therapist. Maybe I shouldn't be talking to you. Look, you've got to keep me out of this. I'm like a Deep Throat informant, see. Journalism ethics and all that stuff—you can't disclose your sources."

I closed my eyes and saw my future exploding like Roman candle bursts. It was a sensational story, but what could I prove? If I told people at the station, how would they react? Joan would probably dismiss the story as a harebrained conspiracy theory hatched by a certified lunatic based on an interview with a man in prison for fraud.

"Thank you, Mary Ann." I got up with my hand extended for a shake.

Mary Ann rose slowly, ignoring my hand, a snarl growing on her face. "It's true—"

"Oh, I believe you. We both know what Jillyn is capable of. Just don't expect to hear this on the news tonight. I'll have to do some fact-checking—you know, get my ducks in a row. This might take some time." I picked up my handbag and turned to the door. I could feel Mary Ann's eyes drilling into my back as I walked away.

On the way to my car, a young, black girl rushed up with a gushing smile.

"You're the news lady—"

"Yes, I'm Peri Holmes," I said, beaming my famous smile and patting her on the head. As I walked on, I took a deep breath of the crisp fall air. I like being Peri Holmes, reporter for the six o'clock news. Periwinkle might expose Jillyn just for the sweet taste of revenge. But Peri Holmes could not and would not risk her career on such a salacious story.

Epilogue

She fights to regain consciousness and shivers against the chill in the room, attempting to make sense of the rhythmic beeping—just out of step with her heartbeat. She squints and a white uniform comes into focus.

"Most excellent. Now, you are awake," the nurse says in a Swiss French accent. With a trained eye, she scans the vitals machine. "Jane, I'm going to listen to your heart." She places her stethoscope on top of the patient's gauze-bound chest.

Jillyn's tongue moves over her teeth; her mouth feels like cotton. "No, wait. I'm . . . ." *Focus—Jane's your alias! Jane Doe.* With a wan smile, she says, "I'm Jane."

"On a scale of one to ten, what is your pain level?"

"My pain?" She tries to prop up on her elbows, still groggy from the anesthesia and pain meds.

"Lie down," the nurse reprimands. "It's vital to protect your stitches."

≈≈≈

For the first time in her life, Jillyn appreciates the clarity of 20/20 vision the Lasik procedure has given her. Chuckling, she recalls the wretched gold-rimmed, round glasses she wore in high school. Standing in front of the full-length mirror, she touches her high cheekbones, runs a thumb over the new cleft in her chin, and admires her freckle-bleached face. Smoothing her silk tunic, she admires her new silhouette. A 32DD now. No one could ever call her flat-chested again!

The private surgical suite door opens, and the world-renowned plastic surgeon, Dr. Fischer, strides in. "Aren't you a vision? Your body is healing with swiftness. It's been a privilege to work with you, patient 292996," he says with a wink.

"You've done a brilliant job." Jillyn turns to marvel again at her reflection. "How can I ever thank you for my transformation? I'm grateful for your handiwork, but most of all your discretion."

Sliding a sealed envelope from the breast pocket of his tailored jacket, he hands it to her. "Swiss surgeons are like Swiss bankers—numbers are all we need. The more zeros at the end of a check—the happier we become." Smiling, he leaves.

After the suite door closes with a *thumpf*, Jillyn opens the envelope. The blue Australian passport and driver's license slide onto the table. Each bears an identical photo of her unsmiling face. She runs her thumb over the passport photo, then scans the document for accuracy. Meticulous attention to detail, just as requested. Name: Olivia Nicole Ellis. Birthdate: 17 March 1975. Country of Origin: Australia.

Not only has she turned back time, but she has also been transformed.

≈ ≈ ≈

The driver opens the door of the black Town Car at Geneva International Airport and assists her to the curb before he lifts her bags from the trunk. A porter hoists the mound of leather bags, each with gold-foil letters stamped O.N.E., onto the dolly. She tips the chauffer with pound notes, her French scarf billowing in the wind.

"Private terminal, please," Olivia says in a measured tone with the hint of an Aussie accent. Her first and last public red carpet walk, as a bombshell instead of a coding nerd.

"Of course, ma'am," the porter nods as he pushes her belongings through the concourse doors.

She walks to the airport Starbucks, hoping to pass a newsstand. Am would appreciate the irony that he'd featured Jillyn's cover story the month her death made international headlines.

"Anything else, ma'am?" the cashier says, sliding three copies of the English language *Vanity Fair* into a plastic bag.

≈ ≈ ≈

Jillyn sprays a fresh layer of sunscreen over her transformed self and adjusts her red string bikini, the lounge chair cushion warm against her legs. Picking up her cocktail glass, she scans the Indian Ocean as colorful parrots chatter in the palm trees. "Just water for a thousand miles," she says, as she takes the hand of her co-conspirator and faithful corporate pilot, Nikolas.

He puts down the copy of *Vanity Fair* and picks up his drink. "Welcome to Oz." He says, clinking glasses with Jillyn. "Here's to off-the-grid living. Well, at least for me. You'll never give up coding life," Nikolas says. "The writer turned your interview into a long form obituary. The article talks about Shamrock's bankruptcy. Apparently they haven't figured out the embezzlement yet. He makes it sound like you were God's gift to Silicon Valley."

Nodding, she lifts her glass again. "God's gift indeed. I'd like to propose another toast. Here's to Mary Ann—your squadron mate and my Franklin High classmate. To the whakadoodle. Thanks for the ten grand you loaned me for my first startup."

Nikolas adds, "That's a bit harsh isn't it? Mary Ann's eccentric, but her heart's in the right place. And she did bring us together."

"Right, there is that. Do you think she bought your Key West story? A diehard Buffett fan retiring to the Keys is plausible—just crossing my fingers she doesn't try to track you down."

Lifting his guitar from a black, sticker-covered case, Nikolas begins strumming a Buffett classic. "I'm indebted to Mary Ann for mentioning you were hiring a pilot, or I wouldn't have met my life's love."

While he segues into another tune, she wonders if Nickolas has outlived his usefulness. *What if Mary Ann sniffs onto his trail like a bloodhound? How and when should I dispose of him?*

"Any regrets retiring to Oz with me?" Jillyn asks.

"You're kidding me, right? Two-plus years—planning our getaway, living apart, texts on burner phones. If I'd doubted the satisfaction of waking up with you every morning in this paradise, I would've hit the road for Florida. I'd be playin' dive bars, living off tips."

Tracing her finger along his jawline, Jillyn says, "Nickolas, you are my Adonis."

He picks up the guitar and begins plucking another favorite—something about changes in latitudes and attitudes.

"I believe we'll go undetected here." Jillyn twists a garnet sea glass pendant. "The middle of the vast Indian Ocean. Nothing for thousands of miles but deep blue water meeting a pale blue sky. I can do without a lot, including an umbrella in my margarita—but Wi-Fi is my oxygen. I'm going to have to figure out to how to crack that code. But we have time. Lots of time." She savors the exotic brown-berry sweetness in her glass, recalling the Loveless Café sorghum.

Refilling her glass from the pitcher, he says, "Here's to island life."

Taking his chin in her hands, she kisses him deeply on the lips, relishing his rough five o'clock shadow. "Nikolas, what do you think about doing a digital currency startup? I've even thought of a name. CimONE."

"Olivia Nicole Ellis, you truly are a genius. Long live Oz."

A satisfied inward smile fills her body with warmth she hasn't felt since she shed it all and dove into Forbidden Lake.

ABOUT THE HARPETH RIVER WRITERS

Sandy Ward Bell grew up in upstate NY. Radio was her first love. After college, she became an announcer and promotion director, married, had a daughter, and the art of storytelling became her new passion. Her freshman novel, *In Zoey's Head*, reflects her experience with the media and pop culture. Her second, *Parked at the Mansfields'*, highlights her appreciation for Jane Austen's timeless story. Her third book, *Bold*, honors women's courage through a collection of short stories. She also contributed to the anthology *By Blood or By Marriage*. Bell spent many years living in Augusta, Baltimore, and Pittsburgh. Today, she calls Nashville home. Visit sandywardbell.com.

A native of Maryland, **Suzanne Webb Brunson**, has lived in New Jersey, Georgia and Tennessee, where she learned about country stores, local politics, and strawberry festivals while a reporter on the state desk of The Nashville Banner. Her roots are in the Deep South, and Florida, which is not Deep South but further south. A former newspaper reporter and editor, she earned a journalism degree from the University of Georgia. She has been a freelance writer for newspapers, magazines, nonprofits, a guest blog for Killer Nashville Magazine. She is now writing short stories and a novel. These things she can control with the luxury of imagination. Her short stories appear in By Blood or By Marriage and Gathering: Writers of Williamson County, and the online e-zine, Muscadine Lines, A Southern Journal. She was a member of two literary groups representing Tennessee and Williamson County Authors, and is a founding member of the Historical Novel Society (Midsouth TN/KY Chapter).

Catherine R. Caffey is a wordsmith who left her poetic pen behind when she left her native Nashville. Following college, she dove headlong into a corporate communications career. After decades of making waves in the advertising agency, marketing, and Fortune 500 worlds, she circled back to her youth and hometown, intent on rekindling literary fires. Caffey began by co-authoring a nonfiction volume, part of an award-winning series, housed in the Library of Congress. Her current manuscript, a collection of heartening personal essays recounting life transitions, keeps her up at night, and her hand moving across the page by day.

A product of the sandy hills of West Tennessee, an area east of the edge of the Mississippi Delta and west of the Tennessee River, **John Neely Davis** spent most of his working years in U.S. government land acquisition projects stretching from the Appalachians to the river valleys of New Mexico. Previously published novels include *Stephen Dennison, The Sixth William,* and *Bear Shadow,* winner of the Janice Keck Literary Award. In June of 2018, Five Star released *The Chapman Legacy,* a multiple-generational novel of the American West. He has also contributed to numerous anthologies: *Filtered Through Time, By Blood or Marriage, Comanchero Trail, Western Trail Blazer* Series, *Showdown,* and Five Star Publishing May 2019, future release: *Contention and Other Frontier Stories.* He lives with his wife, Jayne, in historic Franklin, Tennessee. Visit his website at johnneelydavisauthor.com.

Micki Fuhrman grew up in a river town in northwest Louisiana, where stories hung in the air at church picnics, back porch singings, and country store counters. She first wrote poetry for a school newspaper, and by her teens was a professional singer/songwriter, appearing on the Louisiana Hayride and guest-starring on the Grand Ole Opry. Now a Nashville resident, Micki segued into literary writing in 2013. Her short fiction works (written as Vonn McKee) have been recognized by both Western Writers of America (Spur Finalist) and Western Fictioneers (Peacemaker Finalist). Micki is at work on a novel set in the Cherokee Territory of Appalachia. She loves driving backroads, antiquing and cooking for crowds.

Catherine Moore is the author of four chapbooks and the poetry collection ULLA! ULLA!, as well as a co-editor of FIOLET & WING: An

Anthology of Domestic Fabulist Poetry. Her work appears in Tahoma Literary Review, Southampton Review, Mid-American Review, Broad River Review and in various anthologies. A Walker Percy and Hambidge fellow, her honors also include the Yemassee Journal's Fiction Prize, The Southeast Review Poetry Prize, as well as nominations for the Pushcart, the Best of the Net, and the VERA Awards. Her fiction has shortlisted in several competitions and was selected for inclusion in the juried BEST SMALL FICTIONS, 2015. Catherine holds a Master of Fine Arts in creative writing and she teaches at a community college. Her upcoming collection of lyrical pieces in the voices of bog bodies is forthcoming from Unsolicited Press.

Michael J. Tucker, born and raised in the cold northern climate of Pittsburgh, PA, and as an only child, he was often trapped indoors and left to his own devices, where he would create space ships out of cardboard boxes, convert his mother's ironing board into a horse and put on his Sunday suit and tie and his father's fedora and become a newspaper reporter or police detective. This experience left him with an unlimited imagination and the ability to write electrifying short stories and novels. Mike is the author of three critically acclaimed novels, *Aquarius Falling, Capricorn's Collapse,* and *Summer Haze.* His work also appears in the Civil War Anthology, *Filtered Through Time,* and *By Blood or By Marriage,* a Harpeth River Writers Anthology. He lives with his wife Lynn and their dog Teagan in Brentwood, TN. For more information on his short stories, you can visit his website at michaeltuckerauthor.com.

Tom Wood is an award-winning journalist, author, and screenwriter and who informs, inspires, and entertains. His debut novel *Vendetta Stone,* a Nashville-based fictional true-crime thriller, is followed up by *Turn to Stone: A Vendetta Stone Thriller.* His *Vendetta Stone* adaptation was a Nashville Film Festival screenwriting competition semifinalist, as was *Death Takes a Holliday.* A longtime sports writer and copy editor at *The Tennessean,* he's freelanced for the *Ledger* newspapers in Nashville and Knoxville, the *Knoxville News Sentinel, Country Family News,* and other publications. Tom has mystery and Western short stories in several anthologies, and was an extra on *Nashville, Still the King* and various movie/TV projects.

Bill Woods lives and writes beside the Duck River in Columbia, Tennessee but considers Grand Case, Saint Martin, FWI his second home. His novel, *Orient Beach*, was a finalist in the 2018 Faulkner – Wisdom Competition. He is the author of *The Muse of Wallace Rose* and short stories published in the anthology, *By Blood or by Marriage*.